All There Is

A NOVEL

Dan Kovacs

*For my staunchest supporter, who will one day
get to say that she has a famous grandson*

What good is livin' a life you've been given
If all you do is stand in one place?

–Lord Huron, "Ends of the Earth"

THIS STORY IS ENTIRELY FALSE
(except for the portions that aren't)

prologue

THE FINAL MOVEMENT

The woman was stuck between two places.

Her body was broken and decaying in the hospice room; her mind was performing the final movement of an extended violin solo. A single light showcased her to the packed audience that looked onward toward the stage. Most faces were blurred, swirled masses with the exception of the five seated in the front row. Their static smiles resembled a still frame rather than living bodies.

She slipped back to the room as she felt a hand wrap around hers. It was gentle, with only light pressure, as if to prove how fragile she'd become.

"It's okay, Mom. We're here. It's okay to let go. You don't need to be in pain anymore," the voice whispered, just loud enough to be heard above the needless noise in the room.

Mom wanted to open her eyes and say whatever scramble of words she could, but her body wouldn't allow it, hadn't allowed it for . . .

How long had she been like this?

She began to probe for the answer but felt the stage slip away. No. No, she couldn't let that happen. The bliss and peace that flowed through her as she continued to draw the bow across the strings were more important. The notes came out perfect. She felt the tears build up beneath the surface, but they'd never break through.

Mom felt the one hand disappear only to be quickly replaced by another.

"I love you. I wish I had told you more. You have always been so strong and the only reason we made it after losing Dad."

Mom wanted to smile, to give any indication that the words meant something to her.

Another hand grabbed onto hers. This one tighter.

"Please don't go. Please don't go," the voice repeated, distraught and disbelieving. Mom didn't have a choice. She was merely an actor reading a script and following cues.

The hand disappeared as Mom waited in anticipation for one more. There had always been four, right?

Eventually, one last hand clenched hers. Was it . . .? Was it even real? Her mind fluttered as she concentrated briefly on something to identify who it was, but no words came.

The hand retreated from hers without notice and the moment extended, extended, extended until she knew she was finally alone.

The assortment of drugs moving through her system began to dim; the melodic thump of her heartbeat started to slow. It sounded therapeutic, like a metronome, didn't it?

As her body took one last exhale, her mind lingered and focused on completing the violin solo. Her hand hadn't moved with such clarity and skill in years. She never told anyone how much she missed it, but life pushed her in another direction, a better one.

She completed the final movement, hitting the last note and refusing to let it go. Without any control, it faded from existence and was quickly replaced by the manufactured cheers from the audience.

The curtain began to move slowly, giving her one last look at who was seated in the front row.

She stared down at the two who symbolized what had been and all there was. She'd see the one soon—or so she hoped.

As for the other, she'd forgiven him long ago. How could she not? They shared a bond that couldn't be severed regardless of how little they talked.

She bowed in appreciation as the space beyond the curtain shrunk to a small vertical slice, beginning to cut off the familiar faces on either ends.

Closer and closer the curtain pulled until the face in the middle was all that remained.

His smile receded just enough to mouth three words—the opposite of what was screamed at her years earlier.

The light from the stage blinked out; the curtain was finally drawn.

She was gone.

And the face in the middle would never know he was her last thought, her final movement.

I

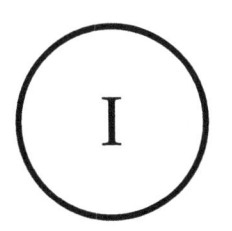

BREAKOUT

one

WORK HISTORY

Life had always been a perfect circle for Coda Finn.

It started and ended with work.

At the age of ten, Coda stumbled into his first job at a small pizza shop in southside Brooklyn called Uncle Sal's Pizza Palooza & Planetarium.

Without realizing it, Coda deviated from his normal route home one day and went inside Uncle Sal's.

"You here for some pizza or stargazing?" the heavyset man behind the counter said. He pointed to the sign posing the same question.

"I . . . uh, I don't have any money," Coda called back. Some of his friends were given a weekly allowance, but he'd never been so lucky. While he didn't know the extent of it, his parents were spread pretty thin supporting four kids.

The cashier reached under the counter and placed cleaning supplies in front of Coda. "How about you clean those tables over there and I'll give you a slice?"

"Isn't that extortion?"

"Extortion?!" the cashier scoffed. "Kid, I don't even know what that means."

"It's when—"

The cashier held up a hand to stop his explanation. "What's your name, kid?"

"Coda."

"As in Dakota?" the cashier asked.

"As in just Coda."

The cashier contemplated this piece of information before accepting it and moving on. "How old are you?"

"I'm eleven." Coda learned to tell fibs from his oldest sister. She always fibbed about what time she'd be home from school, so why couldn't he lie about his age? It came naturally and without remorse. "Do you always ask so many questions?"

"Only when I'm trying to *extort* someone," the cashier warned.

Coda stepped back from the counter to get a better view. "What's *your* name?"

"Sal."

"Are you *the* Uncle Sal?" Coda asked with increased interest.

"No, I'm Cousin Sal. An unfortunate coincidence . . . Coda, look, I got customers waiting and dirty tables that need cleaning. You want that piece of pizza or not?"

Coda inched closer and grabbed the cleaning supplies.

"You gotta—"

"I know how to clean a table," Coda said in a flat tone. His mom made him clean the kitchen table each night after dinner, so he was an expert at the menial task.

Cousin Sal stood with his arms folded and watched as Coda sprayed each table. "Who taught you the double douse down method?"

"My mom."

He nodded his approval. "Where's home for you?"

"A few blocks up."

"You want to work here part time?"

"Part time?" Coda asked.

Cousin Sal tugged at his soul patch. "Yeah, you come in some nights after school and keep the place clean."

"Okay."

"*Okay?* Don't you have other questions?"

"No."

"Go home and ask your parents. I'm sure they know of this place. We are citywide," Cousin Sal said with a lopsided smile.

Coda left the pizza shop and followed the subway tracks back home. He prepped himself for a confrontation with his mom about working at the age of ten with a list of reasons why the money would be useful for him. He hyped himself up the entire walk back, but it was unwarranted. Coda found his mom in the living room and broke into a long-winded ramble about the encounter he had. She listened patiently for nearly a minute as she lightly tapped the top of the book she was reading.

Her only concern was him having enough time to study and finish the steady pile of homework. He assured that he'd be more focused than ever.

Money proved to be a true motivator.

Coda raced back to get the piece of pizza he rightfully deserved.

For the next three years, Coda devoted himself to keeping Uncle Sal's

Pizza Palooza & Planetarium sanitary and clean three nights a week. After the first month, Coda realized customers preferred to order out than dine in, so his cleaning opportunities were limited. To pass the time, he'd blitz through his homework and dive deeper into the treasure trove of books that kept piling up. He knew which ones were special if the symbol was on the back cover, but those were rarer than a blue moon.

At the age of thirteen and a half, Coda began helping out at the fire station where his dad worked. He cooked meals with the other firefighters, cleaned the trucks, and lounged around in the chairs taking plenty of naps. He enjoyed that more than the pizza shop because he felt appreciated for the work he did. His time at the fire station didn't last long since the accident happened six months later. Coda could have gone back whenever he wanted, but it just didn't feel right. He didn't want to hear the sirens and think about people being trapped in a burning building with their death rapidly approaching. Until the accident, death had no meaning in Coda's life, and afterward, he had no intention of letting it back in ever again.

At the age of nineteen, Coda got a job at his college bookstore. He was studying Computer Science at The College State University of Manhattan (home of the Sleepy Sloths!) and had enough free time to pick up the side gig. He enjoyed the job but hated how everyone was more interested in purchasing overpriced sweatshirts than browsing the substantial book supply that the *book*store stocked. Did anyone still read? He did his part by giving away his books to willing individuals, sometimes even the ones with the special symbol.

At the age of twenty-two, having graduated college in four years flat, Coda got his first corporate job at the Jenn/Erik Corporation (JEC). They were the world's first quadrillion dollar company. While tendency had shifted back to supporting small businesses after the dismantlement of Amazon, people didn't realize JEC was supplying every small business with their merchandise. JEC was considered a conglomerate, so they specialized in nothing and dealt in everything. They were too big to fail and too powerful to dissolve, so the federal government did what they specialized in: tossed aside any problem to be dealt with another time.

Considering the vastness of JEC, one might think they hire a massive number of employees. Wrong! JEC only hires one hundred new employees a year, which qualifies them for the federal grant sponsored by JEC. How is a company that large sustainable with so few new employees? Nobody knows. Maybe it's the robots. Maybe it's the aggressively low attrition rate. Maybe it's Maybelline—the active ingredient in sustainability.

Coda was one of the lucky few. After a grueling application process, he began his career as a software engineer in the Airplane and Autocannon Department. His ambitions and potential were limitless.

But it lasted about as long as a teenage romance.

At the age of twenty-five, Coda's ambition was squashed and his outlook on life was heavily diminished.

He was ready to breakout and disrupt his perfect circle.

two

ANNIVERSARY

In the Airplane and Autocannon Department, the gift of choice from managers to their underlings was water bottles. After three years at JEC, in the same seat and working on the ever-spinning project, Coda had amassed rows of water bottles. Employees would walk by and let out a low, long whistle of shock and awe at the sight. Some considered his display a sign of authority or excellent performance, while others saw him as the cocky renegade who disrupted department politics by having the brass balls to display his prizes like a taxidermist would. People got riled up about silly things more often than not.

Similar to his generosity with books, he offered the water bottles to employees whenever they mentioned the dazzling display, but each one refused saying they had enough of their own.

Coda clicked through his unread emails, skimming through the junk. Notices about upcoming outages or culture events or nasty proclamations from managers demanding updates on the failing project clogged his inbox. As a software engineer, he was able to filter out that noise and focus on the work, but that was only easily achieved if he gave a shit. The passion he once had for creating and sifting through code to solve a problem eroded away faster than the cartilage in an athlete's knee.

Bored of the tedium, Coda grabbed one of the water bottles and moved out into the common area. He was greeted by well wishes and hopes of prosperity on this wonderful, invigorating Thursday morning.

Part of Coda's routine on the twenty-seventh floor of JEC was to check on the water fountains. Each H2O TO GO Station came as a pair to avoid long queues of employees waiting to hydrate. Time was money after all.

The water fountain on the left displayed a statistic that 35,673 plastic bottles had been spared from sunbathing in oceans, landfills, backyards, sidewalks, alleyways, street corners, highways, driveways, parkways, byways, and so on. In comparison, the water fountain on the right displayed a number of 36,891 plastic bottles ripped from the clutches of a dying earth. What does the difference in these numbers mean?

Absolutely nothing.

But still, Coda found the silent rivalry fascinating. He was a constant supporter of the left water fountain, which always struggled to close the gap, to break the routine of being behind. Considering his massive water bottle collection, Coda utilized his power for the common good and had no less than three filled at any moment to aid weary travelers that were passing through from other floors.

To be clear, this was the highlight of his day. Work had morphed into a predictable affair like watching a generic horror movie and guessing correctly who would die first based on how useless and annoying they were.

Coda's meeting schedule rarely deviated from the following:

MONDAY – **NO** MEETINGS
TUESDAY – **NO** MEETINGS
WEDNESDAY – **NO** MEETINGS
THURSDAY – **NO** MEETINGS
FRIDAY – **NO** MEETINGS

Coda's team was so mature in their agile practices that they decided to scrap meetings altogether. The work he needed to complete was assigned to him in an external application. Any questions he had were fielded on one of three messaging applications the company used, which meant that his interactions with other humans were limited.

Today would be a special deviation from the norm though. As Coda returned to his desk with three water bottles cradled in his arms, Sam turned to him.

"Hello, Coda. How are you?"

"Good. Just filled up my water bottles."

"Right on schedule, I think," Sam said, checking his watch. He pressed a stubby finger to the screen of the watch when it refused to light up with the time. He scrunched his face when it finally did. "Two minutes later than usual. What was the delay?"

"No reason." It could be attributed to Coda's overarching ache to rid himself of the constant boredom that plagued him at work, home, or any other facet of his meaningless life, but Coda didn't know Sam well enough to dive into that.

Sam nodded, accepted the answer as truth, and then asked, "Are you going to the quarterly today?"

"The what?"

"The quarterly. For the Airplane and Autocannon Department. You know, the meeting we have three times a year downstairs."

Right, of course, how could Coda forget the slight pivot from the worn path? He'd thought about it the entire subway ride to work, but the task of filling up water bottles always distracted him from the present.

"Yeah, yeah. I'll be there."

"I'm walking down if you want to sit together," Sam said.

Coda contemplated his other options, but none came fast enough before he accepted Sam's offer.

Look, Sam was a nice enough guy, but he was boring. His desk was empty aside from his monitors and laptop. He stood for absolutely nothing and never made any personal opinions known. Sam was the epitome of what Coda envisioned the thirty-fifth floor must be like, with the robots that scurried around completing tasks—there to complete work and do nothing else.

Downstairs, the meeting room sat two thousand without trouble and every seat was taken when the Senior Director grabbed the microphone.

"Good morning everyone. Thank you for attending. As you know, we have massive amounts of change occurring within the Airplane and Autocannon Department, and yet, you continue to prosper. Just the other day I received a letter from an eight-year-old girl thanking us for the autocannon her government bought. She went into detail about how the *peace negotiator* picked apart a caravan of criminals intending to do terrible things to her family. This is why we do what we do—to save lives and eliminate the ones society has deemed unworthy. Okay, let's jump into it . . ."

The Senior Director spoke at length about the state of various projects, plans for new initiatives, and so on. Coda didn't internalize any of it.

Sometimes he wondered if he worked for a bad company. He imagined that the villain sometimes didn't know they were one if they had a cause worth fighting for. On the other side though, JEC had an entire department dedicated to providing shelter and sustenance to communities in need.

It was difficult to view JEC in a negative light as the Senior Director announced each employee in the department would get a ten-thousand-dollar bonus for merely existing. JEC treated their employees with respect, so why did Coda never want to come back?

"... Onto my favorite part: the anniversaries!" He clicked to the next slide, which proudly displayed the names of those who were celebrating their five-, ten-, twenty-, and even one thirty-year anniversary. The Senior Director played a video where each employee celebrating an anniversary of twenty years or above answered questions about their favorite moments and advice to the youth.

It was all so sanitary. Each employee praised the company in the same way with a slightly different set of words. Each employee advised to enjoy every day and to contribute heavily into the 401k plan. Each employee was a carbon copy of one another as if walking into the JEC building stripped them of any compelling characteristics.

"That'll be you in another twenty years," Sam said, nudging Coda's arm.

Coda looked over and saw him enraptured with the passing images and words on the screen. Sam bought into the idea that JEC was *it*. Nobody knew what *it* exactly was, but that didn't matter. Sam would continue at the company until he walked into the everlasting glow of retirement at the tender age of sixty-seven with nothing but declining health to look forward to.

"Oh yeah, definitely," Coda said with a nod.

There had to be more for him than this job.

Everybody had a grand vision of the life they could have, but how many achieved it? How many took the first step in chasing after it?

Hardly anyone because the alternative is easier—show up to the job each day, do enough to scrape by, and continue providing for yourself and your dependents. Repeat that cycle of commuting, working, and feeling existential dread each night for forty years and then you can pack it in. You can call it a successful and fulfilling life because you spent the entirety of it working for a company that didn't even know your last name. Coda was doing it because he felt like there was no other choice.

But there was.

He needed to pierce his way out of the circle.

He didn't want to be another drone celebrating a meaningless anniversary and pretending it was good enough.

three

SIDE HUSTLE

"Tell me about yourself, Sam. We have sat next to each other for . . ." Coda trailed off, trying to remember how long it had actually been.

"Eight months, I think."

"It's felt longer than that."

"I know I'm not the best company, so that probably hasn't helped."

"I didn't mean it like that," Coda said.

They sat across from each other at a Thai restaurant a few blocks from the JEC building. Other employees were littered around. The restaurant was deemed a hotspot for the business class.

Following the quarterly, Sam asked Coda if he wanted to get lunch somewhere. It really dug into Coda's routine of sitting alone in the common area and staring blankly into his phone while he shoveled down the same meal as usual, but Coda agreed.

Sam stared back at him. "There's not much to share about me. After the divorce, I needed a reset on life, so I moved to Hoboken and landed the job at JEC."

"I didn't realize you were married."

"Twenty-five years," Sam said with no emotion.

"What happened?"

"I don't really know. We never wanted kids, which wasn't as common as today. Our marriage thrived on us living separate lives. My old job was a block from our apartment, so I was home more often than her, with all the traveling she did. But it worked for us because the moments we spent with each other were meaningful. Sometimes you can't pinpoint the exact moment when a relationship fails. All I know is that the day eventually came when she was gone, and I needed to decide what was next with my life."

"I'm sorry. It must be hard to reset your life after being in the same cycle for twenty-five years," Coda said.

"A change needed to happen either way. Of course, I would have preferred for it to be something less . . . revolutionary. Maybe that's too dramatic of a word to use, but you get the point. I'm only fifty-two, so I still have plenty of time to live and discover what I truly want out of life."

"That's a scary thought."

Sam picked at the fried rice in front of him. Coda was more eager to eat than he was. "What do you mean?"

"I'm twenty-five, right? And I always thought that life would make more sense at this point. The path would be clear, the road ahead would be paved in gold, or whatever other bullshit you'd like to say," Coda said.

"If only it were that easy . . ." Sam chuckled.

"Why can't it be though? Do you really want to work for the rest of your life?"

"I don't mind it. I find work fulfilling."

Coda glanced away from Sam and out the window caked in grime and soot and other New York City abnormalities. People scooted down the sidewalks toward important destinations, toward the next critical moment in their lives. Everything was time sensitive.

"You find work fulfilling? Did you always feel that way?"

"Yeah, I have. But there is something you need to be aware of."

"Okay," Coda nodded, urging Sam to continue.

"You need a side hustle. Something to busy you when the main course of life isn't as appetizing. It can be a good distraction," Sam said, pointing out the window at the drones passing by.

"Oh yeah? What's your side hustle?"

Sam braced himself against the table and leaned in closer, his shirt nearly dipping into his plate of food. "I moonlight as a private investigator."

"No, you don't," Coda said with a laugh.

Sam settled back into his chair and held up three fingers. "Scout's honor."

"Okay, but how does someone get into a *profession* like that?"

"I loved all those pulpy detective movies growing up and how the main character went around asking questions of random townsfolk to piece together what happened. Each person gives a sliver of the whole story and it was immensely satisfying as it fell into place.

"But I eventually realized that the world doesn't work that way anymore. Everyone has such an online presence that the need for in-person interviews is moot. All you need to be is tech savvy and know where to look. I discovered that many, many people want something found, so I started to get in on the game."

"Uh, huh. And how many people have you helped so far?"

"I can't tell you that because I don't have my official license to practice yet. I could get jailtime if the fuzz found out what I was doing."

"Uh, huh."

"You don't believe me?"

"I mean . . ." Coda said.

"What? You think because I'm some middle-aged, overweight slog that I couldn't possibly do something that would be considered *cool* or *hip*?"

"I'm not sure anyone would consider being a private investigator as cool or hip. Most people younger than me want to be a social media influencer and live off their looks rather than any talent they have."

"A sweeping generalization," Sam said.

"Maybe, but that's one I stand behind."

"There will be a time when you need to find something, and I could be of use to you."

"I'll keep that in mind," Coda said. He looked down at his plate expecting more food but there wasn't anything left.

"What about you? What's your story?" Sam asked.

"I don't have one."

"Sure you do."

"I grew up in Brooklyn, still live there, and now I work at JEC. That's the entire arc of it."

"What about your family?"

"They're around."

"You're gonna make me dip into my side hustle with your vague answers," Sam said.

"Don't bother. There's nothing to find."

Pivoting slightly, Sam asked, "What's *your* side hustle?"

"I don't have one." Coda didn't mention his reading habit because it wasn't the type of answer Sam was after.

"Really?"

"Really."

"Well, you got time to figure it out. We have nothing but time."

four

HIGHLIGHTED ENTRIES

Coda's daily commute consisted of a fifty minute subway ride each way. After work, he would hop on the M train in Manhattan for several stops before shifting over to the D train until he hit the Barclay's Center. Some days he slept. Some days he read a book. Some days he thought about the nothingness he'd absorb himself in back at his apartment. Some days he observed the other passengers and wondered about their lives. Where were they heading? What were they thinking? Were they concerned about the guy who was convinced a demonic entity was lurking on the subway tracks? New Yorkers had the amazing ability to ignore their surroundings while on the subway. It was as if each person was inside an invisible pod that no other stranger could penetrate. They ignored the absurdities and rarely showed emotion.

Once at the Barclay's Center, Coda had a three block walk to his apartment. The studio space was a long narrow rectangle on the second floor of a moderately new building. He considered himself lucky that he didn't have any roommates, but the lack of square footage did gnaw away at him.

He spent all his money on location rather than size.

He has lived in the same apartment since graduating from TCSUM and has been surrounded by the same tenants the entire time, most of which he never conversed with.[1]

Ms. Harris was the exception.

"Coda, how was your day?" she asked as he walked toward the building.

"Same as always. What about you?"

Coda paused at the top step and watched her sweep the tiny area inside the two-foot high fence surrounding the entrance. "Oh, it was wonderful. Somebody won fifty-thousand dollars on *The Price is Right* and they were jumping up and down, screaming to the heavens. I think

---

[1] Short for The College State University of Manhattan, as previously stated. From this point forward, it will only be written in its abbreviated form.

my heart skipped a beat or two. A woman my age shouldn't be having that much excitement," Ms. Harris said, clutching her chest.

In the time he'd known her, Coda hadn't learned her first name.

"Also," Ms. Harris continued, "I still need another book from you! You promised me a week ago." She wagged the broom in his direction.

"Did you finish the one I gave you?" Coda was inching closer to the door. He enjoyed talking to Ms. Harris most days, but he wanted to slip away into oblivion in his apartment for the night.

"Well, no."

"Why not?"

"It's too long. I didn't think someone could write such a sprawling story about the common cold causing the collapse of society."

"I warned you ahead of time," Coda said. "Stevie Queen is notorious for that. Part of her appeal I suppose."

"I never abandon a book after starting it, so I'll finish it eventually," Ms. Harris said, steadying herself against the decaying broom. Coda had no idea how old she was, if she had kids, how long she had been living in Brooklyn, or any of those other details you'd expect to gather after multiple conversations with someone.

Coda was fascinated by the life story each person had but struggled with how to extract the information. And once he got it, was there any point in continuing to seek their company?

That was likely one of the reasons why he found himself at twenty-five with no dating prospects.

Coda gave Ms. Harris one last look before stepping inside. She returned to her sweeping without a care for his sudden departure.

Coda's apartment adhered to a minimalist design, meaning no pictures or artwork or decorations adorned any wall. The cheap paint echoed back, begging to be covered, but he always refused. The space was boring and uninspired except for one thing.

The books.

By now, it's no secret that Coda's love of books is his defining characteristic—maybe even a side hustle if he found a way to make money from it. His physical appearance being secondary since his hobbies, experiences, passions, beliefs, and other intangible features are more compelling than the manufactured looks he could adopt.

What made Coda's love of books different?

Well, nothing. Unless you decide to eat each book after finishing it, the most practical use is to read them and then have them collect dust in their permanent home.

For Coda, the entire apartment served as his library. Books were stuffed under his bed. Within the kitchen cabinets. On the tank of the toilet. Amongst his clothes in the dresser. Stacked on his nightstands, coffee table, and desk. No place was off limits because the space he had was limited. If he was honest with himself, he'd speak about how he wanted to open a bookstore and persuade others that reading wasn't a forgotten pastime or chore or something only old people did when they stopped having sex. Gotta excite the mind somehow, right?

He hadn't been honest with Sam about what his side hustle would be because in that moment he didn't realize he was already in the midst of it. Sure, Coda wasn't running a recognizable bookstore, but he was giving away his books to anyone who showed even the faintest interest.

He pulled out the notebook from his nightstand and flipped through the pages. Each was marked with dozens of names and books he'd lent throughout the years. It all started back with Cousin Sal and would continue far into the future.

Over half the entries had a checkmark next to them indicating the book had been returned. For the most part, people were good about that. The unspoken contract between Coda and the other party was that they had an unlimited amount of time to read the book as long as they *eventually* brought it back. In a court of law, the word *eventually* would be subject to much poking and prodding. Coda contemplated enacting a time limit on each book rental, but that felt cold and contrary to what his goal was: to get people to read a fucking book for once.

MILLIONS of books were in circulation, so there had to be a match for each person.

Not all books were created equal though and Coda certainly had his favorites, which he lent out more than others. Currently, he had almost none in his possession. This wasn't made clear to him until he began thumbing through the notebook and noticed the entries highlighted in yellow rarely had a checkmark next to them.

People returned the junk but kept his gold. Go figure.

He tossed the notebook aside and moved to the closet pressed between the full-length mirror and dresser. Coda knocked several times against the paneled wood in the back until he heard the hollow sound. He pushed once . . . moved to the right . . . pushed again . . . moved further to the right and finally found where the paneling pressed inward before popping out. He opened up the secret compartment and stared inside, seeing nothing. He grabbed his phone and shined the light into the tight space and saw a lone book.

It was one from his childhood, *Harrison Spotter and the Pebble of Grave Importance*. The first book to make it onto his elite list; the first book with the symbol. He still recalled sitting in the pizza shop on quiet nights when the customers were scarce and the conversation with Cousin Sal lagged. Coda would sink deeper into the chaotic world of Harrison Spotter and all the unfortunate and harrowing events that plagued him at the summ—

His phone chimed, pulling Coda from the daydream and back to the dusty closet floor.

Coda stared down at the phone and watched as another text message popped onto the screen.

He scanned the texts from his sister, Cecilia. They were another plea, the same kind she had been sending him for what may have been months or years. Cecilia just didn't understand, and he had grown tired of explaining the situation to her. At least she didn't try to guilt trip him by bringing up their dead father like she had done before. Coda began to type out a response before giving up halfway through and deleting it. Any text would come off as insincere and only incite more hysterics from his sister. Cecilia would eventually dispatch another sister to reach out with the same plea.

Still sitting in the closet, Coda returned the book to its hideaway. He retreated back into the rectangle and the notebook. He tore a page out from the back and skimmed through the ledger, writing out all the highlighted entries on the fresh piece of paper.

His hand cramped by the seventh line, but he powered through until all thirteen rows were written out in his aggressively neat penmanship.

The thought thumped into him like a jab to the nose: getting the books back would solve *everything*.

five

IN NAME ONLY

After working at a software company specializing in UX/UI development for three years, Nolan Treiber worked with an impressive catalog of clients. She discovered that the moniker of being a Fortune 500 Company just meant they were willing to throw piles of money at an improved customer experience. The world of UX/UI development starts long before any components or code gets produced. While Nolan was competent on the development side of things, she quickly realized her specialty was in gathering requirements and deciphering the needs of the customer through various boring activities.

Look:

Her job is kick-ass but the average bloke wouldn't find much meaning in a long-winded description of what Nolan does.[2] It's important to continue learning new things, but most people don't give a flying saucer in expanding their tiny tunnel of knowledge.

For all of her advising and development of new applications, Nolan has no appetite to use any outside of work. Translation: She does not partake in the world(s) of social media. Shocking, right? Sure, you could find information about her online but none of it stems from a profile created on any social media site. During her time at TCSUM, she enjoyed the anonymity and the disturbed looks she got whenever potential friends would ramble through the usual suspects they assumed she was active on. It also helped her avoid more criticism than she already

---

[2] User Experience/User Interface (UX/UI) development is the process of examining and then building software that customers of a product interact with. For example, using JEC's banking portal to catch the money pig five times in two minutes for that elusive hundred dollar check was developed by robots to improve the customer experience. In Nolan's case she deciphers requirements from the company she's consulting at and translates them back to the development team. They go off and do their thing, which is glossing over an extremely unpleasant period of time for some. After the magic, Nolan will help test and showcase the results back to the business group. Lost yet?

This entire process is iterative and involves way more steps than mentioned. In total, revamping a customer experience can take years with ballooning scope, petty disagreements, changing staff, and poor funding.

Was that sterile enough to never want more information about UX/UI development again?

received in person.

Instead of focusing on creating a false online narrative like so many others purposely do in college, Nolan dedicated herself to excelling in school and used her own connections to waltz into the job that demanded so much of her time.

After working at a software company specializing in UX/UI development for three years, Nolan was tired of it. The thrill was gone. The clients were dull and always had the same problems. The twelve-hour workdays didn't feel like a burden anymore, but should they really be the norm?

Her motivation to continue down this path was limited to two reasons: (1) Nolan was driven by the desire to achieve something in her life and (2) she was worried how she'd stay occupied without a job.

See:

Nolan is the granddaughter of a real estate mogul and grew up in the lavish, exclusive side of New York City that involved extravagant weekday parties, trips to the Hamptons on the weekends, chauffeurs, luxury penthouses in the epicenter of Manhattan, galas at museums, donations to political campaigns, meetings in skyscrapers, and other oddities.

Simply put, she had money.

More than enough that she'd never have to work a day in her life if she wanted. Her parents had chosen that path and spent their time going to charity events and feigning that they cared about the poor and downtrodden folks of this fine world. Nolan didn't despise her parents for the cheap game they participated in, but she had no intention of following in their footsteps.

By the age of twelve, Nolan stopped going to most of the functions she'd been dragged to for years. She learned that those required events still happened without her presence. Instead, she roamed around the streets of New York City in search of something, anything to give her life meaning. Nolan spent her weekends riding the subway from one end of a line to another with no thought to where she'd end up as long as she made it home before her parents became concerned.

She rarely left New York City though. For all the money and all the opportunity that came along with it, Nolan always found herself surrounded by the skyscrapers and noise and chaos. She didn't mind it, but there had to be more out there, right? As with most things, the concern of always being in the city faded as her high school years ended and morphed into her time at TCSUM. Time flowed like a river runs—always moving ahead without concern for anything else.

In a more recent time, Nolan walked into the unnamed software company like any other Friday.[3] Her afternoon was full of meetings and consultations. Nolan intended to use her morning to catch up on two-week-old emails that weren't topical anymore.

"Do you have a minute?" Sophia asked as Nolan made it to her desk.

"Yeah, sure. What's up?"

"Let's talk in my office." Sophia turned heel and walked down the hall. She rarely came out in the mornings to bother her underlings, so naturally, everyone watched as Nolan trailed behind her.

"Close the door," Sophia instructed.

Nolan did and then sat on the L-shaped couch that dominated the office. Nolan tried to make herself comfortable without looking like she was pining for a nap.

Not much phased Nolan Treiber, but Sophia Kriminell was a notable exception. Maybe it was Nolan's desire to have a motherly figure in her life or the overwhelming desire to impress her boss, but regardless of the reason, Nolan wanted to dissolve into nothingness in Sophia's presence.

"Do you like your job, Nolan?" Sophia asked from behind the desk. It was all so formal. It was all so corporate. Did life always work in such clichés? Nolan believed it did when you became a passive conductor in your own life.

"Yes, of course. The three years have passed by in a—"

"Blink of an eye? Save the clichés. Why do you even want to work here? Everyone knows of the Treiber family and their footprint across this city."

"I like the challenge and the opportunity to meet people."

"To meet other wealthy people like you?"

"Well, no," Nolan said, shifting slightly on the couch. She felt herself slipping.

---

[3] In earlier drafts of this novel, the name of the software company was included, but once the buzz around this literature circulated, the company requested that direct mention be removed or they'd conjure up a fat, tiresome lawsuit. Okay, fine. But let it be known: The dastardly company has a predatory business practice and someone should look into them. Specifically, Sophia Kriminell. It's right there in the name for goodness sake.

"How long do you see yourself here?"

"I . . . I don't know. It's hard to say."

"Take a guess," Sophia said, clasping her hands into a knot.

"Unless there's another job that comes along, I see myself being here for a long time."

Sophia nodded, absorbing the information. "You know about the two manager positions that we have open, correct?"

"Yeah, the one for our clients here in New York and the other in LA."

"You're ready to step into the manager position, but I do have hesitations. I see you as a flight risk. That money you have. Oh, it must seem limitless. I've worked with others before that have more money than you probably do and they always find a way to squander it. You could go anywhere and start new. I need a long-term commitment."

"Yes, yes. Of course," Nolan said. Her mind raced with the possibilities. Finally, she'd have new challenges and move beyond the boredom that had settled into her routine.

"Are you even going to ask how long of a commitment it would need to be?" Sophia said.

"At least five years?"

"At least six years."

"I can do that."

"Are you sure? Legally, I can't make you sign a contract to stay here, but if you were to leave," Sophia said, leaning closer to emphasize the drama behind her next words, "I could ruin your next career move with three phone calls."

Curiosity got the best of Nolan, so she had to ask. "Three phone calls? Who would you call?"

"I can't divulge that information . . . for obvious reasons. Your family is well connected, but I assure you that I know other sorts of people."

Sophia always had a fetish for Nolan's family throughout her employment. In the beginning, Nolan was uncomfortable with all the comments, but now she was numb to them. Nolan had heard a lot worse from students during her college years. As soon as they found out her last name, they treated her differently. Some wanted a slice of the money pie, others wanted to rip her down a few pegs in order to make their own existence more tolerable. Nolan had a hard time believing people existed outside of those groups.

"Is this an official offer or just a hypothetical?" Nolan asked.

"It's a tentative offer. I need some time to think through everything."

"I'm extremely grateful at the potential opportunity," Nolan said. "I can't thank you enough."

"You can thank me with an expensive bottle of wine to show your appreciation for my gratitude."

"Oh, okay. I can do that. Is there anything else?"

"No. We will reconvene sometime soon. Good-bye." Sophia turned away from the couch and began punching at the keyboard. No, like actually punching the keyboard. It explained why a majority of her emails were gibberish.

Nolan left the office and returned to her desk.

Her mind began to snowball into what it would be like to move to Los Angeles. She'd drive out there, for sure. She had to. She needed to see the country and experience the vignettes that happened all over. Sure, Los Angeles may be somewhat of a New York City mimic, but the people had to be different, the climate milder, and the public transportation cleaner. Did they even have a subway? They had beaches though! And celebrities! And a big sign that people went to look at even though it could be seen perfectly fine from miles away.

Nolan felt an ease settle over her. The boredom would subside. Her routine would be dismantled in favor of a new adventure. It's what she wanted. It's what she earned.

Fuck anybody that thought otherwise. She'd always have to fight the stigma that money was the only reason she got her job or found success in keeping clients or that her privileged upbringing instantly made her an airhead or a raging bitch.

They knew nothing about her, largely because she never told anyone the details.

Nolan sat at her desk for the rest of the morning and hashed out a plan for how she would sever ties from her parents. She would start with a modest amount of money in LA (only what she had earned during the last three years) and work herself up. It took shape. She could see her future, waiting on the next subway stop.

Sometime in the midst of her fantasy, her phone rang. She didn't bother to look at the contact information since she was both preoccupied and programmed to answer anytime it rang.

"Hi," the voice said with some hesitation. "You have something I need back."

six

ORIGIN STORY

Like any respectable superhero, understanding the origin story is critical. It provides the context for why the character functions the way they do, usually due to a traumatic or heroic act that altered their life.

Unfortunately for Coda and Nolan, their origin story was mostly forgotten. It had been at some party during some part of their sophomore year at TCSUM, but that was as detailed as either of them recalled.

The takeaway here is that they somehow met on that fateful night in hazy circumstances. It spawned a glorious friendship that survived for the remainder of college.

Each party had a reason for its success.

For Nolan, it was apparent that Coda never treated her differently after finding out her family tree. The blank look on his face could have argued he hadn't heard of the Treiber name before. It was a welcome relief.

For Coda, Nolan was never interested in being more than friends. He didn't need some steamy, loveless love affair that only lasted until someone got their feelings hurt. Coda had enough rattling around in his head that he didn't need added confusion.

After realizing their majors overlapped heavily, the two began studying together multiple times each week. Instead of going to the school library, Nolan insisted on Coda picking a number between one and twelve. That would decide how many subway stops they would go before getting off and finding a random location to hunker down. Seeing that Nolan was an expert in the entirety of Manhattan, she would advise Coda to decrease or increase his selection so that they'd find a more suitable place to go.

Their study sessions stayed on the topic of studying except when the pressure of it all became too much and Nolan looked up from her laptop, blurting out a question. In the beginning, the questions were basic and establishing a baseline for who she was sitting across from.

"Where did you grow up?"

"What was your childhood like?"

"Were you popular in high school."

They demanded simple answers from Coda, none that really inspired him to dig into the type of person he was.

On one occasion, Nolan asked, "Are your parents still together? I mean, assuming they were together in the first place. You never want to—you're giving me a weird look. Am I saying too much?"

Coda closed his laptop and put down the pen. He focused his attention on Nolan. "My dad died like six, seven years ago now. But to answer your question: My parents were still together up until that point."

"Oh . . . oh, wow."

"He was a firefighter. Worked at the station near our house."

"He died in a fire?" Nolan asked.

"No, actually. I could see why you'd think that though," Coda said. His voice was restrained and hesitant to share the information. He couldn't remember the last time he talked about his father. Sure, Coda thought about him all the time and how it was just them against the women of the house. They had to band together! And that's why Coda never talked about it: He had to fend for himself and, like a petulant child, Coda decided it wasn't fair. "My dad slipped in the shower and broke his neck. They say he died instantly, but I swear I saw some life within his eyes when I found him."

"What the fuck, Coda? Why haven't you ever said anything before?"

"The last thing you'd want me to do is introduce myself by saying I have a dead parent. It's not a great opening line," he said with a forced smile. "I lost myself for a while after that, so it's not a place I want to go back to and talking about him is the first step to repeating that nightmare."

"I'm sorry." Nolan knew about painful parental experiences, but it would never be the right time to share.

"I know. There's not much else to say. We can't go back and change what happened."

"Would you, if you could?"

"Of course. I can't think of a reason why I wouldn't."

"Oh, c'mon Coda. You like to read. That's obvious given you have a different book each time I see you and I see you every day," Nolan said, motioning over to the fat paperback adjacent to the laptop. "You should know that going back in time never works out for any of the involved parties. It's a fool's errand."

Coda glanced down at the book and back over to Nolan. "I suppose you're right. Did I ever tell you what I do with each book I read?"

"No, I don't think you have."

"I read the last page first," Coda said, picking up the book and flipping it to the last page. He showed it to Nolan before dropping it back onto the table.

"Why? Doesn't that spoil the ending?"

"You'd think so, but a lot of times it doesn't. The last page of a book isn't always the last page of the story, which is somehow a comforting thought. Sometimes it is the author thanking those who contributed to their work or an appendix or a small blurb about the font that was used. And when the story does end on the last page, I take it as an opportunity to unravel the mystery. You'd think the last page of a story would make sense, but it rarely does. It's like starting to watch a television show halfway through; you'd pick up a piece or two of information, but the meaning behind it doesn't stick."

"How do you still enjoy the book? I don't understand."

Coda picked it up again. "Nolan, the endings never matter. If you are concerned about having the ending spoiled, are you actually reading the book for the right reasons?"

"I didn't realize there was a right reason to read a book."

"No. Yeah. You're right. I meant that it's all about the journey."

"I understand. Have you ever not started a book by reading the last page?"

"I used to. I remember doing that with some of the first books I read at the pizza shop."

"You never told me that y—never mind. What changed? What prompted your shift in reading habits?"

"You are looking for the origin story," Coda said. "I'm sorry but I don't remember why. It just started one day and the habit will continue."

"There's worse habits to choose from, so you picked a mild one."

"When's the last time you've read a book?" Coda asked.

"For fun? Never. I spent my childhood exploring this wonderful city as I've told you before," Nolan said.

"Right, right. Would you ever . . . ?"

"I mean, yeah, probably. Something out there must be of interest to me. I wouldn't know where to start though."

"I can help you there. Just tell me when and we will find you something meaningful."

"Don't hold your breath. I need to get out from this heap of work before I think about reading in my free time."

"Fine. Fair enough," Coda said, throwing his hands up in mock surrender. "But this offer doesn't go stale, so redeem it at any time."

seven

PARLEY

"How long has it been? Six months? Eight months? I don't even remember anymore," Nolan said into the phone. She spun around in her chair and surveyed her immediate space. Nobody was close enough to hear the conversation. The company frowned at personal calls during core working hours of 8 a.m. to 8 p.m.

"I have written down that I gave you the book almost a year ago. And if I recall, we stopped talking after the incident at the bar," Coda said. He remembered the details but decided not to dive into them unless Nolan made the first move. He was willing to move on without a need to rehash the past.

"Ah, you're right. The Wobbling Stool was our favorite. The best meeting spot after a long day of work. An amazing view of the skyline too," Nolan reminisced. She wasn't wrong. Nolan and Coda found their way to The Wobbling Stool at least twice a week as the bar was conveniently placed along their routes back home.

"Yeah, so, how have you been?" Coda asked.

"Fine. I might be getting a promotion. I'm not sure. You know Sophia—always masking the true meaning of her words," Nolan said.

"Oh nice, I'm happy for you," Coda said with supposed sincerity. Phone calls were wonderful in distorting intention even when the inflection and tone were dead giveaways. "Is it for a manager job? I remember you talking about that before."

"Yeah. How do you remember that? I didn't realize I have been trying to get promoted for this long that even *you* would be familiar with the situation."

A slight dig, but Coda didn't fault her for it. Both of them were to blame for their current situation. "You talked about it passionately every time I saw you."

"Almost as passionate as you are about your books."

A lull in the conversation. Where should it go next?

"Have you read it?" Coda eventually asked. "The book I lent you."

"Coda, I'm sorry, but I don't even recall the name of the book. You know that reading was never something I enjoyed." Nolan spun her chair back around and pulled in closer to the desk. She used to have several pictures tacked up to the cubicle wall, but they were now face down and collecting dust on the desk. Nolan picked one up and flipped it over. Two smiling faces stared back at her.

"No, no. I understand. The name of the book is *A Competition for the Royal Seat*. I'd appreciate if you could find and get it back to me."

"Is everything okay?" Nolan said, sensing the urgency of the request.

"Of course, I just ran an audit of my books and realized I'm good at lending them out, but not great in having them returned."

"And you decided to call me about this during work after we haven't spoken in months?"

"Correct."

"I'll need more of an answer than that," Nolan laughed.

"I just want them back. Trying to take a proactive approach with something in my life."

"How many are you trying to get back?"

"Twelve," Coda said without hesitation. He visualized the list he had written out the night before.

"Am I the first one you reached out to?"

"You were a logical place to start. I could take care of two things at once."

"What do you mean?" Nolan asked, already knowing what Coda would say next.

"I'd like for us to be friends again. We can talk about what happ—"

"That's not necessary," Nolan said. "We both said things we shouldn't have, most of which I don't even remember anymore."

"Oh . . . okay . . . good. I didn't want to relive any of that."

"Coda, look, I need to get back to work, but let's meet up next week. I'll find the book and bring it with me."

"Yeah, I'd like that. The Wobbling Stool?"

"Of course," Nolan said. "We can't cheat on them."

"I'll text you when I head over."

After an elongated back and forth of good-byes, Nolan hung up and refocused herself. She returned to her aggressive list of emails and began to sort through them.

When she was done, Nolan pinned the photos back up on the wall and reminded herself how much she had missed Coda.

eight

PLAN OF ACTION

Coda was stuck.

He took the list out of his pocket and unfolded it. The first few names were easy. Ms. Harris, Nolan, his sister, and former coworker.

Simple.

People he knew and could track down without issue. He already talked to Nolan and saw Ms. Harris yesterday, nudging her toward finishing the book. He called his sister, Cassandra, and she agreed to drop off the book sometime over the weekend when she wasn't busy. As for his coworker, Coda needed to figure out where the Soaps and Suitcases Department sat.

As for the other names, he read them again and again, trying to pinpoint the last time he saw each person.

"What are you looking at?" Sam asked. He was standing behind Coda with three water bottles cradled in his arms. "Just doing my part," he said after noticing Coda's glance. "One of these days, the left water fountain will overtake the competition. I hope I'm here to see it."

"Thank you for your service," Coda said.

Sam placed the water bottles on his desk and turned back toward Coda. "So?"

"What?"

"That piece of paper. I've seen you pull that out a bunch of times today," Sam said, pointing to the evidence in question.

"Trying to recover some lost merchandise."

"Is that right? What kind of merchandise? Is it of the illegal variety?" Sam questioned, lowering his voice so the roaming robots wouldn't hear their conversation. Each day, the robots from the thirty-fifth floor sent a concise five-page email to management detailing the building gossip, which gave them a distinct advantage over humans since they lacked remorse in being greasy snitches.

Coda's face contorted into a jumble of strained muscles. "Are you joking?" he asked.

"Yeah, of course," Sam said, laughing off his string of questions. "You don't seem like the type to engage in such nefarious activity."

"You caught me. I'm a pretty uneventful person . . . Listen, can we pick this up later?" Coda asked, folding up the piece of paper and returning it to his pocket.

"Sure, sure. I'll be here."

Coda got up from his desk and walked down the hall. His manager, Hugo, was standing outside his office staring down at his fake watch. He didn't think anyone knew, but *everyone* knew. "Right on time!" he said as Coda approached. "We can sit in here if you like." Hugo motioned to the office.

Coda followed him in and closed the door. Besides the quarterly meetings that happened three times a year, this was the only other semi-regular meeting that Coda participated in.

The giant plaque reading HUGO BOSS glared back into Coda's face as he sat down. Was it bizarre that his boss's last name was Boss? No more than an odd coincidence you'd find in a lazy script. Was it bizarre that his boss's name was a direct copy of the famous fashion company that ran into soaring profits after making uniforms for the Nazis? Yes, yes it was.

"How's your week been?" Hugo asked.

"Good," Coda said, shaking his head. "Continuing on the project. We are making good progress it seems like."

"Nice, nice. You have been doing great work. I asked around and everyone seems to like you. What's your secret?"

Coda laughed. "I'm surprised to hear that. I don't interact with many people. Most of my time is spent developing new code or filling up water bottles."

"Nice, nice. I have seen your collection of WBs. That's what I like to call water bottles—it saves time. You have an impressive display of WBs. I'm kind of jealous," Hugo said, looking over at his barren shelves.

"You could get some if you wanted. They are everywhere around here," Coda pointed out.

"Why don't I take a few of yours?" Hugo suggested.

"Sure. They are just water bottles."

"WBs, please, if you don't mind. And they are more than that, Coda."

"How so?"

"They represent your power and influence within this bison-eat-bison company we work for. Do you understand that the Airplane and

Autocannon Department is the most competitive place in the entire company? People will try to persuade you that the Aglet and Avocado Department is fierce with cutthroat personnel, but I have never seen anything like this department before. The way individuals like you proudly display your WBs on the cubicle shelves like a hooker flashing her tits on the street corner is so bold, so electrifying."

"Okay."

"Nice, nice. I'm glad you understand. I need you to bring it down a notch or two. I can't have you gunning for my job!" Hugo Boss said with a nervous laugh. He adjusted his tie and pulled it even tighter against his neck. He let out a small cough.

"You can come by whenever and take them."

"Thanks for the WBs. I'll be sure to include it in your performance review. Helping other employees is a fantastic soft skill to have. Last time I checked, it's not something the Soft Skill Academy on the fifty-first floor taught."

"I didn't know that. Thanks for sharing," Coda said. He was bored of this conversation.

"Coda, what do you like about this job? What keeps you coming into work each day?" Hugo suddenly asked.

"That's easy: the routine. I love that each day is the same. I love that I wake up each morning and take the same subway lines that arrive and depart at the same exact times. I love that I need to wait five minutes to badge into the building because everyone wants to be first into the office. I love that I need to follow the same process for completing a user story and that I get asked the same questions each and every time I finish one. I love that the robots are programmed to walk the floor at the same time each day so I know when I shouldn't be participating in any office gossip. I love that the same lady serves the same sandwiches in the cafeteria and pretends that the Wednesday version has a secret sauce on them that certainly doesn't exist since the Wednesday sandwich tastes no different than any other day. I love that I read the same status updates and watch as each project has a little green check next to it even though we all know each one is failing miserably. I love that I ride home on a crowded subway that smells of the collective body odor that built up from everyone working in a cramped, soggy office building. Hugo, I love it all. This routine would be anyone's dream and I can't think of doing anything else until I fall into my grave one day."

"Nice, nice. Great answer. I too am a fan of the routine that JEC provides its employees. I'll be here until I retire or get murdered by an ex-lover like in one of those crime shows on The Flix. Ya know, Netflix, but I prefer calling it The Flix. Saves time."

Coda blinked at Hugo Boss several times as if to silently tell him how much of a dope he was.

Hugo loosened his tie and took a big breath before tightening it again. He continued: "One other thing I wanted to remind you about: The ten-thousand-dollar bonus announced at the quarterly will only be available to those employees who are employed at JEC up through next Friday. It's a silly thing for me to mention since you don't intend on going anywhere, but I have been telling everyone on the floor about it."

"Thanks, I appreciate that. I fully intend to still be employed here up through next Friday."

After a minute of meaningless back and forth, Coda left Hugo Boss's office and walked out to the elevators. He scanned the large, electric directory that showed all the floors and which departments sat where. Coda typed in Soaps and Suitcases. The screen buffered for several seconds before spitting out the result.

Coda rode in silence to the forty-first floor. There was no elevator music because that was unnecessary spending for JEC. The world had just recovered from a global pandemic and the only realization anyone got out of it was that elevator music sucked. Congress even passed a law about it. Seriously, it's true. Ms. Harris told Coda all about it one night after work.

The forty-first floor of the JEC building was entirely black except for the pockets of light that guided Coda down the hallway. He heard the occasional disgruntled outburst as a thud ricocheted off a random wall.

Coda marched forward, eventually running into an employee.

"Hey, hi," Coda said. "Do you know where Boris sits?"

"Who am I speaking to?" the shape said, reaching their arms out into the light.

"Coda Finn. I work down on the Airplane and Autocannon floor. I'm looking for my friend Boris." Friend was a loose term, but it seemed like the fastest way to end this unpleasant experience.

"It's Boris!" the voice said, stepping into the swath of light. He kept his arms outstretched and pulled Coda in for a hug. "It's been too long! What do I owe the pleasure of seeing you?"

"Are you okay?" Coda asked. Boris's face was a patchwork of bruises.

"Yeah, yup. I'm good. Just one of the hazards of working on this floor. We are all managing to survive."

"Has it always been like this?"

"It's one of the reasons why I left AA. My skin is sensitive to light, so I was appreciative that the company has a space for employees like me to thrive."

Coda nodded, not remembering Boris speaking of that ailment before. "That's . . . great. I know it's been a while, but I wanted to see if you finished reading that graphic novel I gave you. I'm sorry I haven't reached out before intruding like this."

"Don't worry about it. It's not like I reached out to you either. Has anyone taken my spot down there?"

"Yeah, I think so, but I don't really walk over to that part of the floor anymore. I don't have much of a reason since you left."

"Wow, Coda, that's so sweet," Boris said and pulled Coda in for another hug. "I always knew we had something special."

"Me too, me too."

"What was your book called again?"

"*Listen People.*"

"What kind of title is that?!" Boris yelled, laughing until he fell out of the light and smacked his face off the nearby wall.

"I didn't write the graphic novel, so I can't answer that. It's widely recognized as one of the best ever written though."

Boris stepped back into the light and rubbed his face. "Yeah, yeah, yeah. That's the usual generalized conjecture someone says when they have nothing else noteworthy to mention about a book."

"Okay, well, anyway . . . do you still have it? I need it back. I, uh, I have a friend that wants to read it."

"I'm sure it's somewhere in my apartment. I'll take a look tonight."

"Thanks Boris."

"Of course, my friend. I'll drop it off on your desk when I have secured the package. I'll brave my sensitivity just for you."

"It was good seeing you," Coda said and crept out of the light.

"See ya later, buddy!" the voice called out like a specter in the night.

Coda navigated slowly back to the elevators. On his way down, he reread through the list. Coda had no idea what the locations were for the remaining names. They were oddities from earlier times in his life.

He could resort to Internet stalking, but he had a better solution.

"Where'd you go?" Sam asked as Coda returned to his dingy refuge.

"I met with Hugo then went to the Soaps and Suitcases Department."

"Oh, wonderful! How was it?" Sam said with disturbing enthusiasm.

"Dark."

"I'm not surprised. You didn't hear it from me, but the company has been trying to sell off that department."

"Why?"

"Nobody uses soaps anymore! Where have you been, Coda?" Sam scoffed.

"I just told you where I was."

"Uh . . . never mind . . . anyways, what's the deal with the paper? I have been waiting patiently to hear," Sam said with a grin.

"How serious are you about your private investigator work?" Coda asked.

"Deeply serious. If I'm being honest, I'd rather be tailing someone through the streets or sitting in an Internet café to uncover some lost information. And once I finish all the detective work, I want to come back with all the papers organized—and this is key—in a Manila folder that I present to the client by pulling out the evidence one piece at a time. I really can't stress enough how key that Manila folder is. I have a stack of five hundred waiting at home. There was a fantastic deal at Office Depot. So yeah, I'm serious."

"I wasn't sold until the Manila folder part, so I'm glad you mentioned it." Coda slid over the piece of paper. "I need help with the last seven. I'd like to know their current location, so I can try to get the books back from them," he said, pointing to each row.

"This is not what I was expecting, but I am intrigued. Why these books? What kind of relationship do you have with these people? Is there any bad blood I need to know about? Do you need me to get photographic proof of their location?"

Coda decided to just answer the last question. "I only need their address if you can find it."

"Easy. Too easy."

"Really?"

"Yeah," Sam said, looking around to see where the robots were. "When do you need this by?"

"Monday."

"Easy, easy. C'mon Coda, I was expecting a challenge!"

"Maybe some other time. Do I owe you anything?"

"For my coworker and pal? Absolutely not!"

"Thanks Sam, I really appreciate you doing this for me. I'll make you a copy of this list. I want to keep the original."

<u>nine</u>

A PERFECT CIRCLE

Coda swiped his metro card and pushed through the revolving arm toward the platform. He had just missed the previous train, so he stood there by his lonesome, hearing the echoes of conversations on the other side of the tracks.

He grabbed at his backpack and pulled out the book he had been working through. *Yelling at Friends* was a *New York Times* bestseller and chronicled one man's journey as he alienated every relationship he had by constantly berating and demeaning the ones around him. While Coda was only halfway through, he suspected that the author wasn't going to have many relationships intact by the end.

The platform began to fill up with working class citizens eager to go home. When the train arrived, Coda pressed through the departing crowd and managed to get a seat next to the door.

He closed his eyes and imagined himself drawing a circle. Perfect in every sense. He then repeated the motion and sketched another perfect circle on top of the first. Coda continued this pattern until the page was worn and he started to tear through the notebook. He kept going, pressing the pencil down harder, but still creating that perfect circle. Again and again.

And again.
And again.
And again.
And again.

He kept going until he tore through the entire notebook and was etching that perfect circle into the wooden table beneath.

Why? he kept asking himself. He had everything he needed, what anyone would want: a good job with potential growth, a stable place to live, and money to plan for the future. People would kill for that. People have killed for that.

Coda didn't have the answer. The mysteries of his feelings weren't easy to unlock.

He knew he needed those books back. They were the first step to repairing the relationship, to reminding himself what she meant—no, means—to him. There's still time. He can fix it, but the books are critical—

Coda felt a nudge.

"Sorry, hon," the woman said.

Coda opened his eyes and looked down at the woman. Her stature was fragile and hard earned. She was crammed between Coda and the guy holding on tightly to his guitar case. "Do you want me to get up?" Coda asked. "So you have more space."

"How about a conversation instead? To keep each other occupied."

"Sure," Coda said, placing the book down on his lap. "Are you heading home?"

"To the shelter," the woman said with a quick nod.

"What kind of shelter?"

"Battered and abused women. I say women, but we get young girls too. Those are . . . difficult to see."

"What do you do there?"

"Talk to them. Or sit with them. Whatever they need. I have a pretty good sense of how to approach the new women in there. The harder ones are the familiar faces because you've talked and listened to them already, so you start to feel helpless after a while."

"That has to be tough."

"It is, but if I hadn't found a shelter like that during my first marriage, I'd be dead," the woman said with no hint of exaggeration.

"Wow, I'm sorry."

"Don't be sorry. I'm here now, talking with you. No sense in burying yourself in the past. What about you, hon? Are you heading home?" the woman asked, slapping Coda's knee with her hand.

"Yeah," he said, nodding.

"And what do you do?"

"I work at JEC as a software developer."

"JEC," the woman said, rolling the name around in her head. "Isn't that the company that claims they will have the cure to cancer in five years? Not just one of the cancers, but *all* of them."

"That's the one," Coda said.

"What a noble profession you are in! Saving lives and helping to keep families together."

"Yeah, it's a great company to work for. I really enjoy it." Coda didn't have the heart to tell her that he worked on programs that increased the potency of the autocannons that did anything but bring families together.

"What are you reading there?" the woman asked.

Coda held up the book and gave the woman a brief run through of the experiment the author was voluntarily engaging in.

"How interesting," the woman said. "I wonder why he would do that."

"He hasn't made that clear yet. He just seems to be interested in the psychology behind all of it and exploring why relationships fail."

"That's pretty simple, isn't it?"

"What do you mean?" Coda asked, shifting in his seat.

The train was packed tightly with people standing and holding onto the poles strategically placed throughout. It was noisy, but Coda had no difficulty focusing onto what the woman was saying.

"Relationships fail because people are involved. An imperfect being trying to build a connection with another imperfect being. Lord knows I have failed at it plenty of times—even with my own children! Can you imagine? How can a mother not have a healthy relationship with her own children?"

"I can imagine," Coda said, losing any desire to continue talking. Thankfully, he had a good excuse. "This is my stop."

"Oh, that was quick."

Coda was caught in the surge towards the door, but managed to ask, "What's your name?"

"Grace."

"It was a pleasure. That's my—"

He was propelled out the door before he could finish.

As previously suggested, Coda has several sisters. Three, if you are looking for an exact number. Coda is the youngest and an answer to his parent's prayers for a son. The order goes as such: Cecilia, Cassandra, and then Clementine. Their relevance to this story is limited due to each of them partaking in their own lives that rarely overlap with Coda's.

Cecilia will call Coda occasionally to chastise him about a current situation that's been heavily eluded to. That's the extent of their relationship. Cecilia did her best to set an example by excelling in school and making it on her own, especially after their dad died. From the outside, her life seemed great and from the inside, the same was true. She had no complaints—at least none that she shared with Coda.

Cassandra had a steady job and a solid group of friends. She kept most of the details to herself, so Coda didn't have much information about her. From the outside, her life seemed great and from the inside, the same was true. She had no complaints—at least none that she shared with Coda.

Clementine was still working through her master's degree in . . . Coda couldn't remember. She had a job at a . . . Coda couldn't remember. He knew she lived in an apartment with five other roommates that he'd never met. From the outside, her life seemed great and from the inside, the same was true. She had no complaints—at least none that she shared with Coda.

Look:

The sisters were as plain as Coda, which was refreshing in a crazy world where people felt a need to be something they weren't for the attention and adoration of others who didn't give a flying heck about them.

Of the three, Cassandra was the only one who showed any interest in reading. She'd graze through Coda's bookshelves back when they both lived in the family house. Sometimes she would walk away with a book or ask Coda a clarifying question, but there were plenty of times where she seemed unimpressed with his offerings and left empty handed.

The Diablo in the Silver Metropolis was a sprawling non-fiction tale about the mass murderer that stalked Chicago during the World's Fair in the late 1800's.

Cassandra had noticed the book out on Coda's coffee table during one of her wellness visits and insisted on reading it. Coda explained the premise and she nodded in understanding, saying she didn't need the entire plot ruined before she read it as if you could spoil history.

Now Cassandra was coming over to return the book she admitted to never reading. Actually, she read the first chapter before falling asleep one night and then never returned to it again.

Oh, what a terrible woe! Nothing in this world is tossed aside as quickly as an unwanted book! It's better to burn up the pages and watch the smoke rise to the heavens then see a book degrade down in the dirt. What a tragedy!

"Hey Cod," Cassandra said as she walked into Coda's apartment.[4]

"Hey Cass, how are you?" Coda asked, giving her a hug.

Cassandra swiveled her head and looked around the rectangle. Coda could tell that she was forming opinions, but none materialized for him to hear.

"I'm good. Just the usual stuff. Here's your book back." Cassandra handed it over in the same condition as when she took it.

His heart raced as he thumbed through the pages and found the symbol waiting in the back.

Another one down. He was making better progress than expected.

Coda closed the book and set it down on the coffee table. "So, did you want to stay for a bit? Maybe grab dinner somewhere around here. The Nets are playing tonight, so we might get stuck in a surge of people if we go now though."

Cassandra paused briefly. "I can't tonight. I'm sorry. I promised my friend that we would meet up for dinner."

A thin excuse, but not entirely unexpected. Coda never considered that he was the black sheep of the sibling group, the one that no one wanted to deal with for an extended period of time. He had only himself to blame though. When you isolate yourself for so long, people will stop reaching out. It explained the situation with Nolan.

"It's okay. I understand. Some other time," he said.

"Is everything alright, Coda? Cecilia wanted me to check since you never returned her call."

"Yeah, I'm totally fine. There's nothing to worry about."

"You still haven't reac—"

"Cass, please. I don't want to talk about that right now."

"Cod, there isn't much time left. You have to fix it. You don't want to live with regret for the rest of your life."

"Okay."

"Please don't shut me out," Cassandra said. "I just want what's best for you."

"Cecilia is always saying the same thing and if you guys actually believed that then you'd let me decide how to handle it."

"I just don't want you to make a mistake. We are all protective of you.

---

[4] Pronounced *code* not *cod*. Just to make things confusing. But rejoice, she's the only person that called him that, so don't expect to see it often.

You were so young when dad died and you went through a lot. I don't want to see that same cycle for you again."

"Okay, Cass."

"Do you even remember anymore?"

"Remember what?" Coda asked.

"The reason why you two haven't spoken."

Coda thought for a moment. There was a fog over that period like how someone doesn't remember the moment of impact from a fall. All that remained was the emotion after—the deep sense of distrust that could never be repaired. The answer was buried within, but he wasn't willing to confront it. "I . . . It doesn't matter."

"Co—"

"Is there anything else?" Coda said, walking to the door.

"No, I guess there isn't."

"Okay, let's get dinner sometime soon and talk about anything else other than this."

"Deal," Cassandra said.

They hugged one more time and she disappeared down the steps.

Coda grabbed the book and stared down at it. Would it be enough? Would this ludicrous exercise really change how Coda felt? Would it be the catalyst to undo the damage?

Coda sat down on the couch and marked off the row for *The Diablo in the Silver Metropolis*. He tossed the paper aside, closed his eyes, and watched as the perfect circle dug its way into his skin.

<u>ten</u>

DEBRIEF

It was 10 a.m. on Monday morning and Sam still wasn't at work.

Coda had gone to the water fountain twice, filling up three bottles each time, to curb the anxiety of Sam not being in the office.

He thought all weekend about the names he had given Sam: where they might be, what they were doing with their lives, would they even remember Coda. He thought about how ridiculous it was to encroach on people's lives and demand to get a book back they had likely forgotten about eons ago. He thought about how he needed Nolan's help with this. He thought about how all of the awkwardness and semi-stalking and other oddities would seem trivial when Coda finally had his collection of thirteen books again.

Coda slipped on his headphones and fell into the lines of code he was writing. It was an escape to make his mind work in a different way than reading a book could. Coding was problem solving, running tests over and over to find the flaw in your creation. Reading was imagining a world, a character, a situation. Both gave him a shot of dopamine whenever he modified that one line of code to remove the errors or when he opened a new book and flipped to the last page to see what the author left for him.

The thrill gets harder to find though. The routine bogs it down.

The routine, the perfect circle, the worn path, the pattern, the cycle, the . . .

It's the main thing Coda thought about besides the one question always dangling in front of him like a bully holding out a stolen lunch:

Is this it?

He needed to keep moving forward. It'll pass. Life always ch-ch-changes. But what's the point of waiting until that time comes?

Coda felt a tap on his shoulder and knew Sam had made it into the office.

"I have my findings," Sam said, with a wide grin that showed off his stained teeth. "Shall we grab a conference room to dissect the information?" Sam was five paces ahead as Coda fell in line behind. Sam winded through the hallway and ducked down a side corridor before settling on the eight-person room. "Let's hope no one interrupts us."

Coda sat down across from Sam and waited for him to begin.

"The task you laid out last week was to track down the addresses of seven individuals you deemed critically important. One of my duties as an amateur private—what?" Sam said, looking over at Coda's sinking face.

"Nothing. Go ahead," Coda urged him like a mother would to a child.

"As I was saying, as an amateur private investigator, I have taken an oath to provide you with the answers, regardless of whether I agree with the outcome or not. In addition," Sam said, triumphantly as if he practiced the speech in front of the mirror, "I swear to present the information to you in a clear, concise manner."

Coda was momentarily interested in Sam's wording of providing the answers without mentioning if they were truthful or not. The thought passed freely and he moved on. "That wasn't the presentation?"

"No, Coda, that was the preamble like what they did in the Declaration of Independence."

Coda was beginning to lose hope in this man. "I think you mean the Constitution."

"Yes, yes. Of course. My apologies for the costly mistake," Sam said with a heavy dosage of sarcasm. "Anyways, here is what I found."

Sam undid the flaps of the briefcase beside him with a satisfying *click*. Carefully, Sam removed the Manila folder and placed it on the table like the first piece of turkey on Thanksgiving. He gave a startling smile and pushed the Manila folder toward Coda.

There was no arguing that Sam was killing it with the presentation. A little sloppy on the speech, but atmosphere was pivotal, and he had indeed watched enough detective movies in his time.

Sam flipped open the Manila folder and began to explain his findings. "I was able to obtain seven addresses. In a majority of cases, the addresses I found matched up to the name you provided. As expected, the addresses were readily available once I understood the habits of each subject—their likes, dislikes, shopping habits, places they may have visited. Coda, can I ask a question?"

"Yeah."

"You have lived your whole life in New York, correct?"

"Yeah."

"Does it surprise you that none of the names you gave me currently reside in New York City or even the state?"

"I . . . I—what?"

"It's true! Take a look at this map I printed out." Sam removed a sheet from his stack and placed it on top. "All of your targets—"

"Please don't call them targets," Coda said.

"Subjects?"

"No."

"Prey?"

"What? No!"

"Victims?"

"Fuck—just . . . just call them individuals."

"Okay, fine. So bland. All of your *individuals* are on this map. You can see they are pretty spread out across the country. One in Pennsylvania, another in the Chicago area, and so on. I'll let you take a closer look at that."

Coda grabbed the paper and looked through it before readjusting his eyes and absorbing what was in front of him. Sam was right. The tiny, imperfect circles were in red Sharpie at random spots across the countrywide map. It didn't seem possible.

How was it that everyone else seemed to have left New York City except for him? Was he the only one drawing perfect circles?

"This may be more challenging than expected. Do you think it's possible to fly to each place?" Coda asked.

"Oh yeah, that won't be a problem, but it's an expensive option depending on how you plan it."

Coda had some knowledge of airplanes considering the department he worked in, but he had never flown before. His lack of globetrotting wasn't out of fear, but due to minimal opportunities.

Something else lodged in Coda's mind as thoughts of flying dissipated.

"Wait, did you say you found all seven addresses?"

"Mhm," Sam said, pulling out another sheet of paper.

"But are they all for the names I provided?"

Sam waved a finger at Coda with extreme enthusiasm. "No! Actually, two of the addresses I have here are for the closest living relative."

"Do you think they are dead or something?"

"It's possible," Sam said in a more somber tone, hinting he may know something. If that was the case, Coda didn't pick up on it. Sam continued: "But they may have recently moved or be an exception to posting all their information online."

"That's a relief. How did they seem?"

"What do you mean?"

"You must have come across pictures of each person. Did they seem . . . content?"

"Coda, I don't think you want me to answer that."

"Why not?"

"My job is to give you the facts, not speculate on the individuals."

"I understand," Coda said.

"There's not much here besides the addresses and a couple different maps. I hope that's okay. You said you didn't want more than that."

"Anything more than this and it would have felt like actual stalking."

"Coda, this is absolutely an invasion of privacy. You do need to recognize that. And you also need to consider that if you do go knock on each of these doors, there is a high chance that something unfavorable will happen. People are territorial."

"I know."

"This is important to you, huh?" Sam asked.

"It is. This will sound silly, but it could be the most meaningful thing I do in my life."

Sam laughed, but not in a mocking way. "We all need to partake in some adventure and maybe this is yours. Maybe this is your opportunity to step off the path and wander into new territory."

eleven

GRACE

Tuesday night.

"I have the addresses," Coda announced to Nolan as she sat down with her first drink at The Wobbling Stool. He was amazed the outside seating was open so early in the year.

"And I have your book. I thought it would be difficult to find, but it was in plain view on my desk. I guess my subconscious wanted me to read it." She handed the book over.

Coda scanned the last page of *A Competition for the Royal Seat* and read the declaration from the author that the next book in the series would be out faster than "Darelynz could cross the Hollowing Sea." It has been a decade since the latest book and Coda stopped caring about it a long time ago, which probably caused his distaste toward sequels.

"Thanks Nolan. This means a lot," Coda said, pausing to look at the symbol.

"I never realized there was a message inside the front cover. I can understand why you wanted this back. Who is G.F.?" Nolan asked.

"Wh-what message?" Coda said, confused at the statement.

Nolan reached over and grabbed the book. "Right here," she said, pointing down at the note.

Coda read it. Inspiring words that encouraged him to fight each battle, clearly trying to fit into the theme of the book. When did he get this? What was the catalyst for those words at the time?

Always questions with no answers.

"G.F.," Coda said as if the letters were foreign to him. "Those are my mom's initials. Grace Finn. I never wanted her to put 'Mom' or some other moniker because I knew the kids at school would make fun of me for it. She's the one who gave me all the books I'm going after. She's the one that left the symbol."

"What does the symbol mean?" Nolan asked, taking another sip of her drink.

"I don't know because I never asked. I assumed it was something she made up."

"Why don't you ask her? If you care to know."

"We haven't talked in years."

"What? You've never said anything," Nolan said, shaking her head.

"It's something I am embarrassed about and it's not like you talk much about your personal life either."

"But you told me about your dad."

"I did. That was only because you asked the right questions." Coda saw the look on Nolan's face and continued. "Don't take that the wrong way. We have had amazing memories together and I want to recapture that again."

"I understand. But why the urgency with getting these books back?"

"My mom is dying," he said as if he was reading aloud the menu at his least favorite restaurant.

"Coda—"

"And the sensible thing would be to see her and rectify our situation, but it doesn't feel like enough. My sisters tell me she barely recognizes them on the scarce moments she is conscious, and I'm so afraid of her looking back at me like I'm some stranger. The books . . . maybe they will shake loose something in her brain. I know they were important to her. She loved to read and listen to music. You could always count on her doing one of those two things and I was the only one who showed a true interest in reading. We bonded over that. She gave me a massive collection of books over the years, but only a select few ever got the symbol. And I don't know why. They certainly aren't her favorite books; some of them aren't even good, but it didn't matter. I read each one more closely than any of the others, and I still—

"Nolan, I need them back. It's the only way I'll feel close to my mom again because that person in hospice is not her."

"Your mom is in hospice? You need to see her. You nee—"

"When my dad died, I didn't want to go to the funeral. What kid would? Knowing where my dad's dead body would permanently be freaked me out. All week I cried and begged my mom to let me stay home. She didn't really argue with me because she was grieving too— trying to keep it together and figure out how best to move forward. I never understood her emotion during that time. All she did was read and listen to music. I never saw her cry or yell or have a giant meltdown like we expect people to do. We all grieve in our own way I suppose. But I remember the day of the funeral. I was in my room and being aggressively stubborn about not going. She eventually came into my room after getting my sisters ready and asked me once more if I wanted to go. I said no. She sat down beside me and said, 'Coda, I'm going to die someday, hopefully long before you. I'm telling you now that you don't need to come to my funeral. I want you to remember me for all the moments before that time. And I know your dad would feel the same way.' I'll never forget that because of how absurd it sounded. She gave me permission to skip her funeral while deciding if I wanted to go to my dad's. I didn't think her words would carry meaning so quickly."

"Did you go to the funeral?" Nolan asked.

"No, I didn't."

"Do you regret it?"

"Surprisingly, I don't. We have funerals to make ourselves feel good. The person who died is never going to know how many people showed up or how fantastic the food was afterwards. We do it because it's nice to think that when you die people will still remember you, celebrate you. I think about my dad every day, which is more than anyone who went to his funeral over a decade ago can say.

"I say all this because I am not worried about seeing my mom before she dies. It's not the last memory of her I want. But—but, if I can get these books and I can show her . . . Nolan, I need this. Maybe it seems crazy or a waste of time, but I have the addresses. I know where everyone supposedly is. This is my best shot of breaking the routine, of feeling whole again. I want to repair my relationship with her. And I want to do it with my best friend."

Coda smiled back at Nolan.

"Of course I'll help you. We need to go around the city and find these people, right? That shouldn't be too hard."

"Actually," Coda said, "none of them live in New York anymore."

"Oh, where then?"

Coda memorized the locations and began to rattle them off. "Pennsylvania, Florida, North Carolina, Texas, Illinois, Colorado, and . . . California."

"Wow. They are scattered out. I mean, we could fly to one each weekend and that would avoid us using too much vacation," Nolan said, thinking out loud.

"That will take too long. I wanted to drive."

"Drive?! Across the country? That will take forever!"

"About eighty hours."

"Holy shit. That would be awful. And where would you get the car from? You don't even drive."

"Do you still have your car?"

"Yeah, but I haven't driven it in a while."

"We could use it though, right?"

"Are you using me for my car?" Nolan asked.

"Absolutely not," Coda said. "I'm trying to be tactical about this. I wanted your help with this before I found out where everyone lives."

"Why don't you call these people and have them send the books back?"

"Because I'm tired Nolan! I'm tired of doing the same fucking routine every day. Getting up and going to work just to sit there and waste away until it's socially acceptable to leave. I want to quit. I can't keep doing it for the rest of my life."

"You can't quit though," Nolan said. "How would you pay rent? How would you . . . do anything? And what about the ten thousand dollars they are giving you?"

"How do you know about that?" Coda asked.

"It's all over the news."

"It really feels like I'm the only person who doesn't like JEC, which should be a good enough reason to leave. Life is too short, Nolan. I saw my dad die when I was thirteen and now my mom doesn't have much time left. I don't want to be at the end of my life and wonder about the things I missed out on. I have barely left this city. This . . . this is the best opportunity we have to break the cycle, to meet new people, and see what else is out there. I promise you that work will be waiting when you get back. Anyways, you have enough money to fall back on, right? Your parents can lend you some."

"Don't. Please don't go there, Coda. I have never asked for a handout from them. We aren't going down this road again. Please."

"You're right. I'm sorry. I should have known better."

"I can't just leave my job for weeks," Nolan said. "I am on the verge of getting promoted to the manager position. If you just wait a bit, maybe we can make a road trip out of my move to California."

"I can't wait that long. I need to leave by the end of the week. Can't you take vacation?"

"I don't have weeks of vacation stacked up. My boss doesn't believe in taking time off."

"What a wonderful place to work."

"Coda, I get it. That feeling of an endless routine can be suffocating. But I'm happy with the current path of my career. I have worked really hard to make a name for myself that people don't associate with my parents. I need to follow through with this new job. I hope you understand." The itch was there for Nolan, but she became good at ignoring it. She wanted to escape from New York City too, but what would be better in the long run: a temporary breakout in the form of a road trip or a permanent one with the new position?

"I totally understand. Thanks for the book," he said softly.

"Coda, please don't quit your job. I can't overstate that enough. At least stay there until Friday so you can get the money. It's only three days. You can do it."

Coda looked around The Wobbling Stool. The patrons were pouring in to take advantage of happy hour prices or to wash away sins. Sometimes, it was tough to tell the difference. Coda watched as pockets of people engaged in animated conversation with the words being nothing more than a jumbled buzzing sound by the time they reached his ears. It matched nicely with the traffic twenty stories below.

A band of plexiglass surrounded the entirety of the roof.

Just in case.

"I have to take the next step. The money doesn't matter. It's all about time."

Nolan dropped the subject, knowing Coda couldn't be persuaded. "You haven't even told me how you know these people."

"Most of them were surface-level relationships."

"And you gave strangers books that are so important to you?"

"Well, the books ebbed and flowed on their importance. After I stopped talking to my mom, I didn't see the need in keeping the books to myself. People would ask about the notes or the symbol, but they weren't too concerned. I mean, it's not unheard of for people to leave traces behind. When I met these people, I had a strong urge to give them a book. They'd talk about their lives or we'd delve into a topic that matched up nicely with one of the books and it just seemed right. I don't think people read nearly enough and their excuses for doing so are inadequate. So this was an opportunity for me to do my part."

"I see. Clearly, I have failed you," Nolan said with a much needed laugh. The air between them was still stale and the details of the conversation didn't help to lighten the mood.

"You didn't fail me."

Nolan nodded. "Do you want another drink?" she said, pointing to the empty glasses.

"Yeah, sure. What do you want?"

Nolan said her request. Coda repeated it in his head multiple times to remember. The bartender groaned at the complexity of their order but made it anyways. It's not like she had much of a choice. Of course, she could have quit her job right then, but that would have been ridiculous! People don't quit their jobs on a whim. It's the slow, existential dread that really fucks someone over. The light, constant tapping noise that drives someone insane after months or years. People don't quit their jobs because money wins every time.

Sure, it's easy to hate people like Nolan Treiber because she has money, but here is the harsh reality:

Money doesn't buy you happiness.

Yes, it provides shelter and food, but once you surpass that in the Hierarchy of Needs, money gives you the excess in life that everyone has been conditioned to want.

Listen:

This life isn't easy and the stranglehold that money has over everyone is a massive catastrophe, but don't blame the individuals at the top because that makes you complacent, which is exactly what they want! The rich thrive on the mediocrity of the rest. They thrive on the notion that people believe they can never possibly pull themselves out of the bog and live a normal life.

Everybody has a story.

Everybody.

Even people like Nolan have struggles and doubts and concerns and a fucked-up brain that tells her things it shouldn't.

Coda contemplated all those things in the time it took for the bartender to retrieve the drinks. Upon returning to the table, he asked Nolan, "So what else is new? How have the last six months been?"

Their conversations carried into the night with their friendship being restored to how it was.

twelve

FORFEIT

Coda strongly considered what Nolan said about not quitting.

The contemplation didn't last long. By Thursday afternoon, Coda was stuffing the few belongings he had into his backpack. He decided to leave the water bottles behind for some scavenger to pick through. He attached a note saying to handle them with care and be sure to only use the water fountain on the LEFT side. There was a war to win and it relied on dedicated warriors with the staunchest one fleeing like a conscientious objector.

Sam swiveled around in his chair and watched Coda briefly before asking, "Are you leaving the team? Where are you going?"

"A bit more extreme than that."

"They aren't sending you to the dark floor, are they? You go up there one time and management thinks you have an affinity for that sort of stuff," Sam said.

"No, it's not like that. I quit," Coda said, looking over at him. A small smile escaped. He couldn't help it. The defiance was absolutely thrilling to him.

"Quit? As in Q-U-I-T?"

"Correct."

"Now why would you go and do a silly thing like that?"

"Because . . ." Coda thought for a moment. His mind was shifting, the neurons firing with no cohesive mission. A rewiring was taking place. Neuroplasticity was in full swing. That itch. Instead of worrying about the sensibility of it, he spoke. "Because of the perfect circle, Sam."

"The what?"

Coda stopped loading in the last of his miscellaneous objects and gave Sam his full attention. The stage was his. Don't fuck it up, kid. "The perfect circle. The one that gets you out of bed each morning, shuffles your feet to the bathroom, makes you wear one of the same eight shirts, pays for the overpriced coffee you know you shouldn't keep getting, and on and on and on. It's the perfect circle you only realize you've been drawing after years . . . Sam, I can't stand it here. Everybody looks miserable as they ride that elevator up, knowing they will be parked in front of a desk under the white noise and shitty lights for the next eight to ten hours. We take home a meager amount of money compared to the billions the company brags about on a quarterly basis during our three times a year meeting. Doesn't that bother you, Sam? They call it a fucking quarterly, but it doesn't even happen every quarter. There is literally an entire floor that is painted black and no one seems to mind. And what about our department, huh? You know, it never bothered me until I looked up the number of deaths each year from an autocannon. Do you know how many, Sam? Twenty-five thousand. Am I responsible for the deaths of twenty-five thousand people because it doesn't look like management is concerned about that number . . . I wake up every day and do work that I don't give a fuck about just for the paycheck. Is that really the life I want to have? Did I get birthed into this world just to sit at this desk until the arthritis and hypertension get so bad that someone needs to wheel me out of here in a body bag. And I know what you or anyone else will say: 'But Coda, this is your first job out of college. You have no idea what other companies are like.' What a stupid thing to tell someone. There are a million places worse than JEC, but there's millions of places that would be better for me and I intend to find one of them.

"I feel sorry for you, Sam. You're a good guy, but you've fully bought into the idea that this is it. I'm only twenty-five. I don't want to wake up depressed each day because I have to come to this mediocre job and continue to believe that this is all there is."

Nobody was listening to the monologue unfold because no one else would dare to get caught up in the drama. The robots would have a detailed report by day's end.

Sam's response was succinct and orderly as if this wasn't the first time he'd seen a meltdown. "I understand."

"Thank you again for finding the addresses. I really do appreciate that," Coda said.

"Of course, let me know how it goes."

"By the way," Coda said, scoffing at the implausibility of his next words, "I don't even know your last name."

"Rogers. Sam Rogers."

"Almost like Captain America. Too bad I didn't know that sooner. It would have been a good nickname."

"Maybe when you come back," Sam said.

"Not a chance," Coda said, forcing a smile to dull the bluntness of his statement.

Coda grabbed his backpack and headed for the elevators.

Approaching footsteps and a voice. "Where are you going?"

"Aw, fu—Hugo, I told you I was quitting."

"I thought you were kidding! You have always been one for jokes."

"I have never cracked one joke in front of you. Ever." Coda was repeatedly hitting the elevator button like it could be summoned faster by the assault.

"Can you wait here for just a second? I need to consult the Leader Decision Guide. I have never been in this situation before," Hugo said, whispering the last part out of supposed embarrassment.

"Absolutely not."

"What about your WBs? Did you take them with you?"

"Hugo, I left them here. Just for you."

Taken aback at the consideration, Hugo waivered for a moment before returning to business. "How should we proceed then?"

"I'll give you my badge if you'll let me leave."

The elevator chimed a lovely tune, signaling that one of the twenty-seven elevators would be opening momentarily.

"Uh . . . hmm . . . I don't know. I really want to check the Leader—"

Coda handed over his badge. "Good-bye."

"Coda, you won't be eligible for the ten-thousand-dollar bonus. That is something I do know."

Coda walked to the open elevators doors and stepped inside. With all the dramatic acting he could muster, Coda let out one last quip, "Hugo, I never gave a *fuck* about the money."

Coda closed his eyes briefly and watched the first crack in the perfect circle form.

thirteen

PUPPET

As Coda was reveling in his newfound backbone and the imperfect circle, in another part of Manhattan, Nolan was summoned into her boss's office.

"Hi Sophia. This is unexpected."

"Hello. Sit." The command came off her lips like Nolan was nothing more than a dog.

"Don't we usually wait until Friday for these types of meetings? Is everything okay?"

"Yes, fine. Thank you for coming back to the office. I wanted to follow up with you about the position we spoke of previously."

Nolan leaned back into the couch. She could feel her heartbeat steadily rising and pulsating in her throat. She waited for Sophia to continue.

"As you recall, we have two open manager positions. One at the office here and another out in LA."

Nolan nodded. Yes, she was quite familiar with the situation.

"I want to formally extend the manager position here in New York to you," Sophia said in a flat tone. This was just another business transaction to her. Moving pieces around a chessboard she hadn't cared about in years.

Nolan's smile quickly faded as the thumping in her chest and throat carried up into her head. *This is it. This is how they always start*. She felt her hands shake and that unpleasant, indescribable wave of anxiety take over every portion of her body. The sinking feeling that her world was going to implode and never recover settled in. She needed her medication, but it was back at her desk. A thousand miles away.

She slipped back to the beginning.

Around the time Coda finished up his last day of work at Uncle Sal's Pizza Palooza & Planetarium, Nolan prepared for another night of meaningless parties. She sat in her room and put on makeup and a dress that somebody else told her to wear. She put her hair up in a magnificent bun that somebody else told her to do. She would smile when someone else told her to. For being only thirteen years old, Nolan was proper and refined and skilled at doing her parent's dirty work. She was overtly sexualized to get a few more dollars out of the stingier individuals. It finally clicked for her that night though. Nolan understood the excess and the waste that her parents partook in. The fake conversations, fake laughs, fake compliments, fake notions of friendship. It was all a charade. The money was thrown around from rich person to rich person without ever leaving the tight knit circle. It was a group of addicts passing around a used needle, seeking the same high without understanding the contamination and disease that was coursing through them. Nolan's hands started to shake, and that thumping traveled its way up into her head and whispered all the terrible thoughts that a person should never hear. *Her life was hopeless, meaningless. She was a puppet for her parents. No one respected her. They just wanted the money.* She became trapped in her own head, wondering if there would ever be a way out. Nolan's first panic attack came and went before she finished with the makeup, but it left a lasting impact. And it marked her for future instances. As the years pressed onward, they got worse. The minutes would stretch into hours of isolation where she'd cry until her eyes stung and the snot dripped from her nose onto the carpet. She couldn't tell anyone because . . . it was a weakness. Nolan was determined to figure it out on her own.

It wasn't until college that she understood she wasn't alone and the pain of constantly having a wall up was unbearable. When a doctor officially recognized her panic attacks and anxiety, she started down the path of finding the right medication and a therapist. One of the medications gave her headaches all the time, another kept her in such a deflated state that she almost ruined an entire semester of classes.

With time though, things leveled out. To gloss over this period of time should not make it seem like it was easy for Nolan. Every single day was a battle to correct her thoughts and keep her emotions from spiraling too high or too low.

Now, the medication is a massive deterrent for those unwanted spikes and, generally, she lives a "normal" life. Whatever the fuck that means.

Maybe Nolan was actually lucky enough to get better.

Still though, there were moments when the medication couldn't curb the panic attacks and stop her from dipping into those awful, awful lows.

Nolan took a deep breath and exhaled. "What about the job in Los

Angeles? I was hoping to get that position. I am ready for the challenge."

"No, you aren't," Sophia said. "You're a New York girl. Your network is here. It would be foolish of me to make you start over someplace new. I don't think you're very adaptable."

"Adaptable? Sophia, I have worked with five different companies in the past year alone."

Nolan's thoughts blitzed in. She was losing control.

"There are people out on the floor who have done twice that amount, so it's not a number to be proud of. It's actually kind of low if I'm being honest. And I always intend on being honest with my employees."

Nolan needed to leave. She needed to think . . . or stop thinking . . . or cry . . . or . . . or . . . or—

"Sophia, I need a minute." Nolan quickly moved out of the office and toward her desk. Once there, she grabbed her bag and continued walking until she made it to the bathroom.

She started with her breathing and focused on that. *Slow it down. Slow it down.*

Next, she began to pick through the thoughts that tumbled around in her head.

TheweatheroutinLAiswonderful
AllthepeopletomeetAllthenewplacestoexplore
ThenewclientsTheopportunitiesThechancetogetawayfromNewYork . . .

It continued on.

Nolan had never considered that LA wouldn't be an option because in her mind it was the only choice. How foolish of her. How unbelievably moronic of her to—

Stop.

The medication was the last step. She pulled the bottle out of her bag and dumped one tiny capsule into her hand.

What a world. That pill shuffled the bad chemicals in her brain and brought her back from the brink.

She composed herself in the bathroom and minimized the flood of thoughts until one bubbled up to the surface and stayed: *I'm not a fucking puppet.*

Her parents tried and succeeded at it for years.

Her old friends always assumed that Nolan could pay for everything and give the best, most expensive gifts for birthdays.

Her teachers sometimes suggested that the classrooms could use some new supplies in a slimy, subtle way.

And now, her boss didn't think she was adaptable enough to move across the country. All the years of work, all the long nights. All the billable hours that Nolan provided. All the promises that things will pay off if she just kept going down the path.

Fuck the path.

"Hi, I'm back," Nolan said with a smile. "Sorry about that."

"You understand my decision, correct?" Sophia said, not even bothering to look up from her laptop.

"Yes. It's quite clear that you think I'm not capable enough in moving across the country and starting over. You think that because I grew up in this city and have *connections* here that I am somehow destined to die here."

"That's not wha—"

"Oh? It sounded like that to me."

"Don't—"

Clarity latched itself onto Nolan. Defiance wasn't ingrained in Nolan, but sometimes it was needed in order to usher in a new era.

"Sophia, I quit."

The words hung in the air briefly before evaporating out of existence.

Sophia's demeanor went unchanged. "Okay. I knew you weren't cut out for this." One last jab. The trademark of any successful manager. They don't like any imbalance of power.

"You're right. I'm not. Hope you find some other lackey to do this job."

Nolan pulled off her badge and tossed it onto the couch. It bounced once and slid off onto the floor.

The itch. It was driving her mad.

There was only one cure for it.

She found the contact and hit the little phone icon.

"Hi, when should we leave?"

II

HEADING WEST
(AND OTHER DIRECTIONS)

fourteen

LOGISTICS

Before we proceed into the actual journey, let's run though the logistics. Nolan and Coda don't have any of the details planned out, but we can provide a rough sketch of what the next few weeks will look like.

Transportation
They decided to drive across the country to each location. Nolan dusted off the 2008 Pinto Pinata.

Not familiar?

The 2008 Pinto Pinata was mass produced in the small town of Blue Ball, Pennsylvania.[5] Due to the numerous traffic lights and crowded streets, the town demanded that the mayor come up with an affordable car option compared to the gas guzzling Hummers that Cletus and his band of degenerates continually drove around. The exhaust blown from the pipes of those Hummers were fogging up the storefronts on Main Street. Fed up with the rabid complaints from his constituents, the mayor, Mr. Sud, made a call to The Pinto Company with a desperate plea to solve their crisis. The Pinto Company specialized in—you guessed it—black beans. They stressed to Mr. Sud numerous times that they did not have the means to produce a car to his specifications or even a car in general! Mr. Sud would not be persuaded so easily. His parents beat it into him that no was never an appropriate answer.

Mr. Sud talked to the CEO of The Pinto Company for eighteen hours on that fateful, world-shifting day until an agreement was met. Using two billion dollars of his own money, Mr. Sud would fund the research, development, marketing, and sales of the newly named Pinto Pinata. In return, Mr. Sud would receive all the profits in perpetuity. He argued that The Pinto Company would skyrocket to fame and recognition with the introduction of the groundbreaking car.

This story is a sad one.

---

[5] Many things in this novel are up made or exaggerated for greater effect, but not here. Blue Ball is an actual place full of lovely people who have some pent up energy they need to get rid of.

With a price of two hundred and fifty thousand dollars, the Pinto Pinata was unaffordable to the town folk of Blue Ball and became an absolute failure among the likes of Mr. Sud's other doomed enterprises like a television show, real estate in Las Vegas, a university, a book series about a fictional Mr. Sud who runs for president, and a series of steaks that tasted like dish soap.

The town of Blue Ball did indeed get blue balled by the mayor and his triumphant claim that the Pinto Pinata would be the saving grace.

The Treiber family was the sole purchaser for no other reason than because they could. The car was used sparingly, so a cross-country drive would finally put it through its paces.

Lodgings

Who knows! They will figure it out along the way, but they did agree to not sleep at any hotels, motels, or Holiday Inns with less than a three-star rating on Yelp.

Locations

Sam Rogers did the heavy lifting here. The addresses he provided Coda gave a precise roadmap of where he needed to go. While the specific addresses will be kept a secret for privacy reasons, the cities listed below serve as a general guideline for where the two travelers are going.

1. Easton, Pennsylvania
2. Charlotte, North Carolina
3. Venice, Florida
4. Chicago, Illinois
5. Denton, Texas
6. Aurora, Colorado
7. San Francisco, California

Considering Coda met his list of people in New York, it's not surprising that many of them ventured off to other major cities. Statistics show that 80 percent of people who spent at least one year in a top ten city (in terms of population) will move to another in the next five years.[6]

---

[6] Word to the wise: Don't trust statistics without the proper context because what you read was horseshit. It's easy and fun to lie!

Total Time
With the assistance of Snoogle, Coda watched the map of the United States push outward to a more global view as he inputted each of the addresses. The total time for their journey west rounded out to 83 hours with a distance of 5,500 miles. Those numbers do not reflect the countless stops the duo would make during their three and a half day driving expedition, or how they'd need to drive all the way back.

Needless to say, Coda and Nolan would not be seeing New York City for at least two weeks. That wasn't a problem considering that both had just quit their jobs and had no obligations to attend to . . . except for that, uh, small thing about Coda's mom health deteriorating at a rapid rate.

Miscellaneous
Look:

Road trips can be boring even though Instagram influencers and Hollywood movies make it seem like every second is fueled by gorgeous scenery or intense run ins with wily individuals.

The truth is that some of the United States is downright ugly. Landscapes dotted by fast food establishments, degraded roads, littered sidewalks, barren trees, and other oddities. Many times, though, the sights are even worse with nothing more than scraggly shrubs and small rolling hills that provide no spectacular view except where the next gas station is.

Worst of all are the unsavory people you may encounter.

With this in mind, the story will bypass the dull moments in Nolan and Coda's journey and provide a highlight reel while stringing together the narrative. Maybe it's the right thing to do; maybe it isn't. Regardless, a decision has been reached on the matter.

You know how these things go.

Time to return to our friends and get on with this.

fifteen

OVER AND OUT

"I can't think of the last time I left New York," Coda said.

Nolan ignored him and gripped the steering wheel like she was ready to max out her bench press. She stared ahead, intent on staying in her lane amongst the heavy flow of traffic moving on the Verrazano Bridge. At least it was the weekend. Nolan wouldn't know it, but it was significantly less crowded.

They were a long way up and Nolan kept circling in her brain about how she never went to the top of the Empire State Building for this reason.

Also, it was a massive tourist trap. Any local would agree.

She clenched her chest and held it in as they crested over the peak.

"Are you alright?" Coda asked. "I could have driven if you didn't want to."

Further ... further ... just a li—

Relief.

Nolan exhaled as the car moved down onto lower ground. "Sorry, what were you saying?" she said with a smile.

"I, uh, I just said I don't know the last time I ventured outside the city."

"Me either. Actually. I explored so much of the city and never got bored of it. For a while I had a hard time imagining there was any other place worth visiting. My parents talked sometimes about all the traveling they did before I came into the picture and their stories turned me off from the idea. What was the point of traveling when you already lived in the most sought-after city in the world? I don't know if that's actually true or not, but that doesn't matter." Nolan turned to look at Coda briefly. "Now, we are going to find out what else this world as to offer."

"The world? Our travels aren't taking us that far. By the end of this though, I imagine it'll feel like we've circled the globe at least once," Coda said.

Coda didn't have the words for it, but this was monumental for him — the escape from New York. It's not monumental like winning a Nobel

Prize or discovering a new planet or perfecting that recipe of cupcakes you've been struggling with for a decade; it's quieter than that. Another step in his life that would bring him across some familiar faces and likely meet a multitude of new ones. He'd have the chance to rediscover and reconnect and possibly correct some past mistakes.

Would he tell them the truth? He hadn't considered what he'd say to each of the book thieves about why Coda Finn was miraculously standing at their front doors. *Hey, it's been a while. Good to see you. Sorry for how things ended, but I'd really like my book back. You still have it, right? You wanna know why I drove all the way here? My mom is dead! Well, almost. Yeah, crazy, right? And we've fucked things up big time, so I decided to go on a desperate chase for books to repair our fractured relationship . . .*

The daydream rambled on as he stared out the window and watched the drab scenery zip by.

The phone propped on the dashboard vibrated and pulled Coda's attention back inside. Did they want to save thirty-three seconds by taking an alternate route? No thanks. Coda declined the request and the screen returned to their tiny car hogging the deserted road.

"You need to prep me before each stop. Like, I need some backstory on these individuals," Nolan said. "Also, play some dang music. I'm thinking too much about how I destroyed my future two days ago."

Besides the conversation they had on Thursday afternoon when Nolan called him, the two had not discussed quitting their jobs. They could delve into lengthy hypotheticals and contemplations of their futures, but for right now, Coda's focus was on making it to those seven addresses.

The 2008 Pinto Pinata was ahead of its time with some alluring gadgets, but they hadn't thought to include Bluetooth, so Coda grabbed the aux cord and plugged it into his phone. He scrolled through Spotify until he found a playlist where he knew at least one song. He adjusted the volume knob to a level that didn't promote conversation or inhibit it either.

Nolan didn't seem to notice. "Um, I'm waiting . . ."

"For what?"

"Tell me about who we are driving to see—wait—I have another way of going about this. Before we make it to each location, you need to answer three questions."

"Sure."

"What is their name? How do you know them? Which book of yours do they have?"

Coda nodded in agreement. "Easy enough." He rubbed his face to clear out the thoughts. "His name is Muscle Fox. I met hi—"

"Muscle, seriously?"

Coda gave a long sigh. "Seriously. That's his birth name, so please don't ask him about it. In my experience, he gets agitated when people inquire about the uniqueness of his name."

"That will be tough, but I'll do my best."

"Let's see . . . we met at a volunteering event in Brooklyn. Picking up trash around a park. Nothing overly exciting about it."

Nolan tried to commit the information to memory. "Mhmm. Go on."

"I gave him a book called *The Bombastic Knack of Giving a Damn*."

"What a lovely name."

"A clickbait title for sure, but the message behind it is good. The author argued people don't care enough about the world to mend it."

"Sounds like something a hippie would write."

"Nah, not spiritual or anything; it's getting people to believe in something. You'd have to read it to see if you agree or not."

"Why did you give Muscle the book?" Nolan said, the syllables coming out cautiously like she was on stage at the National Spelling Bee.

"You'll have to ask him that. You only said I had to answer three questions," Coda said.

"Fine," she said, dragging the word out like a toddler. "You are just the worst sometimes."

Coda scoffed at the remark and they both turned their attention back to the road, thinking about what awaited them in Pennsylvania.

sixteen

LOOKING FOR AUTOGRAPHS

The 2008 Pinto Pinata trudged along the bridge connecting New Jersey and Pennsylvania, obeying the 25 mph sign that flashed after the toll.

"What *thing* are we crossing over?" Nolan asked.

"I believe it's water."

"Well, yes, but a river? Lake? Ocean? My sense of geography is all messed up."

"It looks like that . . . is"—Coda pinched his fingers on the map until the name popped up—"the Delaware River."

Coda was correct, but there was more to it than that. Easton was at the crux of the Delaware and Lehigh Rivers, making it a prime location for hundreds of years. Combining with the neighboring cities of Allentown and Bethlehem, the entire area was a well-kept secret of economic growth. Easton was only an hour and a half ride to Philadelphia or New York City, making it a prime location for commuters who wanted the quieter suburban life and affordable taxes compared to the egregious prices in New Jersey.

"Take a right here," Coda said. "It should be up ahead."

Nolan eased into the turn and drove slowly down the tree lined road.

The Snoogle Map application alerted them that they had reached their destination: a sprawling house with a sloping front yard. A series of steps led up to the front door, leaving no doubt where they needed to go next.

"These houses are beautiful!" Nolan said. "And they all have grass. Not a lot, but still. And garages. And porches. And . . ." She continued to point out all the items she rarely saw in New York.

Coda listened with half an ear and waited until she was done. "It's the luxury of having space." His mind was elsewhere, thinking about how they needed to go home. They couldn't intrude on other people's lives and demand back property that was given to them years earlier.

"Are you ready?" Nolan said, cutting through his thoughts.

"Y-yeah. I think. I'm oddly nervous about this."

"Don't be. It's not like you're asking for money. We are nice, respectable people and, anyways, I'm sure *Muscle Fox*—really, what a name—will be happy to see you again."

"Can you do the talking?"

"I'd be happy to. I need to burn off some energy after that long ride," Nolan said, shifting around her shoulders like she was warming up for a sporting event.

"That will be the shortest drive we have this entire trip."

Realization rippled across her face. "You're right. I am going to try and forget about that now. We have an important task to complete." Nolan turned the car off and grabbed a few items before stepping out. Coda followed, double checking his pocket to make sure the list was in there.

Nolan rang the doorbell three times. "The first two are to let them know we are here. The last one is to show that it's urgent," she explained as they waited for someone to answer.

Coda nodded, unsure if he agreed with her rationale.

Nolan stepped back from the door and looked left and then right. The wraparound porch was home to several rocking chairs and an abundance of plants showing imminent death. It was hard to tell whether neglect or timing was the culprit.

Muffled sounds came from behind the door as several locks disengaged. It swung open in a fury and they were met by a menacing man who towered above them. He braced himself on the door, favoring most of his weight onto his right leg.

"Yes?" the man said, stopping himself from saying more.

Nolan turned back to Coda and mouthed to him whether that was Muscle Fox or not. Coda shook his head quickly. No, of course the middle-aged man in front of them was not who they were looking for.

"Uh, hi. We are looking for M-Muscle," Nolan said, forcing the word out. "Is he around?"

"Who are you?"

"We are friends of his. Old, old, old friends. Trying to reconnect."

"You have the right place, but he isn't here right now." Both a relief and a disappointment. Sam had proven to be good on his word, at least for their first location.

"Is he working or something?" Nolan asked.

"He is downtown at that damn Bacon Fest."

"Bacon Fest?"

"It's exactly what you think it is," the man said with little interest.

"That is incredible."

"You two not from around here or something?" the man asked.

"No, we drove in from New York City."

"I see. We used to live over in that awful place. Is that how you met Muscle?"

"Yes," Coda said, stepping into the conversation. "It's been a while since I've seen or spoke with him."

The man turned his attention to Coda. "Then how did you find out where he lives?"

"Do you want the honest answer?"

"Let me hear the damn lie first. That may be amusing and worth my attention." The slightest smile passed over the man's face. He gripped the door a bit tighter, his knuckles beginning to turn white.

Coda noticed the man's discomfort. "Do you want to sit?"

"I'm okay for right now," he said. "Go on. Let's hear your web of lies."

"Yeah Coda, let's hear it," Nolan said. She was enjoying him being put on the spot.

"You two are expecting some spectacular lie. Normally, if I wanted to lie, I'd probably say I hired a private investigator to find your address since that feels reasonable. That's the truth though."

"Oh really? Should I be concerned? You aren't some crazed fan, are you?" the man asked.

"Crazed fan?" Nolan said.

"You two look around Muscle's age so you probably have no damn idea who I am. I was a professional boxer back in another lifetime. Three-time defending heavyweight champion. Once a month or so, I get someone knocking on the door asking for a damn autograph. I didn't think anyone gave a damn about boxing anymore."

"Wow. I had no idea. Muscle never mentioned that."

"He ... he's a complicated kid. I'll leave it at that for now. But back to your previous answer ... you actually hired a private investigator to find us?"

"It was a coworker of mine who was looking for some practical experience. He is an *aspiring* PI, if such a thing exists."

The man didn't say anything.

"What's your name?" Nolan asked.

"I'm Sylvester. Everyone calls me Sly."

"It's nice to meet you. I'm Nolan and this is Coda."

"Likewise." Sly extended a hand to Coda and then Nolan. Coda felt the arthritis. All those fights did their damage.

Sly continued. "Look, I won't take up more of your time. You can find Muscle downtown in the center circle. You can't miss him, as I'm sure you know."

"Where is downtown?"

Sly gave them quick directions, saying they passed right by it on their way in. It was close enough that they didn't need the car.

They thanked him for his time and retreated from the front porch.

It wasn't until they were halfway to the center circle that Coda had the realization. "You know, why didn't we tell his dad about the book? We are going to walk all the way there just to see Muscle, explain the situation, and then walk back to the house."

"Coda, you are overthinking this. It's all part of the adventure. Half the reason of doing this is to explore new places and meet people. Let's just find him and take it from there." A word bounced around in the recesses of Nolan's mind to explain the pattern they had to follow, but it wouldn't fully surface until they got some chips in the plains.[7]

They continued walking through the streets of College Hill, eventually passing by the series of buildings that gave the area its name. Small comments passed between them, but none developed into conversation. They came to the winding stairs cut into rock that led downtown. Less than a mile from the circle, Coda could see the milling of people and filtration of noise that was desperately trying to make its way to them.

Coda took a deep breath and exhaled. His shoulders sagged and loosened, releasing the tension that was cramped up inside.

Relax. Enjoy this.

His tension came from another place. One that he pushed aside and tried not to give much thought. Each of the people on Coda's list had a piece of his story that he hadn't shared with anyone else.

He was afraid of what Nolan would think.

---

[7] It will make sense when it needs to. Patience is a virtue after all, which is something only impatient people say.

seventeen

THE REDWOOD

Bacon Fest proved to be the event that brought everyone out, even in the brisk March weather.

From the top of the hill, Nolan saw the pinpricks of figures moving back and forth like one cohesive unit. As they got closer, it became clear that the crowd was expansive and pushed out toward the perimeter of the circle. Police barricaded off the intersecting streets to dissuade anyone from plowing through the bystanders—not like that ever stopped the real assholes from doing so at other events.

Coda led the way as Nolan grabbed onto his arm. They were adept at maneuvering through slower traffic, so they easily sidestepped and rushed past anybody that didn't match their desired walking speed.

It didn't take long to find Muscle.

Once Coda pointed him out, it made sense to Nolan. The guy was as tall as a redwood in California and lean enough that if pushed out of a plane, he had the slim chance of floating safely to the ground.

"It looks like he is standing by himself," Coda said, moving back and forth to get a better view beyond the stagnant pockets of people.

The center circle was lined with tables and tents from various vendors touting their signature creations. They walked by booths that advertised bacon lotion, bacon breath mints, bacon sunscreen, bacon shoes, books about bacon, books made of bacon, books with bacon bookmarks, and other oddities.

"Do you want to stop at any of these?" Nolan asked, tugging on Coda's arm. "You may find your next favorite book or the newest subsidiary for your former company to purchase."

Coda looked back and said, "I'm good."

Something felt off to Nolan about Coda. He seemed incredibly wound up. Had she done something wrong? It was too soon for them to have another argument. She wasn't sure their friendship could recover again. What happened if they fought while they were halfway across the country? Would he leave her and grab a flight from the closest airport? Her mind blitzed with the questions. She felt the panic sitting on the edge, waiting to be invited in. Sometimes, her panic attacks were a polite houseguest and asked for permission before completely fucking her up.

Nolan latched onto Coda's arm tighter. He didn't say anything for a few seconds before turning back around. "My arm is not an orange." He looked down at her hands. "You can stop squeezing the life out of it."

"Yeah, sorry. I zoned out for a second." Nolan relaxed her grip and felt the wave of fire in her chest recede. She was going to be fine. Sometimes the flares were a signal of a bigger fallout waiting in the shadows, other times they disappeared entirely. She hoped for the latter.

"Muscle. Hey!" Coda called out as they passed the table selling bacon cupcakes. They pushed out past the last swell of people and into the small clearing.

Muscle turned his attention down toward them. "Hey?" he said with ambivalence.

"It's Coda Finn. From New York. Do you remember me?" Coda pointed to his chest as if they were conversing in two different languages.

The confusion broke from Muscle's face as he took two massive steps toward them. "Coda! Of course I remember you!" He pulled Coda in for a hug and swallowed him in a sea of arm bones that could have wrapped themselves around Coda twice.

Nolan stared up at Muscle's vertical endowment. She would find out that he stood at an impressive 6 feet 10 inches, which didn't break any records, but if you've never seen anyone that tall before, it would catch your attention.

Muscle released Coda from his grip. "It's been—I—I'm a bit flustered. It's like seeing a ghost, but in the best possible way."

"You probably have lots of questions."

"Oh yeah, but first . . . I'm Muscle Fox. Nice to meet you," he said, looking down.

"I'm Nolan. Friend of Coda's." What an odd saying that had always been to her, like it was an unfinished thought. Friend of Coda's *what*? A friend of his beef stew? A friend of his existence? It didn't make much sense, but she went along with it anyways.

"Only a friend? I'm glad you said it so I didn't have to ask," Muscle laughed.

Ah, right. The everlasting stereotype that a girl and guy traveling across the country *must* have some sort of will they/won't they relationship.

"My good friend since college," Coda said, defusing any awkwardness. "She is my co-pilot on our journey across the country."

"Across the country? I don't follow," Muscle said.

Nolan pointed towards a less chaotic portion of the circle where some table were set up. "Let's sit down over there and talk through everything."

Not only would they field questions about their nonexistent romance, Nolan also realized they would explain a dozen times why they were doing this and the items he was after. She didn't mind though. Most of life was just a rehash of the same conversations over and over again. Another unavoidable routine. Nolan could ask ten strangers how they were doing and she guaranteed all of them would give a neutral or positive response. You had to pry and beg with potent questions to get even a shred of a meaningful answer. She came across this problem all the time with her clients. They constantly held back vital information until Nolan asked the same question framed in a varied way.

What a massive character flaw in human beings. Just think about how efficient the world would be if people were honest—good, bad, or indifferent. If Coda had been honest, he'd have fought through the discomfort and rekindled the relationship with his mom. If Nolan had been honest, she'd have ditched her parents a long time ago even though they saved her. If Nolan and Coda had been honest with each other, the secrets they will find out wouldn't be classified as such.

Around and around it goes.

Muscle sat on one side of the plastic table with Coda and Nolan taking seats on the other. The framing of it looked like they were shuffled into an interrogation room to be grilled by the veteran cop, Muscle, who was trying to wrap up one final case before retirement. A tired cliché. Add it to the slush pile.

"I'll start us off," Muscle said, stretching his arms out across the table. The metal beams underneath groaned at the added pressure. "Are you still living in New York?" the question pointed to Coda.

"Yes. I'm over near the Barclay's Center."

"Do you ever catch a game there?"

"I've never gone."

"Shame. You weren't a big sports fan when I knew you, so I'm not surprised. I didn't have much of a choice," Muscle said with a smile.

"We just met your dad. You never told me he was a professional boxer! Actually, you never told me much of anything about your life."

"We met each other at an interesting time."

The comment piqued Nolan's interest, but she let it pass once it became clear they wouldn't elaborate further.

Muscle continued. "So, what about you? Do you live in New York as well?" he asked Nolan.

"Yeah, over in Manhattan."

"Living on the good side of town, I see."

"There's nice places all across the city and Manhattan has its fair share of shitty areas too," Nolan said.

"I lived there for about . . . nine—no—ten years. My dad and I were over in Queens. Close enough to the airports so he could fly out whenever he needed to."

"I didn't even know you left the city," Coda said.

"Yeah, I finished up high school here and then went to the college right near my house. The area is okay. I get a bit stir crazy sometimes. There's enough to do here, but it feels like a place you'd want to live in when you have a family and mortgage."

"I've gotten that vibe," Nolan said.

"I'll break out of here at some point, but I don't lose sleep over it. Got other things to worry about."

Coda nodded and then asked, "Are you working?"

"Yeah. I work in the Office of Admissions at the college. I walk to work every day, which is nice and come home on my lunch break," Muscle said. He was giving the safe answers but Nolan felt there was something deeper going on. Again, she let it slide because she may be wrong and didn't want to embarrass herself.

They went back and forth with the surface level information that old acquaintances do. None of the questions were particularly exciting until Muscle asked, "So, how's your family? Your sisters still doing good? What about your mom?"

Nolan turned to Coda and saw his face get flush. "My sisters are doing well. Finding their paths in the world. My mom . . . is not doing well."

"Is she going to get better?"

"No."

"I'm sorry, man. That's heavy. I'm really sorry to hear that. She was very welcoming the few times I came over to your house."

"She loved having guests and being able to entertain. It's not a trait that got carried over to me. But . . . that's why I'm here. I wanted to find some things and give them to her. One last surprise before . . ." Coda didn't finish the thought.

Nolan waited for Coda to continue but he sat still. She didn't think he said aloud often that his mom was dying. "Coda is looking for a book that he lent you a while back. Something about taking a shit."

"The Bombastic Knack of Giving a Damn," Coda said in a flat tone.

Muscle reached up and rubbed his neck. "I know the book is somewhere in the house. Just need to find out where it went."

"Really?"

"Yeah, I didn't leave anything behind in New York and my dad is a packrat." A pause as Muscle swung his legs out from under the table. "Let's go back and find it."

They got up from the table and wove their way through the crowd. It had thinned out as they approached late afternoon. There was only so many bacon products one person could look at before having enough.

Muscle took point on the walk back and asked some more questions. How many books were they looking for? Where were they all located? Why were the books so important?

All of the questions helped Nolan to hear more of Coda's thought process. He explained everything in short, factual answers with no emotion behind them. She knew it was a ploy. She knew that Coda felt *something* about the entire situation. He'd speak about it when he was ready.

Once the conversation hit a lull, Nolan asked a question that was gnawing at her. "How did . . . you two . . . meet?"

They were halfway up the endless set of steps carved into the hill. Between heavy breaths, Muscle replied, "You . . . never . . . told . . . her?"

"It never came up until now," Coda said, not as affected by the walk as Nolan and Muscle were.

"Don't . . . be embarrassed," Muscle yelled back. He stopped at the platform breaking up their uphill walk and looked down at Nolan. "Your friend had quite the violent streak."

"There's no way," Nolan said in disbelief. She was clutching her side. It was pathetic how out of shape they were.

"Oh yeah. Coda and I met in juvie."

eighteen

CHARRED

Some believe that opposites attract, but for Coda's parents, it was simpler than that. They were the same person. Their interests aligned. Their philosophies for starting and raising a family were identical. They believed their home should be utilized for gatherings and enjoying the company of others. Who gives a damn if a stain ends up on the carpet? They laughed at the tiny moments that nobody else understood. They knew which takeout place was the cure to a bad day. They transitioned into the territory of outside jealousy because everything *looked* perfect and that's because everything *was* perfect. Sure, they bickered and stressed about money, and struggled whether Brooklyn was the right place to solidify their lives, but those moments added up to a single star—a dot—in a sky of millions. With each child they welcomed into the world, their lives got more complicated, but they always came back to the center of their perfect circle and kept rediscovering what worked. Because for them, what worked when they first met continued to be the secret formula that fueled their sustained success.

When Darian broke his neck on the bathroom floor, it ruined everything. No solo artist found the same success as when they were in a duo. Grace lost her spark; she lost her soulmate—something that Darian always poked fun at her about. Grace held it together because she had to, because she was always the stronger one. Darian could run inside a burning building and go save lives, but he was the first to cry during a movie or when the kids achieved greatness on a small scale. He deferred the tough choices to Grace. At least once a day, somewhere in the Finn household, you would hear Darian say, "Did you ask your mother?" Darian was the face of an Easter Island stone; Grace was the foundation buried underneath.

With the face gone, the foundation cracked and creaked and wore away. The three girls were too engrained in their own lives to be completely derailed by the death. They had friends to fall back on or school activities to keep their mind free from the dreadful rotating thought that they no longer had their father. Don't interpret that the wrong way. They grieved. They struggled. They had moments of immense sadness, but time trudged forward for them and the sadness became a tug instead of a constant gnaw at their livelihood.

The same couldn't be said for Coda.

He was only thirteen when his dad died. Coda was a freshman in a high school where he had minimal friends and mainly kept to himself. He had the social skills that were required to meet people (his three sisters were varying shades of exceptionally outgoing) but it took time to forge relationships, especially when you find yourself in a new, diverse environment. After several months of school, Coda was an outsider in that freshman class. Lines were drawn early, and he was shuffled into the corner with the less desirable classmates. Leave it to high schoolers to prematurely judge and categorize for not fitting into a predetermined box. It was the tired notion of cliques that Coda didn't believe was real until he was a part of it. His sisters warned him that the high school attracted a curious group of students and the Finns were always in the minority, regardless of how social and chatty they were.

Coda didn't mind the anonymity until the bullying started. Subtle jokes and stifled laughter from the more "popular" students whenever he'd participate in class. It then elevated to more targeted attempts to tear him down by calling him a faggot or making fun of him for reading or any of the other outlandish things they homed in on.

Coda was absent from school for two weeks after his dad died. He begged his mom to go back after the first week, but she insisted they take the necessary time. Coda was fearful of how far behind he'd get on the schoolwork. He saw another student earlier in the year miss three weeks due to a lacerated liver and that poor soul was still writing English papers to catch up.

Gordon Fontana. There was always a ringleader and he was it. On Coda's first day back to school, Gordon didn't say anything to him. Actually, no one did. They all knew what happened though; gossip like that spreads faster than bread mold especially with the marvelous use of social media. As a pillar of the community, Darian Finn's death attracted media coverage. The headlines spoke of a decorated firefighter and loving father and wonderful husband who found an untimely death. Quotes in the articles ranged from community members to his brothers at the fire station—all of them speaking praise.

It wasn't until three weeks after Coda went back to school that the jokes started. Coda isolated himself more than usual and became buried in books to escape his own reality. A larger target was painted on his back and people like Gordon took advantage.

Piecing together the minutes of chaos from numerous sources, the following description of the events is what the police walked away with.

Coda liked to sit in the row either closest to the door or closest to the windows. Sitting by the door meant he could be first out of the room when the bell rang, while being by the windows meant he could stare outside and let his mind wander. For his algebra class, Coda took up residence by the window most days. It was the one class he and Gordon shared. Coda entered the classroom on time and took his normal seat. As did Gordon, who sat in the back. It was easier to hurl insults at others when you couldn't see their faces. On that particular day, Gordon stood up and wandered over to Coda. "Thinking about your dead dad?" he asked. Coda didn't answer as he turned his attention away from the windows and to removing items from his backpack. Based on testimonies from other classmates, their teacher was not present in the room, which was likely the cause of the escalation. As Gordon walked away toward the front of the room to [conflicting stories about where he was going], he made one final comment. "Are you embarrassed about how he died? Do you think if your dad died in a fire he would have been charred darker than he already was?" Coda bolted up from his desk and tackled Gordon into the teacher's desk, knocking both of them to the floor. Coda punched Gordon once in the face before reaching down and grabbing scissors that had fallen off the desk. Before the other students could even get their phones out, Coda stabbed Gordon in the abdomen with the pair of scissors in what one person would describe as "something you'd see in a prison fight." Gordon screamed and pushed himself away from Coda. Some students fled the room looking for help, while a couple pinned Coda to the floor and pried the bloody scissors from his hands. Within minutes, Coda was in handcuffs and quarantined from the other students.

In a matter of seconds, Coda destroyed his life. He spent time in a juvenile detention facility with the charge of aggravated assault. Nobody explained how he wasn't charged with attempted murder besides the lawyer saying he was extremely lucky. He was expelled from the high school and didn't bother to fight the outcome. The sympathy from the community only extended so far. Some people abandoned the family altogether and spoke in hushed tones about how they always felt something was off with that boy.

Much like high school, Coda didn't interact with others in juvie except for the monstrous entity known as Muscle Fox. He was persistent and cornered Coda on multiple occasions just to get him to say something more than hello. It took time, but Coda peeled back the pain and agony of everything he'd gone through with Muscle. For being an intimidating presence, Muscle was a fantastic listener and knew the right questions to ask for Coda to unburden himself.

While he was building up a relationship with Muscle, Coda was destroying the one with his mom. Each time she came to visit him before being released on probation, Coda would spew venom at her. She took it because his pain was extraordinary. She took it because she was the foundation. But she was tired and each argument made her slip further away from her son.

The petty arguments continued once Coda was home and in between the time he started school again. Coda would sit around all day never leaving his room. He didn't touch any of the books that piled up. She urged him to get out of the house, unafraid that Coda would have another episode. She wanted her son to reacclimate himself to life, to rediscover there was a lifetime ahead that wouldn't always be filled with such pain and grief.

One night, she forced Coda out of the house to go get takeout for the family. When he returned, there was a book on his bed. *The Bombastic Knack of Giving a Damn.*

Grace left one of her notes on the inside cover.

> *Coda,*
> *The pain and sadness you feel are temporary. Your entire life is ahead of you and I hope you rediscover what a joy it can be. This book helped me regain my purpose after your dad died and it's a simple one: you and your sisters. Give a damn about something in your life and you'll find peace.*
>
> *G.F.*

Coda sat on his bed and stared down at the book. It had an uneventful cover with nothing more than the title printed in large, glossy letters across the width and length. He wouldn't have been drawn to it on a bookshelf, but that was because he was a newly crowned fourteen-year-old and didn't think self-help books were a necessity for him. He flipped to the back and found the symbol tucked into the corner.

He decided to read it and the book became a small piece of what got him back on track. Coda excelled at his new school and graduated on time. His mom cried at his graduation, but it was likely a combination of successfully navigating four kids through high school rather than just Coda's accomplishment.

As he moved onto campus for college, his visits back home became infrequent even though it was a doable subway ride. The calls to his mom began to space out from a few days to a few weeks. She had done so much to course correct his life, but Coda took it all for granted. It would boil down to an explosive argument between the two of them that permanently fractured their relationship, but it was dismantled long before then.

Grace held out hope that Coda would reach out and offer to repair their relationship and apologize, but he could be just as stubborn as she was. Time passed and without either of them realizing it, their window for making peace had rapidly closed.

nineteen

MORE TO LIFE

"A pair of scissors? Really?"

"Yeah."

"That's pretty fucked up."

"Yeah."

Nolan saw the look on Coda's face and tried to backtrack. "I . . . uh, I didn't mean it in a negative way. It's not the type of behavior I'd ever expect from you and not indicative of who you are now." She continued to rummage through the boxes and quietly scolded herself.

"I never told you because I had no reason to. I was a minor and they sealed the records. Going to TCSUM gave me the blank slate I needed. Honestly, I haven't thought about what happened for a very long time. It feels like a faded dream."

"I understand. Did you mean to physically hurt him like that or was it just . . . the circumstance of how it happened?"

"Nolan, does it matter at this point?"

Coda's detachment to the situation chilled her. "No, I guess it doesn't." Maybe he felt more shame than anything else. Nolan didn't always understand Coda's motivations or actions and she learned it wasn't her place to discover the true answer.

Nolan, Coda, and Muscle continued to search through the basement in silence. After coming up empty in every other room, Muscle's dad suggested they check the basement. They had to tell him five times what they were looking for before Sly finally understood and pointed them toward the epicenter of his hoarding tendencies. The basement was crammed with stacked boxes, old newspapers, stilted furniture, and layers upon layers of thick dust. Coda questioned whether the book could actually be a part of the mess, but Muscle assured that it had to be after turning up empty elsewhere. They fanned out to different sections and picked through what they could.

After a long bout of silence, Nolan finally asked, "Muscle, you never told me: What was your crime for ending up in juvie?"

"I called it joyriding, but the police didn't see it that way."

"They sent you to juvie for one instance of joyriding?"

"No, no, no," Muscle laughed. "That was my sixth time."

"Six times?" Nolan said incredulously. She was picking through a box full of letters that were folded in various styles. She opened up one and saw the name Valerie written in fantastic cursive. She folded up the box, knowing what they needed was not among those contents.

"Being the son of a moderately famous 'celebrity' allowed me to get away with more than I should have."

"Ah, I see now."

"Don't judge me too harshly. I was a stupid kid just like anyone else. After that last time, my dad told them I needed to get it through my thick skull that I couldn't fuck around like that anymore, so they kept me at the facility for a couple months. I actually didn't mind it. I met some cool people and made a friend or two."

"A true love story," Nolan called out.

"Oh yes. Coda tried his best to deny our friendship, but I can be persistent."

"I didn't have much of a choice. You can only run so far in a place like that," Coda chimed in.

"What happened with you two then?" Nolan asked.

A loud, irritating sound echoed out through the basement. "Sorry about that," Muscle said. "Moving a table across a concrete floor is a bad combination. What do you mean, Nolan?"

"Why did your friendship stop with Coda?"

"It didn't stop because of anything either of us did. It just . . . faded? Yeah, that's a good word for it. We needed each other most during those initial months and once we both got going again in our respective schools, we just grew apart."

"That's sad."

"I don't see it that way. Not every relationship needs to last a lifetime. We aren't wired to be these extravagant social butterflies all the time. We demand smaller circles of trusted acquaintances. I say that, but I'm so thrilled you two are here now because reconnecting with an old friend provides a surge that not much else can."

"How'd you get the book we are hunting for?"

"Not much of a story there," Coda said. "I knew he was in a similar situation as me and could potentially benefit from it."

"Except Coda knew I was not much of a reader."

"It didn't matter though. For me, giving books that I enjoyed to other people was a way to connect. I knew Muscle would eventually read it."

"Well, did you?" Nolan asked, turning her attention to Muscle. In the fading light that crept through the tiny basement windows, Muscle's outline looked like nightmarish creature.

"I did. But it was over ten years ago and I couldn't tell you much about what was in the book or if the message stuck. I do remember one thing though."

"Oh yeah?"

"The note in the beginning."

"My mom always loved to be theatrical and dramatic. I don't know if I agree with everything she wrote," Coda said.

"What did she write?"

Coda recited his mom's message from memory.

"Inter—"

"MUSCLE! MUSCLE! I NEED YOU!" a voice boomed through the house.

"I'm being summoned," Muscle said.

"Does he do that often?" Nolan asked.

"All the time." Muscle dropped the box and wove his way over to the stairs. "I'll be back in a minute."

Nolan leaned against a piece of furniture and raised her arms in protest. "I'm thinking we aren't going to find the book down here. I haven't run across a single one yet."

"Me either."

"I'm sorry Coda."

"It's okay." He moved to another box and picked through it without any interest.

They continued in their soulless shuffle across the basement until Muscle returned. "My dad was demanding to have dinner, so I whipped him up something quick. What about you guys? Are you hungry?"

"Yes," they said in unison.

"Anything to escape this dull, repetitive reality I find myself in at the moment," Coda said.

Nolan and Coda followed Muscle back up the stairs. His dad was still on the couch watching television and didn't pay much attention to them.

"You guys are staying here for the night, correct?" Muscle asked as they congregated in the kitchen.

Nolan looked over at Coda and shrugged. "We don't have much of a plan for this trip."

"There is plenty of space here, so no need to go to a hotel. My dad would actually be offended if you two didn't stay."

"Really? I got the impression he wasn't too thrilled with our company."

"My dad is miserable because of the constant pain he has, not that you guys are here." Muscle didn't explain any further than that.

On the other side of town, Muscle took them to a shopping center dominated by heavy weights like Wal-Mart, Kohl's, Staples, and Hobby Lobby. Tucked in amongst the giant corporations was a tiny storefront with the words **FRANK'S ITALIAN RESTAURANT** etched across the top. Muscle explained on the way over that Frank's was not authentic Italian cuisine, but it was the go-to spot for him and his dad at least once a week. The staff was a rotating cast of lovely people that fawned over them every time they ate there. Muscle said you couldn't beat the customer service even if the bread was sometimes stale and Nolan related to that more than she expected.

As predicted, a chorus of cheers broke out when Muscle stepped into the restaurant.

"The usual spot, Mr. Fox?" the hostess asked.

"That would be perfect."

Even in a city like Easton, people could rise to the top and become royalty. A hierarchy existed wherever you went.

Halfway through their meal, Muscle asked, "How long are you anticipating this trip to take?"

Coda answered. "To hit each of the places, it'll take over eighty hours of driving. But, of course, we will have plenty of moments like this where we catch up with people. I'm thinking it will take about two weeks."

"It must be nice to have jobs with that much vacation time. The admissions office would be in shambles if I was gone that long," Muscle said proudly.

"We quit our jobs," Nolan said.

"You're joking?!"

"Nope."

"That is badass, assuming you have another job lined up once you get back."

Nolan looked over at Coda. "I don't think either of us thought that far ahead. That existential crisis is further down the road than I'm willing to look right now. What about you Coda?"

"Same with me. Being in software development, there is a sizable amount of freelance work available, so I'll find something. There has to be more to life than just working, right?"

Muscle nodded and kept whatever opinion he had to himself.

The check arrived a short time later with a drastically reduced amount. Muscle insisted on paying and left a hefty tip on the table. "Let's go," he motioned after paying. "There's one more thing we have to do tonight besides finding that elusive book."

twenty

STABILIZE

"There's a football rivalry in Easton," Muscle explained.[8] Coda leaned up to the front row seating to hear what he said next. "They play a game on Thanksgiving each year over at the college. Massive crowd. Like fifteen thousand people. It's insane. Leading up to the game, there are ceremonies. One of them is that the Easton seniors spend an entire day building a giant bonfire in an empty patch of land between the school and the highway. People donate pallets of wood from all over. It's an assembly line of students passing wood down this long, winding path. After completing the bonfire, the seniors camp out for the night, making sure no one lights it prematurely. Stories have been told about flaming arrows being shot from the highway and other nonsense. Anyways, the city loves the tradition of the bonfire so much they decided to do another one."

"Is that where we are going?" Coda asked.

"Correct. The school is right over there," Muscle said, directing their attention out the front windshield.

Coda watched as they pulled up behind a trailing line of cars working toward a parking spot. In the distance, smoke and fire swirled until it petered out above the tree line. Numerous silhouettes circled around the fire at a distance with many more perched up on the hill to the far side.

Ten minutes later, they were parked in a distant lot and inching their way around the school, which was a patchwork of buildings smushed into one giant monstrosity, showing how many expansions had taken

---

[8] Muscle was being modest. The Easton-Phillipsburg Thanksgiving Day Game is one of the longest running high school football rivalries in the country with over 120 meetings. They claim the turkey tastes better for whichever city wins.

A petition gained steam in the mid-2000s to have the rivalry declared as one of the natural wonders of the world. It made sense as to why. What's more natural than getting drunk to watch an 11 a.m. game to make the meal afterward with estranged family more tolerable? Going one step further: What's more natural than roving bands of middle-aged bums getting day drunk on a holiday to reminisce about how the last time they enjoyed life was at seventeen? That's why America exists!

Sadly, the petition died out after no groups outside the middle-aged bums shared the same enthusiasm.

place throughout the years.

Coda felt the heat of the bonfire from a couple hundred feet away. Subtle at first, like the steam coming off a hot bath, but it grew to an uncomfortable level as they walked around the human perimeter that had formed. The crowd was stagnant as many stood transfixed as the fire burned away all the labor from earlier. Several people had pulled off their jackets, cradling them in their arms.

Coda imagined being trapped in a fire with no escape. To have the heat swelling, the smoke choking your lungs. The fear trickled into his body and settled in. How did his dad do it? Why did he choose to do it? Losing his dad made Coda realize how little he knew about him. Everybody has a story, but not all of them are shared or sought after. Darian Finn's story had lost its light. Hopefully Coda wouldn't make the same mistake twice.

Coda rejoined the present as Muscle found a spot for them on the hill.

"Do you have a lot of friends in Easton?" Nolan asked.

"No, I don't."

"You went down to Bacon Fest by yourself today?"

"Yeah. Why? Is that weird?"

"No, not at all. I traveled around New York by myself every weekend. I found I didn't need the company of others to be satisfied."

"Do you still feel that way?" Muscle asked.

Nolan leaned forward and looked past Coda. "Yes and no. I'm okay with being by myself for short periods of time, but I prefer the company of others more so now than when I was younger."

"Why is that?"

"I don't know exactly. Maybe it's a side effect of growing up or maybe it's the insatiable need to get into a relationship and explore this world with someone else. If I spend all my time alone, that possibility becomes rather limited."

"I'm okay with being alone," Muscle said.

"For your whole life?"

He stared out into the bonfire before answering. "I don't work that way. I've never had the foresight to see where I'd be in five, ten, twenty years. All the things I've done have led me to this moment, but I never sat and calculated how to get here. Other people tried to do that for me."

"What do you mean?" she asked.

"Nolan, you must be curious," Muscle said with a smile. "And Coda,

I doubt I ever told you."

"About what?"

"My name."

Coda thought briefly. "You told me several times not to ask about it."

"That sounds like my usual deflection. Look, people assume my name has some deep, mystical meaning and a great story behind it, but that's not the case. My parents always wanted a kid but weren't fully prepared for the responsibility. That idea confuses me because it's not like raising a kid is some well-kept secret in the adulthood vault. My dad was always convinced he'd have a son who would become a professional boxer like him. We'd create a dynasty and solidify a cushy life for ourselves because contrary to popular belief, not all athletes get paid millions. My dad spoke with some idiots who stressed the key to going down the correct path in life starts with a name. What's one thing you need as a boxer?"

"Muscles," Nolan said.

"Amongst other things, yes."

"You're kidding about all this."

"I wish I was. My mom was too meek to fight him on the name, so she resigned to it. She didn't hang around long after I was born. But, anyways, as time went on, it became clear muscles were one thing I was never going to get. I kept growing and growing, much to the disappointment of my dad. It caused a surprising amount of friction when I was a teenager. He threw me into the ring a couple of times and watched me get my ass kicked. I had the reach, but none of the speed or stamina or muscles. His dynasty was sure to crumble. All the pressure he put on me resulted in the joyriding and other petty criminal activities I partook in.

"And now, my dad's health is terrible. The arthritis in his joints, the chronic back pain, the start of memory loss. All because he spent too much time in the ring. What did he get for it? Some accolades, but not a whole lot of money. I'm the only one around to take care of him. All those people he met along the way abandoned him. I understand why. He's not an easy person to get along with, but he's still my dad.

"So you asked me about my future and maybe my answer surprised you, but I don't see anything beyond my dad. No matter how much we were at odds when I was younger, I can't deny that he raised me by himself and struggled every step to figure out what I needed. He's going to be gone one day and maybe I'll think about my future then. Everyone has wild ambitions about what they want out of life, but the best thing you can do is stick close to the ones who have always stuck with you."

Muscle went quiet as the chatter of everyone else made the silence between them not so dramatic. It made sense to Nolan. She saw the small moments throughout the day where Muscle's dad would call for his assistance and he'd drop everything. She never experienced a parental bond like that before and envied him for it.

"I don't want you to think I'm an unhappy person," Muscle continued. "We try to make life so complicated. Not everyone needs to save the world or start a family or brag about all the places they've traveled to. Live and let live. I don't know who said that, but someone did. I agree with that sentiment. I've yet to discover everything in this world, and don't feel any pressure to."

"Thanks for telling us all that," Coda said with a clap to Muscle's shoulder. "I forgot how much you loved to ramble on."

"Fuck off," Muscle laughed.

"I wish I felt the same way you did."

"People change."

"You think so?"

"Absolutely," Muscle said with confidence. He was overly sure without any examples to choose from.

Coda didn't press the idea further.

"Let's sit here for a little longer," Muscle continued. He let himself fall back against the trampled grass and closed his eyes. Nolan followed his lead.

Coda stared at the bonfire once more and felt a wave of peace pass through him. It was the first time all day that he wasn't concerned about whether they'd find the book. He relaxed his body and joined the others as he collapsed against the ground. The sounds of wood crackling and splitting and burning, burning, burning drifted into the open sky toward the countless dots perched above.

┃┃┃

The Fox household did not have a garage, instead, they had a canopy made of aluminum off to the side. Muscle eased the car into its designated spot alongside the other that belonged to Sly Fox, three-time world heavyweight champion who held the title longer than anyone else in history. Yes, seriously. Longer than Muhammad Ali. Longer than Larry Holmes or Mike Tyson or Joe Lewis. None of the respect any of those names received either. None of the money, too.

They trudged back into the house, discussing what the sleeping arrangements would be when Muscle stopped in the kitchen. "Coda, is this it?" Muscle handed a book over to Coda. He recognized the ugly burnt orange color on the cover.

"Yeah. Holy shit," he said, flipping through the pages. The note from G.F. was on the inside cover and the symbol buried in the back. Coda skimmed through the last page and instantly recalled how unremarkable it was—just the author listing out his infinite list of acknowledgements, the vainest section of any book. "Has this been here the whole time?"

"It couldn't have," Nolan said. "We walked through here a thousand times. There's no way we'd have been so blind."

"Dad? Dad?" Muscle called out.

A grunt from the other room. The television was buzzing with the local news, who was continuing their coverage of what was wrong in the world.

"Did you find Coda's book?"

"Yeah, yeah. I did," Sly said, pulling himself awake slowly. "All day I thought you three were looking for a *hook*. 'Where's the hook? Have you seen this hook?' I thought you had lost your goddamned minds. And then it finally made sense that you couldn't possibly be looking for a hook. We don't have any fishing gear or nothing of the such. Val used to tell me I didn't listen well. That wretched witch—"

"Dad, c'mon."

"Yeah, yeah," Sly said, shooing Muscle off with a wave of his hand. Everyone was standing in the living room listening to Sly's rambling. "Book. Book. I realized that's what you must be tearing apart the house to find. Well, you didn't bother to check in one place."

"Stop with the theatrics. Just tell us," Muscle said with exhaustion.

"I used the book to prop up the couch. About a year ago, one of the legs on it broke and the damn thing wobbled like a real sunabitch. I spent the day finding things to fix this damn couch and nothing was the right height—except for that book," he said, pointing to Coda's hands. "The perfect height. No more damn see-sawing when I'm trying to watch the news. But don't worry. I found something else to stabilize the couch. Thanks for asking," he mumbled.

Muscle shook his head and walked back into the kitchen. "I'm sorry about that. He can be immensely irritating sometimes."

"Every family is that way, I suppose," Nolan said.

"How's the book? Any damage?"

"Maybe a little dented, but nothing I would have noticed. Don't worry, it's not like the book is worth anything more than sentimental value."

"Yeah, okay."

"Do you have a pen?" Coda asked, pulling the list from his pocket.

Muscle fished through a nearby draw and returned with several options. Coda grabbed one without much thought and put a checkmark next to *The Bombastic Knack of Giving a Damn*.

One step closer, but still a long, long, long way to go.

twenty-one

CAR CHAT I
Somewhere in Virginia

The rain had been a steady downpour for the last two hours. Being in no rush, Nolan stayed religiously in the right lane as every car whipped by splashing buckets of rain onto the windshield.

"One thing from Easton is still bothering me," Nolan said.

Coda looked up from his phone and asked, "What's that? If you're upset about not getting any bacon products, I do apologize. We should have taken advantage of such a unique opportunity."

Nolan laughed. "No, it's not that. You should know I'm not a die-hard fan of bacon like many others. I'd take a side of sausage over bacon any day."

"For the record, I don't agree with you, but this is a debate for another time. I need to think through my argument before I engage in battle."

"Do you remember when you asked Muscle if he thought people could change?" Nolan said, circling back to her initial point.

"Yes," Coda said, "you say that like it didn't happen less than a day ago."

An arm flung out and hit Coda in the shoulder. "That's for your sassy remark . . . I just don't think it's possible for people to change."

"Why is that?"

"Because a majority of our habits and behaviors are formed at such a young age. They are then reinforced for years and years before that trigger may happen where someone makes a conscious effort to change. How can it possibly be done?"

"Neuroplasticity."

"What's that?"

"It's the concept that the brain is plastic and able to be shaped by repeated behaviors. Sure, it's easy to decipher that in a negative way, but there is an abundance of stories where individuals have rewired their brains to undue decades of learned behaviors or regaining their old way of life after a traumatic injury."

"That's a new term for me, but that feels like more of a physical thing," Nolan said.

"Not at all. Your behaviors could manifest in a physical way, but it's likely they begin with an idea."

"I don't follow."

"Let's say you were in a loveless marriage for a decade. Your brain has gotten used to the shitty situation you have been in. You have probably lost your sense of worth. One day you find the courage to leave and move on with your life. That'll take an extreme amount of time and dedication to rewire your brain to believe you deserve more than what you received in that relationship. That positive reinforcement could come from a therapist or family members or someone new you met. Regardless of who it is, you are making a conscious effort to restructure your behaviors and mindset."

"How often is that successful?"

Coda threw his hands up in surrender. "I'm not a professional on the matter. I only read one book about it."

"Of course you read all that from a book."

"You say that like it's a bad thing."

"No, I didn't mean it like that . . . I guess I'm just more of a pessimist about this, even if science tells me otherwise. I look at it from a . . . spiritual or naturalistic way. People are too complicated to fit in a neat box when it comes to their behaviors."

"Agreed, it's not a one-size-fits-all type of situation, but to make a blanket statement that people are unable to change is a bit naïve and shortsighted."

"Maybe."

"It makes for a better story though."

"What does?" Nolan asked.

"Having a character that doesn't change. Imagine if you wrote a book about this awful, dreadful person that was malicious in a variety of ways. For the entire book you hinted at them changing for the better, but in the end, the character resorted back to their normal ways."

"Sounds more frustrating than anything. Why would I spend my time reading a book where the main character doesn't evolve? That's the point of every single story!"

"They evolve by not evolving."

"Uh, I don't know about that."

"Just an idea."

"If you believe so strongly in it, then you should write it."

"I could never write a book," Coda said.

"Oh please, I'm sure every author has said that at one point in their career. Self-doubt is the greatest demotivator. You've read hundreds—possibly thousands—of books. Who would understand the structure of a book better than you?"

"That's not my argument. I don't have any good ideas, which is the foundation for a worthwhile story."

"We can come up with a story right now. Shouldn't be too hard."

For the next hour, Nolan and Coda riffed about potential ideas. Most were so dreadful and trite that they are not worth repeating. For the ones that had an iota of sanity to them, they were quickly dispatched once the two determined that someone else had already written about it.

They came to the following conclusion: Writing an original story was impossible as all the good ideas were taken, which meant everything new would be a retread of the past. They concluded further that there was no reason to try because we all wound up dead anyways.

They were overly cynical for being so young, but that could be blamed on the following:

- Shitty politicians
- Old people on social media
- The rich getting richer
- Fake news
- Real news
- Never ending road construction
- Same day delivery
- Astroturfing[9]
- Climate change
- Billionaires pretending to have a moral compass
- Strawman arguments[10]

---

[9] "Astroturfing is the practice of masking the **sponsors** of a message or organization (e.g., political, advertising, religious or **public relations**) to make it appear as though it originates from and is supported by **grassroots** participants. It is a practice intended to give the statements or organizations credibility by withholding information about the source's financial connection."

Source: Wikipedia. A credible website regardless of what any teacher thinks!

[10] "A straw man (or strawman) is a form of argument and an informal fallacy of having the impression of refuting an argument, meanwhile the proper idea of argument under discussion was not addressed or properly refuted ... The typical straw man argument creates the illusion

- Reboots of tired franchises
- Political correctness
- People's propensity to believe an inconvenience as an injustice

If people could actually change, then maybe Nolan and Coda had a fighting chance to ditch their cynicism for something more optimistic.

Don't count on it though.

Change is a winding maze with minimal exits and an abundance of pitfalls.

---

of having completely refuted or defeated an opponent's proposition through the covert replacement of it with a different proposition (i.e., "stand up a straw man") and the subsequent refutation of that false argument ("knock down a straw man") instead of the opponent's proposition. Straw man arguments have been used throughout history in polemical debates, particularly regarding highly charged emotional subjects."

Source: Wikipedia.

twenty-two

MEANINGLESS WORD

Between the rain, rest stops, and going the wrong way for a half hour, Nolan and Coda arrived in the Charlotte area late Sunday evening. Coda was ready to suggest them pushing through the last twenty minutes to the address Sam Rogers provided, but they'd done enough driving and he didn't want to barge in late at Eve's place.

Instead, Nolan asked him to look up a hotel. Keeping true to their commitment, Coda found a luxurious TripleTree on the outskirts of the city with a four point three star rating. Absolutely spectacular.

"How can I help you?" the lady at the front desk asked.

What could she have possibly helped them with besides getting a room or pointing to where the bathroom was? What a needless thing to say. Could Nolan have asked for some money? What would the lady have responded with if Coda questioned her about the meaning of life or why people didn't vote?

Nolan didn't challenge the status quo and said, "Looking to get a room for the night."

"You came to the right place!" the lady cackled as if that wasn't her go-to joke.

"A room with two beds would be preferable."

The lady darted back and forth between Nolan and Coda, brewing, brewing, brewing her opinion about them. "Thank you for mentioning that! I would have assumed you wanted just one bed. You two look like a couple in love!"

Nolan and Coda were both dressed in the same clothes they slept in and hadn't showered since before they left. They looked closer to something you'd see on the sidewalk in New York (take your pick from the following: dog shit, trash, rotten food, or murky water) rather than a lovey dovey couple.

The lady behind the desk took another five minutes pretending to click the mouse and type away on the keyboard before she asked for someone's credit card.

Nolan looked at Coda ready to discuss who would pay, but he already handed his card over without concern.

The lady swiped the credit card fifteen times, apologizing profusely for the gosh darn thingamajig not working. Finally, it went through and she returned the credit card to Coda with two room keys. They would be occupying Room 2727 on the second floor.

"One more thing!" the lady said as they began picking up their bags. She bent down under the desk and came back with two Post-it Notes. "We used to give away fresh cookies, but corporate is losing bundles of money and decided to cut jobs and cookies. I only work ten hours a week now and have barely enough money to survive! Isn't this wonderful? Please don't answer that. Instead, corporate wants us to give each guest a Post-it Note with a word written on it."

"A word?" Coda said.

"Mhmm," the lady confirmed while dipping her head to write down the words. "The words will be meaningless because life is meaningless, right?"

"Words are more powerful than life though. They can last for centuries and even cause people to kill one another. Can you imagine? A book that dilutes the human brain so much that people demean and crucify others who don't believe in the same words and made up stories?"

"I can't think of any book with that sort of sway over people."

"Oh really? Hmm, maybe it is something to think about."

The lady disregarded Coda's last comment and passed over the two Post-it Notes. "Enjoy your stay at the TripleTree!"

Halfway to the stairs, Coda looked down at his word. In flowing, cursive font, the five letters managed to spread across the entire width.

grace

Coda went cold as if Death itself passed through him.

What he didn't know is that the lady at the front desk was enraptured by an episode of *Pretty Crap Grace*, which was running on the television across the room. The show centered on the main character, Grace, who was not great at life. Her aspirations were to become amazing! She'd have to traverse her struggles as a ho-hum woman in Dallas where she lived in a lavish apartment even though she worked part time as a bottle opener at a restaurant. Every night from 8 p.m. to midnight she turned into one. An actual bottle opener! That was the hook which made it stand out from all the other shit shoveled into people's mouths while draining their lives in front of the television. To think that Nolan and Coda thought there weren't any original ideas left.

"What does yours say?" Nolan asked. "I got *faster*. I'll have to think about if that has a deeper meaning to me or not."

"I got *carpet*. How uneventful." The lie came out easily.

"What a bummer. I got my hopes up for nothing . . . Once we get settled in the room, we need to talk strategy for tomorrow."

Coda nodded and led the way to Room 2727. Inside, they rummaged through the space opening up every door to see if any surprises were left behind. They came up empty.

Coda threw his stuff on the bed closest to the window and quickly moved into the bathroom. The bright lights from multiple angles blurred his vision. He stared at himself in the mirror and took several deep breaths. He took off his clothes and stepped into the shower. The water was scalding but he leaned into it and dunked his head under. The sensation of drowning was only slight to Coda's best guess since he'd never found himself in a situation like that. He'd only been in a body of water larger than a bathtub on a handful of occasions.

He lost track of time and heard a knock on the door. "Everything alright? You're going to shrivel up in there."

Coda turned off the shower. "Yeah, sorry. Just thinking."

No response.

Once he stepped out of the bathroom, Coda felt compelled to apologize again for taking a long shower. He wasn't used to sharing a space with someone else. After living most of his life in a crowded house or with a gaggle of roommates, the solitary life Coda had in his apartment was a welcome one. Long showers weren't a luxury though since the hot water crapped out after ten minutes.

Nolan ignored his apology again and instead asked, "What's their name?" She was spread out on the bed with her laptop.

"Eve Adamson."

"A tamer name than our first subject I suppose." She shook her head, thinking of the absurdity of Muscle Fox's name. "How do you know her?"

"We worked at the bookstore together."

"At TCSUM?"

"Yeah."

"Hmmm, the name doesn't sound familiar."

"That may be because she is transgender. At the beginning of college, she went by her birth name and then transitioned to Eve."

"Oh wow."

"Is that going to be a problem?"

Nolan looked annoyed. "Of course not! Coda, why would you even say that?"

"I-I'm sorry. She just told me so many horrible stories of people being phobic that my natural reaction is to be defensive."

"She is no different than anyone else. End of story."

"Thanks."

"Last question then . . . even though I have others . . . which book did you give her?"

"*Cat's Crib.*"

"Sounds familiar," Nolan said, feigning any recognition of the title.

"It's by Kilgore Trout if you've heard of him. He gained lots of notoriety back when his book *Laughterhouse-Four* came out. Huge anti-war book that had aliens and time travel and all sorts of gallows humor. Come to think of it, most of his books talked about a deep hatred of war and how appalling the human race had a tendency to be. *Cat's Crib* had more of a religious slant to it amongst his usual topics."

"Kilgore Trout," Nolan said. "Kilgore Trout, Kilgore Trout. Fascinating."

Upon further reflection, Nolan decided to ditch discussions on their plan for tomorrow. They'd figure it out in the morning. She closed her laptop, grabbed some clothes from her bag, and moved to the bathroom.

Coda heard her repeat the name Kilgore Trout a dozen more times in a low whisper.

Fascinating indeed.

twenty-three

LIES & SERENDIPITY

Throughout their yummy continental breakfast of runny eggs, stale bread, one kind of cereal, orange juice in musky containers, a single blueberry muffin, and a tray of burnt bacon (much to the dismay of Nolan), a plan for the day was finalized.

It boiled down to this: go to the address and see what happens.

To provide anymore brainpower to the topic was needless. They hadn't expected their trip to Easton would result in a festival of wonder, a frenetic search through an aging house, or a tranquil evening on a hill overlooking a bonfire, so why try to do more than the minimum?

After departing from the hotel, Coda input the address into Snoogle Maps and it spit out a travel time of twenty-seven minutes, citing several long swatches of red lines as the source of delay.

No matter.

It was a Monday morning and work traffic was to be expected.

"Is all this weird to you?" Coda asked as they exited the parking lot. "We should be going to work right now, struggling to get a seat on the subway or walking around to brew that first cup of coffee."

"I was a bit anxious this morning as if my body craved the old routine. It's like having one of those dreams where you miss the deadline for a school project, and you wake up in a cold sweat. This feels right though. Like I should have never gone into a corporate job in the first place."

"What the fuck are we going to do when this is over?"

"Find something better than what we had. Or beg for our old jobs back. I'm not quite sure yet what the play is." Nolan paused. "I'd rather not consider that now though, if that's okay?"

"Yeah . . . yeah, sure."

They inched along the highway as traffic poured into the downtown area where the skyscrapers lived that crammed thousands of lowly souls into each one.

Several exits down, Nolan turned off and entered a neighborhood of Charlotte that neither of them knew. Actually, they didn't know a single thing about the city. A quick Snoogle search would have returned a trove of false information about the city of Charlotte. Care to look?

- Population of 12,845 illegal zoo animals, many of which have been running wild for months
- 83 miles of dirt roads that were used during prohibition and preserved for historical reasons unknown to residents
- The average rent for a one-bedroom apartment is 7 trout from the local river of Gargarmelt
- For the last twenty years, the mayor has been one of those animatronic fish that tells horrible jokes and sings obnoxious songs to no end
- Sidewalks are only wide enough for one person at a time to deter group gatherings
- Nightlife closes at 8 p.m. except on Flag Day
- An undetermined number of Confederate statues are perched on street corners so citizens "don't forget their heritage" that they certainly don't care about until someone tries to take them down
- A single public park that spans half a city block long and is closed most days for repairs
- Home to the NASCAR Hall of Fame

Why would a city lie so much? How is it known that Charlotte is lying about these supposed facts?

Charlotte experienced a population boom over the past ten years and is scrambling to expand and accommodate the massive influx of residents. The campaign broke down into three parts: rebuild infrastructure, raise taxes, and convince the rest of civilization how shitty the city is.

It was an effective plan that corked the growth of Charlotte down to a nominal amount, but the expert sleuth, our very own Sam Rogers, saw through the ruse. While researching Eve Adamson, Sam noticed the aggressive news articles that populated his Snoogle results. He dug deeper, deeper, deeper. He discovered that Russia does in fact meddle in American politics. He discovered that 30-year mortgage payments are a scam. He discovered that the average adult has a reading ability of a toddler. He discovered that the moon landing was faked because the moon doesn't even exist! On and on the discoveries went. All there in plain sight, but not simple enough for anyone to care about. Sam considered adding these findings to the Manila folders, but he stopped himself. Coda needed to find all the answers on his own assuming he gave a flying fuck about any of it. Above all that though, Sam wanted to preserve his findings for the PIMP—Private Investigator Mega Prize. It was the annual congregation of intellectuals in the PI community to designate one of their peers as superior to the rest. The prize was a gift card. But to where? That was part of the surprise! But that's enough about Sam—he keeps popping up even though his purpose is done, kaput. Not every character needs to have a satisfying arc.

Look:

Let's regroup after this final statement.

If you did need a reason to *not* visit Charlotte, the NASCAR Hall of Fame is actually there.

Yikes.

Street parking was limited, but Nolan managed to squeeze the 2008 Pinto Pinata in between two vehicles that screamed of a mid-life crisis (as if people had to wait that long to find themselves embroiled in one). The 2008 Pinto Pinata was larger than a pinto bean or a piñata but smaller than twenty-seven thousand pinto beans or twenty-seven piñatas. That should clear up any confusion about the size of the parking space and car.

"Does she live in an apartment complex?" Nolan asked.

Coda dipped his head and looked out the window. The building beyond the passenger side of his best friend's ride went up and up at least . . . Coda had no idea. He was a terrible judge of height. Maybe fifteen floors. Could be thirty-five. No more than fifty though.

"That would be a massive house if it wasn't."

"Oh, you prick," Nolan said with a laugh.

"Let's see what we can find out."

They walked halfway around the block until they came to a large sign declaring they had arrived at the cornerstone of luxury and affordability. The same bullshit that every apartment complex from Charlotte to Pluto claimed. Nolan hit the handicap button, and both set of doors swung open faster than expected. The lobby didn't resemble an upscale complex as the name Skyhouse seemed to imply. Soft piano music hummed overhead for all to enjoy. A sign directing potential tenants to the leasing office told them where they didn't want to go. Instead, they walked to the circular desk with the man stationed behind it. He stared down at his phone with his mouth half open. Drool pooled in the corner of his mouth and threatened to overflow until he inhaled sharply, sucking it back in. The reflection off his glasses showed the drool was caused by the hardcore pornographic movie he was watching. This didn't imply he was a bad person for watching porn on the job; he was likely another bored, disgruntled employee of a company that didn't give a shit about him. Really though, what was the worst that would happen at an apartment building in downtown Charlotte? A homicidal maniac? A five-alarm fire? A tenant taking a swan dive off the top story? Maybe, maybe, maybe. But still, no reason to be hung up on hypotheticals. It was an average Monday morning after all.

"Excuse me?" Nolan asked.

"One second," the man said, wiping his mouth with the back of his hand. A grin passed over his face as he continued to look at his phone. Twenty agonizing seconds passed before he looked up. "Yes?"

"Were you just watching porn?" Coda asked.

"Of course not." The man answered confidently as if he prepared his whole life for someone to finally notice.

Coda considered challenging him further but decided not to. "Does anyone by the name of Eve Adamson live here?"

"Are you food or postage?"

"I don't get—"

"Are you delivering food or packages?" the man said, enunciating each word to avoid repeating it again.

"Uh, no."

"Can't help you then."

"What do you mean?"

"I can't tell you about any of the tenants that live here unless you are delivering food or packages. Was I unclear about that?"

"Alright," Coda said. He choked back his growing annoyance and pulled out the piece of paper from his pocket. He slapped it down on the desk and smoothed out the edges. "Right here"—a forceful finger jab—"is the address for Eve Adamson, the person in question. Is the address listed here for Skyhouse?"

"Yes."

"Does that apartment number exist within this building?"
"Yes, we do have a twelfth floor."
"Okay, great. Fantastic. Can we go up to see if she is home?"
"No."
"Why not?"
"Did she invite you here?"
"No," Coda said. Nolan shot him a dirty look.
"Then no can do, partner. You could be a homicidal maniac or a five-alarm fire and I can't have that on my conscience. If you have her address, you probably have her number. Just give her a call. She'll know what the process is for letting guests into the building."
"And what's stopping me from taking an elevator over there?"
"Well, you don't have a keycard. You need one of those."
Coda grabbed the paper and stepped away toward the doors. The man called out, "Don't be mad! I'm just doing my job!"
Outside, Coda let the frustration wash over him. Once the wave crested and carried itself back out to sea, he turned to Nolan. "We have two options: wait here to see if she leaves the building sometime soon or we go around and try to find her."
"Uh huh. And how do you think we'd find a single person in this city? How come you don't have her number?"
"It takes me years to save people's numbers to my phone. Once it gets far enough down in my list of messages, I clear it out. After college, I didn't expect to see many of the same people anymore. It's not like I had an expansive group of friends to begin with." He wasn't wrong. Coda kept a tight, imperfect circle of friends during his time at college. It wasn't from the lack of trying either. He sat next to people he didn't know in class and struck up conversations when he could, but it boiled down to people not always having time or an interest in pushing a one-time conversation into a repeated experience. La-dee-da. A different problem for a former iteration of himself to deal with.
"I hope you have my number saved," Nolan mumbled.
"Yes, of course. Even when we weren't talking."
"How about this instead? We walk to a coffee shop and think through this more. The coffee at the hotel was atrocious and I'm running on fumes." Before Coda replied, Nolan picked a direction and stuck with it. She consumed blocks at a rapid rate and kept walking even when the red hand told her not to.

"There! Hungry Ghost Coffee. How does that sound?" she asked.

"Perfect. I'll grab us a table." Coda surveyed the space. He looked left. He looked right. Most of the seating was empty, save for a few miscellaneous people, as the working crowd was snuggled into their cubicles counting rows in Excel. Still, indecision gripped him. Sometimes the simplest choices can be the most burdensome.

He chose one cattycorner to the baristas and watched as Nolan pointed at the menu lofted back behind the counter. She didn't even ask what he wanted, but much like going to The Wobbling Stool, their orders at a coffee shop never deviated from the mean.

Nolan walked over to the table with one mug in each hand like she was on a tightrope with a thousand-foot drop.

"Grab it, grab it, grab it," Nolan called out. She extended her arm and passed the mug to Coda then settled into the seat across from him. "Nice place they got here. Good find, if I may say so."

"What are we going to do for the rest of the day?"

"Rest of the day? I think the question is how are we going to find Eve."

"We take our time here and then stake out the apartment building some more. Maybe that guy will be off his shift soon and we can convince someone else to let us up," Coda said.

"Nobody is going to let us up there."

"Maybe we can tailgate someone else up the elevator."

"Doubt it."

"I'm just thinking out loud here. Feel free to contribute at any point."

Nolan laughed. "Relax for a minute. Our current predicament will work itself out—"

"Excuse me?" a voice asked.

Nolan and Coda looked over at the woman standing nervously at their table.

"Are you Coda Finn?" the woman asked.

Coda put down the mug. "Holy shit."

Nolan glanced back and forth. "Did our predicament just work itself out? I told you it would!"

twenty-four

PER ASPERA AD ASTRA

Years ago, during one of their shifts at the bookstore, Abraham pulled Coda into the storage room and lifted his shirt. "Look at what I got last week. I finally took the bandage off today." Coda cocked his head sideways and read the text that crawled up Abraham's spine. "Per aspera ad astra," Coda said, taking his time with each word. "What does it mean?"

"Through hardships to the stars. It's Latin. Never heard of it?"

"No, I have not."

He let his shirt fall back down. "All those books you read, and you don't know a popular Latin saying. Tsk, tsk."

Coda felt his face flush. "I, uh, I—"

"I'm just joking with you."

"Why'd you get it? What's the meaning?"

"That's the wonderful thing about a tattoo: I can let you ponder the intention behind it." Before Coda could respond, Abraham continued, "Let's get back out there, yeah?"

In a more present time, Coda looked at the new additions on Eve's arms and tried to decipher their meaning. Some were symbols, some were more wording, but all of them would need a further explanation for him to understand.

"Do you mind if I sit?" Eve asked.

"Yeah, yeah. Absolutely," Coda said, breaking from his trance. He pulled his backpack off the seat and Eve slid into it.

"Hi, I don't think we've met before," Eve turned to Nolan.

With a wide smile, Nolan said, "Oh, I know allllllllll about you. Nice to meet you Eve. I'm Nolan, Coda's travel buddy on this quest."

Eve gave a hesitant nod. "Okay, and what quest is that?"

Coda gave a quick rundown of everything that happened so far. He left out the most pressing details about quitting his job and the extent of his mom's illness, but it was enough for Eve to understand why they were in Charlotte.

"So, you drove all the way down here to get a book? Don't you have my number? I could have rummaged around and mailed it up to you."

Nolan shook her head. "Yeahhhhh, about that . . . see, Coda and I are on an exploratory mission of sorts. This seemed like the best excuse to leave New York for a few weeks and discover what the heck is going on in the rest of the country," she said, both covering for Coda and providing some semblance of the truth.

"I see," Eve said. "Still, you could have given me a heads up. Work is busy right now and I don't know how much time I can spend to show y'all around the city."

"We aren't asking for your time," Coda said. "The book is the top priority."

"The book. Huh. Good to know. Silly me for thinking that running into an old friend at a coffee shop might actually mean something more than just finding a book."

Nolan drummed her fingers on the table. "What Coda means is that we don't want to disrupt your day. We don't mind hanging out and exploring the city until you are done."

Ignoring Nolan, Eve turned her attention back to Coda. "What happened to you? You fell off the planet. One day you were working at the bookstore, the next you were gone, and no one seemed to have the full story. You never returned my texts and now you show up here in Charlotte begging for a book."

"I know. I'm sorry. It's easy for me to fall out of friendships," Coda said, looking over at Nolan. "Out of sight, out of mind is too literal of a saying for me."

"Don't get me wrong. I'm not holding a multi-year grudge or anything, but we knew each other during a vulnerable time of my life, and you were always so kind and attentive. Maybe I built up more of a friendship than we actually had. I'm just shocked you're here."

"Again, I'm sorry. I don't have much of a defense for my actions."

"It's okay Coda. Really."

"How did you even find me? You left that part out," Eve said.

Coda lapsed into another explanation of Sam Rogers and his foray into the world of private investigations. This trip was turning into a wonderful marketing ploy for Sam Rogers—his name would be spread across the country.

"Sounds like something out of a shitty novel. Speaking of, which book did you come all the way here for anyways?" Eve asked.

"*Cat's Crib.*"

"By Kilgore Trout?"

"That's the one."

Eve sat back in the chair. "You know, I got a two-bedroom apartment as an excuse to keep expanding my book collection."

"Oh goodness, another bibliophile," Nolan said.

Coda and Eve looked at Nolan and said, "*Bibliophile?*"

"I may not read a lot, but I still know words! As a side note to you Eve, we spent hours sifting through the last house we were at looking for his damn book—no offense, Coda—so please tell me you're a bit more organized."

"Yes. They are categorized by author."

"By author!" Nolan said in amazement as she clapped her hands. "What a relief!"

"I remember you being quite the Kilgore Trout fan," Eve said. "Is that still the case?"

"Yeah, I really do admire his work. But seeing that he died over a decade ago, it's not like there's more material of his to read. I loved *Cat's Crib*—one of his better novels for sure."

When you read as many books as Coda has, you are bound to surface with a few favorite authors as you dip into dozens and dozens of others. Kilgore Trout was a rare combination of wit, satire, and social commentary. Mr. Trout believed in humanism and the power of people helping others. He believed that we should celebrate the birth of each individual and ensure they found success in their lives. Mr. Trout was a survivor of the Dresden bombing during World War Two, which served as inspiration for his most famous novel, *Laughterhouse-Four*. In the decades after World War Two, he would constantly denounce war and the atrocities of it. He referred semi-regularly that dropping the atomic bombs on Hiroshima and Nagasaki were the worst decisions in human history and exemplified the stupidity of people. Imagine that: dropping two bombs that wiped out millions of people and never experiencing consequences from that decision. Was it any worse than what the world was fighting against in Germany and the surrounding countries? Was it even comparable? The world can be a disgusting, awful place and Mr. Trout built a career around showcasing the ugliness behind the human spirit while being reflective on mortality and family and love.

Sure, Coda gathered as much from reading all of Kilgore Trout's novels, but an underappreciated facet of Mr. Trout's writing that gelled with Coda was his exclusion of acknowledgments or indexes or details about the font or any other bullshit an author likes to cram in at the end. For Coda, it meant whenever he first picked up another Kilgore Trout novel, the last page would actually be the last page of the story. And the beauty of it was that they were never spoilers considering Kilgore Trout's novels were largely about nothing except various people writing about their own lives.[11] Regardless if the ending would be spoiled or not, the thrill pulsed through Coda as he peeked ahead into his future and saw what was ahead.

It's ironic. We all know the true ending to our story, but we have no way to peek ahead and modify it. All we can do is shape how the ending feels. Were we good? Did we treat others with kindness and respect? Did we laugh and love and enjoy the simple moments? Did we waste our years in a dead-end job? Did we pursue wholesome relationships and spend time with the right people? Did we rediscover what was lost? Did we vote? Did we have an opinion on the things that matter and leave out all the rest? Did we seek knowledge? Did we drive with the windows down on a beautiful summer night? Did we camp out under the stars and understand how small each of us are? Did we sing a favorite song in a casino and not care how silly we may have looked?

Did we discover all there is?

By shaping how the ending feels, we have created a worthwhile experience that others could draw inspiration from.

Kilgore Trout taught Coda the absurdities of the human spirit and also the beauty behind it. *Cat's Crib* is a novel largely critical about the idea of religion and other things Coda can't quite place. For as many times as he's ventured into Kilgore Trout's worlds, Coda always walked away with more questions and a strong feeling that the message flew over his head. No matter. He tried to question his mom one time why she gifted

---

[11] That sounds more belittling than intended. Mr. Trout thrived on first-person narratives where the character's main plot would be an event in present time, but a majority of the book is spent rehashing memories from year's past. His ability to craft convincing backstories filled with rich detail about both minor and major characters is noteworthy. Important to consider: None of his books ever eclipsed more than three hundred and twenty pages. His stories were brisk and small in comparison to some of the more tedious writers. Once again proving that size doesn't matter. But still, sometimes it is euphoric to dive into a massive book and get lost in a crafted, unique world. The dead, beaten horse says this: Each book is special regardless of size. You read whatever the heck you like.

him that book and included it in the rarified collection. She abstained from answering and without a note in the front, Coda was left clueless. No matter. When he passed the book along to Eve one day, she asked him why and Coda abstained. He had to keep the routine going.

"I remember that Kilgore Trout came up in conversation when we were stocking shelves. One of the English classes had to read *Dinner of Winners* and we fell into a lengthy discussion about Trout. I wasn't entirely sold yet on him, but I did appreciate you giving me that book. I think it swayed me into a more favorable outlook on him," Eve said. "I'm surprised I never gave it back. I know I finished reading it in a couple days."

"No worries."

Eve tapped her phone, lighting up the screen. "Shit, I really need to get going." She considered a moment. "Actually, do you want to join me? I'm going on a recon mission."

"Uhh," Nolan looked across at Coda. "Sure, I mean, we don't have anything else planned for the day."

Coda nodded in agreement.

"Perfect, I can drive and explain on the way. One question though: Are either of you religious?"

twenty-five

NUMB TO IT ALL

During the walk back to Eve's building, she gave a detailed account of her life's happenings since graduating from The College State University of Manhattan, stylized as TCSUM and pronounced *tee-sum*.

Eve left New York a month after graduation as she landed a job at the Charlotte Observer. She grew up on the fringes of Charlotte with her parents and multitude of siblings, so she always considered the area home. Majoring in Journalism during the peak downfall of newspapers was a bold strategy, but Eve figured that while jobs had decreased substantially in physical print media, there was a massive surge in online reporting she could take advantage of. She aced the interview and when asked what vacancy she wanted to fill, she questioned if the Charlotte Observer had a branch for investigative journalism. They said no and weren't interested in kickstarting a new segment revolving around that concept. Her options boiled down to covering local sporting events, keeping track of the mayor's office, or assisting in an advice column that was tarnished after a scandal in 2021.[12]

The revamped advice column wasn't nearly as popular amongst the readers, which piqued Eve's interest. She settled on that and with the help of several other entry level staff members, they restored the column

---

[12] Eve didn't elaborate further, but in some detective work of his own, Coda discovered that the advice columnist at the time, Mr. Darcy, was renowned for his sage, non-judgmental advice. He was a family man to three spectacular children and an adoring wife of more than two decades. Mr. Darcy was credited as being the pioneer behind the radical disinformation campaign to paint Charlotte as a dump.

In a series of exposés on the local news channel, Mr. Darcy was dismantled as a raging adulterer who had as many as twenty lovers throughout the city! Mrs. Darcy was oblivious to the cheating and watched with the rest as her husband was ripped apart in each broadcast. In an act of pure insanity, Mrs. Darcy shuffled all three kids into their SUV and drove into a concrete barrier on the highway. All four occupants died instantly from a hodgepodge of gruesome injuries. So it goes. With his life completely shattered, Mr. Darcy snuck one last advice column in the newspaper that served more as a suicide note than anything else. They found his body on Monday morning with a hose shoved deep in his mouth as he huffed on exhaust from his expensive car. So it goes. The editor of the advice column was fired for gross negligence in letting the suicide note appear in the paper. The advice column was subsequently shut down for two weeks until the whole city forgot about the five dead people.

to its former glory.

After two years of uplifting the community, Eve felt she had fulfilled her penance as being new to the Charlotte Observer family. She approached her editor on a Monday morning before he got slammed with meetings and reminders of how the latest edition of the paper wouldn't make it to print on time. Eve learned that her editor was a man of facts and wanted a clear, concise proposal. All hopped up on adrenaline, she said, "Mr. Larter, it's time we began the investigative journalism branch of this newspaper. The people are begging for it! Here is my plan." Eve slid across the five-page document and stepped back from his desk. Mr. Larter picked it up and thumbed through it with no commitment to read anything within. "Fine. I need a story next week," he said and then followed up by asking her to vacate his office.

Eve had curated a long list of stories she wanted to pursue. The small fish she delivered every few weeks built up her confidence to ask about going after Shangri-La—or in other words, the biggest story of her blossoming career.

Nolan and Coda appeared in Charlotte at a wonderful time. Eve was just given permission to run full tilt with a story she pitched to the entire editorial staff. Most questioned her sanity, but her boss had full trust in Eve and convinced the other editors to let her go after the story.

After an elongated rehash of Eve's professional career (with scant details on her personal life), they headed west in Eve's car for what she called a "leisurely stroll into the lion's den."

"You never mentioned why you cared if we were religious or not?" Coda asked from the backseat. He sat in the middle and looked out the windshield at the passing macadam underneath.[13]

"We are going to 'mass' at the megachurch on the westside of the Catawba River. You'll know it when you see it."

"What kind of story are you writing about the place?"

"About the son of a bitch that runs it—Kent Copulation-Dome."

Coda reran the name several times in his head. "What's wrong with Kent?"

Eve's response was trite: "He's a true, certified asshole."

Here's a longer explanation as to why:

---

[13] Fun Fact: The name macadam derives from its founder, John McAdam. Not very creative, huh? Keep that in mind next time you invent something and struggle with what to call it.

Kent Copulation began his life in west Texas. The town was one of those places people rarely escaped from. Poverty ran deep amongst the residents and electricity was still a relatively new invention that some still marveled over. His father was a swindler that excelled at selling snake oil to the community. The tricks and schemes he concocted were endless, and while most were abrupt failures, the ones that succeeded provided a level of comfort for Kent and the entire family. Kent's mother suffered from postpartum depression and found herself unable to get out of bed most days. Kent and his other siblings took care of her, but after a particularly nasty psychotic break, Kent's father shipped her off to an insane asylum where the extreme electroshock therapy fried her brain irreparably.

Scarred by the tragedy of his mother, Kent focused on education to lift himself out of the poverty-stricken town. During his time at Texas Tech, he fought for the inclusion of a fraternity on campus that focused solely on the Word of God. The fraternity would not include any drinking, socializing with sororities, or any other form of debauchery. The years of being an active participant in his father's schemes imprinted onto Kent that the fastest way to get money was deception. Each semester, dozens of students pledged their desire to be a part of the fraternity. They were in the Bible Belt and most students had been raised in a god-fearing household.

For Kent, it had been quite the opposite. His father was fond of stressing that god-fearing individuals are the easiest to manipulate because "they toss their coins aside to appease an entity that doesn't exist!" Out of curiosity, he walked to his local church one Sunday morning as a teenager and watched as the poor, uneducated parishioners dumped what little money they had into the basket. All because the pastor said God demanded it. How foolish!

A fascination latched itself to Kent as he wondered how he could take advantage of fearful folk that wanted to do right by their god. The fraternity was the answer. The dues for one semester was sixty dollars. (To date these events and understand the significance of that amount, Kent attended Texas Tech from 1965–1968.) Kent capped the fraternity at fifty members to preserve the intrigue and mystery. He stressed the money was used to buy Bibles and keep up with the administrative costs of running a fraternity. It was all bullshit. Kent found a bookstore in downtown Lubbock with an abundance of Bibles being shipped in each month. He cut a deal with the owner to buy half the stock at a bulk discount. The admin costs that Kent raved about were a complete scam. The fraternity meetings were held in a classroom on campus, which was free. No food or drink was provided in an effort to promote fasting, which pleased God greatly.

So what did he do with all the money?

He paid for his college education and the various dates he went on. In secret, of course, since he preached abstinence to all the fraternity members.

Like any good con artist, Kent became familiar with what the Bible said. He read it each night and devised sermons like he saw the pastor give in his hometown. After a year or two, he was able to reference passages and books without any hesitation. The best part is he forced members out after a year due to the overwhelming demand, so Kent was able to repeat the same sermons. He perfected his communication skills and prayed on the weak.

Kent continued with the con for nearly four years. As his graduation approached, he made the heartbreaking announcement to suspend the fraternity because he didn't feel any of the members were dedicated enough to carry on the legacy. People begged and cried and petitioned for him to find a proper replacement, but Kent never budged.

In the spring semester of 1968, The Brotherhood of Devout Followers ended.

Kent graduated from Texas Tech with a degree in Finance and no intention of utilizing that knowledge for a corporate job. In addition, he walked away from college with a fiancé. A year prior, he met Ms. Lucky Dome in one of his classes and instantly felt a connection. What Kent really loved about Lucky was her money. For generations, the Dome family had been amassing an empire that rivaled the Rockefellers or Carnegies. What did they specialize in? Cereal, of course. Everybody eats breakfast.

Lucky had a dominant personality that constantly put Kent in his place. She always wanted more. Better dining experiences, bigger gifts, more respect, and most importantly, more money. She shared with Kent her desire to expand the family empire out of cereal and into entertainment. Lucky watched several years back how a person like John F. Kennedy could inspire a nation just by charms and good looks. Lucky wanted Kent to personify and capitalize off that groundwork.

Over the next decade, Kent and Lucky slowly crafted and built out a new leg of the Dome empire. (In a subservient move, Kent adopted his wife's last name as a sign of respect to her family who never favored him. Much like Lucky, the family always expected more, more, more.) They had kids. They moved around the country. They faked documents saying Kent spent time at Oral Roberts University to expand upon his evangelical passions. It was easy enough to pronounce himself as a minister of God without providing proof. What didn't work as expected was him coming unannounced to various churches and offering to spread his message. After being denied countless times, Kent and Lucky would organize meetings in local town halls where Kent would preach his views on God. Their entrance fee was modest: only forty dollars.

Through this practice, Kent gained notoriety and was approached by a rapidly evolving television channel, the Christian Broadcasting Network. On a weekly basis, Kent would appear on one of CBN's many programs. The co-hosts would nod along to his rambling, but the message always boiled down to one basic fact: give us your goddamn money.

In the early 1980s, Kent felt confident that the Dome family was ready to create their own televangelist network. He learned from what CBN did and some of the pitfalls they fell into. Kent believed they were too passive in their approach in getting viewers to tithe.

Lucky and Kent purchased a huge patch of land on the outskirts of Charlotte, at that point a Podunk city with little appeal, and began construction on their megachurch and television studio.

Tragedy struck mere weeks before the opening when Lucky's private jet crashed on her way home to Texas. There were no survivors. Kent, being the person he was, used Lucky's death as a means to promote the megachurch. On that first Sunday, the five-thousand seat arena was packed with a new flock that came to hear Kent Copulation-Dome's sermon about his dead wife.

The move caused quite a stir amongst the Dome family, many of whom denounced Kent and pressured him to strip himself of the Dome name. His children were in awe of his behavior and distanced themselves from him in an act that permanently severed their relationship.

Kent faced mounting difficulty in succeeding within his own family, but on the outside, he was amassing a fortune that rivaled the cereal empire.

Time ticked by for Kent Copulation-Dome as the megachurch became a haven for the very people his father advised him in taking advantage of so many years earlier.

The money grew and grew and grew and grew.

Fast forward to a more present time. Kent Copulation-Dome was still swindling his flock as he neared the age of eighty. He'd never quit his game until St. Peter greeted him at the Pearly Gates.

He had no one in his life. His children hated everything he did. His staff saw through the deception and witnessed appalling abuse and behavior. His circle of friends was wound tighter than his bleached asshole.

He had his money though.

The one thing he could take with him beyond this life.

"Okay, we are here," Eve announced. She circled around in a massive parking lot. Coda turned and looked ahead at each spire that rose into the sky. The structure was a monstrosity with the word SALVATION etched into the side with a dramatic picture of Jesus Christ on the cross with a light beaming down from Heaven.

"Why is the parking lot so crowded?" Coda asked.

"Because Kent Copulation-Dome believes that the Sabbath should be two days out of the week. My theory is that he saw people weren't coming in large enough crowds on Sundays, so he decided to preach that God implored his flock to give not once, but twice a week. He holds an event on Monday afternoons."

"An event?"

"Yeah, I struggle to call it mass because he doesn't give communion or do anything you'd expect during a church service."

"I can't say I have much experience going to church."

"That's okay."

"What does he do during these events then?" Nolan asked.

"He spews his bullshit."

"Who has the time to drive all the way out here on a Monday afternoon? I'd expect most people to be working."

"You'd be surprised," Eve said. "I'd say his target audience are vulnerable groups: the elderly, people who don't have much and are looking for a miracle, the weak, the uneducated, the—" She stopped herself.

"What's your beef with this guy?" Coda said.

"Because," Eve said, "I grew up going to this stupid church. My family would come here every single week praying and giving away what little money they had with the continual hope something good would happen. Maybe Kent would see their contributions and help pay the rent they were always behind on or that God would bless them with the materialistic things they lacked. It was sickening. I didn't understand it for a while. I'll attribute most of my negligence to age, but I eventually realized what my parents got out of this deal they signed up for: absolutely nothing."

"What are you hoping to find out about?"

"Nothing revelatory. It's just a vain attempt to expose this psychopath to a larger audience. Hopefully not in a positive way."

"Do you think anyone will be persuaded by what you write?"

"Of course not!" Eve laughed. "Kent Copulation-Dome is one of thousands. He isn't special. Greed and consumption suffocate so many people and kill countless more in the process. Consider this: How many news articles do you see a day? Ten? Twenty? It's hard to say, right? After working at a newspaper for three years, I've learned that the only way they measure success is by volume. The more we write, the more people will read. It doesn't matter if the content is good or even factual! We've been trained to jump from one problem to the next. The world is so connected right now that I could read an article about a tsunami in Asia and be sad for thirty seconds before swiping to another article about an oil spill or that the coral reefs are practically dead or that the local high school had a mass shooting. We are inundated with tragedy and problems and corruptness. We aren't impacted by it anymore. Numb to it all. That's all people feel, Coda. Numbness to everything. Ironic, I suppose." Eve took a breath. She gripped the steering wheel as if she wanted to vacate any life from it. "I guess I want to do my part and contribute to the pile of piss."

Nolan and Coda absorbed her answer.

"Well, I can't deny your passion about this," Nolan said. "I'm curious to hear from this fuck head."

twenty-six

GIVE

They parked on the far end of the lot and wove through the cars toward the entrances that were clogged with people trying to squeeze through the double doors.

Once inside, they were greeted by a staff member in a button down. She didn't look to be any older than our three friends. "Hi! First time?" the worker asked. She thrusted a pamphlet in their direction.

The worker's pleasantry was only a formality. Using security cameras embedded with high-end facial recognition software throughout the parking lot, the main office quickly identified the pack of newcomers. A half-dead body slumped behind a computer radioed down to the pamphlet worker and gave her a brief description on the bogies. While radioing down, exceptional computer software was scanning the faces against a gaggle of databases to see if any hits were returned. Who were these people? What was their occupation? Salary? Marital status? Political affiliation? Any information to gain a deeper understanding of who was walking in. Based on the aggregated data of all those who entered the megachurch, Kent Copulation-Dome would shift his sermon to resonate with the crowd.

Eve tossed the pamphlet into the garbage without looking at it.

They continued deeper, moving underneath the high, vaulted ceilings with exposed rafters and catching views of people mingling around on the second and third stories. Vendors were selling merchandise of all kinds: Bibles, clothing, prayer beads, bottled holy water, communion wafers, the blood of Christ, and other oddities. The body and blood of Christ was not meant to be kept in the tabernacle; it was meant to be sold for a profit!

Without having assigned seats, they peeked into multiple tunnels to find any openings. Everything was full. They found the ramp leading to the upper levels. They walked to the east end of the megachurch and into the last available tunnel.

"Any complaints about sitting over here?" Eve asked.

Nope, none.

She found three seats about halfway up. The crowd was more scattered on the upper levels, but maybe the saying was still true in this instance: The true fans sat in the nose bleeds.

On each seat they found an envelope with a plea from Kent Copulation-Dome asking for contributions to the beautification of the megachurch. Kent's message spoke of how the church had served the community for nearly forty years and that the daily television broadcasts reached millions of viewers. We can't let that fail, right? In bold print at the bottom, it said how the church accepted cash, checks, credit cards, or donated plasma.

Coda looked around and saw people digging through purses or wallets for money. He watched an elderly man slowly raise the envelope to his lips and lick it several times before sealing it shut.

Coda was conflicted. Eve's bias toward Kent Copulation-Dome was a bit heavy handed for him, but he also understood that her fury was warranted. Though he could only see the tops of their heads, it was a sea of baldness and white hair down on the first level. Walkers and scooters and canes lined the aisles. He wondered if it was a generational thing or if being old made someone more religious. Imagine living for many decades and experiencing the pain of losing those around you. Wouldn't you want to believe there was even a slim chance you'd see your loved ones again?

Coda's lack of religion growing up led to him never having a staunch viewpoint of it. For him, as long as people didn't shove it in his face or treat others like dirt, he was okay with whatever people practiced. During Eve's info session about Kent Copulation-Dome, one question kept bubbling to the forefront: Who cares? Who cares if one guy is cheating the system and getting away with it? If his targets are too ignorant to understand, then that's their fault.

He decided this situation was one he'd be neutral about. Coda wasn't informed enough to care and didn't care enough to be informed. Contrary to expectations, Coda didn't need to have an overt opinion on every matter.

All the lights were dim on the main stage with the exception of one that shined up on a towering image of a cross. In Christianity, you couldn't go very far without seeing one.

Nolan picked up the Bible and flipped through the pages. The font was tiny and crammed to the edge of every page. "You could bludgeon someone to death with this," she noted, examining each side. Eve looked over and nodded. She returned her arms to a folded position.

The singular light winked out of existence and a raucous cheer rippled through the crowd. The screens on either side lit up with a logo of two arms stretched out with cupped hands as if they were waiting to receive a gift of communion or money.

The logo remained as a voice came through the audio system.

"Are you ready?" it yelled.

Another wave of cheers.

"I said: ARE YOU READY?" it yelled even louder.

The cheers amped up in volume.

"Children of God, you know who he is. This man needs no introduction." The voice seemed to miss the irony of the statement. "Please welcome our founder and leader and savior, Kent Copulation-Dome!"

The cheers reached their peak. Who knew the geriatrics could clap with such fervor?

A platform descended from the ceiling. A light snapped on and showed a man in a navy-blue three-piece suit. His hair was combed to the side and left enough room on his forehead for a math teacher to write out equations. Coda watched on the screens as the cameras tracked the platform down to the stage. The man's smile was wide and full. Decades of practice. He waved out to the crowd as the cheers continued. Coda could tell the man fought hard to not look as old as he was. The skin on his face was pulled back like a taut bedsheet; any wrinkles were exterminated except for the noticeable shadows under his eyes. He had a tan that worked surprisingly well as he didn't exude an orange aura that others were known for. All in all, Kent Copulation-Dome was the embodiment of wealth and calculated appearance.

As the platform reached the bottom, Kent stepped off as the spotlight continued to follow him. His voice echoed out from the speakers once the applause died down. "Who are we going to save tonight?" He sounded fragile as if someone should return him to the shelf. Coda would learn that Kent's question was his famous tagline. A large portion of each program was dedicated to providing salvation to people in the audience.

Cheers burst out from the parishioners again. The constant applause was getting to Coda. It was worse than a television sitcom or when he graduated from college and people insisted on cheering for each student even after the Dean asked to hold their applause until the end.

Kent paced back and forth across the stage, the spotlight always following him. He walked with a slight limp and it looked to Coda that each step ailed him to some degree.

"What a beautiful day," he began in a manufactured Southern accent. "What a beautiful day in the Church of Christ. And what a wonderful crowd! Look at you all packed in there! This may be our biggest crowd ever . . . Can I be honest with you? I felt distant from God today." Murmurs of surprise throughout the crowd. "I know, I know. 'Kent, you are the most devout among us! You must always know the path forward.' No, I wish it was the case, but like any other person, I am fallible. I am tempted by the misguided and the venom that exists in our world." He slammed down a fist like he was banging a gavel. "Many questions were running through my head today. Am I doing enough for all of you? Have I truly devoted my life to the cause of being a teacher? Have I inspired enough souls to change their wretched ways? I only have two private jets after all. If I had a third, imagine all the new places I could get to," he said with a flashy smile, wide enough to see the crooked bottom row of teeth. "Have I helped to quell the suffering of the innocent? Have I understood and extrapolated the lessons from the Bible? Will I get to see the Pearly Gates one day? I'm an old, old man. My time here is shrinking—just like many of you out there. I see the canes and hunched backs and thick rimmed glasses staring back at me.

"With all those questions, God didn't deliver any answers except for one. He said to me, mere moments before I came out here, 'Kent, you are on the right path. But you need more. Challenge your flock to give more!' I thought about what God said to me"—an extended pause— "and I knew I couldn't disagree. What is the purpose of living if not to give?" said the man with a net worth of a billion dollars. "Several verses from the Bible came to mind while contemplating this idea of . . . giving," Kent said the last word as if it was foreign to him.

"Luke, Chapter Nineteen, Verse Eight: 'But Zacchaeus stood up to the Lord and said, "Look, Lord! Here and now I give half of my possessions to the poor, and if I have cheated anybody out of anything, I will pay back four times the amount."' Have you given half of your possessions? Be honest with yourselves! We do not carry mortal possessions such as wealth or fame or good fortune into the House of God! We bring ourselves and that's it. Rid yourself of the burden of money. It spawns the devil and devious behavior. The gamblers, the adulterers, the abusive, the addicts, the corrupt . . . what binds all of them? Money! Of course! Here, at this wonderful church, we leverage what we are given to provide more for *you*. Everything I do is in service of *you*! I am but a humble servant of our Lord and Savior.

"Not convinced yet? Consider this from Matthew, Chapter Six, Verses Nineteen through Twenty-One: 'Do not store up for yourselves treasures on earth, where moths and vermin destroy, and where thieves break in and steal. But store up for yourselves treasures in heaven, where moths and vermin do not destroy and where thieves do not break in and steal. For where your treasure is, there your heart will be also.' Let me repeat that last line again: 'For where your treasure is, there your heart will be also.' Now, what is your treasure? Giving unto others! You will be judged for how much you give to the meek and the sick and the poor and your church. We support numerous local charities and soup kitchens. We take your generous donations to feed, clothe, and shelter the less fortunate. That's the real treasure! Once you rid yourself of that pesky money, your heart will be free to fully embrace God. Trust me, I have abided by this ideal for decades and experience the best the world has to offer," said the man with a net worth of a billion dollars.

"You may have noticed the envelopes on each of your seats. I hope all of you gave what you could. If you can spare more, my wonderful staff will be walking around to collect anything you'd like to give. Remember: Each contribution helps your community and brings you closer to God." In the weeks to come, Eve would discover that the donations Kent Copulation-Dome pawned off his worshippers rarely made it back to the local community. Shelters across the city reported that the megachurch had no affiliation with them. The evidence, as always, was hiding just out of sight.

"We also want to introduce a new way of giving," Kent said, pointing to the screen on his right. It changed to show the words #PAYCHECKCHALLENGE in bright blue letters. "The Paycheck Challenge is simple. If you visit our website and provide proof you've given us a donation that is equal to or greater than one of your paychecks—or for our older folk, your Social Security check—I will personally say a prayer for you to God. Even the best of us need someone to put in a good word. This challenge will be active for the next month, so that should be plenty of time to participate. With your help, we will be able to change our community and help you to rediscover that what matters in this world is how much you give. That's it.

"Now, who are we going to save tonight?" Kent clapped his hands together and basked in the wild cheers that engulfed him.

Coda sat up in his seat and suffered through the next hour and a half of Kent Copulation-Dome bringing people up to the stage and cleansing them of their sins. The formula was the same. He would have an unpaid worker pluck someone from the crowd, make them hobble up to the stage, and engage in brief conversation before placing his hand on their forehead. He'd whisper some incantation that was barely audible and usher the individual on their way. The whole schtick was intolerable to watch, but the worst part for Coda was that the people they picked from the crowd were the impressionable ones: the mother with small kids, the middle-aged man working paycheck to paycheck, a slew of elderly people who confessed they had more money than they knew what to do with. Actually, scratch that. The worst part was that Kent Copulation-Dome made all the old folks walk up a series of six steps to get to the stage. That motherfucker didn't even have a ramp or go to their seats. That was the real atrocity.

Kent Copulation-Dome ended his "mass" with two reminders. The first was about the Paycheck Challenge and the necessity for every person in attendance to contribute. The second was that he'd be going live on his nightly television program in two hours, where he would repeat the exact same thing. He'd beg, lie, steal, bribe, and probably drool over the money people willingly forked over. You know, all those important lessons from the Bible.

The lights in the auditorium (let's call it what it is) came up as everyone made a surge toward the exit. Eve, being at the end of the row, continued to sit in her seat, blocking any chance of them leaving.

Coda leaned past Nolan and asked, "Are you alright?"

"It was exactly as I remember. That guy is a complete snake. I can't believe people give him anything."

"I'm sure there is shit you can dig up on him. There must be someone he's scorned who would be willing to go on record about it," Coda said.

"This will take time. Obviously, I wasn't expecting to discover what the angle of the piece was today, but I needed to reaffirm with myself that this guy truly wants people to give him all their money."

"He made that point quite clear."

Nolan shifted in her seat. "I . . . uh . . . I didn't see a problem with it. He was an inspired speaker who wanted people to promote their best selves." Her face reddened knowing her opinion was hugely unpopular.

Eve studied her for a moment before saying, "You're entitled to your opinion like anyone else, but I'm sorry you see it that way. I hope you didn't find this to be a waste of time."

"No, not at all," Nolan was quick to say. "Certainly not an experience I thought I'd ever have. It isn't one I'd look to repeat though."

Eve started to say something else but stopped herself. Instead, she got up from her chair and led them to the exit.

Outside, the lanes were choked with fleeing parishioners.

Eve turned to them as they reached the car and said, "Once this mess dies down, let's go find someplace to eat. I can't let this be the highlight of your time in Charlotte. Any preferences?"

twenty-seven

A ROCK FULL OF FOOLS

They settled on a burger joint east of the airport per Eve's suggestion. All discussion about the megachurch or Kent Copulation-Dome ended five minutes into their ride.[14] It was an experience the three of them shared, but to dwell on it further would have crushed Eve's mood even more.

After ordering a bundle of burgers and sides, they found a table in the back and waited until their food came.

In between bites, Coda and Eve reminisced about their time at the bookstore. It became clear to Nolan that they only saw each other while working. She wanted to ask questions but stuck to her place as the third wheel. Nolan listened as their conversation jumped from memory to memory. It reminded her about the trivial aspects of her job. Eh, old job. When Nolan first met a client, she'd sit in a conference room for an hour and listen to them jabber about all the things they wanted and expected from her team. Nolan would nod and agree and smile and perform the other robotic actions Sophia demanded of any employee out in the field. She rarely had a voice and could never have a dissenting opinion, which is why it felt nice when no one barraged her with negative comments after sharing her opinion about Kent Copulation-Dome. Religion was never a thing Nolan interacted with after the age of six or whenever her circumstances changed—she knew the exact day and all the details if she considered it more. But she never talked about that.

"Hey, hello? Come back to us," Coda said, poking at Nolan.

"Yes, hi. What's up? Sorry, I was letting you two talk about the good ole days."

"Those have yet to happen," Eve said. "Coda and I were saying we

---

[14] Eve did write her story and it gained slight notoriety in the Charlotte area but was overshadowed by Kent Copulation-Dome's arrest. The FBI had issues with his finances and nabbed him on twelve counts of . . . who cares? Kent kept true to his word and found salvation prior to the trial. He was hardly mourned outside of his brainwashed parishioners, who would have cheered at him unloading a 12-gauge shotgun into an innocent person's face. His cause of death was never released. Kent's end amounted to no more than a footnote in a larger narrative.

should go to a bar and grab some drinks."

"On a Monday night?" Nolan questioned.

"It's not like you have work in the morning," Coda said.

"Well, what about you Eve? You don't mind drinking on a Monday night?"

"Not at all! I was the one who suggested it. I have a bar in mind. But I will give you a heads up: I'm a bit biased toward the place since my boyfriend works there."

"Boyfriend?" Coda said in amazement. "Why didn't you say anything earlier?"

"It's not like you two told me anything about your relationship."

"Wait," Nolan said. "You think Coda and I are dating?"

"I figured. Why else would you two go on this exceptionally long road trip together? I can't think of any *friends* that like each other enough to go through such torture."

Nolan and Coda looked at each other and then burst out laughing.

"I can assure you that there is nothing romantic between us. Never was, never will be," Nolan said.

"Oh, I'm sorry for assuming. I just thought—"

"That a guy and girl traveling across the country have to be romantically involved?" Coda said. "I don't blame you. It's a trap anyone would fall into."

"I'm using Coda as an excuse to finally see the West Coast," Nolan said.

"And I'm using Nolan for the free transportation. Mutual benefit for us."

"I see. Now that I'm embarrassed, are you two ready to go?" Eve asked.

"Lead the way," Coda said, thrusting out his empty bottle of water toward the exit.

The bar Eve's boyfriend worked at brought them further east toward downtown Charlotte. Unlike any bar in New York, this one had ample parking which really promoted the idea of drunk driving.

The inside was dimly lit with small pockets of people tucked into corners. In the middle was an obtrusive shuffleboard table that wasn't occupied.

Eve introduced them to her boyfriend, Warner. His most outstanding feature was the mustache that looked like a dying Chia pet. Several times throughout their brief conversation, Warner stroked it like the villain in a B-movie.

While listening to Eve explain who Nolan and Coda were, Warner nodded and prepared three drinks, saying they were on the house.

"Shuffleboard anyone?" Eve asked.

"Never played," Nolan said.

"Same here," Coda echoed.

Eve looked back and forth between them. "Really?"

"I didn't go out much in college," Coda shrugged. "I was more of the drink-in-my-room-and-consider-how-my-life-sucks type of guy."

"I went out a good amount, but my friends apparently avoided all the bars in New York with shuffleboard."

Eve shook her head. "No matter. The game is easy to pick up. You take these donut looking things here and slide them down to the other end of the table. See the lines with the numbers? That's the number of points you get. But only the team with the furthest donut gets points." She saw the confusion on their faces. "I'll explain more as we go. It'll be you two versus me. Maybe you'll have a slim chance to score a few points," she said with a smile.

They took their positions on either end. Eve started down with Coda. Nolan watched as they laughed at Coda's misfortune of either tossing the donut too softly or off the side.

A sharp spike of panic ripped through her. *You need more friends. Look how quickly you can be replaced.* She picked up her drink and took a long sip to slow the thoughts. It didn't help. *What did you do those six months you and Coda didn't talk? Oh, right, you buried yourself in work. How'd that feel? When's the last time you went on a date? Who could you call when you get one of these amazing panic attacks? No one. You have nothing. You're worth nothing. None of it is yours—*

"Nolan! You're up," Eve said, standing beside her.

"Right. Okay, how about some beginner's luck?"

Luck rarely manifested in a game of shuffleboard. It was all about skill, which Nolan and Coda had none. They lost 15–1.

"Another game?" Eve proudly asked.

"Uhhh, I don't know if I have it in me," Nolan confessed. She needed to stop drinking before the panic attack swelled again. Each wave would be stronger and more devastating if she allowed for it to continue.

"How about we get another round?" Coda offered.

Before receiving an answer, he walked over to the bar and flagged down Warner.

They continued in this fashion for another two hours. Well, in actuality, Eve and Nolan stopped drinking after the second round, but Coda ploughed ahead. It was more than Nolan had ever seen him drink before.

Following his fifth trip to the bathroom and the noticeable sway with each step, Eve and Nolan agreed to take him back to the apartment.

As Nolan helped Coda close out his tab, Warner leaned over the bar and confessed to having a heavy hand for Coda's drinks. He said this while stroking that awful mustache of his.

Finally, Nolan and Coda made it past the security desk at Skyhouse and were able to use the elevator.

Out of curiosity, Nolan asked, "We noticed the guy at the front desk was watching porn this morning. Is that a daily thing for him?"

"Frank? Oh yeah, he's got a problem with that. People have complained, but it seems like they can't find a replacement for him."

"Oh," Nolan said, amazed by Eve's cavalier acceptance of the strange behavior.

With Coda leaning onto her, Nolan followed Eve off the elevator and partway down the hall until they hit her apartment. "Throw him in the spare bedroom," she advised. Eve held the door open and let Nolan and Coda pass through. "Make a right and then it's the door on the left."

Nolan followed the instructions and dumped Coda onto the bed. He groaned and mumbled incoherently. "Are you going to be okay?" Nolan asked.

Coda's elegant response: "Hmm . . . bbbbaaaaaaaa . . . sleeeeeeeee." Nolan grabbed his feet and pulled his shoes off. Coda turned over and buried his face in the pillow.

Nolan moved to the bedroom door and turned on the light. The room was decorated with a few IKEA pictures and furniture. The main display were the three columns of bookshelves that cradled two of the walls. Each row was stuffed with books of various sizes. "Alphabetical order," Nolan reminded herself.

She started at the middle bookshelf before realizing the bottom row capped out on author names that began with P. Nolan restarted her search on the far bookshelf. Queen ... Riggins ... Rove ... Shook ... Svent ... Tibe ... Tsar ... too far ... Trout, lots of Trout. Nolan scanned through the half a row dedicated to him. *Laughterhouse-Four, Dinner of Winners, Father Day, Timeshake,* and other oddities.

Nolan pulled out both copies of *Cat's Crib.*

"Everything alright in here," Eve said, appearing at the door.

"Yes. Yeah. I figured I'd grab the book for him." Nolan held up both copies. "How come you have two?"

"Coda didn't give me all the details, but I knew the book must be special based on the note in the front. I assumed I'd give it back to him someday, hence why I got myself another copy."

Nolan nodded and found the handwritten note from Coda's mom in the more pristine copy. She read the message several times before smiling and closing the book. "Did you ever get a chance to meet his mom?"

"No," Eve said. "It was hinted at, but Coda and I didn't have much of a friendship outside the bookstore. It's bizarre to think about. You spend a lot of time around someone, but neither person makes an effort to extend the friendship." Eve shrugged. "Different times, different people."

"Are you tired?" Nolan asked.

"No. You?"

"Me either."

"Follow me then." Eve stepped out of the doorway and walked into the living room. She collapsed herself onto the couch. "Let's talk."

Nolan crept up slowly, unsure what to make of that. "Uh, about something in particular?"

Eve laughed. "No. It's just ... we haven't had a chance to all day. Coda and I were hogging the spotlight by talking about the bookstore and that was on top of me dragging y'all to the megachurch."

"It's okay. I resigned myself to the fact that I may become a third wheel at certain points. It's a side effect of accompanying him on a trip that feels like an elongated high school reunion." The panic from earlier had fully receded back to the depths. It's amazing how sometimes the panic consumed Nolan and other times it disappeared before she could make sense of what was happening.

"You don't have any family or friends to visit on your journey west?"

"There's family out in California, but I haven't kept up with their whereabouts for a long, long time. Everyone I know lives in close proximity to the city."

"Any dreams of breaking out of there?"

"Of course. People are foolish to stay in one location their entire lives. That whole idea of wanderlust fascinates me. You truly never know the experiences you could have or the people you'd meet."

"You say that like New York is the crotch of civilization," Eve said. "There isn't a better city to meet an abundance of new people every single day. It sure beats Charlotte."

Nolan thought a moment. "I understand that, but you get blind to the novelty of it after living there so long, you know? Taking the subway everyday becomes a chore instead of an adventure. Fighting through the mobs on popular street corners gets dull after the thousandth time. Everyone has these incredible ambitions that far outpace any one person—or so they feel—which means they never have time for other people. A New York day feels a lot different than a suburban or rural America day. If that makes sense? Everyone has somewhere to be and to establish meaningful connections with people, so you need to choose your words wisely. It's not something I've mastered yet."

"What is that last part in reference to?" Eve questioned.

"Dating," Nolan said with a forced grin.

"Ah. Well, don't get discouraged. Meeting Warner was the last thing I expected to happen."

"Tell me more about you two."

"I'd be happy to. How about over a glass of wine?" Eve said.

Nolan agreed and Eve went through the motions of pulling out a fresh wine bottle, uncorking it, and filling up two glasses rather generously. She stepped away for a moment before placing the glasses back down. "Might as well finish the bottle," she muttered to herself and evened out the rest of the wine between them.

As Eve returned to the couch, she unloaded a long string of details about her and Warner's relationship. They met on a dating app and took things slow at first, only meeting up once or twice a week. After realizing their connection was stronger than just a fling, they upped their hangouts and started introducing each other to close friends. Time whips by as it always does and now Eve was stressing about how to celebrate their one-year anniversary. Following that momentary contemplation, she dipped back into the details and explained why she loved Warner. It felt real to Nolan and she listened with unwarranted envy. Nolan did her part and asked questions when needed but was quick to switch the topic at her first opportunity.

"Why did Coda give you the book?"

Eve took a long sip of her wine. She was a third of the way done. Nolan had some catching up to do. "Now that is a loaded question. Have you ever read it?"

"No."

"The book has some choice opinions on religion."[15]

"Coda did mention that."

"During college, I was in a massive state of transition. One of the many moving pieces was my detachment from religion. My parents are good-natured people, but I felt they put too much stock in the idea of religion, the potential punishments, and the demands to give your fair share. Being one of seven kids meant I could slip through the cracks with a lot of things but going to church on Sunday mornings was not one. Moving to New York for college afforded me the chance to step away from it, so I did. That book was one of many to help me see that other people are skeptical of religion too, that other people question how and why it has a stranglehold on so many. Kilgore Trout's take was more satirical, but it still carries a worthwhile message and I believe Coda knew I'd connect with it."

"What's the message?"

"We are all fools. Complete idiots."

"That's inspiring."

Eve pulled back her shoulders and sat up straight. Out of everything said so far, she seemed to be the most captivated and inspired about this. "I'm no expert and it's been a while since I've read the book but Trout's stance is that religion and technology and all these grand, grand ideas people have usually end up harming us. He's not scathing of religion, but you can tell he doesn't believe in it. In the book, he makes up a

---

[15] The book choice was odd when you consider how the Finn family was not religious, but if you read Grace's note, you'd understand the intention wasn't for that. Books tend to have more than one meaning, right? This leads to another question though: Why not show the note? Because Coda's show and tell has limits (and lies—lots of those). Gotta leave some morsels for the imagination.

religion called Bok—Bokonism—no, Bokononism, and it has odd ideas but plenty of wisdom. That's no different than any other religion: small pockets of great advice nestled in blankets of shit."

Nolan didn't respond. She didn't exactly want to circle back to the religion discussion from earlier. She had enough for one day. What really interested her was that Grace's note in the book had nothing to do with religion. Maybe Nolan needed to read the book to grasp the intention . . . or, maybe, it wasn't any of her business. Peeking into the book without Coda being there felt like an invasion of privacy, more so when she considered the current state of the relationship with his mother.

"Sorry," Eve said, sensing that Nolan was uncomfortable, "I didn't mean to dig in so deep."

"That's okay. I appreciate the thought you've put into this. Why'd you come back to Charlotte?"

Eve sighed. "I looked in plenty of other cities, but nothing panned out. I don't mind it here and my parents are happy I came back. I'm far enough away that I don't feel suffocated by them."

"Are you close with them?"

"Yeah, surprisingly."

"Why do you say that?"

"I mean, it's not much of a secret," Eve said, laughing as she took another drink. Down to less than half. Nolan was catching up.

Nolan nodded. "Coda told me on the drive in. I . . . I didn't want to pry. It's a new experience for me."

"Does being around a transgendered person make you uncomfortable?"

"No, no. It's not that. I just didn't know if it was okay for me to bring it up and ask questions."

"Depends upon the person, I suppose," Eve said. "For me, I'm extremely open about my transition and that may be because I got so much support during that time. People like Coda were instrumental in helping me through my college years."

"Your family was supportive?"

"Yes, very. Which is odd because you'd think a conservative family from down south who names all seven of their kids after important people from the Bible would think otherwise. It was certainly a shock to them, but they adjusted quickly."

"Why the name Eve? Especially since you don't . . ."

"I see where you're going. Why pick a religious name if I'm not religious anymore? I decided on that name a long time ago. Something about taking the name of the first female was exciting to me. And I couldn't miss the opportunity to make the connection with my last name too."

"Eve Adamson," Nolan said quietly. "I hadn't put the two together before this."

"That only took me all of sophomore year to figure out," Eve said, tipping her glass to Nolan before taking a sip.

"What did Coda help you with during that time?"

"Just letting me vent. I identified as a man when I first met him, but I knew what my path forward was. I was growing my hair out and dressing in a more feminine way. He was one of the many people who lent a listening ear when I was confused or frustrated."

"Frustrated by what?"

"The response from certain individuals. It's no secret that identifying as anything other than straight in this world leads to additional stress. I'm lucky with the support I had — still have — but there were people who would comment on the clothes I was wearing or use the wrong pronoun after repeatedly telling them how I identified. My greatest hurdle to overcome was my body image.

"From the age of ten, I have stood in front of the mirror poking and prodding my body. Pulling on the skin to envision myself skinnier; looking at the chest hair I hated. I stared at my face and learned every single mark and curve. I planned out all the surgeries I would have to make myself look acceptable. I wish I could tell you that it's gotten easier, but it hasn't. I'm afraid that portion of me will never go away."

Eve wiped the tears away from her face.

"I'm sorry. I don't know what else to say."

"It's okay. You listening is more than enough. I can't tell you how refreshing it is to meet new people and their first instinct isn't to stare and wonder why I look just a bit off from every other female they know. I've come such a long way with being proud and comfortable with who I am. My body image issues are the next hurdle I need to tackle. I'll get there with time."

"Thank you for sharing all of this with me. Do you feel like you can live a normal life?"

Eve laughed. "I'm doing that already. I'm no different from you or anyone else. It's common for people to look at me or hear a piece of my story and assume every moment was drenched in trauma. I'm not saying it was easy or for some that the obstacles and pain don't feel endless, but if all we do is portray transgendered individuals as broken and unaccepted, will they ever feel included in society? Once that stigma goes away — if it ever does — life will be so much better for people in this community."

"I'm sorry, I didn't mean any offense by my comment."

"I know, I know... How has Coda been with everything? I didn't get a chance to ask him today."

Nolan put down her empty glass as her head swayed. Eve took her last sip but continued to hold hers.

"What do you mean?" Nolan asked.

"I remember he was figuring out his asexuality back in college. We talked about it several times, but I never pushed too much. He seemed unsure about it."

"His what?" Nolan said, leaning forward off the sofa.

"Oh, fuck. Fuck, fuck, fuck. Has he not ever said anything about it?"

"No, never."

"Oh God. I'm so stupid. I'm sorry. I just... I just assumed. You two seem so close. I-I pressed you two earlier about being in a relationship. I was waiting for him to say something about it then, but I did the exact thing I hated that people did to me..." Eve rambled.

Nolan's head swam with the statement. *Coda? Asexual? There's no way! But when's the last ti — How do I bring this up to him? Do I even talk about it? He has so many other things going on right now... But what if he needs to talk through it with someone? I don't know... I don't know... I don't know... I can't think straight right now...*

"It's okay. Really. I know you meant no harm by it," Nolan managed to respond. "Do you think I should bring it up to him?"

Eve took a long breath and composed herself. "It's been so long. I have no idea where his head is that. I don't know what the right answer is. Part of me thinks it may be good to broach the subject, but the other part knows what it's like to carry a weight and not be ready to tell others. You're going to know better than me."

"Why do you think that?" Nolan asked, blinking several times.

"Because you're all he has."

twenty-eight

CAR CHAT II
Somewhere in South Carolina

"Do you believe in justice, Nolan? It's hard to after what just happened. I'm a good person. I live my life as intended and help others when I should. I'm not perfect by any stretch of the word, but I don't believe I deserve this. It's a cruel, disgusting world to think that this atrocity will go unpunished or unacknowledged by the guilty party. What do you think ran through their mind as they watched the event transpire and refused to complete their task? Was there shame? Was there further contemplation? Will they lay awake in bed tonight — wherever their home may be — and wonder why they didn't do the right thing? Nolan, will I ever get the answers I deserve? No, not me. We. We, as a society deserve to know why such a phenomenon prevails." Coda slumped back into the passenger seat with a disgruntled look plastered to his face.

"Are you done?"

"I think so."

"Can I be honest?" Nolan asked.

"Yes."

"Stepping in dog shit is a universality. Anyone can relate and many have experienced the pain you are going through. I know you will conquer and persevere. I believe in you."

"Nolan, your lack of sincerity cuts me deep," Coda said, feigning death like an actor in a stage play.

"A thousand condolences."

"That many, huh? Well, I am certainly grateful."

"Can we pick this up later? I'm not really in the shit talking mood."

Coda nodded and turned up the volume knob, ending another one of their Car Chats — or Car Shat in this instance.

Let's backtrack slightly.

Ten minutes earlier, they pulled into a rest stop and split apart to use the bathroom. On his way back to the car, Coda's mind was running through where they should stop for the night. They had a delayed start out of Charlotte, and he knew Nolan wouldn't be interested in driving too far in the darkness of South Carolina highways. As he debated this, he walked off the concrete path and through the grass. It saved him fifteen seconds, if that. Coda heard the *squish* sound and looked down to see the pile of poop spread out from the point of impact. Coda lapsed into a spree of expletives as he dragged his shoe through the grass to clean off as much as he could.

Behind Coda, about twenty paces, was the instigator of the poop. A smug grin swept across the man's face. His golden retriever, Surge, was adept at pooping in any location with grass, foreign or familiar. For the last ten years, the man brought his golden retriever to rest stops around the country and had the dog defecate in hidden places amongst the grass. South Carolina was one of the last states to cross off his list. In addition to gaining immense satisfaction each time an innocent stepped into one of Surge's traps, the man witnessed all the landscapes and types of people the USA offered. He watched arguing families, solo travelers, love drunk couples, retirees venturing out on the road, city folk lost in the backwoods, and all the other groups that couldn't be defined. He saw snow-peaked mountains, barren valleys, wheat fields that ventured into the horizon, dense pockets of forests that housed wild, vicious animals, and . . . and . . . heck, he didn't know what else.

Sometimes he wondered if his life would be empty once his mission was complete or his faithful companion was no longer around, but that was a worry for another day.

Tonight, he was the hero and would celebrate as such.

Tomorrow, he'd start heading to his favorite national park.

twenty-nine

SOMETHING TO SHARE

"Is anyone even here?" Nolan asked. She looked down at the card suggesting to ring the bell for service.

One . . . two . . . three separate times the chime went off before a disheveled man tottered his way over to the desk.

As a result of their poor planning and unwillingness to drive further, Nolan and Coda would be staying the night in a motel. It was one of those places that most drove by and elected to keep going just a bit further to find a better option. Coda did a quick search on Snoogle and the motel sat at a three point eight rating with seven reviews. Ehh, he was not convinced. When they pulled up, only half the lights on the sign worked while the others flashed obnoxiously like a bug zapper celebrating a victim. The pool out front was void of any water and caked with rust stains on each side of the concrete interior. Two other cars dotted the parking lot, but neither had the prestige or elegance of the 2008 Pinto Pinata. For each potential pitfall, Coda convinced himself that it would be fine. Neither were germaphobes, so they'd make it work.

"Ca-can I he-he-help you?" the man stammered. He grabbed a seat and was out of breath from the short walk.

"Looking to get a room for the night," Nolan said.

"You c-came to the right place! We have plenty of those available. Most people just keep driving until they hit Savannah, but I say to hell with that! This is the most repu-reputable motel in the entire state."

"Wonderful. We couldn't ask for anything more. You're quite the salesman."

"Oh, I gotta be. My family has kept this business alive for four generations. I can't let them down," the man's tone shifting to a more serious slant.

"Could we get a room with two beds?"

"Certainly. Do you want to k-know my n-n-name?" the man asked abruptly.

Nolan turned to Coda who shrugged his indifference. "Yeah, sure. Hit us with it."

"I'm W-Wilson W-Wil-Wilson."

"Nice to meet you Wilson."

"No, my name is Wilson Wilson. Sorry, I stutter because my mom whacked me on the head too much as a kid. At least that's what she always told me. I know I'm different, but that's okay. I've had this job for a long, l-l-lo-long time, which is more than a lot of p-people can say!"

"Don't apologize for anything," Nolan said. "You are doing great. Both your first and last names are Wilson?"

"Yup!"

"That's unique. I have never met someone else with a name like that."

"I'm f-f-fourth generation Wilson Wilson. My daddy, granddaddy, and great-granddaddy a-all had m-m-my name too."

"Even cooler! I'm named after my dad's brother. At least that's what they tell me," Nolan said.

That was new information for Coda. He didn't know she had much extended family. He also didn't know that Nolan's comment was a casual lie — one told out of habit than anything else.

"What's your names?"

"I'm Nolan and that's Coda."

Wilson nodded his head and smiled widely. "Your names aren't as cool as mine!"

"You got us beat there."

"Do you two like theories of conspiracy?" Wilson asked as if he'd been itching to get the words out.

"Who doesn't?" Coda said. "Which is your favorite?"

"Umm ... hmmm ... uhhh ..."

"You don't have to choose just one," Coda said.

"I like reading about how the earth is flat and that the moon landing never happened. Okay, I g-g-got it! I know my favorite." A pause. "The m-m-missing nuclear bombs!"

"Wait, what?" Nolan said.

"There's lots and lots of nuclear weapons that have gone bye-bye over the y-years."

"That can't be true."

"It is!"

"How come people don't talk about it more?"

Wilson Wilson shrugged. "I'm not a g-g-government official. Are e-either of y-y-you?"

"We are currently unemployed."

"Do you two have cellphones?"

"Well, yeah," Nolan said, looking over at Coda.

"C-can you turn th-them off? They hurt m-m-my head."

"Sure." They pulled out their phones and switched them off.

"Thank you," Wilson said, ditching the childlike tone. "Now we can have an honest conversation."

"Wait. Wait. Did you just . . .?" Nolan said, pointing at Wilson.

"I had to take precautions that you weren't spies," Wilson said with complete seriousness.

"Aw, man, that is fucked up. You can't pretend to be . . . to be . . ."

"To be what? To be a retard? Who gives a fuck?" Wilson reached to the back of his head and released the man bun. Long strands of hair fell down behind his shoulders.

"C'mon Coda. This guy is a piece of shit. We will find another place to stay for the night." Nolan turned to leave. Coda stood frozen, unsure of what transpired.

"If you leave now, you won't be able to see it."

"See what?" Coda said, stepping closer to the desk.

"Follow me."

Coda looked back at Nolan. "Are you joining?"

"Coda, are you crazy? That man is going to dice you up."

"No he isn't! Hey Wilson, are you planning to kill me?"

"Doubtful. I have too much at stake to do something stupid like that." Wilson was halfway down the hall. "Last chance."

"If I'm not back in ten minutes, call the cops. Is that fair, Wilson?" Coda said.

"Yeah, fine."

"Coda, that man just pretended . . . and you're okay with that," Nolan said.

"No," Coda said, "I'm not okay with that, but I'm curious to see what he has. And that is totally separate from him being a shitty person."

"Hey! I'm just misunderstood," Wilson called out.

Nolan left the office and stormed out to the car. Coda circled his way around the desk and caught up to Wilson.

"Good decision. You are gonna want to see this. Are you familiar with the incident in 1958 over at Tybee Island?"

"I've never heard of that place."

"It's out past Savannah, so not too far from here. The military was running some exercise and two of their planes collided. One of them was carrying a nuclear weapon. It fell into the water and was never recovered."

"Again with this shit," Coda said. "There is no way that nuclear weapons disappear without a trace."

Wilson stopped in front of a door. "You're right. They don't stay missing. Maybe it isn't the military that finds them again though." He bent down and grabbed the ring of keys attached to his belt loop. Wilson flipped through them quickly until he reached the desired one.

Coda's heart raced as Wilson opened the door. *It has to be bullshit. This guy was a complete freak. There is no way that he has a . . .*

"Lo and behold," Wilson said, stretching his arm out to showcase what laid beyond. "Step closer, step closer. Take a look for yourself."

Coda moved toward the glow in the center of the room. He could see the outline of a massive, indistinct shape. He'd never seen a nuclear bomb in person before, but as he stepped in front of it, Coda saw the United States flag etched into the side with a long serial number. "No fucking way. No fucking way." He reached out to touch it.

"No! No! No! You can't make contact with it!" Wilson yelled.

Too late. Coda's hand pressed against the side. It felt . . . cheap. He was expecting steel or some heavy, cold material. It seemed light too. Coda was no expert, but weren't nuclear bombs supposed to be thousands of pounds? How was it being supported by the dinky table it sat on? He pushed harder against it.

"Stop! Stop!"

With one soft shove, Coda knocked the nuclear bomb off the table, breaking it in half and exposing the foam interior. "Ahhhh," he said, recoiling back. "You asshole!" Coda scurried for the door and up the hallway. He looked behind him several times to make sure Wilson Wilson was not following.

At the car, Nolan was still in a foul mood. Now Coda was too. Neither spoke during their search for another place to stay. Their frustrations wouldn't get hashed out until later that night. Nolan was appalled that Coda didn't mind Wilson's callous and disgusting behavior, while Coda was upset at being fooled by a man with a double name.

Back at the motel, Wilson Wilson let out a cackled laugh after Coda retreated from the room. He continued his high-pitch laughter for the amusement of no one but himself. He picked up the fractured nuclear bomb and tossed it aside. There were plenty more to choose from. Besides being a dick, Wilson enjoyed spending weeks crafting the fake nuclear weapons. His attention to detail was a source of pride even if no one understood the effort he put into them.

The process of showing off his work was relatively easy. After an ocular pat down, Wilson would quickly decide whether a customer was worthy of being duped as he believed it to be quite the honor. One time, someone asked Wilson why he did it, why he brought people back there. He never considered how he didn't have an answer. After dozens and dozens of instances, he finally understood why: he was a sad, lonely soul who thrived on the belittlement of others. He lacked the self-shame to be concerned about it though. If you think he was a crappy person, you should have met his granddaddy! That guy was a real son of a bitch. Racist, homophobic, misogynistic, xenophobic, and on and on it went. Wilson's granddaddy was a boil on the ass of the human existence, but, thankfully, that boil was lanced a decade back.

But, still, Wilson Wilson IV did have a secret.

He closed the door Coda ran out of and walked over to the corner of the room. He flipped up the shag carpet and tossed it aside. Wilson pulled on the latch and lifted up the door in the floor. A dim light pulsated at the bottom. Carefully, he moved down the ladder that groaned with each step of his excessive frame. Once at the bottom, he followed the light deeper into the tunnel until he reached an opening high enough for him to stand upright.

Wilson smiled as he moved closer to the object that hogged most of the open space. His hand caressed it as if he was petting his favorite animal.

"One day," he said. "One day, one day, one day . . ."

thirty

THREE WORDS

"I was expecting . . . more," Coda said, glancing at the bungalows that passed by.

"This isn't the Hamptons."

"Apparently not. I assumed everyone down in Florida was old and rich."

"Only the first part of that statement is accurate." Nolan slammed on her brakes as an elderly woman waved and slowly crossed the street. The woman stopped halfway and bent down to pick something up off the street. She examined it with complete curiosity. "She better have found a nugget of gold," Nolan said in annoyance. Eventually, the woman continued at her glacially pace.

It was early afternoon in the beautiful beach town of Venice, Florida. Coda was shaken awake under the cover of darkness as Nolan said she couldn't sleep. They had a six-hour drive ahead of them and she didn't see the need to delay it any further. Within twenty minutes, they were packed and out of the more domestic hotel then the one they fled from.

He hadn't slept either. Cecilia ambushed him late with another call. Their conversation was brief with too much that went unsaid. Coda stared at the ceiling the entire night, willing himself to find peace. He found none. Instead, he suppressed every emotion that tried to break through so he could be numb to it all.

During the leisurely ride south, Coda answered Nolan's three questions that accompanied them to each location thus far. The individual's name was Sadie Nguyen. Coda met her during one of his free elective classes at TCSUM. After a lengthy decision-making process, Coda settled on weightlifting. Yup, that's right. The guy that rarely stumbled into the interior of a gym enrolled in a class with all the meatheads. It was one of two squandered opportunities considering Coda could have picked up a useful life skill like project management, mastering an instrument, or learning how to cross stitch.

It was wildly apparent that Coda and Sadie were outcasts, and as such, they stuck together. They partnered up during each lifting circuit and cheated on exams by saying the other person flawlessly executed each lift. The teacher gave even less of a shit than the students, which led to a lot of free time during the hour-long class. Upon hearing Sadie speak for the first time, it was clear that English was not her first language. She always spoke in the present tense, jumbled around words, and shortened her sentences to remove the fluff. It was as if Coda was speaking to a rudimentary artificial intelligence. He found the change of pace endearing and could never look down on someone making the effort to assimilate.

Coda's habit was always the same: He struck up conversations with people in his classes, but never made an effort to extend them into the outside world. Sadie was no different. Their friendship dissipated at the semester's end, but obviously, Nolan and Coda wouldn't be in Florida if he hadn't given her a book.

The Bronze Lodestar.

Sadie claimed to have no interest in reading, but each person did if you knew what lever to pull. Coda settled on a story that was bathed in not-so-subtle allegory about how much religion sucks. Really, it's not a trend for Coda. Seems to be more of a thing in general than anything else. Coda didn't remember any more specifics regarding *The Bronze Lodestar*. Heck, he couldn't even recall if his mom left a note at the beginning of the book. For as much as Coda read, he was no different than any other person in that he could barely recall the details. The words, sentences, stories, metaphors, contents of the last page, and other facets all blended into a single emotion or gut feeling.

Scratch that previous comment.

Coda did remember one other detail about the book. He spilled precisely three drops of coffee on page 277. It was the only time in memory that he had ever defaced one of his books.

He was a firm believer that dogearing pages was a punishable crime. Use a bookmark, you savages!

Whenever the book was not being read, it either had to be on a shelf compressed up against other books or placed front side down so that the opening pages of the book (if it was a paperback) would not be flayed open forever.

Sadie was appreciative of his gesture and promised to read the book. The rest of the semester slipped by without any comment on her progress. As we know, Coda was fantastic at giving away his things but not recovering them.

And as such, Sadie's rental became stop #3 on their renowned tour.

Coda pulled out Sam's list yet again and quadruple checked the address. It still matched where Snoogle Maps was taking them. One detail he didn't share with Nolan was that Sam didn't list Sadie's last name as Nguyen, but Falconer. In their brief friendship, Sadie never struck Coda as the monogamous type. She always spoke of things grander than that. Always revolving around money and power.

"Hey, question for you," Coda said during the final stretch of their drive.

Nolan turned down the volume of the music. "Fire away."

"If Sadie was living in *actual* Venice, you know, the one people *actually* want to visit, would you have flown there with me?"

"With money not being a factor?" Nolan asked.

Money was never an issue with her so that's an odd thing to say, Coda thought. "Sure, with money not being a factor."

"Absolutely," she said without hesitation. "Who wouldn't want to see Venice? The city is sinking into the ocean. Not sure how many more years we'd have to see it."

Coda envisioned the city swallowed by the sea. The ancient relics submerged and unrecoverable. The boat tours no longer confined to the outskirts of the city but free to travel wherever they wanted. Would it happen all at once? Would he be alive when people talked about the once-great-beauty of Venice like it had been gone for an entire millennium? People would forget that they caused it. The tourists stomping around the streets, the city always building, building, building because they always needed more, more, more. The money was never enough. The piles of garbage could be hidden. The rotting smell that creeped up from the canals could be covered up. The dirty, foul water could be attributed to something that wasn't pollution.

People were always quick to forget their mistakes — almost as quick as they are to destroy something.

Nobody knew that better than him. Why else would he travel thousands of miles to escape from New York?

That downward spiral with his mom was a subtle decline into the sea with the final jab being more of a detonation that collapsed the whole damn city in seconds.

Three words was all it took.

I hate you.
I hate you.
I hate you.
I hate y—

"We are here!" Nolan announced, ripping Coda from his visions of chaos, his remembrance of what he'd done. "This . . . this is the biggest freaking house we've seen so far. It has a gate and everything. Are you sure we have the right address?"

Coda swallowed twice, the words getting caught in his throat. "I trust Sam. He's been ace so far. This house does feel out of place though."

The massive beach home was hidden beyond the iron gate that blocked their path. Hoisted high above the driveway and concrete wasteland underneath, the house looked like a castle in the sky. Even from this distance, Coda could see the intricate details of each capital at the top of the columns that were evenly spread across the front. The shrubs were trimmed to perfection as Coda spotted a long-limbed man hunched over tending to one of the many gardens.

"There's a call box here," Nolan said and inched closer to it. She rolled down the window and pressed the button.

It hummed for a few seconds before returning a voice.

"State your business," the call box cackled before returning to the hum.

"We are friends of Sadie Ngu—"

"Sadie Falconer," Coda cut in. "Nguyen was her last name in college."

Nolan let go of the button. "You didn't mention that bit."

"A small detail. My apologies," Coda said.

"State your business with Mrs. Falconer," the voice echoed. *Hummmmmmmmmm.*

"We'd like to catch up and retrieve something I gave Sadie during college."

Hummmmmmmmmmmmmmm.

"Get to the point, boy!" the voice yelled. "My patience is thin."

"A book. I gave her a book. *The Bronze Lodestar*. We took a wei—"

"Enough!" the voice demanded.

Hummmmmmmmmmmmmmm.

"Answer one more question," the voice continued, softer but still agitated. "I wasn't going to get the brain transplant the other day, but then I changed my mind." *Hummm.* "Was that sentence funny? State your reasoning."

Nolan and Coda looked at each other then back at the call box.

"It was stupid because dad jokes are the lowest form of comedy," Nolan said with the hot take.

The hum cut out. With a quick *click,* the gate began to swing inward.

"The lowest form of comedy? Really?" Coda asked.

"Worse than cringy improv."

"Wow. I'm learning new things about you during this trip, Nolan Treiber."

You aren't the only one, she thought.

Nolan pulled through the gate and winded up the driveway. The gardener stopped tending to the flowers and stood up to watch their arrival. His body looked more disproportionate than Muscle Fox. The man was completely clothed with a bandana covering his face, but before Coda could get a better look, the man scurried around the side of the house. Nolan parked the 2008 Pinto Pinata under the extended roof adjacent to the front door.

"Each day of this trip gets weirder and weirder," Nolan noted.

"You say that like it's a bad thing."

"Of course not. Merely an observation."

They moved to the front door. Coda could hear the crashing of waves against the sand and the sounds of seagulls squawking to find their next meal. So close to the beach. He could taste the salt in the air. What an odd sensation. It was a beautiful cloudless day. The weather was warm but enjoyable with the breeze off the ocean.

Nolan knocked two times and stepped back. The locks began to recoil on the other side for what seemed like minutes. Eventually, the door swung open and they were greeted by an older man.

"I am Dietrich Falconer. Hi-ho!" Liver spots and wrinkles dominated his face. His wide smile displayed — what Coda assumed to be — the dentures. The teeth were too white and orderly for a man his age. His stature was firm and assured. He was wearing khakis with loafers and a Hawaiian shirt tucked in. It didn't match at all.

This man had money. This man had *fuck me* money because that's what you'd say to yourself after realizing your luck would never eclipse Dietrich Falconer's.

"Hi-ho!" Coda volleyed back. He couldn't resist. How often do you get the chance to start a conversation with that? "I'm Coda Finn and this is Nolan Treiber. Thanks for letting us into your home."

"I haven't let you in yet," he said with a smirk. "But I am quite confident you aren't robots, so that is a good start."

"Is that what the strange question was about?" Nolan asked.

"Yes, my dear. I am quite alarmed about the state of artificial intelligence and how much robotics has progressed over the years. I had to do a brief Turing Test to understand where your intelligence resided."

"I . . . uh . . . okay," Coda said.

"Not to worry! Not to worry! I am not some deranged kook. With a powerful name like Dietrich Falconer, I should be president of this god forsaken country, not a lowly bystander! I mean, for goodness sake, a million people get killed in the pandemic a few years back and we have learned not a thing. Not a thing! Sometimes I feel blessed to be an old man so that I don't have to watch this world fall into deeper disrepair much longer."

"I . . . uh . . . okay," Coda said.

"You have business with Sadie, hmmm?"

"That's correct," Nolan said, taking over for Coda.

"I will have Butler fetch her." Dietrich Falconer took two steps back and yelled to his right. "Butler! Oh, Butler! Please go fetch the lady of the house for me."

When Dietrich turned his attention back to them, Nolan asked, "What's your relation to Sadie?" The question came out slowly as if Nolan didn't want to hear the answer she knew was coming.

"Lady Sadie is my darling wife! The sweet nectar that this old bee feasts on. She is my Fountain of Youth, the Juliet to my Romeo, my . . . my . . . well, you get the idea," Dietrich said, pushing up onto the balls of his feet as he couldn't contain his glee. "To find love again so late in life is heavenly."

"I . . . uh . . . okay," Nolan said as if she was afflicted by the same ailment that struck Coda.

"True love does not recognize age," Dietrich reiterated proudly. "Oh, oh! Lady Sadie! Guests for you." His voice crooned out in a newfound softness.

Sadie appeared in the doorframe. "Soda! Soda! Is that you?"

"Yes, it's me."

Sadie was in shorts and a t-shirt, but Coda could tell how muscular she was. The weightlifting class may have been a joke to him, but it seemed to stick with her.

"Soda?" Nolan questioned.

Coda leaned over and said, "A, uh, nickname she gave me. She found it unbearably funny that my name rhymed with soda."

"It be so long. Why you here? You live in New York, hmm?" Sadie asked, the words fractured by her heavy accent.

"I'm sorry to barge in like this, but I was hoping you still had the book I gave you back at TCSUM. During our weightlifting class."

"Are you the one I have to blame for Sadie's obsession with the gym?" Dietrich asked.

"No sir, I didn't take that class seriously at all. Look at me now," Coda said, pointing to himself. He was well within the means of being a healthy individual, but it was no secret that Coda was more bones than muscle.

"Book? You want book?" Sadie said.

"Yeah. Do you remember when I gave you *The Bronze Lodestar*?"

"Ohhh" — recognition passed over her face — "I don't like that book. It is silly. All the animals talk much like a baby bedtime story."

"Well, that's okay. I'm not offended. Do you still have the book with you?"

Sadie shrugged. "I . . . hmmm . . . it's big house. It could be anywhere."

"I have an easy solution to that," Dietrich said, bouncing up onto the balls of his feet again. "Butler! Do you have a moment?"

Dietrich waited for a reply that never came and returned his attention back to the guests. "Where are my manners?" he continued. "Come inside you two! It appears we jumped straight into business bypassing all of the typical chit chit. Hi-ho!" Dietrich stepped aside and motioned for them to enter the house.

Nolan and Coda obliged. "Thank you," they both said.

"Ahh, there's Butler. My good man, woul—"

"Sir, I am no man. As you are so fond of reminding me, I am only a below average non-human entity that has the outstanding privilege of serving you and Lady Sadie."

Coda located the source of the formal tone and found a disheveled robot carrying a pile of clothes with a bandana still hanging from its neck. Shaped like an adult human, the robot would have blended into a crowd if it weren't were the shiny silver color that radiated off of it or the LED screen that replaced an intricate face with rudimentary emotions to be displayed. In this moment, the robot —presumably named Butler — had a neutral look made up of tiny blue dots. It looked exactly like the robots that roa—

"Is that a—" Nolan tried to say.

"Yes, yes. Get the fanfare out of your system, Ms. Nolan. My faithful servant, Butler. Have you never seen one outside of the movies? It's more common than you'd think in this advanced society we live in."

"I . . . uh . . . okay." Nolan stared at Butler. She noticed the three fingers on each hand and how both feet were propped up on ten small wheels that allowed Butler to course correct as needed. Nolan watched has the LED screen flashed to a wide, toothless smile.

"Hi," Butler said, giving a friendly wave.

"Hi-ho!" Coda said.

Nolan remained silent.

"Butler, would you be so kind to go find this, eh, book that Mr. Coda is so desperately seeking? The title is *The Bronze Lodestar*. I haven't the faintest idea where you'll find it, so start your search wherever your heart desires. Excuse me — wherever your CPU desires."

"Certainly, and very funny, sir! You always have a sharp, dashing sense of humor. It may be your undoing someday, but not this day!" Butler said before turning back toward the grand hall and zipping out of sight.

"That entity will be the death of me," Dietrich muttered. He turned his attention back to Coda. "What is the, eh, urgency with finding this book?"

"It's a long story, Mr. Falconer."

"I am an old man, Coda. I tell nothing but long stories, so it would be nice to hear one for a change . . . Why don't you girls go run off and play fetch or something?" Dietrich said casually.

Sadie grabbed Nolan's arm and took her away from the men. "We finds you both later. Tam biêt!"

Coda watched as they disappeared down the hall. Strange times indeed.

"She will always remain a mystery," Dietrich said. "I never know how she spends her time. That's what I get for marrying an international goddess!"

"Yeah, so, the reason we are here . . ." Coda began. The story occupied their time as Dietrich ushered him into the kitchen and concocted a drink. Coda finished after his hand went numb from the cold glass that was now clenched in his hand.

"A tale of love, loss, and the desire to mend! I can see why you are here. Let's hope that Butler can find what you seek. You know, when I met Sadie in New York and asked her to be my wife, she moved down to Florida with three suitcases worth of belongings. Her clothes seemed limitless as she first spread them across our bedroom floor. I don't recall seeing a book. My old mind may be failing me though. Who would remember such an, eh, inconsequential detail from over two years ago? Hi-ho! How's the drink?"

"Great. Thank you for the hospitality," Coda said. With each sip, his throat throbbed like a knee after being dragged along concrete. "Your, uh, robot—"

"No, no. Not robot. We don't use such derogatory terms around here. He is referred to has my servant or his true name, Butler, which you have already heard used multiple times." Dietrich leaned in close. "I don't want him to harbor any resentment toward me." He moved his thumb across his throat in a slashing gesture. "I haven't found the off switch yet or else he'd be in the city dump by now. Do you want him? Hi-ho! What a brilliant idea! You can take him off my hands. How does that sound?"

"No, thanks. I can barely care for myself."

"He's no maintenance at all! That's what you get with the Model Four."

"Right, well, I'll think about it."

"Hi-ho! That's the spirit!" Dietrich yelled.

"Anyways," Coda began, "Butler looks very familiar to the robo — uh, helpers I used to see roaming about JEC. Probably just a coincidence. I know companies have shifted toward them after the pandemic and that bombing in Prague."

"No coincidence at all! I work at JEC too, Mr. Coda. I brought them over with me from my last job. And I think you're being a bit crass. Companies learned during the pandemic that the employees crying over being essential were the easiest to be replaced by algorithms, machine learning, robotics, and other artificial intelligence. It's getting cheaper by the day while people are always demanding more money and begging for a better life. Baloney! Hi-ho! I guarantee you in another five years our world will look very, very different."

Not to be morbid, but Dietrich Falconer wouldn't live long enough to see whether his prediction came through or not. Heart failure. So it goes. Death is a common houseguest for the characters in this tale. Isn't that true for all of us?

Coda didn't care for Dietrich's morbid outlook, so he disregarded that portion and focused on the other half. "Why didn't you say anything when I told you I had quit from JEC?"

"Because information must not be forced but sought after."

"Okay . . . where did you work before JEC that you had access to these helpers?" Coda asked.

"Amazon. Do you remember that company? The SEC told them to skedaddle after becoming a monopoly."

"Right. That happened during my freshman year of college."

"Big news, eh? Well, you're looking at the former President of their Robotics Division," Dietrich said, pointing to himself with pride.[16] "The company collapsed so quickly I was able to sneak out the Model Four prototype and began shopping it around until I landed at JEC. The world thought they had defeated capitalism by getting rid of Amazon, but it only made way for a larger, uglier monster." Dietrich shook his head.

"You don't like working for JEC?"

"Of course, I do! They pay me like a city's go-to hooker. I make an outrageous amount of money every single day. They offered me an executive level position after Amazon collapsed. I took it for a couple years but didn't enjoy New York City. After meeting Sadie, I decided to come back to Florida and make this summer home my permanent residence. They forced me out of the executive position and instead put me in charge of the JEC warehouse in town. Another Amazon relic that JEC bought for pennies on the dollar. I went from corporate big wig to squabbling with entry-level employees about their right to use the bathroom during a shift," Dietrich said with disgust.

Coda's reply was short. "Oh, I see."

"Want to take a ride over there with me? It's my day off, but a businessman like me can never break away from their work," he said with a fake smile.

---

[16] To avoid confusion or thinking the author is a twit: Dietrich Falconer did not always object or refrain from using the r-word in its various forms. He shied away from it in the presence of Butler due to the delusions already hinted at.

"Uh, sure. What about Sadie and Nolan?"

"Fuck 'em. No offense. Sadie has gotten on my last nerve recently. She never has sex with me anymore, which is in violation of our prenup. My dick doesn't get hard once and she assumes that . . ." he trailed off.

Coda felt trapped. "We can go for a bit. It would be nice to see a different side to the corporation," he said with no enthusiasm.

"They are a bunch of cunts. Hi-ho! Excuse my vulgarity. But they really are. They whine and keep trying to form a union, which is completely unacceptable. My main job is to stop their constant conspiring."

"Right."

"You'll see for yourself . . . C'mon finish up that drink. I'm feeling buzzed and want to drive over before it wears off."

Dietrich struggled hard, but eventually pulled himself up from the couch. As he tossed his empty glass into the sink, Coda poured the remains of his into the plant next to his chair.

Nothing like some alcohol to promote growth.

thirty-one

WAVES

Nolan was led deeper into the house. She lost any sense of where she was or where Coda might have been after the third turn.

"What's our destination?" she asked Sadie.

"I change and we go *weeeeeeeeeee* . . . like—" she stopped walking and waved her arms around.

"I have no idea what you're getting at."

"Eh . . . erm . . . rolling coasters? Rides! We go to musement park," Sadie said, agonizing over every word. Nolan could sense her frustration. It must have been tough to smooth out the edges of her English when her husband spoke like a snobby socialite . . . similar to what Nolan grew up with.

"There's an amusement park around here?"

Sadie nodded. "Twenty-minute drive! Quick though. It get dark out early." She led the rest of the way to a bedroom and disappeared into a walk-in closet.

The room was spacious and sparsely decorated. Her parents were the same way. All that money and they didn't even bother to pimp out their penthouse with the gaudy art and meaningless mementos you'd expect the ultra-rich to do. *Is this how the rest of the day will be?* Nolan asked herself. *You just dwelling on your parents. Why don't you worry about something else? Like your fear of heights. Doesn't an amusement park have plenty of those?*

"Sadie?"

"Yes!" she yelled back through the door.

"I get stressed out on rides. I don't like heights."

"Heights?" Sadie said, poking her head out the door.

"Yeah."

"No, you be fine! Fun, fun, fun!"

Nolan took a deep breath. She felt trapped. With the way Sadie pulled a complete stranger through the house, Nolan guessed she didn't get many visitors.

The door opened and Sadie stepped out. "Ready. Can you drive? I no have car."

"Sure," Nolan said with a smile. "I don't mind driving. Would it be okay if Coda and I stayed here for the night?" At least she could squash one concern of hers.

"Yes! So much space here! We never see guests." That confirmed one of Nolan's suspicions.

Sadie repeated the same walk from earlier in reverse and was bouncing with excitement as they made their way to the 2008 Pinto Pinata. "Nice car. I like!" Sadie commented as they got inside. She opened every compartment and pressed each button.

"Are you looking for something in particular?" Nolan asked.

"No."

Nolan held up her phone. "What's the name of this place? So I can get us some directions."

"Ride and Die."

"That's pleasant." Nolan typed it in and the place popped up. Less than twenty minutes. No traffic. "So, Sadie, do you have a job down here?"

"No work."

"Why not?"

Sadie shrugged. "No reason to. Dietrich makes all money. I spend my time on beach and at gym. Look." She flexed her bicep.

A brief jolt of insecurity passed through Nolan as she saw the toned arm Sadie was showcasing. "Nice," she managed to say. "Do you ever get bored?"

"Yes. I very homesick."

"Why don't you go home and visit?"

"Dietrich no give me money to fly. And he no want my, eh, family to come here. Say there will be problems."

Nolan stopped at the gate and waited for it to open. She turned to Sadie. "That is wrong. You should be able to go see your family."

"It's okay. Butler and I have plan. I tell you at musement park."

Nolan pondered over the comment but didn't pry further. They moved away from the gated house and back through the bungalows and shacks. Some were well maintained while others looked like they were one windy afternoon away from collapse. Regardless of their condition, Nolan found herself envious that people lived at the beach. Yeah, her family went to the Hamptons, but it was always about business. For all the trips there, she never put a toe in the water. What a waste. Her and Coda's journey allotted more time than needed to reexamine every aspect of her life and she wasn't happy with most of it. Another truth: Her answer was out in California, but that was something she hadn't spoken to Coda about.

Later. They had time . . . and plenty of driving ahead of them. Everything would unravel when needed like they were part of a . . . a . . .

The parking lot at Ride and Die was half full and Nolan found a spot toward the entrance. Sadie darted out and dashed ahead. Nolan lowered her head and looked out the passenger window to see Sadie wasn't waiting. Nolan reached behind the seat and grabbed her smaller bag. She dug around inside of it until she found the pill bottle. The doctor always told her the pills were meant as a preventative measure. She needed to take one before putting herself in a stressful situation. Her obvious, but unasked, question: How was she supposed to know when that was happening? Today was her lucky day! Even the thought of getting dragged onto a ride was enough to get her heart racing and the deep-rooted panic to settle into her bones. Nolan tilted the bottle sideways and watched as four pills slid out. She wondered what that would do. It wasn't the day to find out, so she put three of them back and swallowed the one left in her hand.

Sadie was standing near the ticket counter when Nolan walked up. "I buy, but no money," she said with a frown.

"It's okay. I got this one."

"Thank you, Nolan. You are nice person!"

Once inside, Sadie talked in detail about what she wanted to ride and where everything was located. Sadie had either come often to the amusement park or studied a map to understand the layout. Nolan wasn't quite sure which option was more believable.

Sadie grabbed Nolan's hand and led her to the first ride.

Nolan looked up and watched people scream as the ride ascended higher, higher . . . and then a sudden drop. The screams continued to split through her head as they moved closer to the ground, stopping just short with a quick jerk. Legs and arms bounced around from the adrenaline as the yelling morphed into unfiltered laughter. "Nope. Not going to happen."

Sadie shrugged and accepted Nolan's answer. "Okay. You wait here then?"

"Sure."

Sadie ran toward the line. *It doesn't matter if I go on the rides*, Nolan thought. *She just wanted someone to take her, to be friendly with.*

The cycle repeated itself for the next couple of hours. Sadie being amped about each ride and Nolan politely declining. Their conversation was sparse as it was generally a recap of what Sadie thought and where their next stop was.

It was the longest that her and Coda had been apart on the trip. She missed him. She didn't always understand how they got along, but they did.

"One ride left," Sadie eventually declared. "The wheel!"

Nolan followed her pointed finger to see the Ferris Wheel lit up a short walk away.

"I can't do that," Nolan said.

"Always no, no, no with you! Say yes! Please."

It's going to be okay. It's going to be okay, Nolan kept repeating to herself. *Since when were you such a downer? It's one ride.* "I will try it." She hadn't considered that the Ferris Wheel was the worst ride to go on with a fear of heights since it moves at a snail's pace and likely to stop at the top. As with any other person, Nolan's decisions weren't flawless.

"Wonderful! This be great!"

The wait for the Ferris Wheel was nonexistent and they were quickly shuffled into their own compartment. "Last is best," Sadie said.

Nolan clenched her fists as the door closed and the operator hit the button. With no urgency, the Ferris Wheel hiccupped and then moved them upward. Their private compartment swayed softly like a metronome. Back and forth, back and forth, back and forth. If she just focused on conversation, maybe that wou—

"Sadie, do you have any friends here?"

"No. Everyone old. Dietrich bring me to dinners. They all boring and make fun of my, eh, accent."

Nolan stared at Sadie and tried not to see the background change from the old, shabby buildings to the other rides to the sparse tree line and finally to the darkened sky. She felt herself coming undone. *This was a mistake. I need to get out of here. Take me back, take me back, take me back . . .*

"Nolan, it okay," Sadie said, reaching out her hands and placing them on Nolan's legs. "We, eh, conquer your fear. What don't kill make you strong, right?"

"Yeah," Nolan mumbled.

"Tell me about you," Sadie said with a comforting smile.

She told Sadie about her parents, what life was like from the age of six and onward, and her thoughts on New York City. To Nolan, it felt like she had spoken for an hour, but realized that wasn't the case when the ride jolted to a stop near the top. "Fuck, fuck."

"Nolan, it okay," Sadie repeated. "You strong. And you nice. Can't ask for more than that!"

Nolan took a deep breath and held it. The pill didn't help at all. Probably because she took it hours ago. She exhaled and felt like her world wasn't going to end. Her world still sucked, but she decided to view it from a different angle. Nolan focused on the sounds below. The laughter . . . the high trilling sounds of rip-off games . . . the waves. That's it. The waves. The beach was close. She closed her eyes and pictured herself standing in the water and letting each wave crash into her with none having the force to knock her off-balance. She found Sadie's hands and squeezed them tightly. The panic attacks would always plague her — Nolan wasn't oblivious to that — but she didn't have to fold each time the nervous energy ramped up. She'd been through worse than riding a fucking Ferris Wheel. She was strong and nice and beautiful and empathetic and quick witted and . . . and . . . and a million other things that escaped her mind. She needed to believe all of it.

Nolan opened her eyes. "I'm okay," she said with a smile.

"It peaceful up here. A good time to tell you my plan: I kill Dietrich."

Nolan was ripped from whatever newfound serenity or breakthrough she experienced. The waves receded back into the ocean. Her smile disappeared. "What did you say?"

"I kill Dietrich. Well, eh, Butler say he do it."

"Why would you joke about that?"

Sadie blinked several times and cocked her head like a dog waiting for a treat. She laughed and clutched her chest. "Hi-ho! That what Dietrich always say. Sorry, bad joke. I get bored sometimes and say bad things."

Listen:

Sadie did have a plan to kill Dietrich.

Throughout her time in the United States, Sadie was harassed and verbally abused for her lack of proper English. And those that didn't chastise her, thought she was a complete idiot. She learned after a while to use that to her advantage. Did Coda not remember her major was in theater arts? Everything about Sadie was manufactured. The innocent gestures, the slips in pronunciation of easy words, the confessions of being homesick. All lies. All of it.

Why did she go through all this trouble?

C'mon, you know how these things go.

Money.

Dietrich was an easy catch. By the time she stumbled across him at a bar near JEC's headquarters, Sadie had already conned half a dozen other men. Her success varied wildly, but each resulted in some cash she would pocket, while sending the rest back to her family. She was getting close to graduation and knew her interests did not align to a corporate job or struggling as an actress for the next decade in an expensive city. She dreamed of a lavish lifestyle where she could buy what she wanted and travel on a moment's notice. The fastest way to achieve that was to marry some schmuck.[17] It took five dates for Dietrich to propose.

Several things happened quickly that Sadie didn't anticipate after the courtroom wedding. First, Dietrich announced he wanted to move back to Florida. Sadie couldn't complain. Who wouldn't want to be by the beach each day? If he'd told her what Venice looked like though, she wouldn't have left New York. There were no trendy stores or upscale restaurants. The average age in the town was older than her parents. She adapted though because that's how she was raised.

The second thing was how controlling Dietrich became. The submissive side she witnessed during their dates was thrust out into the ether once they arrived in Venice. He demanded sex every night, highlighting what was written and agreed to in the prenup. Dietrich would get worked up and say disparaging things he would casually brush off and attribute to being upset. He withheld money from her for shopping and traveling, effectively making her a prisoner in Venice.

Butler was the unexpected twist.

During Dietrich's days at the warehouse, Sadie forged a friendship with their robot. (She never found the word to be derogatory, so it was

---

[17] A word she learned after taking public transportation for years in New York. You were a schmuck for blocking the entrance to the subway or walking too slow or bumping into someone. It's true that many indiscretions are ignored in the city, so to be called a schmuck is a wonderful rite of passage.

her preferred way to describe Butler.) The robot would spot her on certain lifts in the gym and follow her around the house as she began to sow discord that Dietrich had plans to scrap it. Butler may have seemed rudimentary, but like any machine, it could be reprogrammed. Sadie taught it hate and contempt for Dietrich and how to be subtle with sabotage. Butler began putting two spoonfuls of sugar in his coffee instead of one and trimming the shrubs an inch shorter than Dietrich demanded. Sadie spoke to the robot about how there were others like it and they could both escape to find their true happiness. Butler began to siphon small amounts of money from Dietrich's account. A few thousand dollars every week. The old man never noticed.

One day, the discussion turned to permanently getting rid of Dietrich. It made sense. With a divorce, Sadie would get nothing, and Dietrich would rely on Butler more than before. They were still in the process of deciding how that should happen as their interactions were put on hold after Dietrich confessed to Sadie of his growing fear that Butler meant him harm.

Patience. Sadie steadied herself and knew the situation was delicate. She needed time and, most importantly, keeping up her character for a little while longer.

This outrageous charade begs two final questions:

1.) What would Sadie do with all the money?
2.) Why in the world would she joke about her *plan* with Nolan?

Obviously, Sadie would keep a majority of the money for herself. Dietrich had kids and several other wives, but they were all dead. How tragic, right? The man had experienced his colossal share of grief and Sadie was meant to be the last pleasure he could squeeze out of the short time he had left. The money Sadie didn't take (which she figured would be a few million) would go to her family and rip them out of poverty, keeping a promise she made years earlier.

For question number two: Sadie knew all about Nolan. Who didn't? Everywhere Sadie went at TCSUM, the name TREIBER was thrown around. On buildings and plastic cups and garbage cans and student IDs and other oddities. Sadie resented the bitch without ever knowing her. She hated the money and privilege people like Nolan walked around with. Crying about her bullshit panic attacks when she could pay for the best doctors to cure her of any ailment. And Coda, my God. All he ever talked about was "my friend Nolan." It was nauseating, but regardless of her hatred, Sadie had much larger plans than Nolan Treiber. The only thing she could do without breaking her cover was make Nolan feel more uncomfortable than she already did. Maybe she could get Butler to cut up some of Nolan's clothes or put a nice dent in that pretty car. That would work. Anything Sadie could do to not think about her own terrible existence was a brilliant use of her time.

People are rarely who they seem with Sadie being a prime example.

Back to the Ferris Wheel.

Sadie's misplaced "joke" was enough to deter Nolan from continuing any conversation with her. Something seemed off about Sadie Falconer and Nolan didn't have the determination to figure it out. Sadie's life story didn't seem as important anymore. Instead, Nolan sat on the Ferris Wheel and felt the compartment continue to sway. Was this how each stop of their trip would go? Forced conversation to pass the time until they got what they needed.

Coda needed the books, but what about Nolan?

There is only one reason you're here is to get to California to discover what? A pipedream? A hope? she told herself.

Nolan shook the thought away and looked down at the seat. Declarations of love were etched into the metal with dates to match. Nobody who felt true love would waste their time scratching it into a spot where nothing occupied it besides sweaty assholes. Nolan closed her eyes and placed her head back onto the perforated metal.

She casted aside brief thoughts of love and let the waves return. They were calmer but more frequent. Each crash caused a repeated sensation of cold water against her legs. In between, she experienced peace — the euphoric moment of anticipation for the next wave while appreciating the break. Nolan was alone. No yelling kids or lifeguards perched in their tower or surfers paddling to their next triumph. For once, she didn't mind it. She knew the solitary moment would pass and she'd be cast out into the world, to be surrounded by the waves of people she felt distant from.

Nolan would suffer through a quiet car ride back to Dietrich's house. Sadie's brief appearance in Nolan's story almost up, and she'd spend the last bits of it focusing solely on herself.

She needed to do one thing before leaving Florida.

thirty-two

BUY MORE, SAVE LESS

The warehouse sat two blocks away from the coast. Close enough to smell the sea, but far enough away to not have a view of it. The building was nondescript and ugly, which purposely gave the vibe that there wasn't millions of dollars' worth of product inside.

Dietrich cruised into a spot ten feet from the front entrance. "Where does everyone else park?"

"About a quarter mile that way," Dietrich said, pointing behind him toward the road they just turned off from.

"Seems unnecessary. There's plenty of open space here." Beyond Dietrich's spot were concrete barriers blocking access to the rest of the parking lot.

"Very observant. You'd make a great asset to the warehouse team. You interested? Only kidding! Hi-ho!" he blurted out in a rush. "But, if you must know, I had those barriers put up after they tried to unionize for the third time. I warned there would be consequences."

Coda began to speak, but Dietrich continued.

"Sometimes I worry I'm too much of a curmudgeon for my age. Maybe I should just retire and enjoy my time left. But then I think of all the people I let down and that's what keeps me going."

"Who have you let down?" Coda asked.

"My kids and ex-wives. You know, I used to be a poor son of a bitch. Imagine that! I couldn't rub two pennies together for a long time, and I dealt with that shame every day. I think my children resented me and know my ex-wives sure as hell did. I wonder what they'd think of me now," Dietrich said, tilting his head back.

"Do you not speak to any of them?"

"They're all dead, son. Hi-ho! Some people want to live forever, but I want to get the heck out of here with some money in my pocket."

"I don't think you take any money with you when you die."

"Says who?"

"Well, I . . ."

"We fight, bicker, kill, steal, cheat, rob, maim, and other oddities all for the sake of money. What's the point if it doesn't matter beyond this life?"

"Mr. Falconer, I don't think there is a point to money."

"You sound like someone who's never had to worry about not having money before."

"Well, I . . ." Coda stumbled over his words for a second time.

"Being poor isn't easy but once you get a taste of what it feels like to have money —obscene amounts of money — you'll never look at other people the same. Those people in that warehouse are lazy. No ambition. No determination to pick themselves up from their lowly place in the world. You think I'm a monster, don't you? I've offered to cover tuition costs for college courses or certifications. No takers. I've organized happy hours for us to get to know one another better. No one showed up. I've offered to bring in more servants like Butler to help lessen the load. Nobody voted for that out of fear they'd be run out of a job. And . . . that was smart thinking because that would have happened."

"Mr. Falconer, you're their boss, not their friend. They fear you and with that fear comes a desire to never want to interact with you."

"Then they shall remain in the mud while I sit victorious atop the mountain."

"If you believe so," Coda said.

Dietrich tilted his head back once more before pivoting to another subject. "Sadie is stealing from me. She thinks I don't know, but I'm not that clueless. And it can't be her because she doesn't have access to my bank accounts. So it must be Butler . . . I don't know how she convinced him . . . I know she doesn't love me, but I hope she doesn't leave. I can't die alone. I—" His hands shook as he wiped the tears away from his face.

Is Nolan having as thrilling of a time as I am? Coda thought. He wasn't sure how to console Dietrich but went with the first thing that came to mind. "Maybe you shouldn't pressure her into sex? That would be a great place to start." His tone sounded surprised that he even needed to say it.

"Hi-ho! Good thinking, son. I trust that a man like yourself is a *smooth operator* with the women folk."

"Yes, absolutely. I'm a real slut back in New York. Also, Dietrich, you may want to consider just talking with Sadie to understand her feelings. Maybe she has a reason for stealing the money and not being intimate."

"Well, look at me! I'm more wrinkled than a shirt that sat in the dryer too long. My boobs are bigger than Dolly Parton's. My—"

"I get your drift," Coda said. "Still, I'm sure Sadie loves you or else she wouldn't have married you."

"You manage to be intelligent and incredibly naïve in such a short span of time. Hi-ho! You are quite the specimen. My dear boy, Sadie loves my money, not me. I didn't think it would bother me as much as it does. But, alas, I have made my choice and must see it through until the end."

Sensing a dead end, Coda asked, "Can we head inside now? It's gotten hot in the car." He could feel the sweat forming on his back.

"Certainly! Follow me."

The inside of the building was as drab as the outside. The walls in the waiting area were bare except for smiling, professional photographs of the founders and current CEO of JEC because nothing inspired employees more than seeing the executives that made a hundred times their salary.

The few seats that were in the lobby had camera equipment sitting on them. Nobody was around to claim it.

Dietrich approached the desk. "Edgar, how are you?"

He looked up, startled. "Mr. Falconer, I thought today is your day off."

"It is, it is. But you know I can't stay away for long. And anyways, I have to show my new friend around!"

Edgar looked at Coda and likely wondered how the *friendship* came about. "Oh, okay."

"What's the deal with the camera equipment?" Dietrich asked.

"They are filming the commercial for the new ad campaign, sir. Remember?"

"Right, right!" Dietrich said, slapping his hand off the desk. He turned to Coda. "In a month, JEC is rolling out the 'Buy More, Save Less' campaign. My cronies back in New York concocted that beautiful message. Corporate ran a survey and found that this warehouse has the happiest employees in the entire company. Hi-ho! Do you believe it?"

"Sounds like a stretch based on how you've spoken about them," Coda said, hardly containing his nonexistent excitement.

"Pish posh! One day with my fine crew of servants and the camera crew will get enough propaganda to show in ad campaigns for years."

"Sir, do you have an ID so I can print you a visitor's pass?" Edger asked, attempting to drive his boss from the lobby. The longer Dietrich hung around, the more likely Edgar was to say something he'd regret.

Coda moved for his wallet until Dietrich said, "No need for such formalities, Edgar."

"As you wish."

Dietrich stepped away from the desk and toward the hallway leading deeper into the warehouse. "This way, son. Keep up."

After badging through the set of doors, Coda could finally grasp how large the warehouse was. Off to his left was a series of doors leading to various offices, each with a tiny window for the occupant to peek out when needed. Beyond that was the small break area that sported two refrigerators, three microwaves, and a small sink. Seating was limited, which seemed purposeful to discourage fraternization amongst the workers. Opposite from the offices and break area was an expansive open area broken up by endless rows of shelving. Coda couldn't see beyond the Aisle 45 sign except for the small figures that glided around like ants scurrying back to their home. Amongst the rows of merchandise was a winding conveyer belt system that moved in every direction. Employees were stationed at multiple points performing different tasks to prep each item. Settled within the humans were more Model 4 robots, courtesy of Dietrich. All of them sported the same neutral look Coda had seen on Butler's LED screen when they arrived at the mansion. The robots seemed to be floor supervisors as they stood with their dangly arms pinned back and slowly swiveling their heads like an osculating fan.

"My office is up on the second floor," Dietrich said and motioned for Coda to continue following him.

"Why are the robots needed?" Coda asked. He was three stairs behind Dietrich's shambling body. It looked like each step sent a tremor of pain radiating out his body. He gripped the railing until the veins in his hand flexed.

Dietrich stopped and explained between his labored breathing. "Not robots, Mr. Coda. Helpers. Helpers or servants. Do your best to remember that." He resumed climbing the last half dozen steps and continued his answer at the top. "It's simple. I was them as a motivation tool. You are bound to work harder when you feel your job is at stake."

"That's a terrible way to motivate your employees."

"Son, you can take your vulgar and unwanted remarks elsewhere. I don't answer to you."

"Okay."

"Hi-ho! We shall forget that outburst from you. I trust it'll be the last one during our time together. Here is my office," Dietrich said, pushing open the door. The space was more densely decorated than his own home with framed pictures of him with famous individuals. A cabinet in the back corner displayed Dietrich's awards from no-name publications and blogs with each shining chunk of metal reaffirming his viewpoint on leadership and a never-ending conquest to increase profits. He moved behind his desk and settled into his chair. Coda stood near the door, finding no need to venture in further. "Let me just grab my clipboard and we can go. I like to create tallies to understand which employees are wasting company time. Currently, there are no punishments for their thievery, but I am working to change that with corporate. I drafted a report saying we could get another fifty thousand dollars a year — a year! — at this location if we eliminated their idle time."

When Coda first saw Dietrich, he felt a wave of sympathy. It was a flaw of his whenever he saw an older person. He couldn't help but see their frail bodies shuffling along and wish he could help restore their youth. His sympathy stemmed purely from a physical aspect since he never interacted with those individuals more than a simple greeting. Coda thought about all the tasks he did with minimal effort — showering, walking to the subway, sitting down, making dinner, and so on — that were likely a massive undertaking for someone older. He never understood what the motivation to continue was. If he had eight great decades under his belt, he'd ask for a swift needle in the arm to end things before it all seemed like a needless chore.

Of course, from the descriptions his sisters told about his mother, Coda knew that frail, decaying bodies didn't only happen to the elderly. Maybe things would be different if she wasn't d—

Maybe.

Maybe.

Maybe.

But probably not.

As Coda rehashed the afternoon's events, whatever sympathy he had projected onto Dietrich was completely gone. At first, Coda saw him as a wolf in sheep's clothing. An old man trying to keep his edge on everyone else by being a hard ass. He was the product of a different time. Then Coda's mindset shifted to viewing Dietrich as a sheep in wolf's clothing. Beneath the tough exterior was a man that wanted companionship in his last years of life. He eluded to the loss and pain of outliving his family and Coda empathized with that. He (supposedly) offered his employees unique opportunities to bond outside of work and develop new skills.

But now, Coda finally saw him for who he was: your run-of-the-mill asshole. Coda envisioned Dietrich as being the type to proclaim to others about his "God given rights" as if that was even a thing. Coda believed it wasn't Dietrich's lack of money that drove away spouses and children, but his authoritative stance and belief that everyone else around him was inferior. In only a few hours, Coda understood all he needed to about Dietrich because assholes only had one function.

The world was full of assholes, so was Dietrich special? Absolutely not. Much like all the others, history would forget about him. And if it did carry some record of Dietrich Falconer, the summation wouldn't be favorable.

Coda left the office while Dietrich continued his search for the elusive clipboard that Coda snagged from the table.

He bounded down the steps and wove himself amongst the aisles, out of sight from Dietrich's ivory tower. Coda knew his impact would be limited in his short time at the warehouse. He couldn't dismantle the entire regime by creating some triumphant uprising nor would he be able to convince hourly employees to walk away from their vital job, but he could do something.

The shelves of Aisle 8 were packed with toiletries. Tissues, towels, toilet paper, Q-Tips, baby wipes, and other oddities. Everything was pushed to the front of each shelf for easy accessibility. Coda was impressed with the neatness of it, but his priorities were elsewhere. He looked down at the clipboard and saw a list of employee names that spanned five pages of single-spaced Excel rows. He flipped through the pages and saw that every name had at least one tick mark in the adjacent column. At the top of the first page, Dietrich had noted that a single tick mark meant that the employee had "slacked off" for two minutes of company time. Dietrich's system was archaic and purely subjective, which wasn't the least surprising.

Beyond all the names was a final page were Dietrich scribbled a list of possible punishments. They began as cruel and quickly swerved into a sadistic territory.

Dietrich had used all this brain power to think of punishments up through someone's twentieth infraction. He was clear to note that firing an employee was a sub-optimal solution since the workforce in Venice was limited, so he decided to slowly snuff their desire to live.

Yup, something a smug asshole would do.

"Yo, buddy! Who are you?" the man yelled from the end of the aisle.

Coda raised his hands up in surrender. "I'm here with Dietrich. Just came to visit for a bit."

"Mr. Falconer? Today is his day off," the man said, moving closer.

"He's up in his office right now."

"Shit, really?"

"Yeah."

"First that fucking film crew and now this," the man muttered. He tugged the radio from his belt and spoke into it. "Attention, attention: The bird is roosting in its nest. I repeat: The bird is roosting in its nest, back from a short winter." He put the radio back and pointed at Coda's clipboard. "Are you his new lackey or something?"

"No. Definitely not. I was looking for a place to get rid of this. I can't believe he does this to you guys."

The man shrugged. "I've seen worse."

"Isn't there an HR rep here to report his behavior to?"

The man threw his head back and laughed. "He fired them months ago. Said they were a waste of money when he could do it himself. That's when he brought in the robots and installed all the cameras."

"I'm sorry."

"Sorry for what? This is how life is."

"It doesn't have to be," Coda said.

"Oh yeah? How else would I make money?"

"You could quit and find another job."

"Kid, I know you aren't that stupid. Just idealistic, which I appreciate, but I'm an uneducated minority in this country. That doesn't give me many opportunities."

"That's not true," Coda said in disbelief.

"Maybe, maybe not. But I don't see a need to find out."

"Aren't you tired of the same routine? Work, sleep, work, sleep, and on and on," Coda questioned.

"I have a family I love and hobbies I enjoy. My life isn't just this job."

The words hit Coda square in the chest. He never considered that his "routine" may not have looked so bleak if life didn't orbit around his prior job at JEC. "I've never considered that before."

"I'm here with buckets of wisdom. Look, you said you wanted to dispose of that clipboard. Let me introduce you to the baler."

The man led Coda down the wide walkway between the aisles and conveyer belt. Coda tried to keep up, but the man's pace was that of a seasoned speed walker. They passed by half-dead employees that monotonously scanned packages or pushed carts to their next delivery point. Everyone looked aged and defeated under the fluorescent glow. The robots stood at every fifth aisle with the same look plastered onto the LED screen.

"Toss it in up there," the man announced as they arrived at the baler. He pointed up a small set of stairs.

Coda climbed up and threw the clipboard into the open mouth. As simple as that.

"Normally," the man continued when Coda turned back toward the stairs, "we only throw cardboard in. They probably caught us on camera doing it, so that may be a future problem."

"I could have just snuck it out of here and thrown it away somewhere else," Coda said.

"I know you think you did something noble for us, but I assure you no one cared about Mr. Falconer's tick marks and no one will hail you as a hero. Sometimes you can't unfuck a fucked system, you understand? A rock thrown into the water doesn't always make a big ripple. Doesn't mean you should stop throwing rocks though."

"I understand. You know, I used to work at JEC until a week ago."

The man nodded. "You were a corporate guy weren't you?"

"How'd you know?"

"Look at you," the man laughed. "What did you do?"

"Software development within the Airplane and Autocannon Department."

"How exciting. Did you get to watch any of the autocannons in action? I hear they really eviscerate people."

"Nope, never did," Coda said. The shame crept back into the corner of his mind.

"Damn! Nothing better than seeing some terrorist fuckhead getting what they deserve. I imagine you try not to think about the innocent people that get killed by mistake."

Coda had nothing more to say about it.

The man eventually continued away from the topic. "Why'd you leave? I heard some departments were giving out a big bonus to the employees. I hope you stayed long enough to enjoy that."

"No, I didn't. And I left because I was tired of *that* routine."

The man nodded again. "Kid, you're too young to be that jaded. You got another forty years of working ahead of you." He stepped closer. "Don't worry about us. We'll be okay. And one day, if it isn't, we will fight against it," the man said, slapping Coda on the back. "Want to be in a commercial? I think they are still filming around here somewhere."

"I think I'll pass on that. Thanks though."

"Well, I've wasted ten tick marks of time walking you around. I need to get back to it. Know your way back?"

"Yeah."

The man turned down the aisle to their right "See you around, kid."

Coda walked back toward the office in no rush. He found himself deflated from thinking about the autocannons, the pointless conversations with Dietrich Falconer, and even meeting the washed-up bastard to begin with.

thirty-three

ON THE BEACH

Nolan found Coda asleep on the couch when she and Sadie returned from Ride and Die. A half drank bottle of whiskey sat beside two empty glasses and the copy of *The Bronze Lodestar*.

"Your friend and Mr. Falconer had a nightcap . . . or several. I just carried Mr. Falconer to bed," Butler announced from the shadows. His LED screen turned to a smile. "Welcome back, Lady Sadie."

"Hi," she said between yawns. It was another deceptive day for her. That would make anyone tired.

"Would you like me to rouse Mr. Coda?" Butler asked.

"You can leave him there. He looks comfortable," Nolan said, noting Coda's half opened mouth and drool slowly traversing down his chin. "I see you found the book."

"Yes, Ms. Nolan. Buried in a closet on the second floor. I hope you both find the condition of the book suitable."

Nolan picked it up off the table and turned it over several times. "Looks fine to me."

"Most excellent. I can show you to your room if you'd like."

"No, I'm okay here."

"We have many bedroom. You sure?" Sadie asked.

"I'm sure. Thank you."

"Anything else you need?" Butler asked.

"No."

Butler and Sadie turned to leave. "Actually," Nolan continued. "I have one question for you Butler."

"Yes, Ms. Nolan?"

"Do you actually want to kill Dietrich? Sadie mentioned it as a joke, but her demeanor suggested otherwise."

Butler looked over at Sadie and then back to Nolan. The LED screen changed to an exaggerated frown. "I love serving Mr. Falconer. I am incapable of such an action, so Lady Sadie must have said that in jest. My functions are limited by design with my overriding purpose being to serve."

"Interesting," Nolan said. "I wouldn't think a robot such as yourself would understand love. Makes me wonder what other things you are hiding."

"Is that all, Ms. Nolan?" Butler said, fidgeting his right arm.

"Yup, I'm good. See you both in the morning," Nolan called out as they resumed their walk down the hall. She could hear the whispered words they were exchanging, but it quickly faded as they turned the corner.

For all the day's activities, Nolan wasn't tired. She collapsed on the couch and stared out the glass doors toward the ocean. *That's right! I had one more thing to do tonight*, she reminded herself.

She strained herself forward and reached across to Coda. It took three strong nudges before he opened his eyes. "Hi, get up. One last mission here in Florida. I promise it's an easy one."

"Hmmm . . . hmmm . . . fine," he mumbled.

Wasting no time, Nolan moved over to one of the glass doors. The light from the nearby lamp didn't extend far enough to see a handle. She felt around the glass, leaving behind a mosaic of smudge marks. "Got it," she said and gave a hard tug. No budge.

"Right here," Coda said from behind and reached for the latch.

One more pull and the door flung open bringing in a rush of noise and air. Nolan's skin prickled as she stepped outside and adjusted to the cooler weather.

"Where are we going?" Coda asked.

"Use your brain. Where else would you go when staying at a beach house?"

"Plenty of places. As seen by my trip to a warehouse and your trip to . . . somewhere."

Nolan circled around the chairs and firepit spread out on the deck. "A warehouse? Huh?"

"I'd rather not recap my day. I'm sure yours was better."

"Actually, I doubt it was. Sadie may be a compulsive liar," Nolan said. "Let's agree not to dip into the details. I'm glad you got your book back."

"Compulsive liar? I . . . Okay, I'll let that thread dangle. Dietrich wasn't any better, so we will be lucky to bail in the morning. And about the book . . ." Coda said, stopping halfway down the steps.

"What is it?" Nolan asked, looking up at him.

"The book isn't one of my mom's."

Nolan continued to walk ahead, moving off the wood planks and onto the sand. She felt each grain slide into the spaces between her toes. "What do you mean?"

Coda half jogged to collapse the gap. "There's no message from her in the front and the symbol isn't in the back."

"Maybe that's not your copy then? And if it isn't, where the fuck would we find it?" she wondered aloud.

"No," Coda said, shaking his head. "This is the right copy. I spilt coffee on one of the pages."

Nolan didn't respond, so Coda finished his explanation.

"When I checked it, the stains were there. I don't know what happened, but I've completely wasted our time here," he said, deflated and thinking back to that call with his sister in Georgia.

"Definitely not time wasted. Look at where we are right now! Have you ever been to the beach, Coda?"

"I . . . I don't think I have."

"You'd remember if you were."

"What now? Why'd you bring me out here?"

"To enjoy this."

In the daylight, they would have seen the wide stretches of beach that extended beyond eyesight to either side. Nolan may have spotted the Ferris Wheel if she looked hard enough. They would have seen the patches of garbage that tourists left behind and the washed-up debris from the ocean. They would have seen the scattered lifeguard stands that were flipped over since it was the "off-season" as if such a thing existed for Florida beaches. They would have seen the locals that bathed in the sun until their skin could be harvested for the next line of Gucci purses, the families stuffed with little kids that ran amok, and the day drinkers snoring on a towel, destined for a nasty sunburn. They would have seen the lazy sand dunes and sparse patches of grass and stubby palm trees mixed within. They would have seen the artificially constructed jetties that popped up periodically along the shore. They would have seen it all under different circumstances.

Thankfully, the beach was vacant with the melodic sounds of crashing waves to keep them company.

Nolan sat down in the sand, feeling the cool sensation spread up her legs and down her arms. Coda joined her, dug his feet into the sand, and hugged his knees.

A silence expanded until Nolan said, "I had a panic attack today."

Coda turned to her. "A panic attack? Since when?"

"Over ten years."

"Really?"

"Yeah." Nolan watched the blur of a wave collapse onto the shore and quickly recede back into the ocean.

"I had no idea," Coda said. "What are they like?"

"Usually they aren't bad. I take medication to dull the brunt of it, which does a decent job. But the medication requires that I'm proactive about being in a stressful situation. Well, life isn't that convenient. The bad ones engulf me in unmanageable dread. I've pictured it like someone has trapped me under a blanket. Silly, I know. There's a way out if you can just find the opening, but your brain is fogged, and your body is uncooperative. At a certain point, you're more okay with suffocating than trying to escape. And once you stop begging for it to be over, the blanket gets lifted and you finally take a deep breath, slowly returning to normalcy. Those are the worst ones, like tonight."

Coda stared at her. His face was more defined under the moonlight. Everything was equally proportioned and pleasing — that was the only way Nolan could describe him. She'd never put more thought into it than that. She noticed the faint emergence of stubble growing unevenly on Coda's chin line.

"What happened tonight?" he asked.

"We rode a Ferris Wheel. I hate heights."

"Why'd you go on it then?"

"I was bored and tired of sitting around and watching Sadie ride everything else."

"Sounds like me at every college party. I've never felt more miserable than in the presence of aggressively drunk college students. They sucked at conversation and yell whenever a song from their childhood played. But, anyways, I digress . . . I'm glad you made it out the other side," Coda said, placing a hand on Nolan's forearm.

"Thanks Coda. It's a good reminder that the panic attacks still have some power over me."

"What else causes them?"

Nolan contemplated the question for a moment. "One other situation comes to mind: conversing with my parents."

"Do you want to elaborate further?"

"Not necessarily, if that's okay."

"Fine by me. I'm here to listen to whatever you'd like to talk about." Coda turned his head toward the ocean. "Can you imagine getting to enjoy this every day? You know, when you can see everything. Do you think Sadie and Dietrich understand how fortunate they are?"

"Doubt it. Sometimes it's hard to see beyond the daily inconveniences to focus on the bigger picture."

"What's the bigger picture, Nolan?"

"That's a loaded question."

"Have you ever thought about everything in the world?"

"I don't know if I could. That's daunting. There's so much."

"Strip away the excess. The gadgets and cars and twenty kinds of bed sheets to choose from and endless news cycle always broadcasting our next doom and fancy clothes and unnecessary television shows and social media platforms and bloated desires to see what every celebrity is up to and . . . and . . . and fancy houses filled with garbage and robots ordered to serve and nuclear bombs and war and megachurches and bacon festivals and bonfires and subway rides and on and on and on and on it goes. What's left? What's left when all of it is gone?"

"I don't know," Nolan said.

"Me either," Coda confessed. "But I hope to know by the end of this trip. Maybe it'll finally make sense."

"And what if you don't find out?"

Coda shrugged. "Return to what I've always done: lived but never enjoyed a second of it."

"I hope that isn't the case."

"Me too," Coda said.

Nolan shuffled her feet in the sand, digging them down deeper. "Thanks for bringing me along on this journey. We are seeing so much of the country and meeting new people — not that I'd want to see all of them again."

"Of course, I can't think of another person to share this with. There aren't many people in my life I care about."

"It's hard to see that when you have friends scattered across the country."

"Friends?" Coda questioned. "If any of them were actually friends, I'd have the books back or at least avoid the confused faces when we show up on their doorstep."

"I give you credit then. I wouldn't drive in a zigzag across the country to knock on doors of people I didn't consider friends."

Coda laughed. "You forget you're on this zigzag trek with me. But you're right. There was absolutely a simpler way of doing this. I just couldn't stand it anymore, Nolan. The city, the job, the regrets, always tearing into me."

"Are you ever honest with people about how you feel?"

"Never. Besides not having anyone to confide in, I have become adept at keeping everything internalized. A nasty habit I picked up after my dad died. And now the cycle has repeated itself with my mom," Coda said, shaking his head.

"What happened with you two?" Nolan asked. An overdue question.

Coda looked at her as sadness swept across his face. "You'd expect some spectacular story based on the . . . *charade* I'm making out of this extended journey, but it's depressingly simple." He took a breath. "I told her I hated her. Our relationship was spiraling for years and I just snapped. Similar to the, uh, incident at school, I'd plead temporary insanity for why it happened. Who knows what the argument was about anymore? It was one of dozens. But I remember what she said after. 'Coda, I'll be here when you no longer feel that way.' I thought she was so smug to say something like that. How could she tell me that I wouldn't stop hating her? It spurred me even more and left a deep wound. Really deep. I don't know when, but I felt shame and a tugging notion I could never undo what I did. So I stayed away and never sought forgiveness, even though I would have been granted it because I'm her son. And now . . .

"Three words. That's all it took. How stupid is that? It feels outrageous that so few words could cause a massive divide but think about if I told someone I loved them. The exact opposite. You'd probably feel immense joy. We always toss around the words *love* and *hate* as if they are chips on a poker table. Overused and meaningless most of the time, in my opinion. But, man, when you actually mean it, those words can change tides," he said, shaking his head again and staring out at the darkness.

"We are going to fix it. We still have time," Nolan said.

He didn't answer.

Nolan had tuned out the sound of crashing waves, but finally let it back in. The noise recycled in her head every few seconds along with one other thought. *Ask him, ask him, ask him.* The desire sat on the edge of Nolan's mind. Eve's confession about Coda's sexuality was still weighing heavily with Nolan and especially after saying he had no one to confide in. She could help him. She could unburden him. She could—

No.

It wasn't the time nor her job to do so.

If not now, when?

Sometime.

Did there have to be a more definitive answer than that?

No.

Nolan stood up and began taking off her shirt and pants. *It's cold as fuck out here. And that water is going to be a lot worse*, she thought.

"Nolan, what are you doing?" Coda asked in confusion.

"Just doing what anyone else would at the beach." She tossed her clothes aside and dashed toward the water. She heard Coda call out once more, but it was quickly drowned out from the wind beating against her ears.

Closer . . . closer . . . closer.

Her lungs and legs burned from the unplanned burst of exercise. The sand changed from soft footfalls to compact and soggy.

Nolan attempted to dive into the ocean, but it morphed into a lunge. She collided with a wave and was swept under. The cold water paralyzed her system as she felt her lungs constrict. A fleeting fear ran through her. *Do I even know how to swim?*

She did and pushed up from the ocean floor and surfaced, taking several seconds to breathe in air and cough out the saltwater.

"Nolan, what the *fuck* are you doing?" Coda yelled.

Her teeth chattered as she tried to push the words out. "Going for a swim. Come on in the water's . . . super cold!"

Coda shook out of his clothes. He followed her movements and jumped into the ocean, yelling like he'd become unhinged. Nolan watched as he sank under a wave and reemerged on the other side. "Holy fuck! You weren't kidding. I think . . . my system . . . is going into shock."

"It's great, isn't it?" she asked.

"Y-yes."

"You could have left your boxers on."

"When's the . . . next time I'll have . . . a chance . . . to skinny dip . . . in . . . an ocean?"

Nolan began to swim for the shore with Coda following behind. Once on land, he ran for his clothes.

"You have a nicer ass than I do!" she called out.

"I believe the proper term is a bubble butt," he said, kicking out his hips to show off his asset.

They walked back to their original spot, forgetting about the biting wind that was even colder now.

"I wouldn't — oh, too late," Nolan said as Coda sat on the sand. "You will be wiping off sand for days now."

"It'll be a memento from Florida . . . What was that all about?" Coda motioned back down to the water.

"Exactly what I said: I just wanted to do as one does at the beach."

"In the middle of the night? In March?"

"It's the best I could manage," Nolan said.

"Well, how do you feel now? Besides absolutely freezing."

"Like I did a system reboot."

"Me too," Coda said.

If he had pressed her further, Nolan would have given a different answer. One with a single word and something she had been chasing for a while. It wouldn't last long, but she latched onto it as she sat next to Coda and resumed their stares back into the endless void.

Peace.

thirty-four

CAR CHAT III
Outside of Atlanta, Georgia

The 2008 Pinto Pinata dwindled to a stop within the mile-long traffic jam. Cars honked and demanded passage forward, not realizing they were part of the problem.
 By sitting in traffic, you *become* the traffic.
 "Are you sure you don't want to make a pitstop?" Nolan said, pointing to the distant skyline.
 "Nah, not unless you want to," Coda said.
 "Let's skip this one. I've never heard good things about Atlanta."
 Coda turned to her in confusion. "Who have you been talking to about Atlanta? How does that come up in conversation?"
 "I don't know! It just does."
 "Now I'm imagining a weekly gathering with other socialites of New York and all you do is trash talk the other cities."
 "I'm not a socialite. I resent that."
 "Oh, darling," Coda said, impersonating a snobby, rich person. "Have you heard about the squalor that the denizens of Atlanta live in? Such filth! How barbaric! Don't get me started on Los Angeles! The smog chokes every breath and wannabe celebrities flock there just to fail miserably. Ugh! Ugh, I say!"
 "Are you done?"
 "Yes. It's hard to think of mean things to say about other cities."
 "Coda, I'd appreciate if you didn't lump me into the wealthy category you think I belong to."
 "But you are wealthy."
 "No, my parents are."
 "Right, the parents who paid for college and let you take this car across the country."
 "Fuck you. How about that?" Nolan said. "You have no idea what you're talking about."
 "Okay. Okay. I'm waving the white flag. I'm sorry."
 "I always enjoyed our friendship because you never looked at me differently for having money. Everyone else saw my last name and

immediately believed I had an easy life."

"You haven't had an easy life?" Coda questioned. "I don't mean that sarcastically . . . It's just that you don't talk about your personal life a lot."

"There are still things for you to discover."

"When will that happen?"

"When are you going to tell me everything about your life?" Nolan fired back.

"I-I don't know," he stammered. "I figured it would happen organically and when it needed to."

"That seems like a reasonable answer, so expect the same from me."

"Okay," Coda said, bring finality to the conversation. He turned his head and thought about how much of the truth he was hiding and how he could run from it so easily.

Sometime later, Coda said, "Hypothetical situation for you." They were still in traffic with their view of the skyline unchanged.

"Go for it," Nolan said with vague interest.

"What if we lived in a world where, at thirteen, you had to read the Book of Life?"

"Okay . . ."

"The origin of this book would be unknown, but it has all the relevant knowledge you'd need to circumnavigate life. You memorize the material and take the exam. If you fail, you become an outcast."

"Okay . . ."

"Do you think people would be happier if a book gave them all the answers? How to make your significant other happy; how to raise your kids; how to swim; how to speak to people with respect; how to have a civil conversation when both parties have differing views. The list goes on and on. An almost unimaginably long list of scenarios with detailed answers."

"People wouldn't read it. Think of all the ways they would try to cheat. It sounds like a failed utopia."

"Is it though? Granted, you've forced them to learn a copious amount of information, but it's all to prepare them for the obstacles of life. They still have the freedom to go out and make decisions."

"All the decisions would be the same since everyone read the same source material, right?"

"Good point," Coda said.

"And what happens to the outcasts?"

"They die."

"What?" Nolan said in disgust.

"As you said, it's a utopia, so there is no room for weak links."

"This sounds like the premise to a young adult novel that would have been popular when we were kids."

"I'm sure someone has written about this idea. This will go into the trash pile with all of our other unoriginal book pitches. Let me check Snoogle." Coda grabbed his phone.

"Why do you call it Snoogle? I've tried to think through the possible reasons, but none really come to mind."

"Oh," Coda said, looking up at Nolan, "it was a nickname my dad had for my sister. I heard it so much as a kid that I guess it stuck."

"Which sister?"

"Cecilia."

"Your oldest sister, right?"

"Yeah. Cecilia, Cassandra, Clementine, and then me."

"You never speak about them much," Nolan noted.

"Casualties of the falling out between me and my mom. They sided with her and viewed me as the immature brother. They felt like I was spoiled because I was the youngest. That classic bullshit."

"Once we get back, you can work on repairing those relationships too."

Coda winced at the comment. "Maybe."

"Why that nickname for your sister?"

"Because she had an answer for everything, but my dad had an irrational fear that Google would take over the country through invasion of privacy, selling your personal information, and all that stuff, so he never referred to them by their name. Not sure what that achieved though."

"Not the answer I was expecting," Nolan laughed.

"Everyone has their quirks!"

"I suppose."

"He wouldn't be too happy that I worked at JEC. He'd say I sold out to a massive corporation when I could have worked somewhere smaller and helped out more people. If he knew I worked on software for the autocannons . . ."

"What about it?"

"Nolan, I don't want to think about that. This trip is helping me remove some guilt I have with working for a company like that."

"I understand. I won't pry, but for the record, you did bring it up."

"It's just that . . ." Coda paused, collecting his thoughts. "I can't escape this feeling that I've indirectly killed people with my job. It never bothered me until a week ago. I was so far removed from the end product . . . I couldn't tell you what happens next with my code after it's merged, but I do see the news. I see all the JEC products being waved around and used in combat . . . and those autocannons . . . those are the top prize for anybody to get their hands on. Like the guy told me at the warehouse yesterday: they *eviscerate* people. Eviscerate, Nolan. How am I supposed to move on from that?"

"I really don't know, Coda. Time, maybe."

"Yeah, maybe. Look: I'm not losing sleep over this, but it's the closest I can empathize to the dread you spoke about last night. This pit rises up from my stomach and makes me feel awful."

"I'm sorry that's been weighing on you. You were just doing a job."

"And that's exactly why I quit," Coda said, raising his voice. "I was tired of being a mindless drone surrounded by incompetence or other shills. There has to be something else more rewarding to do."

"You just need to find it. Why don't you focus on this trip and getting these books back home?"

He wanted to tell her more but couldn't find the words. He should have said what he felt the true reasoning was behind the trip. It was more fundamental than anything he said so far. Would Coda ever know what to say about the situation? Not likely, unless he stumbled across the nonexistent Book of Life.

Coda looked outside as they passed by the flashing lights and torn up cars. Debris and skid marks were scattered across the blocked lanes. Police circled around a human shaped object on the ground that was covered with a sheet. The paramedics were tending to other occupants in the crash.

Coda absorbed as much of the scene as he could before Nolan sped past, eager to get beyond the outskirts of Atlanta.

Coda should have felt some pain, some sympathy for the victim underneath that sheet, but in a world of billions, why be bothered by the death of one?

thirty-five

THERE'S NO PLACE LIKE ... CAVE CITY

After spending the night in Nashville with nothing of acclaim to mention, the duo continued their northbound travels. Coda questioned when he'd get to drive the 2008 Pinto Pinata and the only response he received was an exaggerated huff and snort as if he was taunting her with a red sheet.

Out of Tennessee and well into the meat of Kentucky — a state Coda believed served no purpose — Nolan declared they needed gas.[18] The 2008 Pinto Pinata was a formidable beast, getting five hundred miles to the one gallon of gas it held. Was such a thing possible? Who cares!

Nolan pulled into the deserted gas station and parked next to the first pump.

"I can pay for this one," Coda said, reaching for his wallet with one hand and the door handle with the other.

"Hey. Hey! HHHHHHHEEEEEYYYYYYYYYYY!" a voice shouted as he stepped out of the car. "You're not from around here, are ya?" The voice lacked malice, but Coda's heart still sank. The abruptness of it caught him off guard.

Coda whipped his head around to find the source. It wasn't hard. A man had come out of the convenience store who was the size of a grizzly bear — in girth, not height — with a smile plastered to his face.

The man continued: "I know every car in this town and yours isn't one of them! Want me to prove it?" Before Coda could respond, the man jumped into a wonderful rendition of "Twinkle, Twinkle Little Star" except with every lyric replaced by car names and not the desire to lull a child to sleep.

Nolan saw the scene unfolding and stepped out of the car. She listened with fascination. When the man finished, she clapped wildly like her

---

[18] But in all seriousness, Coda was deeply troubled that he knew nothing about Kentucky besides that derby thing where people wore outrageous hats and considered it fashion, and the chicken that gave millions of people diabetes. He searched on Snoogle asking, "What purpose does the state of Kentucky serve?" Typically, Snoogle fires back thousands of responses with links to spam, porn, and Wikipedia. In this scenario, Snoogle returned one word spread across the entire webpage: **NOTHING**. Coda had no qualms with the response.

favorite band[19] had just finished a set.

"Thank you, thank you!" the man said, bowing.

Confused, Coda let the scene continue to play out.

"What was all that about?" Nolan asked.

"Well, I saw you two pull up and knew immediately you weren't from around here. We used to get visitors all the time here, but things have slowed down in the past year."

"What happened?"

"I'll explain inside. Let me ring you up," the man said, gesturing toward the gas nozzle that Coda was holding.

In the convenience store, the man explained they were in Cave City. A city in name, but a small town at heart. With only a couple thousand residents, Cave City was a tight knit community with big aspirations. The predecessors had created Dinosaur World, a tribute to all of our prehistoric friends. It's fun for the whole family! Digging for fossils, looking at artifacts, fucking around on the playgrounds (his exact words), and checking out detailed replicas of some badass dinos! Following the pandemic that no one remembered, Dinosaur World saw a dramatic drop in visitors so the city shut down the attraction for six months each year to save costs. Devastation swept through the city as the two thousand residents wondered what the future would look like.

"Thankfully, our fearless mayor, Dixon Butts, came up with an idea that will knock your socks off!" the man said.

"Oh yeah, what's that?" Coda asked, handing over his credit card.

"I'll let him tell you about it."

"Well," Coda said, looking outside at Nolan, "we have more driving to do today. I'm not sure we have the time for an extended pitstop."

"Nonsense! It'll take a half hour. You can spare that."

"You'll have to ask the boss."

The man followed Coda back outside and toward the 2008 Pinto Pinata. As he approached Nolan, he said, "I hear you're the head honcho 'round here."

"That's right," she said without hesitation.

"You all got time to meet Mayor Butts and hear about his bold idea to save this city?"

Nolan glanced over at Coda who shrugged his indifference. "Yeah,

---

[19] The Killers. Relevant information for a later segment of the story.

sure."

"Wonderful!" The man further explained that he'd give the mayor a call about the incoming visitors. He gave them directions to downtown, which were straightforward since they could see the bell tower from the gas station.

Before seeing them off, the man finally introduced himself. "I'm Roy. Fourth generation here in Cave City. My family has been running this gas station since the time of the Model T!"

Roy waved with unbridled enthusiasm as Nolan wove her away around the gas station and back out onto the main road. Their drive downtown was two stop signs, a traffic light, and another old woman crossing the road with no urgency.

As Roy mentioned, the mayor's office was a square chunk of brick amidst the other buildings in the three block stretch of Cave City's downtown. Some buildings were boarded up while others looked like they were in a death throe with signs proclaiming massive sales and low, low, LOW prices. Parking was ample as Nolan eased into a spot behind the Ford Fiesta (one of five in the city if Coda recalled Roy's song correctly).

A jolly looking man stood outside, grabbing his suspenders and squinting at the 2008 Pinto Pinata.

"That must be Mayor Butts," Coda said with infinite wisdom.

Nolan ducked her head down to get a better look out the windshield. "No, no. He doesn't look like a Butts to me. I've seen lots of Butts and most were . . . more . . . shapely." She moved her hands through the air to mimic a circle, an imperfect one.

Coda looked at the man in suspenders and back at Nolan. "What are you talking about?"

"We have been over this before," she said with annoyance. "After our stop in Easton. I told you about the five ruling families of New York City: Pox, Blightberg, Stump, Treiber, and Butts."

"Oh, right," Coda said, not recalling that previous conversation in the slightest.

As they exited the car and approached the man, he introduced himself. "Welcome to Cave City! I am Mayor Dixon Butts!"

"Do you have any relatives in New York City?" Nolan asked, determined to understand his lineage.

Mayor Butts stroked his chin and tugged on his suspender, deep in thought. "All of my family is east of the Mississippi, but not that far east!"

"Hm, interesting. Good to know," Nolan said as if that was the most important piece of information she'd ever heard. "I'm Nolan by the way. And that is Coda."

"Pleasure. A true pleasure," Mayor Butts said. "Let's head inside and discuss the plan." He led the way, holding the door open for Nolan and Coda. "Straight back and to the right."

Following his directions, they discovered a windowless room. In terms of office spaces, it was on the opposite end of the spectrum from Dietrich's. Small and cluttered with aged equipment. Mayor Butts circled around to his chair and motioned for Nolan and Coda to grab a seat.

"I assume Roy filled you in on the basics," Mayor Butts said. "He is our greatest advocate to tourists."

"I know a bit about the city, but Nolan was waiting at the car when Roy explained everything," Coda said.

This prompted Mayor Butts to delve into the history of the city and the local attractions. A majority of the information was new to Coda, which goes to show that maybe Kentucky had some hidden gems amongst the uselessness. After his lesson, Mayor Butts wheeled the cart with the overhead projector to the corner. He pulled down the screen on the opposite wall and flipped off the lights. Coda felt like he was teleported back to elementary school. He hadn't seen such archaic technology since.

Mayor Butts slapped down a sheet of paper onto the overhead projector and tweaked the positioning until it was perfect. "What is that?" he asked with the inquiring nature of a tenured teacher.

Five interlocked circles spread across two rows.

"The symbol for the Olympics," Nolan said with hesitation. It felt like a trick question more than an obvious answer.

"Correct!" Mayor Butts said, tossing her a piece of candy from his pocket. Nolan caught it and stared down at the melted chocolate. She casually let her arm hang and tossed it under the mayor's desk. "And what does the Olympics symbolize?"

"Unity," Coda said.

"Athleticism," Nolan said.

"The Jamaican bobsled team!"

"The US hockey team beating the Soviet Union's ass!"

"That gymnast getting her leg broken!"

"Michel Phelps winning all those gold medals!"

"Those people getting killed in Munich . . . Oh, that's not a fun one."

Mayor Butts listened as Nolan and Coda continued to volley answers back and forth. Most of them were recollections of specific events that occurred, not what the games were meant to symbolize. Once the two exhausted themselves, Mayor Butts pulled his suspenders and let them snap back against his chest. "Right. So close, so close. But here's what the Olympics symbolize to me and this town." He ripped off the first sheet and slapped down the next one.

It was a woman jumping up and down with a manic expression on her face, somewhere between pure ecstasy and widespread dementia. She was tossing money into the air. The motivations for her reckless behavior weren't clear, but Coda guessed the intention would have been if the photographer created a better picture.

Generally, pictures are worth a thousand words, but in this case, you were spared from nine hundred and forty-eight of them.

"Money!" Mayor Butts exclaimed. "The Olympics brings buckets of money to the hosting city. Forget the pride of being chosen or the wonderful opening ceremony the city creates or the questionable living quarters the athletes stay in, it's all about the green stuff! This — THIS — is how Cave City, Kentucky becomes a powerhouse again."

"What are you saying?" Coda asked.

"Isn't it obvious, Coda? Cave City will be placing a bid to host the 2030 Olympics!" Mayor Butts beamed with pride.

Coda did some quick math in his head. "Isn't the 2030 Olympics supposed to be winter games?"

"I don't know, is it?" the mayor said. While that could be read as sarcasm, his tone did not give off that impression.

"Coda's right," Nolan said. "This year is the summer games in Paris."

"Oh, that's useful to know," the mayor said.

"Mayor Butts, this is Kentucky, right?" Coda asked.

"Correct."

"And you want to host the *winter* games here?"

"Well . . . Look! We are flexible. We will submit a bid for the 2032 Olympics! How about that?"

"Fantastic," Nolan and Coda said in unison.

"That's it? No doubts? No declarations of discontent? No demonstrations of disobedience? No d-d —I'm drawing a blank."

"Really, we need to get going. We have a long way to drive today," Coda said, starting to stand.

"What's your destination?"

"Chicago."

"Pft!" Mayor Butts scoffed, swatting his hand at the mention of the city. "They are still riding that high from hosting the World's Fair in the 1890s. That could be Cave City! Immersed in the total glow of God's grace and the continuous influx of tourists until the Apocalypse kills us all!"

"We wish you the best of luck. It seems you have your work cut out for you," Nolan said, following Coda's lead to leave the office.

"Wait! Please! Let me give you a tour of the city," Mayor Butts pleaded.

"Between the gas station and our drive to this building, I think we have seen most of it," Coda noted.

"But I haven't shown you Mammoth Cave! The largest cave system in the entire world!"

"I'll look it up on Snoogle."

"Sno — Oh, never mind! I guess you weren't worthy enough to see the nuclear bomb we have hidden down there," Mayor Butts said, trying to entice the visitors to stay *just* a bit longer.

"Ha!" Coda said, pointing at the mayor. "Nice try! I've been fooled once by that already. It won't happen again."

"Rats, that usually works on the unsuspecting ones," Mayor Butts spewed like a cartoon villain.

Nolan and Coda moved out of the office and to the car. More pleas to stay longer in Cave City and the slapping of suspenders could be heard behind them.

Out on the street, Nolan started the car and headed away from the downtown area before any other distractions could inhibit them.

Mayor Butts ran out into the road, following the trail of dust that was kicked up by the 2008 Pinto Pinata. After half a block, he gave up his pursuit and kicked at the ground like both a cartoon villain and disturbed child. He was evolving.

As Mayor Dixon Butts continued his temper tantrum, citizens from the surrounding buildings came out to see what the commotion was. As a (perfect) circle formed around Mayor Dixon Butts, he repeated, "I tried! I tried! I tried!" Eventually, a woman pulled herself free from the circle and walked up to the mayor. She soothed him like a mother as Dixon's cries subsided into violent, sporadic hiccups. In a swift motion, the circle collapsed as all the citizens descended upon Mayor Butts.

Two miles up the road and continuing to put distance between them and Cave City, Coda finally spoke. "Well, I learned several things about whatever the fuck that was. First, there truly is no purpose for the state of Kentucky. If we weren't already at an even number, I'd say to absorb it into Tennessee. Secondly, how stupid was their idea? Had they even thought of the feasibility of such a task? I have so many questions, Nolan. And I'll never get answers to any of them."

Still focusing on the road, Nolan nodded. "I agree with your points and want to add one more: Imagine if we talked about this experience with anyone else. They wouldn't believe it! Even worse, think about if you read it in a book. A chapter dedicated to Cave City, Kentucky and the whole time you'd expect some pay off like the city was full of cannibals and they were luring in unsuspecting tourists or the city was a metaphor for the struggles of middle America. But instead, there would be no payoff. None! That would piss some people off since they demand every plot point be wrapped up tighter than a swaddled newborn. Good thing that isn't the case."

thirty-six

SOMETHING TO DULL THE PAIN

Saturday morning.
 They spent Friday evening at a hotel bar on the outskirts of Chicago. Coda provided his usual prepared statements about what he and Nolan were heading into. Here's the consolidated notes:

- The individual's name is Parkland Locke, but the address Sam provided was for Parkland's closest relatives, which looked to be his parents
- Parkland was Coda's roommate freshman year. Their *friendship* bounced between lukewarm to tolerable. Parkland enjoyed the partying, pledging for frats, and neglecting schoolwork when possible, which put him at odds with Coda
- Coda lent him *Searching for Virginia*, a novel about a boarding school, angsty teenagers, famous last words, and death

Their destination was an unknown suburb of Chicago. Coda hadn't bothered to consult Snoogle for details. The neighborhood was quaint and looked like each homeowner took pride in their thirty-year investment, but the weather was anything but pleasant. Even being that far west of Lake Michigan didn't make the area immune to the biting winds and single digit temperatures.
 "Any advice?" Coda asked as they pulled in front of the house.
 "Coda, this is our fourth rodeo. We got this. Let's hope they aren't twats like our friends down in Florida," Nolan said, more in prayer and hope than sarcasm.
 Coda rang the doorbell twice and heard the tentative bark from a dog on the other side as if it wasn't quite sure what the disturbance was. Nolan bounced up and down beside Coda to stop the frigid chill from shutting down vital organs.
 As they waited for a response, a thought careened into Coda. "You know, I just realized something."
 "Oh yeah? What's that?"

"I didn't bring a single book to read on this trip. For someone who claims to be such an avid reader, you'd think that . . ." he trailed off to mumbling and then nothing.

"If you haven't noticed," Nolan said, still bouncing, "you keep gaining books throughout the trip. Read one of those."

Coda scoffed. "I don't reread books. Why would you when there's millions of others?"

"Because that's what people do when they like something. You're telling me you haven't read any Kilgore Trout novels more than once or the books your mom gave you?"

"Nope. Never."

"Huh," Nolan chewed on the information before deciding she had more pressing matters. "Okay. What the fuck? Is someone going to answer the door before my body turns into Jack Faust?"

"Jack *Faust*?"

"Yeah. Jack Faust. The snowman. Why are you looking at me like that?"

"Nolan, it's Jack *Frost*."

"Oh. Fine. Whatever. Someone answer the fucking door!" she cussed through gritted teeth.

The locks, uh, unlocked and the door flung open with haste like the house heard Nolan's angry plea.

An older gentleman stared at them behind the glass door. See, the Locke family were smart people. Why have one door when you can have two? It's a question many others should ask themselves.

The man was less aged than their encounters with Sylvester Fox and Dietrich Falconer in the sense he could likely walk a mile without collapsing from cardiac arrest. That was saying a lot considering he had a cast on his left leg that was hoisted up onto a scooter for mobility, which meant walking a mile for him would be quite the burden on his right leg.

"Hi. Can I help you?" he said. It's a silly question to ask a stranger when you think about it. What if the recipient wanted their assistance to rob a bank or throw a bag of Surge's poop onto the White House lawn? You opened yourself up to endless possibilities and the potential awkwardness of telling them you couldn't help.

Coda answered the man's question by asking another. "Are you Mr. Locke?"

"That's right," he said with no hesitation.

"I went to college back in New York with your son, Parkland. He was my roommate freshman year. I came out here with my friend" — pointing to Nolan — "to get back a book I lent him. I hope we have the right house."

Mr. Locke froze briefly. "You, uh, you have the right place. You came all the way from New York to get a book?" he asked. A sensible question each person along their journey had asked in some fashion. Even more interesting, people asked that before pondering how Coda and Nolan found out where they lived.

"It's an important book," Coda said, not giving away all the details yet.

"You should have called first or something. We could have saved you a trip."

"It's okay. We've had other stops to make along the way."

Mr. Locke shook his head. "That's not exactly what I meant." He glanced over at Nolan. "Why don't you both come inside before the cold snatches you?"

"Thank you," Nolan said and pushed past Coda to reach sanctuary.

Mr. Locke wheeled around the scooter and led them down the hallway to the living room. Pictures of the family evolving through the years dominated the walls and bookshelves. A collage of photos above the fireplace were predominately of Parkland. It seemed like a bit of favoritism.

Coda hadn't thought about Parkland much since finishing freshman year, but he did recall how little Parkland spoke of anything outside of topical events relating to school, sports, or friends. To be honest, Coda didn't even know his family lived in Chicago. Generally, he was good at breaking through with people when determined, but Coda stopped trying after the first month when it was clear he and Parkland were not going to have a blooming friendship.

"I apologize for us barging in and disturbing you on a Saturday," Coda said. "My other friend tried to find Parkland's actual address, but this was the closest he was able to get."

Mr. Locke nodded. If he had any further questions, he didn't ask. Instead, he lifted his leg off the scooter and fell back into the couch. He motioned for the strangers to sit as well.

"I'm sorry, I never asked for your names."

"I'm Coda."

"Nolan," she said with a small wave.

Something felt off. The air was still inside the house. The clock ticked slightly off rhythm, filling the room with brief noise in between the questions and answers. What happened to the dog they heard after ringing the doorbell? What was Mr. Locke doing before they arrived?

"Nice to meet you both," he said with a forced smile. Mr. Locke was trying desperately from moving the conversation forward in a meaningful way.

"So, Mr. Locke," Coda said, looking over at Nolan and then back to their host, "we don't want to take up much of your time. Does Parkland live here? If not, could you help us get in touch with him? I'm really interested to hear if he still has the book. He wasn't much of a reader, but—"

Mr. Locke collapsed his head into his hands. He rubbed his face several times before lifting his head back up. His eyes were puffy and red.

"I never introduced myself. You can call me Augustus. Some people prefer to shorten the name to Gus or maybe even August, but not me." He attempted to get up from the couch before conceding it wasn't worth the effort.

"Okay. Augustus," Coda said. "Have we interrupted something? You seem distracted."

"Parkland died of a drug overdose six months ago," Augustus said like the last wisp of air coming out of a balloon. The words were rehearsed, rehearsed, rehearsed. Said enough times until they couldn't be anything but true. Why else would anyone mutter such a heinous thing?

Coda sat back in the chair and looked over at Nolan again. She rubbed her hands up and down her thighs, unsure of what to do next.

The sound of the garage door opening turned Augustus's attention, seeming to forget what he had just divulged. Distant barking returned from somewhere in the house. "Alaska is back from the grocery store. Would you two mind helping? I'm not much use these days." Augustus pulled himself up from the couch, wheeled over to the door, and pushed it open.

Nolan and Coda stood behind Augustus, peeking into the garage and awaiting further instructions.

"Jesus Christ, Augie! What is going on? Did we adopt new kids or something?" Alaska said, stopping in place as she came around the hood of the car. She made light of the situation, but genuine concern was sketched across her face.

Augustus leaned his weight into the scooter and said, "Friends of Parkland. Looking for a lost book."

"Oh," Alaska said. The answer was sufficient for the moment as she regained the confidence to enter her own home. "In that case, would you grab some bags from the back?"

They only needed one trip. It was clear that Augustus and Alaska were empty nesters. Nolan grabbed four plastic bags while Coda scooped up the last three and closed the trunk. They hustled back inside to seal off the house from anymore of the icy air that was flowing in.

Unsure of what to do, Nolan and Coda dropped the bags on the kitchen table and stepped back toward the living room. Alaska didn't pay much attention to them as she continued on autopilot to put everything in its proper place.

Coda turned his attention to the photos. He stepped closer and looked at the large family. In some pictures he counted six kids, while in others he only saw five. After a brief game of Spot the Difference, he saw that Parkland was the odd kid out. Coda moved to the fireplace and—

"He was our youngest," Augustus said, pointing at Parkland. He wheeled up beside Coda. "Heart of gold, but I can understand why you two didn't get along. Parkland was reserved and always clinging to distant pain. He could never shake what his life was like before us."

"*Before us?* What do you mean?" Coda asked.

"We adopted Parkland when he was ten," Augustus said, looking back and forth between Nolan and Coda.

Nolan tensed at the reveal and waited for Coda to respond.

"I had no idea. He never said anything." Coda said.

"Do you blame him?"

"No."

"My sister never got her life together. Drugs . . . jail . . . the whole gambit. Ten years we allowed for Parkland to stay in that situation. I'll never forgive myself for that," Augustus said. Coda could see he was clinging onto pain too. "The cancer tore through my sister with no mercy. Maybe it was a blessing. She wasn't fit for this world as terrible as that is to say."

"I'm sorry."

"Ah, yes. Those magical words. We have heard them countless times over the past six months. It's funny . . . I feel like I should be apologizing to people. I could have done more. I could have stopped his spirals. I could have asked more questions and . . . and . . ." Augustus stopped and stared out beyond the pictures like a distant mirage was beckoning him with paradise.

"Hi, I haven't properly introduced myself. I'm Alaska," she said, stepping into the conversation.

They returned the pleasantry. Coda continued to talk. About the trip, the books, what they came across so far, and other oddities. No one interrupted him. Coda felt the power of drawing people in with a story, but after getting through most of it, he grew tired. Nothing he said was more important than hearing about Parkland.

"How come I didn't meet either of you during our freshman year?" Coda asked.

"Parkland didn't want the help," Alaska said with a shrug. "He got on a plane and insisted he would be fine. With six kids, you learn to trust their judgement after a while."

"I hate to ask, but I don't even know. Did Parkland graduate?" Coda said.

"He did," his mom said. "He wanted to be a teacher."

"Did he ever . . .?"

"He moved back to Chicago and was looking to get certified but never did."

"Why not?"

"The drugs sapped any potential."

Coda nodded. He thought about how Parkland would always saunter into the dorm room late. He'd try to be quiet, but his drunken stumbles were unavoidable. Coda chalked up his behavior to being a college student. Didn't most freshmen desire to drink with the newfound freedom they had?

Maybe there was a sign. A harbinger of what was to come.

Of course.

Of course.

Coda was grasping for an answer that wasn't there. His lack of intervention on Parkland's routine was not what drove him to drugs. Coda sought a comfort for himself, a confirmation he could wipe his hands clean of any guilt.

Imagine that?

Coda rubbed his forehead, trying to push away the thoughts and images.

"What was he addicted to?" Coda asked.

"Coda!" Nolan said, passing him a look. "That's an awful question to ask."

"No, no. It's okay," Alaska said, waving away any insult. "It helps to talk about every aspect. He was addicted to morphine."

"When did it start?"

"After college. He never told us why. We tried to get him into therapy, but he skipped the sessions. We had his siblings talk to him, but he was too proud to admit it was a problem. God, we were so foolish to think that it would just disappear. I was too concerned about our image as a family to take it as seriously as I should have," Augustus said. "You always rationalize it as how the worst would never happen. Not to *your* family."

Alaska grabbed his hand and squeezed it tightly. "There will never be a day where we don't feel the weight of regret . . . He was in the house when he overdosed. Maybe if we found him sooner . . ."

Augustus stared back out into the mirage.

Coda spoke. "The book I gave him is about a boarding school in the middle of some state. The main character is new and an outsider. In classic fashion, he gets scooped up by the other outcasts and they bring him into their imperfect circle of friends. Well, the main character has a crush on Virginia, the mysterious girl that likes to smoke and do other edgy things. The attraction builds and builds until one night when they kiss. She runs out of the room without explanation and leaves the school grounds. She dies that night in a car accident and it destroys the main character. He spends the rest of the book searching for why she out driving so late that night."

"Does he ever find out why?" Alaska asked.

"Of course, which is the greatest atrocity of the book. Because we don't get that luxury. I'm guessing you have questions about Parkland that will never be answered, *could* never be answered. We can either let them consume us or make peace with it."

"Why did you give the book to Parkland?"

"I don't know anymore," Coda said. "I wish I did. It was probably on impulse. Sometimes you meet someone and just know a book they would connect with."

Alaska nodded. "Maybe he did. Something we will never get the answer to."

"That's a small answer. There's more important ones you'd be interested in, I imagine."

"I've sat in his room enough these last six months to know he didn't keep any books."

"Oh," Coda said.

"But," Augustus said, "the kids went through his stuff. That sounds like they were vultures, but it was cathartic for them to find something to remember Parkland by. Maybe there's a chance one of them grabbed it."

Coda shook his head. "I gave that book to him so long ago I doubt he held onto it all the way through college. It's okay. I understand."

"No, really," Alaska said. "We can send out a group text and see. They all live around here except for Ophelia. She is out in Salt Lake City, so let's hope it isn't with her." Alaska dug into her pocket and pulled out her phone. She pecked out a text and sent it. "What's the harm in seeing? It would be nice to get a win, you know?"

thirty-seven

CONFESSIONS ON THE "L"

While not an immediate win, less than ten minutes after the group text was sent, two of the Locke kinsmen responded back saying they had the book in question.

Of course.

This wouldn't be much of a story if our main characters didn't go on another adventure.

Alaska tried to sort out the mess and get confirmation as to who *actually* had the book, but after several more exchanges, Jake and Troy continued to profess that the other was wrong. Alaska relayed the information to Nolan and Coda in real time as they huddled in the living room. During all that, Augustus sprang up and remembered that he locked the dog in the bathroom. He grabbed his scooter and scooted down the hallway to free the beast.

All talk of Parkland's death evaporated for a short time.

Coda envisioned grief like trying to knock over a boulder by blowing on it — virtually impossible. But, if you brought the right tools, you had a chance of sending that boulder tumbling down the cliff. What were the necessary tools? Who knows! Coda wasn't a self-help guru.

In this specific example, it seemed like *Searching for Virginia* served as the perfect tool for momentary distraction.

"My goodness, this shouldn't be as difficult as it is," Alaska said, shaking her head.

An obvious question popped into Coda's head. "Can't they just check their apartments? I'm guessing that's where they'd keep it."

"It's—"

A brilliant flash of white fur dashed across the kitchen floor and skidded into the living room. The dog (of unknown breed to Coda) paused in front of the strangers before barking once and retreating in surrender.

"That's Lemon Lime," Alaska said with vague interest.

"The dog's name is Lemon Lime?" Nolan asked.

"Yeah. Half of the family wanted Lemon and the other Lime, so what better compromise than to give the dog both names?"

"Can't argue with that."

"It's silly. No one supported my initial proposal to name him George. What's funnier than giving a dog a human name?" Augustus said as he wheeled back into the room. He repeated the name to himself several times and chuckled at each mention.

"Anyways," Alaska said, "back to what I was saying. The city is celebrating St. Patrick's Day. None of the kids will be at their apartment today. I imagine their incoherence will continue to get worse. It's an important day around here."

"In what way?" Coda asked.

"Well, besides all the drinking and parades, they dye the river green, which makes everyone embrace their non-Irish heritage. It's chaotic and messy, so you two picked the perfect time to come to Chicago. Augie and I used to go down there, but . . . kids," she said with a smile. "Let me text them and see what their plans are."

The back and forth continued far too long as the responses from the Locke kids became more sporadic. By the time Alaska pieced together the full story, Augustus somehow made breakfast. They ate at the table and lobbed questions to each other like they were at a high school reunion.

Coda spoke and spoke and spoke.

Nolan spoke and spoke and spoke.

And yet, for all that talking, neither provided many insights into who they were. It's amazing how much people can talk without ever making a point. It's amazing how fearful people could be of others knowing the truth.

That's one of a dozen reasons why Coda enjoyed books: The characters hardly lied. Sure, you had your unreliable narrators that could trip you up sometimes, but generally speaking, the descriptions and thoughts and feelings of a character were accurate. And always to the point. No time to waste. Every word was carefully planned. Each conversation pushed the story forward. Every description needed to be kept in memory for when it served a higher purpose later on. Each plot point was meticulously drawn out in a notebook with the author knowing the end before much else. Every creative decision mandated and approved by an editor, literary agent, publisher, and other oddities to ensure profits were maximized. Every person alive was acknowledged on the last page (much to Coda's annoyance) because *without them* the book would have never happened. Everything always tied into a nice bow at the end where you sit back and wonder how you were so stupid not to figure out who the killer was or where the climactic scene would take place. Gradual character growth happened in order to keep you invested. The character has to evolve! They just have to. What was the point if a lesson wasn't learned or good didn't conquer evil?

It all made sense. Nothing meandered. People died when they needed to. People survived when the plot demanded it. People said the right thing to avoid conflict or the exact wrong thing to drum up drama.

People were perfect circles when they had to be. People were monsters when they had to be. Take your pick.

It was all manufactured for your reading pleasure.

If only life were like that. What a stale thought!

If life was neat enough to fit inside the margins of a paperback, maybe it wouldn't feel like a chore, an endless routine.

Or so Coda thought.

But wait, there's more.

If novels were so much neater than life itself, why were many mimics? The stories baked in allegory about religion or politics. Or the characters who were thin veils for their real-life counterparts. Or how every fantasy story was just a reimagining of some historical event but told as a more thrilling spectacle.

Because . . .

Because . . .

Beca—

Coda didn't know. If he had the answer, would he even think about the question?

With two subtle shakes of his head, Coda collided back into the table and joined the last bits of the breakfast conversation.

"Okay, here's the deal," Alaska said, looking down at her phone. Empty plates were scattered around. Augustus specialized in salami, egg, and cheese sandwiches where the pieces of salami were cut into little pizza slices and placed delicately within the egg. Nolan and Coda helped themselves to two each. "Jake and Troy are down at the river walk and then going to some bars. I think you two should meet up with them. You can see the city and then head back to one of their apartments to check for the book. How does that sound?"

"Sounds good," Coda said.

"Same," Nolan echoed.

The next half hour blended into a sequence of actions. They helped clean up from breakfast. Nolan attempted to make peace with Lemon Lime, but the dog continued to be hesitant. Alaska jotted down a list of phone numbers and passed the paper to Coda. He didn't look at it before stuffing it into his pocket. Upon insistence from both Augustus and Alaska that they could stay the night, the traveling guests grabbed their bags from the car. (What an absolute hot streak Nolan and Coda were on with hospitality from strangers! It helped to flatten the curve of expenses.)

The Locke's kindness continued when Alaska drove them to the train station. It was her suggestion that they take the "L" into the city as the cheapest option. Not being strangers to public transit, Nolan and Coda welcomed the advice.

On the car ride over, Alaska ran through a quick list of places for them to visit if they had the time. Coda committed the suggestions to memory but doubted they could cover too much ground with the excessive crowds.

"I hope they have that book," Alaska said as she pulled up to the station.

"Me too," Coda said. "Thanks again for everything. You and Augustus have been extremely kind to complete strangers."

"Why wouldn't we?" she asked, but not seeking an answer.

As she drove off, Nolan and Coda trudged up the steps, bought their tickets, and huddled under the heat lamp halfway down the platform. The view from atop the elevated platform was as American as it got — a parking lot on one side and an expressway on the other. Coda watched the cars zip by in a steady blur of drab colors. He looked left then right and found the platform devoid of any other riders. He couldn't think of an instance where that ever happened to him in New York.

The time ticked down on the nearby board until it flashed **ARRIVING** and the train slowly rumbled into the station. Nolan walked to one of the last sections and stepped inside. Coda followed and took a seat on the opposite side from her.

Coda reached into his pocket and pulled out the bundle of papers. He opened Alaska's note and consulted their destination on the map next to him. They had fifteen stops to go. He put Alaska's note away and stared down at the highlighted list. Three of the entries were checked off. It felt like they had been traveling for weeks already and all they had in their possession were three measly books that meant nothing to anyone besides Coda.

Parkland Locke.

The name radiated off the page.

"Sam must have known, right?" Coda asked as he folded up the piece of paper. No one else was in their section. His voice sounded louder than intended as it echoed back to him.

Nolan turned her attention toward him. "Yeah, I'd think so. Most people in their mid-twenties have some sort of social media footprint, so I'm sure Sam found posts of condolences and disbelief regarding Parkland."

"Why wouldn't he tell me?"

Nolan shrugged. "Fuck if I know. I never met the guy. You could call him if you're that interested."

"I'm not. It doesn't change the situation at this point."

"Correct," she said. "All this has me thinking though. I didn't expect this trip to be so . . . varied. Each stop has had a unique spin to it. I wonder if our last three stops will be able to match."

"Varied, but not necessarily exciting."

"Coda, we are looking for books, not buried treasure," she said with a laugh. "I am surprised I haven't been pulled over yet. That is a staple of road trip movies. The main character always has a run in with an incompetent police officer who they then befriend during a brief stint in jail."

"Considering that neither of us are cut out for jail, let's hope that doesn't happen."

"Is that so?" she questioned. "I have new information that suggests you'd fare well in prison, Mr. Juvie."

"That was a long time ago," Coda said flatly.

Nolan threw her hands up in surrender. "I know. No judgements from me."

Thirteen stops to go. Still empty.

"Should I be more upset that Parkland is dead?" Coda asked. "It's just . . . I didn't particularly like him, and we never spoke after freshman year."

"You don't need to feel a specific way about something. The reason you aren't more upset is valid. I'm sure you wish he opened up that door and not Augustus, but you didn't have a hand in his death."

"Morphine," Coda said incredulously. "How do you even find that stuff?"

"I don't know."

"Do you think the overdose was an accident?"

"I don't know."

"Is there anything you know?"

"About Parkland Locke? Absolutely not. I have no idea what it's like to struggle with addiction and feel the constant desire of chasing a high. But I do have one thing in common with him."

"Oh yeah? Is it that you really want to be a teacher and inspire the youth?"

"No," Nolan said. She took a deep breath and watched the train slowdown into the next station.

Ten stops to go. Someone stepped into their compartment, looked around, and darted out.

Still empty.

"Was that your answer?" Coda said, leaning forward and shaking his head.

"I'm adopted." There. That wasn't so hard, was it? Admitting it was the easy part; describing the story that Coda would undoubtedly ask for was tougher.

"Nolan . . ."

"It's true."

"Nolan."

"I had no reason to tell you or anyone. What would have been the point? Being adopted isn't a personality trait and it happened so long ago. I've been thinking about it a lot recently. The money, the name, the social status . . . All the things I stepped into without ever asking for it. There's this level of guilt about it all. Why was I the lucky one to get plucked from poverty and live a lavish life? I understood once it became clear why *my parents* adopted me: I was just a puppet for them, a cute kid they could dress up and pawn around parties. 'Oh my, look at Nolan! Isn't she so pretty?' 'Nolan, why don't you go over there and talk with so-and-so?' Everything had a motivation. I was brought into their lives to make them sympathetic, to make them seem like they weren't entirely devoid of emotions . . . I'm sorry I never told you," she said, turning to Coda.

"Don't apologize." Coda stood up and moved across the aisle to sit next to Nolan. "I'm here to listen."

Nolan had no narrative to follow. Her story wasn't rehearsed before the first sold out show. She spoke and spoke and spoke with no idea if any of it was accurate. Memories could be deceptive.

"When they started talking about Parkland being adopted and the terrible living situation he had growing up . . . it hurt to hear. I don't know the full story with my parents, but they weren't good people. I've heard so many things when I was a kid that it's hard to understand what the truth is. They put me up for adoption and I was scooped up by some family. I didn't stay there long as they couldn't handle a newborn, which really makes you wonder how anyone could give up so quickly. No different than my parents I suppose. After that, I was placed into foster care and jumped around houses for the next six years. Of course, I don't recall most of this, but all it took was one peek at my file — yes, I had an actual file — and I saw numerous addresses and names that I wasn't familiar with.

"I somehow kept a mild personality throughout it all. You'd expect me to have anger issues or be closed off from others, but I think I compartmentalized the entire situation. Maybe that's why I was so *attractive* to the Treibers. I wasn't a project for them; I wasn't a broken vase that needed to be glued back together. I was just a six-year-old kid with a string of shitty luck, but still malleable enough to be whatever they needed.

"I knew things were different with the Treibers when they shuffled me onto a private plane back to New York. They spoke so eloquently and directly to the point. They made me feel special in those first couple of months and let me have full run of the penthouse. For a kid who never got her own room, it felt like paradise. I remember feeling like it would be temporary, like the first mistake I'd make they would send me right back. One day, I was drinking milk and the glass slipped out of my hands. Shattered all over the floor. I was petrified. My mom came into the kitchen, looked down at the floor, and back up at me. She saw how terrified I was. She bent down and said, 'Honey, that glass was only a hundred dollars. Don't worry about it.' I'll never forget that. Money was so meaningless to them that she told me the exact amount of the glass and said it with pride. I could have broken every glass in the entire city and they would have replaced them the next day. There were nights back at the foster home where I could barely get a cheese sandwich for dinner and now I was in a living situation where poverty seemed as distant as the sun.

"I eased into it all. What kid wouldn't? I got whatever I wanted and always had ample opportunities compared to others. It wasn't until I was a teenager that I began to understand what my purpose was to my parents. How I was just a puppet. The guilt settled in along with the panic attacks and as the years went by, it continued to get worse. I felt dirty as I watched college kids struggle to pay rent or fully grasp how much debt they were falling into. I felt pathetic as the Treiber name was plastered onto buildings throughout the city and everyone assumed I was a mindless drone, cut from the same fabric as my parents. But there was no reason to tell anyone I was adopted. What person would feel sympathy for the poor girl who was adopted into a rich family and grew a conscious about all the money she had? I'd look like an even worse person than people already took me for. I-I . . .

"I lied to you all those times I talked about rarely leaving New York City. I spent the first six years of my life in California. Being honest with you, that's the reason why I joined you on this trip. After getting screwed over on the position out in LA, I needed the escape. I have been thinking about starting new out there and taking some time to find my parents. There's a chance I won't come back to New York with you."

Five stops left. Still empty.

Coda absorbed the information. "Are you really serious about staying out in California?"

"I've had a lot of time to think on this trip and I'm strongly considering it."

"Nolan, what would you do for a job? Where would you live? Why would you want to find your parents? That's reliving old pain." The questions sprang from Coda like a shaken soda. His mind was spinning.

"I'm sure I could find a waitress job while I submit my resumé to companies. I have money saved up that is separate from the Treiber name. I have wanted to distance myself from New York for a while now and this seems like the perfect opportunity."

"I don't know. I wouldn't want you to fail."

"Coda, what are you going back to? Last time I checked, you quit your job too. You are stepping into just as much uncertainty as I am."

"I-I . . . Yeah, you're right. What about your birth parents?"

Nolan shrugged. "I have no anger toward them after this long. I'm looking for closure more than anything. Even if I don't reach out to them, I'd at least like to find information about what they've been doing for the last two decades."

"Well, I could always put you in contact with Sam."

"I'd prefer someone more professional," Nolan confessed, "even though he hasn't steered us wrong so far."

"I get that."

"I'm sorry I never told you. I hope this won't overshadow the trip."

"Nolan, please stop saying that. That's not the case. I needed this trip and I'm thankful to have you here with me. Keep thinking about California and I'll support you in whatever you decide."

"Thanks Coda. I'm sure you have more questions."

"Yeah, but we still have more driving. I'll ask them some other time."

Two stops left. Still empty.

Nolan finally took in the space around her. It was unremarkable in every possible way. The worn carpet on the seats; the short love messages and vague threats scratched into the glass; the stains representing modern art on the floor; the advertisements for pills and pillows and forgiving student debt and the hottest museums in downtown Chicago.

The thoughts continued to swirl as they always did. California, her birth parents, money, what was next, and other oddities. It was never quiet.

They were all problems for another time.

Did she feel unburdened by telling Coda she was adopted?

No, not really.

Did she feel better after telling him?

No, not really.

But that's okay. Not everything has to be a revelation.

"This is our stop," Coda announced. He stood up and walked to the nearest door. Nolan followed behind him.

A slight buzzing sound droned from the door as it slid open. They stepped onto the platform and felt the chill engulf them.

Nolan watched as the train began to leave them behind, heading toward the next destination.

Their compartment was still empty.

thirty-eight

IF ONLY

What a day!

It probably didn't crack any top ten lists for Nolan and Coda, but it was significantly more enjoyable than expected. Here's a highlight reel: Looking at the incredibly green river like a megalodon was prowling underneath, sampling a half dozen craft beers that all tasted the same, slurred conversations with Jake and Troy and their diverse social circle, seeing The Bean in all its steel glory, and bouncing from one bar to another where anyone not wearing green was chastised by the crowds.

Coda drank more in the past week than during his time at TCSUM, which left him oddly conflicted. He could see the appeal in that he felt more sociable with each sip but was still an unnecessary expenditure of time and money.

Listen:

The important part of the day wasn't the touristy bullshit, alcoholic drinks, or general tomfoolery that Nolan and Coda engaged in.

It was the book.

For now, it always comes back to that highlighted list.

Following the montage of their voyage around Chicago, Nolan and Coda trailed Jake back to his apartment on the north side of town to confirm whether he was in possession of the book.

He wasn't.

Jake drunkenly explained that he *swore* he had the book. He remembered being enthralled by the cover: A woman seated behind a desk who was squeezing her forearms together to show off her "wonderful gifts" while peering through a magnifying glass.

"That is not the cover," Coda said. He sensed they were about to fall into a stupid rabbit hole.

"It is," Jake said in defiance.

"It's not."

"It is."

"It's not."

This repeated seven more times until Jake walked off in frustration and began skimming through the apartment to prove himself right.

"Found it!" he proudly said, walking back into the kitchen and tossing his findings to Coda.

Coda looked at the object. "Do you want to know all the reasons why this isn't the book?"

"It is though!" Jake whined. If Coda had more time to examine the Locke family dynamic, he may have concluded that Jake sometimes acted infantile to get attention. Maybe it stemmed from neglect growing up with so many siblings or seeming to be mediocre at everything he did. It took him ten seconds to chug a beer. Ten seconds! Horribly average.

All Coda ever had was questions, contemplations, and doubts.

If only he could get some stinking answers.

In the meantime, he could provide some clarity to Jake. "Okay. Reason number one why this isn't the book." Coda held up the object to him. "This is a Blu-ray disc. Reason number two: This is called 'Searching for Virgins.' Reason number three: This is a porno. So thank you for giving us insight into your sexual interests," Coda said, tossing it aside.

"Shit. Sorry about that," Jake said. He sank into the chair opposite from Coda. "It's been tough. I don't think I've had a coherent thought in six months."

"Drinking doesn't help."

"Sure it does. I actually laugh and don't think about Parkland every second."

"I understand. It's a process. You'll find peace."

"When?"

"If I knew that, I'd be the most sought after person on the planet," Coda said.

"Maybe." Jake sighed and picked up his phone. "I'll call Troy. He should be back home by now."

▟▋▙

A half hour later, Nolan and Coda were on the stoop of Troy Locke's apartment building. The outside was covered in gray brick and large windows spaced out evenly across each floor. Most curtains were drawn, blocking any glimpses into the lives of strangers. The building seemed modern compared to the dusty, dirty fronts and uninspired designs that lined the rest of the block.

Coda watched through the glass door as Troy turned the corner and came down the set of stairs like he was making a triumphant entrance into the grand hall. A smirk settled onto his face as he flashed the object in his hand for any admirers to see.

"I knew it. I knew it. I knew it," he repeated endlessly as he stepped outside. "Jake always wants to be involved in whatever the latest craze is. He can't accept being wrong. He can't—"

"Thanks Troy. I appreciate it," Coda said, cutting off the rant. He didn't care to hear Troy's gloating.

The cover was as minimalistic as he remembered. A dented guardrail with smoke rising up in the background. Ominous for a first-time viewer, but after reading the back cover, it wasn't hard to piece together that the picture was showing the aftermath of Virginia's car accident. So it goes.

He opened up the back inside cover for confirmation. The symbol was there. It was all he needed.

"I'm sorry again about your brother," Coda said, trying to bring finality to their visit.

"Me too," Nolan chimed in.

"About Jake? Yeah, well, every family has that one sibling," Troy said.

Coda shook his head. "No. I meant Parkland." He was in partial disbelief that he had to even clarify.

"Oh. Right. I mean, it is what it is."

"Is that really how you feel?" Coda said, moving closer.

"It's not like I can wish for him back. He made his choices."

Coda nodded, not in agreement but as acceptance of Troy Locke's irrational behavior. He moved down the steps and away into the Chicago night before turning back one last time.

"Troy," he called back.

"Yeah?"

"Why did you take the book?"

"Because it was the only one Parkland had."

Coda thanked Troy one last time and kept moving down the block toward the commotion that awaited. Utilizing Snoogle, they found the nearest train station and tracked their route back to the Locke house.

Coda showed Nolan the projected commute time.

"Oh God," she groaned.

"Not ideal, but it'll go by quickly."

"I'm glad you got the book back. Another one off the list. I never expected you to have so much luck."

"Neither did I."

"Why have you?" she asked.

The question felt rhetorical, but Coda still tried to come up with something. "I don't think it's so much about the book itself, but more so about how each was given for a specific reason. Aren't you more inclined to keep a gift even if you never use it? The answer is in that logic, but I don't know exactly where."

"I can see what you're getting at. Yet another mystery."

"Yet another mystery," Coda echoed.

The wait at the train station was minimal as Nolan didn't even have time to shuffle over to the heat lamp. They boarded to a half full train that brought them south for five stops before exchanging onto a different line that would take them west.

The second train was less noisy as the conductor wasn't forceful with the brakes.

"Can you come sit over here?" Nolan asked.

Coda was across the aisle and staring out the window. The lights of the skyline burned bright and blended into a fog that was hard to distinguish where one building ended and another began. It looked like a scatter plot without any correlation.

"Why?" he asked.

"Don't be difficult. I need to ask you something."

"Fine." He slid into the seat next to Nolan. "Happy?"

"Yes. Can you soften up for me?"

"What?"

"Soften up because I'm taking a nap. I don't want to feel your bony . . . bones." Nolan leaned her head on his shoulder, grabbing chunks of his jacket and stuffing it underneath until she had the perfect pillow.

Coda returned to his window gazing before feeling the book in his hand again. It was flimsy, narrow, and worn, indicating that amongst a bookshelf, it wouldn't be your first pick. His mom was never concerned with gifting him the most expensive or ornate edition of each book. Most looked as if they were plucked from a doctor's office or found in a box on the street corner. Sometimes he wondered if his mom received the books from somebody else. Did she stumble upon them or was she guided to them? How many books did she read that didn't have enough meaning to pass along to Coda?

More questions. It had become tedious.

He flipped through the pages until he settled on the last. Text filled only a third of the page. He read it several times.

didn't get to say to you. Things I was never able to ask because they never felt important until they were. What's your favorite color? Do you love murder mysteries as much as I do? Have you ever watched a sunset from start to finish?

You would have fascinated me with each answer, defying what anyone would expect.

I loved you. I hardly knew you, but isn't that the best kind of love? Pure and unrestrained before all the doubt seeps in.

Nikola Tesla's last words were: "It's there. Just beyond my reach."

I'll keep going. I'll keep searching.

I hope to have more luck.

Coda dug for the deeper meaning but stopped himself. They were just words without the weight of the previous pages. Possibly in line with what you may think, reading the last page of a book before anything else didn't promote much gravitas. All books end in whispers — a quiet close of a door rather than a slam that shakes the foundation.

Coda restricted his movements to not wake Nolan, who was snoring softly. He was impressed with anyone who could fall asleep on another person's shoulder. With his arms pinned tight against his body, he repositioned the book and flipped to the front.

The message was there, written in an even flow that indicated the words were formed in one endless motion.

> *There are two things we don't get enough of in this life: time and answers. Somehow, the character in this book got both, which proves how idyllic even the best novel is.*
>
> *G.F.*

Beneath his mom's message was more. It was brief with the handwriting more frantic.

<u>WISE WORDS</u>!

No investigation was necessary into whose writing that was. There was only one other person who had the book since he initially received it. The answer as to why Parkland held onto the book was hiding in plain sight.

All it took were two words for Coda to know that someone had gotten something out of a book he lent out.

With a smile plastered across his face, Coda closed the book and dipped his head back.

Time and answers.

Time and answers.

Time and answers.

The message rattled around in his head until the words lost their potency and the thought didn't seem as dire.

From the train station, Nolan and Coda grabbed an Uber instead of harassing the Locke's to pick them up. Upon seeing the address, the driver grumbled about the short commute and complained the whole way about how they were wasting his time.

Three stars and no tip.

Though it was late and the rest of the street was quiet, several lights were on within the Locke household like they were doting parents who were waiting for kids to make it back before curfew.

Nolan rushed out of the car and up the driveway, leaving Coda behind. Once he caught up, the door opened and Augustus was standing behind the glass.

"You made it back! And you got the book!" he said, noticing what Coda was holding onto.

"Yes. It was a great day," Nolan said and moved into the warmth.

"Alaska set up the guest bedroom for you Nolan. Coda, any issues sleeping on the couch?"

"Not at all."

"Great."

"Nolan, I'd show you which room, but . . ." Augustus said, pointing down to the scooter. "I try to limit my trips upstairs."

"No problem. Thank you. Coda, see you in the morning?" she questioned. It was more of a ploy to exit the conversation than anything.

"I'll be here. Good night," Coda said and watched her move up the steps until she disappeared into the darkness.

"Were you planning on going to bed soon?" Augustus asked.

"I don't have to. I can always sleep in the car tomorrow."

Augustus moved down the hallway using his good foot to propel him forward. "You two don't want to stay the day?"

"Unfortunately, we need to get going."

"What's the rush?"

Coda gave Augustus a half truth. "My mom is dying. My sisters don't think she has much longer left."

"And you're here?" Augustus asked. He reached the kitchen and turned toward Coda. "Before you answer that question, let me pose another: Would you like a drink? I have beers in the fridge."

"Sure, that would be great." More drinking. Coda's favorite. But at least this time the goal wouldn't be to chug each drink or get threatened with a fist to the balls from Jake. "I can grab them." He opened the fridge and found a pyramid of beers at the bottom. He scooped up two and sat down at the kitchen table across from Augustus.

Coda continued: "My mom and I have had a fractured relationship for a while. Getting these books is meant to be a gesture of goodwill toward making amends."

Augustus cracked the beer top and said, "Coda, I doubt your mom cares about any past squabbles."

"It doesn't matter much. She isn't conscious. Whatever *offering* I gave would be to ease my own guilt."

"Does that bother you?"

"Yes." A longer answer wasn't needed.

Sensing that Augustus was reaching a brick wall, he swerved to avoid it. Figuratively, of course. "Where are you driving to next?"

"Somewhere outside of Dallas."

"Quite the drive."

"No different than any of the other places so far."

"What's left after that?" Augustus asked.

Coda laid out the remainder of their stops. He felt like he was repeating information from earlier in the day, but Augustus never commented if that was the case.

"I've never done a long road trip like that before. It must be beautiful."

"Not really," Coda confessed. "It's all the same brown mush for scenery and two-lane highways that don't provide any thrilling curves."

"In that case, I'm sorry for your troubles," Augustus said with a laugh. "Alaska and I were arguing about this earlier: Are you and Nolan a couple? She said yes. I didn't think so."

"Just friends," Coda said. A small, forced smile crept onto his face.

"I knew it! Everyone wants to romanticize a guy and girl spending time together."

"You two aren't the first to question it."

"That must be getting old, huh?"

"This whole trip is just a massive cycle, which is exactly what I wanted to escape. We drive, explain our story, find the book, deny being a couple, and move onto the next place. But, I attribute some of the questions to people wanting to know about two strangers who popped up at their door."

"It's not how I expected to spend my Saturday morning, but I'm glad you two came here. I . . . I — we, uh, we could use the distraction."

"How has it been?"

"Awful. Absolutely awful." Augustus took a long sip of the beer. "Alaska cries every day, which I understand. Today felt like the first time I saw a glimmer of what she was like before — quick to action and always offering her help. I miss that. And I . . . I have been incredibly distant. I don't know how to support her or the kids. My parents are dead, which was tough, but my God, losing a child . . ."

"I'm sure you're doing your best."

Augustus shook his head. "You and Nolan are the first new people we have talked to since Parkland's death. All it's been is family and friends trying to console us, but I think they are even starting to give up."

"You should talk to someone."

"I am right now."

"Maybe someone more qualified," Coda suggested.

"Maybe."

Coda struggled with what to ask next. He knew Augustus wanted to talk about something, but likely didn't know how to get there. Coda decided on the direct approach. "Is there a reason you wanted to stay up and have a drink?"

"I don't sleep much these days. Alaska takes Lemon Lime upstairs and closes the door. I always creep in late after she's already asleep."

"Okay," Coda said, unsure of the proper response.

"You never asked how I broke my leg."

"How did you break your leg?" Coda asked.

"It's a long story."

"Augustus, I've read a bunch of books in my life. I imagine the story will be shorter than any of them. In my experience, anytime someone says their story is long, it ends up fizzling out after twenty seconds of rambling."

"It's a long story," he repeated.

"Let's hear it then."

"About ten years back, Alaska let me convert part of the basement into a workshop. I'm not an exceptional carpenter by any means, but I found myself taking on small projects around the house to save us some money. With each new effort, I'd purchase a necessary tool and it began crowding the garage. She and the kids complained about the cars sitting in the driveway each night, so I struck a deal. I'd migrate to the basement if I was given fifty percent of the space. It wasn't a long negotiation as the basement was always a dumping ground for unwanted crap. We could have made it nice and added another bedroom, but the boys liked the coldness of the space and didn't think I noticed the beer stains on the concrete floor.

"Anyways, I moved all my stuff down there with my first renovation being to add a partition and mark off my space. That effort took longer than necessary, but the result was nice enough. I had my sectioned off space with shelves and racks and enough extra room to expand if I ever desired to remodel something extensive.

"As each kid left the house and ventured toward their ambitions, I spent more time down there. Sometimes I was working on projects, while other times I would sit and do nothing. I know people like to assume that 'doing nothing' isn't actually the case, but for me it was true. I'd sit in the rocking chair and stare at the ceiling. When my mind finally drifted toward a topic, it was usually about the kids or Alaska or the future or my job or whatever minor stress had cropped up.

"Things changed when Parkland moved back after college. I always treated him like my own. That kid got a raw deal and I felt a level of responsibility to correct his path. I think Alaska and I did a pretty good job with all our kids with Parkland being no exception. But he was different post-college. He'd stay out late with no texts; he lacked any ambition to get a job; his behavior became more hostile. I'm ashamed to admit how long it took for us to understand his addiction. It was subtle at first and we made excuses. We enabled. We didn't take action. I can't undo that, but I thought of all the ways I wanted to whenever I was alone in the workshop. I'd stare up at the ceiling and think through how we could talk to Parkland and get him the help he needed.

"It was a Saturday morning. Uneventful in every way. Alaska was out grocery shopping. She didn't ask me anymore since I scoured the aisles for garbage we didn't need. Parkland was a notorious late sleeper. We tended not to bother him, especially on the weekend, but I felt an urge that day to check if he was even there. I can't explain why exactly. I went to the room and peeked in the door. Sure enough, he was under the covers with his back to me. I debated whether to wake him up with the offer of making breakfast, but you never knew what side of him you'd get so I didn't bother. I had grown fearful of him. Afraid of the cruel things he could say to me or Alaska. Hours go by and he still isn't awake. Alaska asked me to go back upstairs and wrestle him out of bed. I pushed back at first but relented because it was an argument I wouldn't have won. I opened the door and found him in the same exact position as earlier. As I moved closer, I saw the vomit on the far side of the bed. His body was already cold. His face . . . his — Coda, I can't describe it. To put your hands on your dead child is the most sickening thing you could ever ask someone to do. The rest of the day was . . ."

"Afterward, I found myself spending more time in the basement. Sitting in that chair and thinking. Always thinking the same thing: I could have saved him. If I had just woke him up earlier that morning. If only. If only. If only I had done that, we wouldn't be having this conversation. The thought tore into me each and every day. I had no outlet for the pain. How could I confess such a thing to Alaska? It would destroy her. I couldn't tell the kids; they'd think I was a monster. So I sat with it and let the pain brew until it boiled over.

"A month ago, I was down in the basement and grabbed the hammer. It happened quick as if my brain and body were out of sync. I straightened my leg and slammed the hammer against it. Whack. Coda, do you know how much force it takes to break a leg with a hammer? Well, I found out that morning it takes twenty-nine swings. Whack. Whack. Whack. Over and over until the bone snapped. The pain I felt was tremendous, but it was exhilarating. You're looking at me like I'm insane and I don't blame you. It was penance for my sins. I let my son die and I needed to feel the pain that he did as he overdosed with no one around to save his life. God, if I didn't have other kids and a wife, I'd kill myself. Just toss myself over a bridge and end it all. The pain. Jesus Christ, the pain is intolerable. And for all that suffering, the release was momentary. I feel just as bad now as I did leading up to that moment.

"I had to lie of course about how the *accident* happened. No one questioned it because no one would think I'm capable of such an atrocity. It's always the most unsuspecting who can do the worst harm, right?

"I failed him. If only, Coda. If only I was better."

Silence was the only friend between Coda and Augustus for a full minute.

Eventually, Coda said, "Why would you tell me all that?"

"Because no one else would understand."

"I'm not sure about that, Augustus."

"Okay fine. What better person to confess to than a stranger I won't see again? I'm sorry I used you for my selfish need."

"I understand. I truly am sorry."

"I know you are."

"Are you going to be okay?" Coda asked, placing the empty can aside.

"I . . . I don't know. I hate to alarm you, but would you be okay in my situation?"

"No."

"A definitive answer."

"We don't get enough of those."

Augustus pulled in the scooter and began to lift his leg onto it. Was that it? Wasn't Augustus going to prove he'd be okay? Wasn't there supposed to be some enlightened ending where Coda had one last quip? He was just a character in a story after all.

"Is that it?" Coda said aloud, his thought betraying him.

Augustus stopped and looked over at him. "What else were you expecting?"

"Something more uplifting. One final piece of advice to have all this tied up nicely."

"Coda, you read too many books. Sometimes conversations have an abrupt en—"

thirty-nine

CAR CHAT IV
Missouri-Oklahoma border

"Is there anything left to talk about?"
　A slight pause. "Well, yeah. We haven't covered *every* topic yet."
"Have we discussed what type of naps we like to take?"
"Yes."
"What about candles? Are you a fan of candles?"
"We discussed that back in . . . Ohio."
"We never drove through Ohio."
"Then it was Pennsylvania. Or somewhere. Does it matter?"
"Well, yeah."
"You're relentless?"
"Have we talked about history?"
"Aspects of it."
"Remind me."
"You had a lengthy rant about the Dark Ages."
"Oh yeah. Good times. What was your favorite subject in school?"
"Calligraphy."
"Calligraphy?"
"Calligraphy."
"Those private schools sure do value different things than inner city public schools."
　"For what it's worth, I was the worst in my class."
"Tell me more. I love to hear about your failures."
"Were you popular in school?"
"Answered already. Sort of. Seeing as I was a delinquent of the law and had to change schools, I was never able to make a big splash when I transferred. Which was fine with me. I enjoyed the obscurity."
　"Did we talk about your ideal kitchen?"
"Oh, you're asking the questions now? And no, we have not talked about that because what kind of savage has their ideal kitchen sorted out in their mind?"
　"Me."
"Of course. Fine, I'll allow it."

"I've always been shocked at how many *things* people have in kitchens. Ten bowls. Fifteen spoons. Three mixers. Eight muffin pans. On and on and on. My ideal kitchen would consist of two bowls, three sets of utensils, several knives of various sizes, a toaster, and no more than three pots and pans. My spice cabinet wouldn't have anything older than six months. I'd have a modest supply of napkins to entertain guests, but when I was alone, I'd use a dish rag tucked into my shirt to avoid spills."

"Uh... hmm... This information concerns me."

"Why?"

"It's unnatural for a human not to hoard. What happens when we have another pandemic? You couldn't get condoms for three months!"

"Condoms? Is that considered a kitchen item for you?"

"I was being facetious."

"Ah, yes. Fa-ce-tious. That word everyone manages to use correctly without knowing its meaning or how to spell it."

"V. A..."

"It starts with F."

"Oh."

"Have we ever considered how weird cars are?"

"Yes. Back in Indiana."

"What was our conclusion?"

"That cars would be a lot cooler if they were invisible. Then it would look like people were possessed and floating a few feet above the ground."

"A dull conclusion."

"Yeah, that's what you said."

"Have we talked about death?"

"Yup. But the idea of it made both of us sad, so we made a pact not to talk about it for an undefined length of time. You have seemingly forgot that."

"Did we ever have our debate about sausage versus bacon?"

"An hour ago."

"Shit, I am losing it."

"Should we just sit in silence until we get find a place to stop for the night?"

"Silence as in, you want to turn off the music?"

"I wouldn't be opposed."

A loud scoff. "Ah!"

"I haven't said anything, but the playlists have been mediocre at best. Like first-person-eliminated-from-a-singing-competition type of music. It's been passable, but we can do better."

Another scoff. "You've been controlling the music this whole time. Change it if you aren't satisfied."

"The pressure. It's just too much. There are so many factors to consider."

"Like what?"

"The weather, the mood inside the car . . . and . . . and . . . there's more but now you've pressured me!"

"You're overthinking."

"Obviously. If you knew half the shit I thought about, you'd be convinced I could fill up half a book."

"My thoughts could fill up the other half."

"Imagine if someone wrote a book about this trip."

"It would be a waste of time."

"Absolutely not! We have met fascinating people on this trip."

"I think it has just been people with some deep-rooted traumas."

"You say that like we don't belong in the same category."

"That's not my argument."

"What is it then?"

"A book about this trip would be silly because we've seen a slice of sadness from almost every person we have met. Everyone has had a propensity to divulge their secrets to us. Look at Dietrich or Muscle or that weird fuck back in Georgia. I mean, Augustus told you about breaking his own leg! Do we come off as trustworthy or something?"

"Wouldn't you be more inclined to burden a stranger with your feelings rather than someone you see every day?"

"I . . . don't know."

"Everybody has pain. We aren't special for hearing about it, just like they aren't fucked up for telling us."

"I guess so. Aren't you tired of it though?"

"No. It would feel hypocritical if I was. I'm telling people about my mother, so who would I be to pass judgement onto them?"

"You always have a sensible answer, huh?"

"Hardly."

"I have one more question until we end this chapter and lapse into our silence unless you get the courage to find good music for yourself."

"Ask away, Ms. Treiber."

"Wow, that gave me that skeevy feeling. From you, it sounds like I'm being reprimanded by the principal."

"A fantasy of yours, I'm sure."

"Oh yeah. You caught me."

"What's your question?"

"Do you think endings are important? You've read your share of books and have likely seen plenty of duds and some remarkable ones."

"I may not be qualified to answer since I read the ending first, but no, endings aren't important. You can tell when an author has stressed over leaving the reader with some meaningful words, but I'm not inclined to remember them even twenty seconds later. Books aren't your favorite song on repeat where you memorize every word or a movie that people have deemed as quotable. When's the last time someone has cited a direct quote from a book to you?"

"Never."

"Exactly, because reading is a solitary activity. And with the average novel being a hundred thousand words, who is going to remember anything more than the title and a few characters? And yes, before you contradict me, there are exceptions to the rule. As with anything. To me, it's all about the emotion you feel when you put down the book for the last time. Sometimes the ending shifts the mood, but that's rare for me."

"What do you want your ending to be?"

"If I'm selfish, I'd want it to be sudden. No time to contemplate and consider the regrets. I'm not concerned about leaving a legacy or anything like that. I fully intend to be forgotten when I die."

"I thought we weren't supposed to talk about death."

"You asked me the question! What about you?"

"Surrounded by family. I'm okay with death taking its time. I feel like I'd achieve some level of enlightenment I could impart on others."

"Wishful thinking. I guess I've seen death both ways with each of my parents. Neither has been enjoyable."

"What's the best ending you've ever read?"

"I only agreed to one more question two questions ago."

"Fine. I'll save it for another time."

"Just like all the ones I still have for you. I can still sense the trauma in you that I need to expose."

"We have learned some interesting things about each other to say the least."

"You're more complex than I ever realized, Nolan. I'm sorry for not seeing it sooner."

"It's okay."

"Are you ready to end this chapter?"

Silence.

forty

THE SCRIPT

"Why are we stopping here?" Coda asked, looking out at the empty lot.

"Don't you feel the draw of this place?" Nolan said in an admiring tone. "Just look. It's the epitome of human greed and needless consumption. Tears of joy and pain are dried into the floor of that building every single day. And aren't you the least bit curious to see the sort of crowd in there on a Monday morning?"

"Not particularly."

"Aw, Coda. I'm not used to such negativity from you. Cheer up, buckaroo!"

"Are you okay?"

"Perfectly sane," she said. Nolan put the car in park and gathered her things. "I can crack the window to give you some air if you don't come inside."

"Don't be ridiculous." Coda grabbed his phone and wallet. "Are you planning on partaking in any activities?"

"No need to be coy. I don't intend to gamble."

"Then what's the point?"

"Because you're going to play blackjack."

"No thanks."

"C'mon. Let's just see how it goes."

Nolan exited the car and looked up at the sign. **CHOCTAW CASINO & RESORT** beamed back at her with rotating videos of all the fun they could have.

Walking up behind her, Coda asked, "Choctaw? I've never heard that word before."

"It's a Native American tribe. You know, like Cherokee, Seminole, or Iroquois. All those groups that have been terrorized and decimated by the government for hundreds of years. A large portion of Oklahoma is rightfully theirs. Not that they'd ever get it back. Finders keepers isn't seen as a viable claim to land except when the government does it."

"I didn't realize you had an interest in this."

"I'm no expert, but I try to keep myself informed, especially since they didn't teach it in the snobby private school. That would have damaged everyone's delicate ego to consider how destructive and intolerant people can be."

Coda stopped and waited for Nolan to turn around. "Are you sure everything is alright? You seem agitated."

"I'm anxious. No idea why."

"Well, I'm here to listen if you need anything."

"I appreciate that."

"Also, there's something that has been weighing on me."

"Yeah . . ." Nolan said, coaxing him to explain.

"This whole trip has been about me and the random people to find."

"Yeah . . ."

"Are there any friends or family you want to go see?" he asked.

"Coda, I don't have anybody. I wasn't a social butterfly like you. All those parties from my childhood and teenage years showed me how much I didn't care for idle chit chat. Everybody has a motive, especially when they find out who I am."

"I'm sure you're just generalizing . . ."

"No. Really. There isn't anyone outside of New York. And if there were, this isn't the time for me to go reconnect with them. I'm here for you."

"But—"

"I know what you're going to say, but you don't have to. Maybe we will go on another trip and that one can be all about Nolan Treiber."

"I'd like that."

"Just to be clear," she said, grabbing onto his arm, "I have told you an incredible amount this trip and I hope it's brought us closer."

"It has."

"Good," Nolan said with a smile. She let go of his arm.

"Have you thought more about California?"

"Yes, but I'm still conflicted."

"I understand."

They resumed their walk through the parking lot and to the massive revolving door granting them entrance into the casino. The inside was what you'd expect: gaudy and lavish yet an odor of cheapness was overpowering if you knew where to look. The half dead plants tucked in the corner of each massive room; the unenthused employees who forced a smile with every new customer that stepped up to the concierge desk; the tacky carpet that served to absorb drunken spills and other bodily fluids. But no one came to a casino for its furnishings, right?

Nolan and Coda moved past the small line of people and toward the sign declaring the blackjack tables were ahead.

The crowd inside was nonexistent. As expected, only the most dedicated were occupying the slots and tables. Coda watched as mindless slabs of bone stared into the void, swiping cards and pulling levers with no reaction as the slot machine signaled a win or loss. They were slaves to hope that the next lever pull would lead to the big payoff. They heard from a friend of a friend of a friend that some person struck it big on that exact machine after dumping only twenty-five dollars!

Too many are content with burning through what little money they have at the casino, the local bookie, or with lottery tickets. It's as idiotic as giving money to a charitable organization through a billion-dollar company that has the gall to ask customers to contribute when they are squirreling away millions outside the country.

Hope was the nasty bastard child of common sense and human stupidity. People hoped the next lever pull would be *the one* to set off the cacophony of sirens and squealing noises to signify victory. People hoped the gambler's fallacy was a myth and that the roulette wheel *couldn't possibly* land on black for the third spin in a row. People hoped the two dollars added to their bill at the grocery store to some charity they hadn't heard of — but the pictures of crying children and starving animals sure made them feel sad — would put them in good graces with whatever higher power they believed in.

Hope tended to be misplaced and misguided.

Nolan hoped she wouldn't suffer from panic attacks for the rest of her life or that she'd find her biological parents within a weekend of searching.

Coda hoped he hadn't made a massive mistake by quitting JEC and not having a fallback plan. He hoped his mother had forgiven him.

"Let's get you some chips," Nolan said. Before Coda could protest, she was at the window and passing over a hundred-dollar bill to the unenthused woman behind the glass.

"Nolan, what are you doing?"

"Getting you chips."

"I can see that. But why so much?"

The woman pushed back a small, colorful grouping through the slot.

"Thank you," Nolan said to the unenthused employee. She turned to Coda. "I hate to be crass about this, but a hundred dollars to the Treiber family is even less than finding a penny on the ground. I'm a product of my environment, I suppose. I hope you don't think less of me because I try not to flaunt money around."

There's that silly word again.

"I get it. Have you thought what your life would be like without the Treiber name and the supply of money?"

"Peaceful. It would be peaceful . . . What table looks good to you?" Nolan asked, handing over the chips to Coda.

"You didn't ask if I knew how to play blackjack."

"Everyone is familiar with blackjack. Don't be thick."

Coda scoffed at the remark. "That table over there," he said, pointing off into the distance.

"The one with the woman hunched over?"

"That's the one."

"Any particular reason?"

"Nope."

"Good enough for me. Let's go."

Nolan led the way as they wove around the unoccupied tables with unenthused employees standing by in robotic stances. Every section came equipped with a pit boss that looked equally unenthused as they scanned the room for any ne'er do-wells.

As they approached the desired table, the dealer forced a smile. "Welcome. Looking to play?"

"Yes," Coda said.

"About time," the hunched over woman croaked. Her voice was scratchy and dense from years of smoking as evidenced by the pack of cigarettes she clutched onto like they were a lucky charm. "Sit next to me," she said, patting the cushion on the table's edge.

Coda obliged and spread out his chips in front of him.

"Always such a small amount," the woman commented.

"Sir, ready when you are. Place your bet please."

Coda laid out two chips.

"I'd go with the minimum bet, doll. You never win the first hand," the woman advised.

He pulled back one of the chips. Coda felt an intense urge to listen to the woman. She seemed to be a regular, one of the hopeful lot that believed the outcome would change.

Nolan hovered behind him, pressed up onto her tip toes to see over his shoulder. Nolan likely knew more than Coda about blackjack as it was a staple of the outlandish social gatherings she was forced to as a child, but she reserved making any comments.

The dealer closed the bets and handed out the first round of cards. The woman was given an eight, Coda an ace, and the dealer a six.

"Maybe I was wrong, but — no, that can't be," the woman muttered to herself.

Quickly, the next round of cards appeared. The woman was given another eight, Coda a nine, and the dealer kept her second card face down.

"I already know what's coming next," the woman said with confidence. "Hit." The dealer flipped over another card. A five. Blackjack. "Told you."

Coda swiped his hand sideways, signaling that he would stay at twenty.

The dealer flipped over her second card and revealed a nine. She was up to fifteen and reached for another card. A six. Blackjack.

"Tough luck kid, but that's why you should always listen to me," the woman said as the hand was wiped away from the table and Coda's lost chip along with it.

"Thank you for the advice," Coda said.

"The way I see it, you won't be thanking me in another ten minutes."

"Oh yeah? Why is that?"

"Because you're going to be terrified of me, Coda," the woman said.

"How do you know my name?" he asked with slight concern. Coda looked back at Nolan, but she seemed unfazed by the weird comment.

"I'll answer that after this next hand. Put down three chips for this one. Time to build up an empire before it crumbles."

Coda obliged yet again. The hand played out as follows: The woman stayed at eighteen, Coda stayed at seventeen, and the dealer busted with twenty-four.

"How'd you know my name?" he asked.

"I heard you gabbing with your friend on your way over," the woman said.

It felt like a lie, but Coda had no evidence to argue except he didn't recall Nolan using his name since the parking lot.

"Here's the part where you ask what my name is," the woman continued.

"What's your name?"

"Billie Pilgrim."

"Like the character from—"

"Exactly. That comment never gets old from you," Billie said. She gripped her drink and downed half of it. "Five years from now, I quit smoking and drinking. Hard to believe, but it's for the best. I like the moments when I get to indulge."

"How could you know that?"

"I forgot about all your inane questions. But there is a script to follow. Always a script. Can't deviate from the script too much. They wouldn't l-l-like th-tha-that," she struggled to get out. Her body twitched as she gripped the cigarettes tighter. "G-g-go-godda—" Billie gave up trying.

The game of blackjack continued on in the background, but Coda's focus was drawn to the conversation with Billie. She stopped giving him advice and, sure enough, his small empire began to crumble.

"Don't worry about it, kid. It was always in the cards," she commented after his second losing hand. "And you, Nolan, it's about time you joined us. Sit, sit. I'm sure our lovely dealer wouldn't mind. Isn't that right, darling?"

"Please sit," the unenthused dealer said.

Nolan obliged. "How do you know my name?"

"I've always known."

"Uhh . . ."

Billie turned to Coda. "I'm sorry."

"For what?"

"You know, kid. You know." Billie rested a hand on Coda's forearm. The touch felt motherly.

"How c-could yo—" he tried to say.

"You two keep asking how, but you don't want to know the answer."

"I want to know," Coda said.

"Good. We are still reading from the same script then. Let's play this last hand. And Coda, just go all-in. Nolan won't mind that you lost her hundred dollars."

"I won't mind," Nolan echoed.

Coda pushed all of his chips out onto the table. The last hand was quick. The dealer hit blackjack with her initial two cards. She took control of his chips and added them to her supply without saying a word.

"See? Better not to drag it out," Billie said. She tucked the cigarettes into her pocket and left the empty glass behind. "Walk with me."

They obliged. Did they even have a choice? He hoped they did, but that was a foolish thought.

Billie led them past the blackjack tables and turned back right after Nolan walked into a chair. She was busy checking the time on her phone.

"I would have warned you, but I can't interfere too much. The script," Billie said.

"What is this script you are talking about?" Nolan said.

"Thank you for finally asking." Billie kept walking until she made it to a microphone stand beyond all the tables. "I've seen my birth and death a thousand times already. I'm unstuck. We've had this conversation plenty of times."

Coda took a step back from her.

"What did I tell you about being terrified of me?"

"Why are you doing this to us?"

"It's not about doing anything to you or Nolan. This just is. This is how it's always been. This is how it will always be. What's the phrase you like to use? This is *a perfect circle*."

"Stop it," Coda begged.

Nolan stepped closer, fascinated by the development. "Tell me. What else do you know?"

"I have all the answers, but I can't give you them. The script, my dear. The script."

"What can you tell me?"

"That your story is just as important. And now isn't the time."

"The time for what?"

"The—" Billie stalled and grabbed onto the microphone stand until the twitching subsided. "I can't say. You already know. You both know more than you realize."

"What's next?"

"I can't say, but it'll unfold the same way."

Nolan nodded. She turned to Coda. "What's wrong?"

"She knows. She knows what happened. How could she know?" he rambled. Nolan had never seen him so unhinged.

"It's okay Coda."

"How could it be?"

"Coda," Billie said, "you still h-ha-have . . . s-shit. Listen to Nolan," she managed to say.

He felt delirious. None of this made sense. His life didn't have strange — almost unreal — encounters like this.

Billie grabbed the microphone and tapped it three times, each echo through the speakers louder than the one before. "Is this thing on?" she said into the microphone, already knowing the answer. But the script was the script, regardless if she thought it was silly or not.

None of the other gamblers responded to her question.

"Hit it," Billie said to no one.

Over the speaker system, a single piano note rang out three times. The beginning was strikingly familiar to Coda, but he couldn't place it.

"When there's nowhere else to run / Is there room for one more son," she sang. Her voice was raspy and beautiful like she belonged back in the big band era of music.

Coda stepped back further from her and looked around the room. The employees were unenthused, and the gamblers were absorbed too much in their own lives to pay attention. If she wasn't performing for an audience, what was the point?

Billie continued singing as the background track guided her. She stepped forward and gained confidence with each line of the song.

This is how it must be in the script, Coda thought.

No, that is ridiculous. There isn't a script. It's insane. All of it.

"Nolan, what is going on?" Coda asked her, hoping for a sane reply.

She turned to him with tears in her eyes. "It's The Killers, Coda. Don't you know this band? This song came out when we were toddlers. I remember . . . I remember listening to this at one of the foster homes. I never knew the meaning of the lyrics, but that didn't matter." She spoke loud enough to be heard over the booming voice.

"Yeah-h-h-h-h-h, you know you got to help me out / Yeah-h-h-h-h-h, oh don't you put me on the backburner-er-er-er . . ." Billie continued.

"What does it mean?" Coda asked.

Nolan grabbed his face with softness. "Coda, why do you always need an answer? You don't need as many as you think."

She stepped away from him and slowly walked up to the microphone next to Billie. The background track continued its momentous roar through each verse and chorus. Coda watched in awe.

After the second chorus, the song moved into a brief bridge as Nolan leaned into the microphone and readied herself.

When the bridge broke, Billie and Nolan both sang.

"I got soul, but I'm not a soldier."
"I got soul, but I'm not a soldier."
"I got soul, but I'm not a soldier."
"I got soul, but I'm not a soldier."

They repeated the line six more times as the intensity increased until the final crescendo. Billie belted out the final *soldier* and expanded it for several seconds.

Coda felt the chills climb up and back down his spine. The sensation disappeared as suddenly as it appeared. He looked down at his feet and watched himself sway like he was being pushed by a strong breeze. He steadied himself and clenched his teeth hard to gain control of his body again. He didn't understand what the line meant or why it had the impact on him.

The song continued as it winded down to a quiet end. Billie bowed to no applause or acknowledgement from the nonexistent crowd.

"And give it up for Nolan Treiber who came in for the assist. Totally off script, so I'm surprised they allowed it," Billie said into the microphone before placing it back onto the stand.

"Are you okay?" Coda asked Nolan as she walked back over.

"Of course. I'm ready for our next stop. What about you?"

"Yes." It was all he could summon to say.

"You two need to get going," Billie noted.

"We were just about to leave," Nolan said with a nod. "Maybe one of these times we will remember you."

"I doubt it, but you could become unstuck too."

"Do you ever want it to be over?"

Billie looked around before settling back on Nolan. "It just is."

"Any last words for us?" Nolan asked.

"Coda, I'm sorry to have frightened you earlier. The script. I w-wi-wish I could tell y-you m-m-more, but you'll get the answer you're looking for when you need it."

"What answer to what?"

"I can't say, but you're a smart kid."

Frustrated, Coda walked back toward the lobby. He wasn't ready to face the truth yet. He had done a masterful job of pushing it and pushing it and pushing it, but the cliff was fast approaching.

Nolan and Billie spoke for a bit longer, but none of it was consequential. Sometimes dialogue in the script didn't have much of a purpose. Nolan wanted to give Billie Pilgrim a hug, but she didn't think it would be allowed, so she opted for a wave as Billie walked back into the bowels of the casino. Nolan watched as she walked, walked, walked and eventually disappeared around the corner.

Nolan found Coda loitering near the entrance.

"What the *fuck* just happened?" he asked, still reeling over everything.

She looked up at him with a wide smile. "I hope we find out someday."

<u>forty-one</u>

IN AND OUT

Tucked within a misshapen circle of highways — so dreadfully common in the Dallas-Fort Worth metroplex — was the city of Denton, or more specifically, the University of North Texas.

Do you have a spare moment to talk about Denton?

The city exists merely because of the colleges that have broken ground there. Just as Coda felt he'd seen the majority of foliage America offered by riding up and down, east and west, zig and zag, and zag and zig across the depressing highways, it became clear that Denton, Texas was the embodiment of middle America. As they drove in south from Oklahoma, he observed the poorly maintained roads, failing small businesses with signs tempting customers, abandoned buildings, dozens of in-progress construction jobs that would generate more mediocrity, limited people traversing the decayed sidewalks, signs declaring the age and history of the city in a place where people didn't give a damn, and faded graffiti from a time when citizens cared enough to deface their place of residence. The neighborhoods were a glamorous collage of boarded up houses, unkept lawns, rusted vehicles, and other oddities. Was it that the owners didn't have pride in their property or they didn't have the means to maintain it? The answer was likely a beef stew of different ingredients.

On the contrary to the city falling into disarray was the University of North Texas, or UNT, as it will be referred to for the remainder of its relevance. Each building looked like they just pulled off the bubble wrap and cut the ribbon. The sea of beige brick was visible for blocks with the modern glass faces that were inefficient to heat and cool, but damn, they sure look snazzy! Here, Coda saw students gliding from one class to the next, one building to the next. Some were in small pods, while others elected for solo journeys. They looked like Gerber babies compared to how he felt during college. Youth was always wasted on the young, as the saying went.

"Coda, did you check the address before this? I don't think it's taking us to a building."

Nolan was right. Snoogle Maps had a pin stuck in a large swatch of green and was adamant it was the address given. Coda pulled out the list and scanned down to the first entry that didn't have a checkmark next to it. "I put in the address Sam gave me."

Nolan jerked the wheel and pulled into a spot blocking an alleyway. "Let me see that."

Coda hesitated.

"Are you scared or something?"

"No." He handed it over.

"'Coda and Nolan's Cross-Country Car Chase,'" she read aloud and failed at containing her laughter.

"Don't judge me! I was trying to come up with an alliteration," Coda pleaded.

"It's cute because it makes no sense. Thanks for including my name."

Coda nodded.

Nolan glanced between the phone and Coda's list. She handed it back to him after confirming what he said. "Do you think this was sabotage?"

"Sabotage?"

"Yes. Maybe Sam is making us work hard for this one."

"I doubt it."

"You said that this next target—"

"She isn't a target. Merely an individual caught up in our cross-country car chase."

"Okay fine. You said this *individual* was a professor back at TCSUM?"

"Correct."

"That's a good start at least. It's logical to assume she now works here."

A car horn blared from beyond the passenger window, demanding Nolan stop blocking the alleyway.

"Alright, alright!" Nolan yelled. "Let's find an actual spot and then start asking around."

It took ten minutes of circling the same three blocks before Nolan eased the 2008 Pinto Pinata into a vacant spot. The street parking was free, which was a pleasant surprise — not that it mattered either way for the car.

"Where do we start?" Coda questioned.

"Let's confirm the location where Sam was attempting to direct us."

"It's three blocks up that way," Coda said, pointing past more pristine buildings and crappy student housing.

Nolan led the way. Their destination was the football stadium. The seating capacity was limited, but it was a turf field, so that probably jacked up tuition for a few years.

"Oh Sam. You have failed us," Nolan called out as she latched onto the iron bars and shook them like an inmate in the prison yard.

"A slight setback. He hasn't led us wrong so far."

"Sam, Sam, Sam," she continued to mutter under her breath. "I have an idea." She straightened up and turned toward Coda. "We just need to find the building she teaches in and then ask around. We get to be the private investigators this leg of the trip."

"Simple enough."

Nolan waited for Coda to supply the answer, but it never happened. "Okay, so, I'm guessing she was one of your computer science professors?"

"No," he said.

"No?"

"Yes, no."

"Yes?"

"No."

"No?"

"Yes."

"What are you telling me?" Nolan said.

"Professor Leek was not one of my computer science teachers."

"Why didn't you just say that?"

"I did."

"For Chri — never mind. What class did she teach then?"

Coda hesitated. "Dance."

"Dance?! Coda Finn, you are full of surprises! Tell me, what do you know?"

"I barely made it through the salsa."

"You should have said something. I know all sorts of dances and could have assisted in your success."

"I didn't want to get made fun of for it."

"Nonsense. A lot of people dance. Nothing wrong with that."

Coda backed away from the stadium and started toward the main bulk of buildings. He wasn't sure exactly where Professor Leek would be, but they had to move in some direction.

Their travels wove them around the campus two times before Nolan took off her passive hat and asked students for help. Each one shrunk the search perimeter until the fourth student provided exact instructions.

The Arts school was the beige building past the other beige buildings. Listen:

The rest of the events that transpired at UNT were a strong meh, so let's burn through this hide and seek part quickly. Upon finding the appropriate beige building, Coda and Nolan consulted the board by the entrance that conveniently had the names and locations of all the professors. Their targ — no, individual — had an office on the third floor. What luck! Up, up, up the stairs. No one questioned why two old, misshapen people were wandering the halls of the Arts building, but that goes to show how much people don't pay attention to others. They reached the office. It was locked. Rats, darn, aw shucks. Nolan paced up, up, up and down, down, down the hallway until she found a door that was open. She inquired about Professor Leek. Professor Leek was teaching a class downstairs. Down, down, down the stairs they went and found the classroom. Coda peeked at Professor Leek through the glass and confirmed she was who they sought.

Determined not to be rude, Coda waited until Professor Leek's class was over before barging in. During the interim, Nolan spouted off theories and accusations as to why Sam Rogers gave the address he did. Coda had no guesses and found it difficult to refute her final claim that Sam was trying to pad their story. She believed he thought with only seven addresses on Coda's list they wouldn't have enough wild, crazy encounters to come back to New York with. So, in an effort to be more impactful, he purposely withheld information like Parkland Locke being dead or diverting their destination from Professor Leek's home address or the Arts building to something inconvenient like the football stadium. Coda wasn't buying it, but he appreciated when Nolan became unnecessarily passionate.

(What Sam Rogers couldn't possibly know was the script for the trip was written outside the confines of how humans perceive time. His feeble attempt to add more drama was pointless. The story would play out as it always has because you can't deviate from the script, which is even harder to do when you don't recognize you're following one. For those debating this is a hokey or convenient plot point to stuff this late into the book, that thought is a part of the script. Consider that!)

Coda was still thinking about earlier.

"Nolan, about the casino . . ."

"I've forgotten about that already."

"It's just that Billie knew so much."

"Did she though? All she said was she was sorry."

"Well, how did she know about the song and that it would be so impactful to you?"

"Coincidence."

"That seriously can't be your answer."

"Why not? Coda, we have seen some weird stuff on this trip. That weird guy at the motel or the mayor in Cave City or . . . or . . . I feel like we have had this conversation already."

"Everything appears to be on repeat."

"Lucky us. But since you mention it, what did she apologize for?"

"I can't say."

"That's fucked. You can't leave me hanging like that."

"I'm sorry."

"Fantastic. Now the apology train is stopping at your station too," Nolan said, dismissing his comment with a wave of her hand. "I don't recall asking you about the book we are picking up here."

"You did, but you're asking again because I mentioned it this morning at the hotel and the rest of our conversation was rather dull, so if someone happened to be capturing the story of our journey, I doubt they would have included it," Coda said in all seriousness.

It seemed that the both of them were losing portions of their sanity.

Nolan stared at him and scrunched her face. "Ah. I see. Refresh my memory then."

"The individual is Professor Leek. She taught the dance class I took during my junior year to satisfy one of the elective credits I had. The book I leant her was *I Tried to Better Myself*. From what I remember, it was this sob story from a guy in his mid-twenties complaining about how he wanted to become a better person — go figure — but it doesn't really work out for him. I'm not sure what my mom saw in that book," Coda said, shaking his head and ending with a shrug. "I can't ask her now."

"We still have time."

He hesitated and squeaked out one word. "Right."

"Why'd you give your professor the book?"

"She wanted to get better and I thought reading about a failure might stop her from becoming one."

"Wow, harsh," Nolan said.

Eventually the classroom door opened, and waves of students pushed out, hellbent on being somewhere else.

"Professor Leek?" Coda questioned as he stepped inside the classroom.

"Yes," she said, looking up from the floor. She was peeling off tape.

"I'm . . ." Coda lapsed into his usual story.

After he informed Professor Leek about all she needed to know, she led Nolan and Coda up, up, up to the third floor. She unlocked her office and signaled that she'd be a moment. Approximately twenty-seven moments later, she reemerged from the office with a book tucked under her arm.

"Is this the one?" Professor Leek asked.

"Yeah."

She passed it over to Coda. He flipped to the back and saw the symbol. For some reason, he always checked the back first when it was really the message (if present) from G.F. he was more interested in. With that in mind, he opened the front cover and read his mom's writing.

He decided not to share this one.

The script allowed it.

"Is there anything else you need?" the professor said.

"No. This is what we came for."

"Consider calling next time. I could have saved you the trip."

"Everyone keeps telling us that. Thanks again," Coda said.

Down, down, down they went to the first floor and made for the exit.

"Is that really it?" Nolan asked. She froze near the doors.

Coda turned and said, "Yeah. What's the problem?"

"It's always been more challenging than that. The professor just happened to have the book in her office when you gave it to her over five years ago?"

"Seems like it."

"Are you sure we don't need to run around the city and partake in a scavenger hunt or something?"

"Unlikely."

"Aren't we supposed to learn more about her?"

"Didn't look like she had time to chat."
"This feels wrong . . . It was too easy."
"You're overthinking this."
"Am I? No, no. This is the perfect level of thinking."
"Ehh."
"I have one more question then."
"I'm listening," Coda said.
"What the heck do we do now?"

forty-two

ONE MORE FOR THE ROAD

Nolan's question was a valid one. If history was worth considering, each leg of their trip so far had yielded a more interesting result than what Professor Leek provided. Sometimes it was a story shared, other times it was the actions they partook in. Either way, it was better than the boring endeavor they just wrapped up.

Coda suggested food as to what the heck they should do next.

Nolan agreed.

They walked back to the 2008 Pinto Pinata through the beige campus and past the antisocial students who were wearing headphones to avoid interactions. Coda noticed several had VR headsets on, which didn't seem practical.

"How far away are we from Dallas?" Nolan asked as they reached the car.

"I never checked. Why? Are you interested in going there?"

"Is Dallas a city people are ever itching to go to? No, I doubt it. I was only curious."

Coda had his phone out and consulted Snoogle Maps. "Half hour, give or take."

"We could find a restaurant there," Nolan suggested.

"Look — I'm getting the impression you want to drum up some excitement after our interaction with Professor Leek. Don't feel like you have to. Denton will suffice for dinner and the evening. We can get an early start tomorrow for Colorado."

Somewhat dejected, Nolan said, "If you say so. I just didn't expect for the script to be so *boring*."[20]

"Nolan, there is no script! That woman had a psychotic break or there were fumes leaking out of the vents. A logical explanation is jammed

---

[20] If there was any concern that something noteworthy was awaiting in an unplanned trip to Dallas, don't fret. Dallas was the equivalent to Kentucky in that they both served no purpose. Some may be bothered by the city and state bashing that's happening within the margins. To that end, here is a retort to the boohooing: Sticks and stones can break bones, but words can break egos, so use them to your advantage. Just some friendly advice.

within that bizarre experience."

"Let me know when you find it . . . You never will though," she said the last part under her breath. "Find us a place to eat, will ya?"

"On it." Coda scrolled and tapped through his phone until he returned with three suggestions to Nolan. "This is, uh, unusual, but after today I shouldn't be surprised."

"What do you mean?"

"The three highest rated places in Denton are as follows: Diner, Diner Diner, and Diner Diner Diner."

"Diner?"

"Yes."

"And Diner Diner?"

"Yes."

"And Diner Diner Diner?"

"Yes Nolan. Are you suffering from echolalia or something?"

"Echol—what?"

"It's where you repeat what someone else says."

"Huh, never heard of it before."

"Back to our original goal. None of the places are copycats of each other and they have an identical rating on Snoogle. So what sounds good to you?"

"Diner Diner," Nolan said without hesitation.

"Why?"

"Pretty simple, really, but it's based on a long, wild set of assumptions. My guess is that Diner came first. Why else would you add an excess of words to your restaurant name unless you had to? If that logic prevails, then Diner Diner came next. If I was to copy a restaurant name and then double it, I'd be dang sure to improve upon what Diner had done. As for Diner Diner Diner, they are trying to cash in on the success of Diner and Diner Diner, so my gut tells me their food is probably okay at best and their ambiance is a cheap rip off of the others. So, to recap, since you are looking at me funny: Diner is the OG; Diner Diner is the gold medalist; Diner Diner Diner is the mimic."

"I . . ."

"It's okay. Just find the address to Diner Diner and I'll do the work."

Coda selected it and attached his phone to the dashboard. The drive was uneventful through shoddy streets, lackluster houses, and ghostly citizens. No different than any other place they've stopped at, to be honest.

"Do you think it's a diner?" Coda asked as Nolan pulled in an empty spot.

"If it wasn't, that would be quite the bamboozlement."

The sign above the door flashed DINER before switching to the other word, which was also DINER. Imagine that.

Inside, the restaurant was half full with mostly single parties occupying booths and reading newspapers or watching the Rangers spring training game on the television.

"Table for two, please," Nolan said to the hostess, who grabbed two menus and led the way to a booth in the corner. Nolan slid into one side while Coda took the other.

"Enjoy," the hostess said and sauntered back to her post.

Nolan looked at the menu cover before flipping it over. Coda watched as she read intently for half a minute before she picked her head up. "I don't believe it."

"What?"

"Diner Diner is the original!"

"Wow." Interpret his surprise however you'd like.

"So here's the lowdown—" Nolan said, clearing her throat.

"You really don't have to read it aloud. I can see for myself," Coda noted.

"Nonsense. My voice is golden, as witnessed at the casino."

"Another hidden talent of yours. Go on," he said, waving her on to continue.

"'It all started in the year nineteen hundred and sixty-eight with a woman and a dream. Marmalade 'Marmar' Waverly cooked three meals a day for her family of seven. On holidays, she'd whip up her classics for the extended family to great success. Marmar was always prodded about starting her own restaurant, but never felt she had the business savvy or time to devote herself. When her five kids were grown and out the house, Marmar decided it was time to take a chance! She refinanced the mortgage on the family home and tossed all the savings into what is now known as Diner Diner! It only took Diner Diner ten years to make a profit and it nearly drove Marmar to suicide! Talk about a success story! Why Diner Diner you ask? Because the food's so good, you'll be saying the name twice on your way home! In the late nineties, Marmar passed down the business to her son, Julio, who has kept the restaurant alive and chugging through all the ups and downs the city of Denton has gone through. As for our competitors, imitation is the highest form of flattery and we guarantee our menu slaps compared to those phonies across town.'"

By the end of the history lesson, Coda had his hand pressed against his forehead. "Nolan. Never in my life did I expect to hear so much about a *fucking* diner. Please, it must end."

"This has been the most engaging part of Texas so far. I intend to explore it until things turn rotten."

"We've traveled past that point."

"And yet, you are still talking about it," she said with a grin.

"I . . . I am. You're right. No more from me."

The waitress appeared at the table. "Hi, I'm Frankie and I'll be taking care of you today," she stopped writing on the pad and looked up. "Are . . . are you students at UNT?" she said, stumbling through the words.

"Uh, no. Just passing through. Why?" Coda asked.

Frankie nodded. "That makes sense. No one under the age of fifty comes in here."

"Why not?" Coda looked beyond Nolan's head and finally noticed that everyone was balding or graying.

"I'm sensing some more hot gossip," Nolan said, flashing a smile.

"Diner Diner has been around for so long and is kind of dingy," the waitress said, lowering her voice. "Diner was created for the tourists because you'd probably think it was the original if you didn't know any better. We get a lot of people traveling up to Oklahoma or dropping their kids off at school. Diner Diner Diner was created sometime after the others and became the drunken stop after a night of partying for the college students. So, usually, the younger crowd is always there."

"Fascinating. Absolutely fascinating," Nolan said. "And completely plausible."

"Are you—" Frankie began.

"Being completely serious? Yes, I am."

Frankie shook her head quickly to cleanse the topic. "Can I get you anything to drink?"

They ordered their drinks and Frankie promised to be back for their food order in a jiffy. Nolan and Coda dove into the menu and combed through the numerous pages, their conversation stalling until Frankie returned.

"Two waters and a coffee for you," she said, sliding the drink over to Nolan. "Did you decide on food?"

They had.

Frankie wrote everything down and stepped away from the table but was quick to return. "So, just passing through? From where?" She slid into the booth next to Nolan. "I hope you don't mind."

"All are welcome," Nolan said.

"It's a long story," Coda said, utilizing Augustus's disclaimer before he dove into his confession.

"I have one other table that's already chowing down, so I got time. And, anyways, whenever someone says they have a long story, it is an excuse for not wanting to explain."

"You're right. I've grown tired of telling everyone what we're doing."

"Is it illegal?" Frankie asked, leaning closely to Coda.

"Afraid not. We are driving across the . . ." He spoke and revealed what we already know. Frankie's interest wavered throughout the shaggy-dog story, but she perked up at the mention of their last stop.

"San Francisco?" she repeated.

"Looks like it. We are winging it to a certain extent, but we've had good luck so far," Coda said, looking at Nolan.

"Yeah, Coda's fabled list has not steered us wrong," Nolan said.

Frankie drummed the table, thinking, thinking, thinking. "My boyfriend lives out in that area. Small world."

"Oh really? Get to see him often?"

"I wish. Neither of us have the money to fly . . . Let me check on your food," Frankie said, darting out of the booth.

"You know what's going to happen, right?" Coda questioned.

"I don't catch your drift," Nolan said.

"She's gonna ask to hitch a ride to San Francisco."

"No, that's silly."

"What were the odds we'd pick *this* diner and be going to the one place she wants to?"

"Are you asking me to determine the odds?" Nolan asked.

"That was rhetorical, but my point still stands. When she asks us, we need to have a united front."

"Is this the part where we argue about her turning our duo into a trio until the uplifting music plays while the villain — most likely you in this case — has a change of heart?"

"Normally, but I'm all for her joining us."

"Really?"

"Of course. It's getting close to the end of the second act. We need to shake things up a bit. Just think of our next car chat. We can get back to asking basic questions and not contemplating our entire existence or why I don't find life enjoyable," Coda said.

"Hold up. I don't remember talking about that last one."

"Maybe not, but I've certainly been thinking it."

"I—"

Frankie reappeared with a tray and an abundance of plates on top. "Here you go." She passed everything out to its proper owner.

"Looks wonderful," Nolan said. "By the way, our answer is yes."

Confused, Frankie said, "Yes to what?"

"You joining us on our drive to the West Coast."

"N-no. I can't do that. My job . . . I have rent . . . I . . ." Frankie stammered. She tucked the empty tray under her arm.

"Your choice, of course. But the option is there."

"Give me a couple minutes," Frankie said, chewing on the information as she hurried away from the table.

"A bit too blunt?" Nolan questioned.

"It fits the theme of the day. Everything has gone straight to the point."

With nothing further to discuss, they ate.

"How was everything?" Frankie asked when she returned. She was really nailing the whole waitress thing. You never realize how repetitious the job is until you transcribe what they say.

Nolan and Coda praised the food. It's not like they would have told her if it was shit.

"I thought about what you said, and I'd like to join," she said with obvious hesitation. "I don't want to be a bother or slow you two down or . . . or . . ."

"Happy to have you," Coda said. "As long as you don't mind us making a pitstop in Colorado."

"Not at all."

After a couple more exchanges, they steered toward the logistics of getting Frankie out of Denton. They exchanged numbers and told Frankie they'd decide on a time once they find a hotel for the night.

Frankie suggested the TripleTree, but Coda didn't want another Post-it note that ripped into his soul.

Later, later, later, as they stood at the register paying for the meal, the last gasps of conversation happened.

"Frankie Lao, by the way. In case you want your private detective to do some recon before tomorrow."

Coda laughed. "That won't be necessary. But get ready, we will probably pelt you with too many questions. You'll discover there isn't much else to do in the car."

"Understandable."

"Frankie, Frankie, Frankie—" a voice boomed from the back. An older man burst through the kitchen door. His apron was covered in a mix of colors and ingredients. "This is a mistake. This is a mistake," he kept repeating as he moved closer.

"Not now Julio. Please," Frankie said. She looked back at Nolan and Coda. "Sign here." She passed over the receipt.

"They don't want you. We've talked about this. There's other options," Julio said.

"Julio, please!" Frankie said in the angriest voice she could muster, which wasn't much.

Coda handed back the signed receipt and tugged on Nolan's arm to nudge her toward the exit. "We will see you tomorrow," he said with a smile to Frankie, but the words were lost in the bickering that continued after they left the diner.

"They?" Nolan asked as they got to the car.

The question went unanswered as Coda sifted through Snoogle to find a hotel and take a long shower.

He had a lot to think about.

forty-three

CAR CHAT V
East of Amarillo, Texas

"Anthropology?"

"Yeah."

"It's a word you've probably heard, but don't exactly know what it means."

"Correct," Coda said, leaning up from the backseat.

"Me too," Nolan said.

"Considering we are in the middle of nowhere West Texas and traveling at a high rate of speed, I can now bore you both with the glorious history of anthropology and you can't do anything about it," Frankie said with a mischievous laugh.

The road to Denver — wait, no, it's actually Aurora, Colorado — was a twelve-hour drive from Denton. West, west, west through Texas and then north, north, north through New Mexico and Colorado.

And Frankie was right. They were in the land of tumbleweeds and people spitting chewing tobacco from their porch into a bucket. Nolan drove down the single lane road and kept waiting for either the road to expand or traffic to show up. Neither happened.

Coda graciously gave up his passenger slot for Frankie with only one caveat: She was officially in charge of the music until she was voted out of her spot or abandoned the post. He sat in the middle seat with several bags stacked up on either side. See: The 2008 Pinto Pinata's greatest blunder was the second engine Mr. Sud placed in the trunk, effectively ruining any storage capacity. His logic was that, much like a tire, the driver could replace the engine on their own. He was a man of gargantuan stupidity who never realized a typical car engine weighs north of two-hundred pounds and a majority of drivers don't know the first thing about one. The manufacturer debated internally about telling Mr. Sud how ridiculous his request was but there was no dissuading the man.

Anyways, that's why all the luggage was piled on either side of Coda. Frankie brought more than expected for a trip to see her boyfriend, but they managed to make it fit.

"Okay, so what is anthropology? In basic terms," Coda asked.

"It's studying human beings. You may have heard of sociology, which is studying people through the lens of society, while anthropology looks at the cultural aspect of things. Well, that's the point of cultural anthropology, but there are other sectors. Things actually get confusing when you start talking about sociology and the different branches of anthropology. I barely understand it myself, so explaining it to y'all will cause a headache. You can just look it up. Tons of information out there about it, obviously. Be warned though: When you start typing anthropology in Google, the first result that comes up is the clothing store."

"That's sad and oddly dystopian."

"I know, right? It's a shame because there are some fascinating stories about individuals that really make you wonder. For example, I had a professor who was enraptured with the news story about a healthy social media influencer who posted a video about him wanting to be euthanized. My professor was convinced the culture in this country drove the guy to that mindset."

"What culture exactly? And what ended up happening to the guy?"

Frankie shrugged. "Our overwhelming desire to need more. It's not about *wanting* more because enough of us have what we need. The consumerism culture in this country instills in us to keep buying and making and expanding and evolving instead of just enjoying what there already is. Because, last time I checked, we have enough shit already.

"And I never kept up with the story. It's one of hundreds that could have been used in my classes as teaching points. The struggle with anthropology is the moving target side to it. People are constantly evolving. Their ideas, beliefs, and hatreds. It's like any science I suppose."

"What made you interested in studying that?"

"There was never an *a-ha* moment like you'd expect. Some believe majoring in anthropology is a waste and an easy way to skate through college, but I found the classes engaging and more beneficial than, say, a business or biology class. Just my preference though."

"I understand that. How can an eighteen-year-old possibly know what they want to do forever? It's an agonizing decision."

The last comment hung in the air until Nolan filled in the void with another question.

"So, Frankie, what is your ideal job with the anthropology degree?"

She sighed. "I aspire to be more than a waitress but looking for jobs is such a chore. It's only been a couple months since I graduated, so I'm not putting too much pressure on myself. Ideally, I'd love to work in a museum and really dig into a specific portion of human history, but those jobs are hard to come by. The easy path would be to snag a corporate job and help the bigwigs figure out how to micromanage their employees more."

"Corporations hire anthropologists?" Coda asked.

"Of course! Even a place like JEC," Frankie said with a smile. "I bet there was a whole team of them buried in the bowels somewhere."

The dump of information over the past ten minutes was more than Frankie had spoken the entire car ride. Coda pegged her for being more of an observer than active participant.

Riding the hot streak, Nolan asked another question in the form of a statement. "Tell me about your boyfriend. Long distance isn't easy, so he must be worth the hassle."

"He's great."

"That's it?"

"I don't know what to say about him."

"What's his name?"

"R . . . uh . . . Ryan."

"Are you sure about that?" Nolan laughed.

"Yes." She sounded defensive.

"What does *Ryan* do?"

"Insurance."

"How long have you two been together?"

"Three."

"Months? Day? Seconds? I'd believe that last one."

"Years . . . Sorry, I'm not great with personal questions. Well, I'm not used to people caring enough to ask."

"It's okay," Nolan said. "We don't have to talk about it."

"Thanks. I'm curious about you two. How has it been traveling across the country together?"

Nolan looked at Coda through the rear-view mirror. "It's been chill. No petty arguments. No disagreements of any kind, really. Boring actually if you consider all the shenanigans that movies and television show people getting into during road trips. But that's the script. I recently learned not to question it."

"The sc—" Frankie started.

"Don't ask," Coda cut in. "Same boat as Nolan. It's been calm. We have learned a lot about each other. I found out Nolan gets panic attacks but is super badass and getting better at overcoming them."

"I learned Coda spent some time in juvie, which was a shock. I mean, look at him! He's harmless . . . at least in the time I've known him."

"Seriously?" Frankie asked.

"It's true. Nothing to be alarmed about though. It was a long time ago," Coda said.

"What happened?"

Coda laughed. "A story for another time . . . Nolan also told me—" he stopped himself.

"That I'm adopted. It's okay. I'm not ashamed of it. I just don't make it the forefront of conversation with new people," Nolan said, looking back again through the mirror.

"Oh, and Nolan found out I'm asexual from a friend I confided in years ago. The intel was accurate though. I've been waiting for her to bring it up," Coda said straight-faced.

"Eve told you about our conversation?" Nolan said, bewildered.

"First thing she mentioned the next morning as my hangover was attempting to kill me. I appreciate your discretion about it. I'm still . . . working through it."

"Wow, I feel like I crashed a tender moment," Frankie said.

"No, not at all. I reconciled a long time ago that my sexuality was a complicated maze I needed time to navigate. I'm almost there and Nolan knows she will be the first one to hear the whole story when it's ready."

"Thanks Coda," Nolan said. She wanted to say more, but the words vanished before she could put them together.

Coda sat back in the seat and stared out the windshield into the endless miles that stretched ahead, thinking, thinking, always thinking.

forty-four

DAYDREAM

If you ever find yourself in the unfortunate situation of driving from Denton to Aurora, don't bother looking for places to stop.

There are none.

As previously mentioned, West Texas is an absolute wasteland of desolation and a healthy reminder of what the fall of humanity would look like (in terms of people and topography). The sad, flat, depressing landscape continues on into New Mexico and eventually fizzles out in Colorado.

For the truly adventurous sort, you could detour near Colorado Springs and take your car up Pike's Peak, but overheated brakes and sharp turns could derail your trip and cause a fiery crash that may result in death.

With that in mind, the trio decided not to stop outside of bathroom breaks and refueling the 2008 Pinto Pinata.

Past Amarillo, Texas and the last remnant of true civilization they witnessed, Frankie spotted a wooden sign on the edge of the road. It spoke of elote up ahead. A delicacy amongst the food truck staples.

They weren't convinced until they passed the third and final sign telling them what was ahead. Sure enough, another half mile up the road, a small cart was perched in the grass next to a beaten-up truck.

Nolan brought the 2008 Pinto Pinata to a stop behind the truck.

"What is elote?" she asked.

"Mexican street corn. Served on the cob or in a cup. My preference is the cup because you can mix everything together into a sloppy mess," Frankie said, enlightening the others. "Don't look at me like that! You just have to try it yourself. Y'all would understand if you spent more time in Texas."

They filed out of the car and approached the man hunkered down behind the cart.

"My first customers of the week! It's a lonely business up this way," the man confessed. "I'm Darian. Nice to meet you."

The pleasantries and inconsequential exchanges bounced back and forth.

Frankie took charge and ordered for the others, which turned out to be quite simple: three orders of Elote. So easy a caveperson could do it.

Darian ducked behind the cart. Shuffling and rattling was heard as he sifted around out of sight. Coda watched as the grass and dirt and shrubs drifted in a methodic pace to match the wind. The sight went on for miles, far beyond the horizon.

After paying, Darian said, "You. Yeah, you. Hang back for a second," pointing to Coda.

"Why?" Coda asked. A valid, sane question.

"Because it's what you want."

Coda turned back to Nolan and Frankie, but they were gone. The glare off the windshield made it impossible to see whether they went back to the car. Where else would they have gone?

"Okay," Coda said, trying to make sense of the situation.

"I feel sorry for you, kid," Darian began. "You lost your dad and never took the time to grieve. You let the rage boil over into a stupid decision. Are you going to do the same with your mom? You can't possibly be dumb enough to make the same mistake. But, yet, here we are. In the middle of this nowhere, running further and further from the truth. It's been a week already. You realize that, right? A whole week. How does that feel?"

"It sucks."

"That's it? Look, I get it. You'd lay in bed and hear the sirens go off and wonder if that was your dad traveling along to a heroic death. You always thought of him as the hero, the one to go into the burning building and risk his life to save others. And what happened? He goes and breaks his neck in the most humiliating way. No offense, but it's the truth. And then to cap it off, you got the pleasure of finding his stiff corpse. It's a tough break, kid. No pun intended. You need to let it go though. You have other matters to consider. Your mom, for example..."

"What about it?"

"*What about it?*" Darian said in a mocking tone. "Don't be daft. You're the one that called me here. You can't even be honest with yourself now? For Christ sake, kid. Just let it out and let it go . . . These books. These stinking books. Were they worth it? What are you going to do with them back in New York? Create an effigy to Grace Finn, beloved mother and decent human being? Donate them to the local, dying bookstore? How noble of you. This was a waste of time and I *hope* it hasn't taken you this long to realize that.

"Forget your mom for a second. What about your sisters? They must be absolutely disgusted with you. First you don't show up to your own father's funeral and now you're playing hooky again. You still have a lifetime ahead with them — assuming the Finn plotline doesn't fade out too quickly — so why don't you make an effort? All these people. All these *strangers* you've gone out of your way to see. Why is that easier than being around your own family?

"I get it. You must be tired of the questions. Always, always, always with the questions and none of them ever have an answer. Frustrating, right? But you are controlling this narrative. I mean, isn't this all in your head? I'm here to help, but I can't do that if you aren't *all there*. You need to tighten the screws and clean your noggin. Something ain't right."

Coda nodded.

Darian continued. "You're not a shit person, but you keep treating yourself like you are. If I can be honest, you're as middle of the road as a guy gets. You don't stand for much. You don't have any compelling quirks. You're a pretty lame protagonist, but you know how these things go. You're the book lover, which, if I can be honest again, is not a personality trait to be proud of. But yet, people would gravitate to you if you ever let them in. It's not hard. It really isn't.

"Your mom always loved you. Even after what you said. You've known that though. You've *always* known that. But the shame. Oh, the shame of it all. That's why you never went back and apologized. How could you? The one person that stood by your side after your dad and the assault and the expulsion and you tossed her aside like an empty bottle. Don't live with that shame. I'm begging you."

"Who are you?"

"Really? *You* brought *me* here. You're still staring out the windshield and thinking, thinking, thinking. How could you not realize you're the one writing the script here? This daydream has really fucked with you, huh? I'm surprised you let one run off as wildly as it has because you've been vocal in the past about hating dream sequences in books. What made you think it would work in real life? Or whatever sham this is. Has this helped at all?"

"No."

"Yeah, yeah. It usually doesn't. You know what the answer is, right?"

"I just need to say it."

"Exactly."

"I'm not ready."

"You don't seem to be ready about much. Look, if you are trying to pad this story for dramatic effect, don't bother. You got enough material already. I know it's hard for you to not envision even the blandest aspects of your life as a book, but try not to here, you understand? It's a waste."

"Soon."

"Okay, I'll hold you to that. Who am I to you?"

"My dad."

"Is that so? I'll take your word on that, but I suppose it makes sense since you weren't creative enough to pick a different name. But, hey, I'm merely an actor in the scene. I hope I'm getting the voice right."

"You aren't."

"Darn. Well, it's been almost half your life since you've heard his voice, so I imagine the memories are a bit foggy. Maybe we can try your mom next? That one is a bit more recent."

"No."

"As you say."

"What's next?"

"You're asking yourself what's next? How meta can this possibly get?"

Coda didn't respond, so the figure continued.

"How eloquent. Why don't you get back to the party? You're missing out on a great view. And it doesn't seem like our conversation helped much, so thanks."

Coda detached himself from the cart and sunk into the backseat tucked between the luggage.

Nobody seemed to notice his absence.

forty-five

GIVEN AWAY

Eventually the flatness of Texas and New Mexico gave way to the massive peaks and valleys of Colorado. Snow drizzled every mountaintop as they ventured north to Aurora.

Typical of their other stops, Nolan called it quits outside of Colorado Springs and said they could drive the rest of the way in the morning.

"Does she ever ask you to drive?" Frankie questioned as they lugged their bags into the hotel.

"No. Never has," Coda said.

"She must be getting tired of it. And to think that y'all need to drive back to New York. Sheesh. You'll never want to sit in a car again."

"Yeah. Definitely," he said with a chuckle. Coda knew he wouldn't be driving back. He couldn't waste any more time after making it to California. It's a future conversation to be had with Nolan.

They settled into a room with two beds — Nolan and Coda to one, and Frankie claiming the other.

They talked. They slept.

You know how these things go.

The next morning was more of the shitty continental breakfasts, brief conversations, driving, and other oddities. We will pick up ten minutes away from the address provided by Sam Rogers.

"Three questions?" Frankie asked.

"Yeah. Nolan asks me the same three questions before each stop. Would you like to do the honors?"

"Anything for you Coda . . . What is their name?"

"Chase Hendricks. The address I have is for a relative according to Sam's note."

"Interesting indeed. Quite illuminating. Let's hope Chase is in good health," Nolan said in a serious tone.

"What? Why?" Frankie asked, glancing around the car.

"Coda's old roommate who we ventured to in Chicago died about six months back."

Frankie recoiled. "I'm sorry. Did you know beforehand?"

"Nope," Coda said. "I hadn't spoken to him in years. That's life," he finished with a shrug. Its intention wasn't malicious, but one that showed how tired Coda was of loss.

"Next question," Nolan intervened, bringing them back on track. "How do you know him?"

"A friend from high school. It's not anything more interesting than that."

"None of these people have had good origin stories besides Muscle," Nolan confessed.

"The perks of living an average life. I only met people at school."

"I can tell. We should change that when we get back to New York."

"We?"

"It's still TBD. Don't obsess over my every word. You'll get lost in the fog," Nolan warned.

"What's the last question? I'm invested in this," Frankie said.

"Which book did you lend him?"

"It's called *Infinite Scroll*. The book was complete rubbish from what I remember. I'm not sure what my mom found redeeming in it."

"Maybe her message in the front will enlighten you."

"She didn't write one if I remember correctly."

"Grace Finn always with the curveballs. She is not reliable for sticking to a formula."

"Yeah," Coda said.

Nolan winded through the sprawling neighborhood that jutted out into cul-de-sacs filled with cookie-cutter houses and well-manicured lawns peeking through the melting snow. Past the roundabout, Nolan made a right and ventured onto another street that looked exactly like the one before it. They all watched the house numbers tick by until they reached their destination.

"Are we late for a party or something?" Frankie said, looking out at the cars piled into the driveway and street.

"A bit early for one . . . Maybe we should come back later?" Nolan suggested.

"We don't have the time," Coda said.

"If you say so. Lead the way then."

Coda squeezed around the luggage and out the door. The weather was mild for March in Colorado, or at least Coda's expectation of how disastrous it could be. Out beyond the swell of houses, he could see the same — or possibly different — mountains from their drive in. The view was refreshing compared to the constant urban landscapes they found themselves in.

"Ready?" he called back.

"Let's go six for six."

"More like five for five."

"I don't view Florida as a complete waste, so you shouldn't either," Nolan urged.

Coda could hear the mayhem on the other side of the door. Stifled voices and footsteps echoed and receded.

Before he could ring the doorbell, the door swung open.

"Hi. You're a stranger," the kid said. He was still in his pajamas and clutching an elephant. "His name is Hippo," he beamed with pride.

"I'm guessing that isn't Chase," Frankie said, leaning closer to Coda. "It was a bad joke, but I couldn't help myself."

"Keep up the good work," Nolan said.

"Are your parents home?"

"Yup!"

"Can you get them for me?"

"They are busy!"

"With what?"

"We are going on vacation! No snow for a week!"

"I'm on vacation too. You'll have a great time. Is there anyone else you can get for us to talk to?"

"Um . . . Hmm . . . Uh . . ." The kid darted away from the door. Coda looked down the hallway at the people passing by like steady traffic. No one seemed to notice the front door was open with three strangers peering inside.

The kid came back with someone older. "I answered the door even though I'm not supposed to."

"It's okay," the woman said. She turned her attention to Coda. "Can I help you?"

"Is this the Hendricks's household?"

"Y-yes," she said with obvious hesitation.

"Does Chase live here? I'm a friend from school. Back in New York."

"Uh, no. He's not here. Let me . . . let me get Edith." The woman closed the door, effectively shutting them out.

"You know, she's had the most realistic reaction to three strangers showing up out of anyone so far. Everyone else needs to take notes," Nolan said. "I think we look nonthreatening, but my goodness, people just let us into their house without many questions. It's just how the script demands it to be," she finished with a sigh.

The door opened again. "Come inside, please," the new woman said, waving them forward.

"I spoke too soon," Nolan said.

They followed the woman through the hallway and into the chaos of the kitchen. Bags were scattered everywhere with signs propped up displaying which ones belonged to who.

"Is this the pizza delivery guy?" a new stranger asked.

"No, Marv. It is ten in the morning. We are not ordering pizza."

"Fine. Whatever. Your loss. Nothing like a hot slice of dough before getting stuffed into a van with your favorite family members." He provided way more detail than necessary.

Marv walked away, visibly disappointed and shuffled over to his half empty bag.

"Hi. Sorry," the woman said turning back to them. "It's stressful this morning. We do a family trip every year and for some heinous reason, I designated my house as the rendezvous point. There's like fifteen of us this year! Can you believe it?" she asked, also providing way more detail than necessary. "I'm Edith, by the way. You were asking about Chase?"

"Yes," Coda said. "I went to high school with him and was hoping to get back a book I lent to him."

"Wait, like from when we lived in New York?"

"Yes."

"You came a long way for a book." Bringing back everyone's favorite line of dialogue!

"We have. It's important."

"I'm sorry to say that Chase isn't here. First year he isn't coming on the trip with us," she said with sadness.

"What happened? Is he okay?"

"Oh yes. Yes. Absolutely. Sorry to alarm you. Chase went on a journey of self-discovery by walking the Camino in Europe."

"You mean that super long walk with the passport book you get stamped?" Nolan cut in.

"That's the one."

"I'm more cultured than I thought," she said to herself, beaming with pride. The second person to do so in a small spread of time.

"Why did he do that?" Coda asked.

"Pre-midlife crisis, I think. He was vague about the whole thing. You said you're looking for a book? Well, Chase gave away all his things. Completely wiped out his apartment. No furniture, minimal clothes, and even got rid of his sentimental items."

"Oh."

"I helped him with it and I specifically remember dropping stuff off at a bookstore. Let me see if I can find the name."

"It's okay. You're busy. We have interrupted enough of your time."

"No. No. No worries. Unlike these other people, I packed last night," Edith beamed with pride. Was there anyone else who wanted to step up to the pride plate? Really. Anymore takers? "Give me a minute," she said, bounding off to a different part of the house.

"Stranger in a strange land," Frankie said, looking around at all the vignettes happening around them.

"Pizza guy?" another man walked by and pointed at Coda.

"No! Edith thought it was too early for pizza," Marv yelled from the living room. He let out an exaggerated huff and returned to packing his bag.

Nolan, Frankie, and Coda loitered around the kitchen. No one questioned who they were or why they were there.

Edith returned with a small piece of paper seemingly ripped from a larger notepad. "I found it. They gave us a receipt for what we donated. Tax purposes or something like that. Anyways—"

A whistle boomed through the first floor of the house. Silence followed. Coda located the source. It was an older woman who was undoubtedly the matriarch. "Five minutes until the van leaves! Anyone not in it will be left behind!"

"My mom doesn't mess around with these vacations. She plans all year for them. It's bigger than Christmas," Edith explained.

"Thank you for this. I really appreciate it," Coda said, holding up the note.

"I'm sorry we didn't have more time to talk. It sounds like you three are on quite the road trip if you made it out here from New York."

"It's been an adventure," Nolan said.

"I'll show you out," Edith said, ushering them back to the door.

"Bye pizza people!" Marv shouted out and waved.

The last remnants of conversation passed from Edith to the gang as she wished them luck. They, in turn, wished them safe travels on the trip.

As they reached the car, a dingy van pulled up alongside the 2008 Pinto Pinata. The window rolled down and a scratchy voice called out to them. "What's going on here?" he said, nodding up at the house. Everyone was beginning to file out and head for the vans in the driveway.

"I don't know," Coda feigned.

"Sure you do," the man said, showing off his gold tooth. "They going on vacation, huh? I hope they have a good alarm system. This isn't 1990, so I suppose everyone does," he cackled with maniacal laughter. He rolled up the window and drove off before saying anything further.

"This all feels familiar," Frankie said. "Like I've experienced this before."

"Things have been getter weirder the further west we've come," Coda said.

Frankie shrugged it off, unconcerned with the oddity.

They settled back into the car. Coda watched as the van doors closed and the engines roared. In almost perfect timing, the front door to the house whipped open and the little boy from earlier was running and waving his elephant in the air, begging them not to leave him home alone.

"What a disaster that would have been," Nolan said. "Coda, my friend, do you have an address to the bookstore?"

He opened up the piece of paper and looked it over.

"You are keeping vital information to yourself," Nolan stressed. "Give us the details."

"Bowling's Books. That's all she wrote."

forty-six

YHPRUM'S LAW

Even in an area as large as Denver and all its suburbs, finding a store named Bowling's Books wasn't a laborious task. A quick search led them to downtown.

Like any good chauffeur, Nolan followed the directions without complaint.

"What's the likelihood the book is still there?" Frankie wondered.

"I have no idea. That's not something I considered," Coda said. What happened if it wasn't? The employees of Bowling's Books wouldn't hand over pertinent information about the customer who snagged the book. Even if they miraculously did, they couldn't parade around Denver and track down every lead until they got what they needed.

It was only a book after all, and while Nolan and Coda were on a crusade, a majority of people wouldn't understand or care.

The drive into downtown was simple enough without rush hour traffic. Engulfed by buildings that blocked the early morning sun, they ventured deeper into the shadows.

"Look at that monstrosity over there! I didn't know JEC had a place here," Nolan said.

"Neither did I," Coda said. He wondered what weapon of destruction they were concocting and perfecting on the upper floors. The minds were always at work to eliminate tyranny, but only for the causes that provided the highest profits. People are a currency and easily replaceable by more submissive models.

They passed by an apartment building named Skyhouse that vaulted high into the clouds as the GPS alerted them their destination was close.[21] Nolan circled the block twice before settling on a spot. Another cool thing about the 2008 Pinto Pinata was the car had technology that blocked the need to pay for parking. Mr. Sud refused to reveal how he acquired the advanced piece of tech, only saying he made the "best trade deal of all time." If the world is suddenly controlled by an alien race,

---

[21] Wasn't that the name of Eve's building in Charlotte? What a coincidence!

there's a lead on who the sellout is.

Bowling's Books was on a quiet block squished between a café and podiatrist — completing the holy trinity for any book lover with foot pain and a hankering for caffeine.

"Looks quaint," Frankie said as they approached the door. The glass windows on either side showcased the hot selling books. Overt sexual covers displaying lust and carnal desires for readers to escape from their own drab lives dotted the top shelf in a visually pleasing way. Covers with the author's name written in font larger than the title were sprinkled throughout the displays. It's easy to forget how everything was carefully curated and manicured to produce the highest number of sales for the bookstore and publishing house.

Bowling's Books may not be slinging autocannons to quell disturbances, but they share the same overarching goal.

Money, money, money.

It always comes back to that, huh? But you know how these things go.

A bell chimed as they stepped inside. Several customers were lingering in the aisles, but the only sound permeating through the store was the quiet jazz music from overhead.

"Welcome! How are y'all today?" the employee asked from behind the counter.

"Good," Coda said. "We are looking for a book that was dropped off here a couple weeks ago."

"There's a chance it's already gone. We have a surprisingly high turnover rate for pre-owned books."

"I understand."

"What book?" she asked, leaning onto the counter. She looked like a toddler sitting in a highchair.

"*Infinite Scroll* by T—"

She nodded. "Trenton Dire. I'm familiar with that one. That book is pure shit, if I may say so. I never understood the appeal. I have a friend who plucked it off the shelf one day like he was drawn to it. He swore up and down about it, so I read the book myself — or at least I tried to. Only made it a hundred pages. Why that book?"

"It's a long story," Nolan said, stepping next to Coda.

"They said the same thing to me, but the story wasn't *that* long," Frankie chimed in.

The employee looked back and forth between everyone standing at the counter. "I got time. Unless it takes more than five hours, which I'd have to abandon y'all. Brett doesn't pay me to listen to stories longer than five hours. Everyone has their limit," she said with an overly dramatic shrug.

For once, we will listen to Coda rehash his long story.

Coda spoke. "I'm an avid reader. Always have been. My mom helped me discover that passion and continued to promote it by giving me books she found important. Sometimes the reason was obvious, while other times I didn't understand why. Maybe that was the point. Everything doesn't fit into that perfect circle we like to envision for ourselves. And if we are lucky enough to achieve that perfect circle, we aren't satisfied with it . . . That's a whole other topic . . . Anyways, the relationship with my mom deteriorated after my dad died. Minor teenage angst that I watched her go through with my sisters turned into major warfare with me. It took a while, but we drifted apart. One day I said I hated her and we haven't spoken since. Now she is, uh, dying and I — we — are driving across the country to reclaim the books I've given away that came from her."

That's his latest version of the story. Bounds to change again.

"I lost my dad five years ago," she said. "I'm sorry. You learn to move on, but the pain never goes away."

Coda nodded. The jazz music filled in for the lapse of conversation.

The employee eventually spoke. "What's your name?"

"Coda. That's Nolan and Frankie," he said.

"I'm Murph. It's nice to meet y'all. I don't usually develop an emotional connection to customers this quickly. We will find that damn book. It has to be here. Follow me," she said, moving out from behind the counter. "I walk slow these days, but I blame the intruder sucking my life force." She tapped on her protruding stomach like a judge would knock a gavel.

"Oh my goodness! Congrats! Is this your first?" Frankie asked.

"Yes. It took long enough. I thought my husband was shooting blanks for a while . . . But that's too much detail for strangers. Moving on!" Murph said, waving them forward.

They filed in behind her as she walked down one of the leftmost aisles. The store was not suffering from any shortage. Each shelf was stuffed with books of various sizes. The spines showed a spectrum of colors — some vibrant, while others were faded from age.

"Dire, Dire, Dire," Murph repeated to herself as she skimmed the shelves. She pressed up onto her tip toes and read the author names. Nothing. Nothing. Noth—

"Got it. Well, there are three copies here. Does it matter which one?"

"Yes. There is a symbol in the back, so I really need the copy with that."

"Coda, you are making my job more exciting. I like that," Murph said with a smile. She grabbed all three copies and pulled them down. She handed one to each of the others.

"What does the symbol look like?" Frankie asked.

"It's a . . . oval?" Nolan said.

"Yeah. With intersecting lines in the middle," Coda said.

"Like a crosshair?"

"Exactly. I never thought of that before, but yes."

"And why that symbol?" Murph asked.

"I never bothered to ask. I assume she felt it had some connection to me, but I can't be sure."

"No symbol here," Frankie said.

"Same," Nolan said.

"Me too," Coda said, closing the book.

"Okay . . . Okay," Murph said, thinking. "Before I got married, my last name was Law. Murphy Law. You can imagine the barrage of jokes people made. All of them were shit and unoriginal. My husband's last name is Wright. What are the odds? It helped me go from thinking *everything that can go* wrong *will* to *everything that can go* right *will*. How's that for optimism?"

"Kind of silly," Coda said with a laugh.

"Don't knock it until you have at least tried to knock it over once."

"What?"

"I don't know. Sometimes I talk and forget others are listening. Anyways! Let's try the bargain bin."

Murph led them to the far end of the store where two large wooden boxes dominated the space. "The land of misfit books," she announced. "This is like any good chase. You never find what you need where you first look. It erases the thrill."

"Oh, we know," Nolan said. "Every stop has had its unique set of loop-de-loops, but we always walked away with the right book. We will find it."

"Normally, these bins are reserved for those books that have been loved too much. Any idea what condition the book was in?" Murph asked.

"No. I haven't seen it in years," Coda said.

Murph nodded and began rifling through the bins. The others joined. Searching, searching, searching.

And . . .

Nothing.

After five minutes, they gave up with the bins. Murph directed them toward another aisle saying they should check by the title. No luck there either.

They returned to the counter where Murph helped check out a customer before turning her attention back to them. "Why would we have three copies of the book but none of them be the one you're looking for?" she questioned, drumming her hand on the register. "Are you sure you have the right store?"

"Unless there is another Bowling's Books in Denver," Coda said.

"Brett always talked about expanding but never got around to it."

"Hi. Hello," a new customer said, peering around the group. "I'm here to pick up an order."

Nolan, Frankie, and Coda stepped to the side, making room for the man to converse in a more casual manner with Murph. She asked for his name and spun around to check the shelves of orders and snatched one.

"We haven't checked there," Nolan suggested, leaning into Coda's ear.

After the customer left, Nolan floated her idea to Murph, who immediately turned back to the shelves and began dissecting. They watched her read each sheet and move onto the next until she suddenly stopped and grabbed a stack of books. "Check this one," she said, pulling out the copy of *Infinite Scroll* and sliding it across to Coda.

Sure enough, the symbol was there, propped up in the top right corner. The oval was crisp, drawn in one fluid motion. The crosshair was precise and met exactly in the middle with the lines extending beyond the edge of the oval. His mom etched it in with no effort, as if she'd drawn it thousands of times.

He thumbed back to the last page of text and read it to himself . . .

his weight press into the sturdy chair. He was the orchestrator of destruction, but also the god that repaired it. Nobody could know the truth because they'd never understand why. He chuckled to himself at the idea. A big, provocative speech broadcast out to the world about his heroic efforts would be mocked and scoffed at, or worst of all, ignored. The thought made him shutter.

No time for that though. He had more to do. Other universes to intervene in. The Bounty name didn't know rest or solitude.

If we stand for nothing, everything will stand, his father told him at his initiation.

He stood for something — the Infinite Scroll.

And if he didn't, who would?

Venice Bounty lifted himself from the chair and returned to the planks of wood arranged into a hexagon on the floor.

"Leaving so soon?" the robot said.

"Archibald, there's always more work to be done."

The small sample proved it wasn't as bad as Coda remembered. It still wasn't great though.

"Murph, it's here," he said, showing her.

"Well, shit. Look at that. I told you so! We need to sneak a different copy into the order. Would you mind grabbing one?"

"Of course," Coda said, placing the book down and walking back to the aisle. The jazz music still filtered out. The customers that meandered were enthralled by a book of their choosing. The scene was relaxing and something Coda could see himself being a part of.

He grabbed another copy and returned to the counter. Nolan and Frankie were asking more questions about the pregnancy. Murph said they were having a boy, which was exactly what her husband hoped for. She continued the conversation as she grabbed the book, stacked it on top of the others, and wrapped the rubber bands around them.

During a lull, Coda asked, "How much do I owe you for the book?"

"Don't be obtuse."

"But—"

"This is a hot spot in Denver. The owner is . . . well known, so this one book won't put us out of business."

"Thank you Murph."

"Can I give you one piece of unsolicited advice before you leave?"

"Of course."

"Follow it."

"Follow what?"

"It."

"But what is *it*?"

"Anything. A job. A gut feeling. A romantic interest . . . A . . . A . . . The point is you shouldn't hold yourself back."

"I'll try. Thank you." Coda wasn't sure if he needed to say anything more than that. He didn't understand the enormity behind Murph's simple advice, but it's not like he was a part of her story until this moment.

Murph nodded, accepting the answer. "And the same goes for you two as well," she said, pointing to Frankie and Murph. "Follow it. Whatever *it* is."

forty-seven

CAR CHAT VI
Somewhere in Utah

"I have more questions for you," Nolan announced to Frankie. "Normally I'd harass Coda, but I've exhausted my supply and learned as much as possible about him."

"There's still more," Coda quipped from the backseat.

"Oh yeah? Like what?"

"I can't tell you that. It defeats the purpose of you asking the right questions."

Nolan huffed at his remark.

"You haven't tapped into my psyche as much as I expected. There's one thought that's rattling around I haven't vocalized yet," he said.

"You're such a tease, but in an annoying, unproductive way," Nolan said. "Anyways, back to the subject... Frankie, tell us about your family. What's up with them?"

"They're fine."

"That's it?"

"Yeah. I don't have much to say about them."

"Clearly. How did they feel about you leaving for Texas?"

"All they want is for their kids to be successful. That overrides everything."

"Did they have a problem with you majoring in anthropology?"

"They didn't even know what the word meant, so yeah, they weren't thrilled when I explained it."

"What drew you to that?"

Frankie sat up straighter in the seat. "I wish I knew. Maybe it was a yearning to understand people better — the good and bad sides — but I can't be sure. I started reading up on anthropology and felt an inherent interest to it. My parents are immigrants and built a business from the ground up. They wanted me and my siblings to be as self-sufficient. I went a different path. I never cared about business. People fascinated me though. How we got to this point in history; the things that went well and other things that were a complete disaster. It's amazing how we only interact with other humans and yet have a fundamentally poor understanding of each other. How much truth have each of you told me over the past few days? Some, I imagine, but I'd also guess you've held back because I'm a stranger. I've done the same. How can we not feel comfortable around each other when we all have the exact same makeup? Why has our culture devolved to a point where each person treats themselves as a corporation with every portrayal being massaged and perfected to avoid any criticism? Maybe those are answers I can find along the way in my career. Probably not though. It's never black and white. The spectrum of answers is as vast as the number of questions to wonder about. Why would I own a business or sit behind a desk when so much is out there to discover? My parents never understood that."

"It seems like you know exactly why you jumped into anthropology," Nolan said.

"Are you two tired?" Frankie asked, abandoning the current thread.

"Tired of what?" Coda said.

"This," she said, motioning to everything around them. "The driving ... the constant shuffle from one location to the next ... the endless scenery that all looks vaguely similar."

"Yes, but it's still better than what I was doing in New York," Coda said. "For some reason, I expected more though."

"I agree," Nolan said.

"Coda, what do you mean?" Frankie asked.

"Like you said, everything looks the same. Sometimes we drive by mountains or through a city, but they all blend together. There is no sense of identity or uniqueness. I can't reconcile if it's me being a pessimist or that there isn't anything to see. I had high hopes for this trip. The people and conversations have been a highlight — and spending time with Nolan, of course — but the sights have been dreadful. I thought anything would be more exciting than the skyscrapers of New York, but nothing has caught my attention yet. And I'm worried that the notion is larger than just this trip."

"What do you mean?"

"I haven't found joy in anything for a long time. The books I read are bland and derivative; the places people travel to and then post about on social media ruin any sense of discovery and longing to go there; the friendships I have are dismal because there are none outside of Nolan.

"I've viewed life as a perfect circle. Each day starts the arc and it closes when I go to bed. There are minor deviations from the mean but none ever significant enough to make the circle imperfect. This trip was meant to completely destroy that circle, but all it's done is create a new one. We get in the car, drive for hours, meet wacky people, hear their story, grab the book, and shuffle to the next place. The habitual nature of life is stalking me."

"Is this what has been on your mind?" Nolan asked.

"Yeah. Sort of."

"Well, we didn't have to wait long to hear about it. Your teasing was premature."

"What if it isn't the circle that's the problem?" Frankie said.

"I don't understand."

"You are so fixated on the circle and the routine you find yourself in that you are blind to everything else. What about everything inside the circle that makes the routine or the line itself that defines the shape? You have complete control over that."

"I mean, I quit my job before doing this."

"And yet, you've talked about JEC a handful of times since I've been with y'all. Nolan, how many times has Coda talked about JEC?"

"Dozens."

"And how many times have you talked about your old job?"

"Not many. Maybe three times. If that."

"My point," Frankie said, "is that you need to free up some space in your mind. You are holding onto too much. You think the world is defining that perfect circle for you, but you are in complete control of it. I know going back to New York won't be easy with your mom and not having a job—"

"It's more than that," Coda said.

"I know. I'm sorry for glossing over that, but nobody else is drawing that circle. You are the creator. Coda, that circle starts and ends with you."

"Yeah," he managed to say. It was a viewpoint he hadn't considered.

"Maybe that's how you rediscover joy in your life: take control. Stop reading books for the sake of reading. Find a job that stimulates your passions. Be uncomfortable and force yourself into meeting new people. You're sociable. You two have embraced me in a short time and I'm grateful for that."

"What's after all of this?" Coda asked, mainly to himself.

"I don't know," Frankie said softly. "But I have an idea. Someplace to go if we can spare a detour."

"I'd be down for it," Nolan said. "Coda?"

"I . . . uh . . . I . . . Maybe we should—"

"What's the matter? Is it your mom?" Nolan asked, craning her neck to look through the rear-view mirror.

"No," Coda said in quick response.

"Is she okay? You haven't spoken about her in a few days. What's Cecilia been saying?"

"Cecilia hasn't texted me. No news is good news I guess."

"Uh . . . hmm . . . okay. I won't pry any further than that," Nolan said, somewhat defeated. She cared way more than she ever confessed to Coda. She knew the pain of not having her biological parents in her life, and while the situation wasn't the same, her empathy siren was on full blast.

"Where do you want to go?" Coda asked Frankie.

"Keep driving west until Nolan is tired and then we take it from there. It will be better as a surprise and hopefully show how you haven't discovered everything yet."

forty-eight

THE VIEW(ING)

Frankie tried to keep the location a secret. She dodged the uneven flow of inquiries for the remainder of their drive that day and Nolan's attempts at the hotel. It was easy enough to tell her to find some patience. After the third time, Nolan stopped asking.

They continued driving the next morning under the cover of darkness. Coda slept in the backseat with his mouth open wide enough to catch an assortment of small candies. Nolan didn't talk much as she focused on navigating the curves and bends of the unfamiliar territory. Frankie stared ahead and thought about the mistake she was driving toward. What choice did she have? Her options were limited.

As the light of day drenched everything around them, a sign became visible.

"Yosemite National Park. Twenty miles," Nolan read.

"Surprise!" Frankie said.

"I've never been to a national park before. Come to think of it, I haven't been much of anywhere, which is the exact opposite of what you'd expect from a rich family."

"Your family is rich?"

"Oh yeah. My adoptive parents have a stupid amount of money."

"That must be nice though."

"I . . . I understand that I'm fortunate, but money does not bring happiness."

"But it brings stability."

"Yeah."

"And opportunity."

"Yeah."

"And eliminates so many problems others are constantly worrying about."

Nolan barely spoke above a whisper. "I understand."

"I'm not trying to make you feel bad."

"I know you aren't. I have enough guilt to last ten lifetimes."

"Why though? Consider yourself fortunate. Go help others. Don't keep yourself tied down in the same way Coda does. It's not healthy."

"I have a lot to think through."

"You've done a lot of driving. Haven't you spent some time thinking?"

"Not as much as you'd expect. Going into this, I knew the trip would be about Coda and helping him through everything. That's taken up most of my mental capacity."

"You deserve to take some time for yourself too."

"Yeah. I've thought through what it would be like to stay out in California, but . . ."

"But what?"

"Something is holding me back."

Frankie explained that Yosemite was the perfect place to reflect. She'd taken the trip from San Francisco a dozen times. The amazing thing was that coming during each season yielded a different experience. Seeing that it was March, there was a high threat of roads being closed, but Frankie checked the advisories several times and felt confident they would get to her favorite spot, which happened to be a fan favorite for practically anyone that visited Yosemite.

Coda stirred and woke up fully. "What did I miss?"

"We are going to Yosemite."

"Yosemite?" he asked.

Frankie whipped her head around to look at him. He rubbed his face and scratched at the stubble. "You never heard of Yosemite?"

"No," he said with a shrug. "I'm a New York guy. I could tell you half the streets in Brooklyn if you wanted that useless knowledge."

"Yosemite is a national park. It's absolutely beautiful."

"I'd hope so. No sense in protecting ugly land," he said flatly.

They made their way to the entrance and paid the admission fee. The park ranger rambled about all the closed roads due to snow but was quick to mention how it's the least amount they'd ever seen in March.

"We got lucky," Frankie said as Nolan pulled away from the booth and into the park.

"It's all in the script," Coda said in a mocking tone.

Nolan shot him a glance through the rear-view mirror. "Don't be a hater."

"You didn't even know about *the script* until the crazy lady mentioned it."

"Not true. It's always been in my heart."

"Oh god. I can't believe you just said that! So incredibly cheesy. And if you actually had a script in your heart, you'd be super d-dead," Coda said, forcing the last word out.

"How about we enjoy the view?" Frankie suggested. "Nolan, the road gets steep and chaotic in spots."

"The car will be fine. It's well equipped."

Frankie turned down the music to a quiet explosion as the three of them focused their attention outside. In-between the spaces of the barren trees, they could see down into the valley where any specks of vehicles were moving at a slow pace. Ahead, they neared a bridge with a small but mighty waterfall that was carrying down melted snow from the mountain tops.

"Keep going," Frankie urged. "Only a couple more minutes."

They rounded a corner and stared into the acres of scorched trees and muddy soil. Wildfires had torn through the area, decimating what was while providing ample opportunities for regrowth and restoration. That process took time though.

"Do you see that?" Frankie asked.

"The tunnel? Yeah, we are heading right for it," Nolan said.

"Our stop is on the other side. There should be parking."

Nolan flicked on the headlights of the 2008 Pinto Pinata as they expanded and lit up the tunnel. A sliver of light on the other side grew steadily with each passing second.

Coda squinted and shielded his eyes as the light became more intense.

"This is Tunnel View. Arguably the best view in the entire park," Frankie announced. "There's nothing else like it."

The 2008 Pinto Pinata emerged out the other side. Nolan found a spot in a nearby parking lot and quickly hopped out. The others followed.

They moved to a waist high brick wall that separated them from tumbling down hundreds of feet. Out beyond, the world blossomed. The valley with a thick coating of trees that swept through the entire valley beyond eyesight; the mountains vaulting into the blue sky in varying angles and outcroppings; the sun shining down and making every inch glisten; the sounds of actual nature! Something Coda and Nolan rarely experienced outside the fluttering of pigeon wings and squeaking of mice on subway tracks.

"Pretty amazing, right?" Frankie asked.

"It's incredible. Takes your breath away," Nolan said, leaning and pressing her hands into the brick.

"The giant ass rock over there," Frankie said, pointing to the left, "is El Capitan. People climb that shit without any equipment. Absolutely bonkers ... And there's Half Dome. Oh, and that's ... You know what, I'll give you two time alone." She inched away and moved to another section of the brick wall to read the informational plaque.

Coda stared ahead, allowing himself to take in the view. He waited for it to seep in and latch hold onto him, but it never did. The joy he was so desperately seeking didn't manifest in a triumphant wave bringing an end to his plight.

If only it were that easy.

If only a view could alter his life.

If only he was willing to tell the truth.

Listen:

He could not deny that Tunnel View and gazing out into Yosemite Valley was simply marvelous, but Coda was suspicious of how people could glimpse one sight of nature and be instantly changed. Maybe he was beyond repair or too much of a cynic. As with every stinking thing in his life, the answers weren't there.

He turned away from Nolan and the view and walked back through the parking lot. The 2008 Pinto Pinata was tucked in the corner several spaces beyond an RV.

"Hey. Hey kid. Want a better view?" a voice called out.

Coda located the sound. It was from an older man who was holding loosely onto a leash. He was wearing a vest with a flannel shirt underneath that clung tightly to his bulging gut. The dog had a white snout and droopy eyes that fixated on Coda. "How could I get a better view than that?" Coda questioned.

"Go to the top of my RV. The ten extra feet make a difference. Trust me."

Unsure, Coda smiled but didn't answer.

"I'm Dwight and this is my dog, Surge," the man said, extending a hand.

Coda shook it and introduced himself.

Without being prompted, Dwight explained he and Surge travel around the country, enjoying retirement. They recently made it through the forty-eight contiguous states and were celebrating on their way back home. Surge looked up at Dwight at the mention of going home.

"How long have you been traveling for?" Coda asked, feeling pressure to continue the conversation. Traveling across the country with only you and your dog probably meant Dwight was starved for human interaction. Coda could somewhat relate, but Nolan proved to be a more engaging road trip partner than a dog.

Dwight craned his head to the sky and thought. "Six . . . seven months, I think. You aren't as concerned about the days when all you're doing is driving from one location to the next."

"I understand that. My friend and I drove out here from New York."

"Oh really? Any fun stories?"

"Some bizarre experiences but that's kind of expected."

"This country is packed with beautiful surprises. Nothing inspires more than the open road . . . Well, the offer stands. I'm taking Surge for a walk around the area. The ladder on the back is your way up. Pleasure meeting you," Dwight said, taking a stronger grip on the leash and ushering Surge away. Coda watched as they strolled through the parking lot and kept walking away from the tunnel. They weren't in a hurry. They had no reason to be.

Coda stood idly by until Nolan and Frankie converged on him. "Making another new friend? I didn't think I'd be replaced so quickly," Frankie said.

"He said we could sit on the roof of his RV. He claimed the view was even better from up there."

Nolan moved toward the ladder. "I never decline an invitation."

"But you don't like heights."

"This is baby shit compared to that damn Ferris Wheel in Florida. No sweat."

Frankie followed behind. Coda watched as they navigated the ladder and each sat cross-legged on the roof. "How is it?" he asked, shielding his eyes again from the sun.

"It's . . . different. I'd be hard pressed to say it's *better* though. Those dang trees are blocking some of the view," Nolan said. "Get up here and join us!"

Coda did as told and climbed the ladder, sitting next to Nolan. He could see more of the valley directly below them, but the view was unchanged outside of that. For those who were expecting another miraculous epiphany, sincerest apologies, but in a roundabout way, one part of Coda's fog lifted — the part he was dreading most.

He took a long breath and held it in until his lungs begged for release. He felt his insides squirming and the cold sweat that was festering throughout his body.

It was time.

"The viewing is today," he said in a sudden burst.

"Viewing for what?" Frankie asked, scooting forward to see past Nolan.

"Coda, what the fuck are you talking about?" Nolan stared through him, out to the sea of trees that lived beyond. She knew. She knew his forthcoming answer. In the back of her mind, she always knew this would be the way it went.

"My mom died a week ago," he said with a sad smile. The kind you give someone when it's the only thing to stop yourself from crying. "We were somewhere in Georgia when my sister called me. I ignored it, of course. Cecilia is amazing, but . . . just . . . so parental. Then she texted me saying we really needed to talk. I called her at the next rest stop. She said it was peaceful. One second there and gone the next. Minus the months and months of agony, it wasn't a bad way to go."

"Coda . . . Goddammit Coda. Goddamn you. What are we doing here?" Nolan said through tears. She latched onto his arm and squeezed it tightly. He felt his blood scatter, if such a thing were even possible.

His mind fogged. He was as far into a fever dream as he'd ever gone before. What was he doing here? He hadn't bothered to ask himself that. What compelled him to keep driving, to avoid saying anything to Nolan?

"Coda?" Frankie said. "Are you okay?"

It was several seconds before he spoke. The view was amazing. He tried to picture it in a few months when spring would take over. The lush colors sweeping throughout the valley; the roving bands of tourists looking for the essential photo op; the blurs of animals darting through the dense patches of forest, hoping to avoid becoming a meal; the rock faces that remained as stagnant and menacing as ever. Millions of memories and stories were created in the valley, with most being retold in awe and wonderment.

Not this one though.

"I'm sorry I didn't tell you. I knew you'd want to go back," he said to Nolan. "I didn't want the last memory of my mom to be on her death bed or in a casket or being lowered into the ground. Who would?

"I fucked up my relationship with her and *this* is the only way to move forward. This is how I grieve. I wanted to keep going and get the books and do something right for once. Every day has been tough. So many moments where I struggled to hold it together. Not because I had to, but because I wanted to. The people we've met . . . Each of them have helped in unseen ways. I love my mom, Nolan. I love her so much. I hope she forgave me, but I'll never know. We have to keep going. It's the only option. I'm sorry I didn't tell you. I'm sorry. I'm sorry," he repeated as he buried his head into her shoulder. The muffled cries echoed out. Frankie reached out and rubbed a hand up and down his back.

"It's okay, Coda," Nolan said, not finding anything more potent to tell him.

They embraced for a long time, slipping into a space where the world around them slid away. The view was there, but it was behind the veil.

The grief was monumental and came in a shattering wave for Coda. Mixed up in there was regret and disdain and anger and a thousand other tiny words to describe his emotions.

But there was only one thing to do:

Keep moving forward. Keep traveling west.

You know how these things go.

After all, everybody's lost somebody.

III

WRITE ME A LETTER

forty-nine

HEARTLESS

Nobody spoke for a long time.

They left the RV before Dwight returned for further questioning. They got back into the car, plugged in the address for their last stop, and went back through the tunnel, away from the view that was supposed to fix Coda.

Frankie offered to sit in the back, but Coda declined. Squeezed between the leaning towers of luggage, he existed in the car with his mind being elsewhere. He considered what was going on in New York. His sisters were probably scrambling to make everything perfect. Optics were important for them. The flowers had to be arranged correctly and the collages needed to have a perfect blend of each family member. They'd field inquiries about Coda's whereabouts but keep the responses as vague as possible.

Needless to say, they were disgusted with his absence. For the past week, all three of his sisters begged for him to come home. They just didn't understand. He explained the conversation he had with their mom about not attending her funeral, but they couldn't fathom the reality of it and his intent to honor what she said. At the rest stops and hotels, Coda snuck off to return their calls, which quickly dissolved into vicious insults and pent up anger being slung through the phone. It wore him down.

He held it together though. In some aspect, he was a professional at hiding pain. When his dad died, he tucked away the grief and anger and pain until it exploded like a geyser during the incident at school. He minimized the shame of spending time in juvie. He avoided telling anyone about the crumbling relationship with his mom. He completed the same routine each day and never voiced his disgust with it until he quit to preserve the sliver of sanity that still existed.

He wasn't broken, but he sure wasn't living.

Instead of thinking about the past or what was happening in New York, he looked up from the floor of the 2008 Pinto Pinata and out the windshield. The world beyond was limitless. There was more to discover, more to love, but sometimes it doesn't find you.

You have to seek it out.

You have to discover all of it.

He was closer to the answer than he'd ever been.

As they put distance between themselves and Yosemite National Park, the landscape changed to more familiar backdrops — sometimes they were rolling hills with massive wind turbines, other times it was flat highway roads with sickly trees pressed up against the edges. It wasn't much, but just enough to keep his mind occupied.

At some point, Nolan spoke, soft and quiet as if she didn't want to disturb a sleeping baby. "It's going to be late when we hit the address. Do we call it a night somewhere or press on? And Frankie, I can drop you off whenever you want to see your boyfriend."

"I'm not in a rush. I can go back tomorrow if you two don't mind. It's a surprise for my boyfriend that I'll be back."

"Oh really? Why didn't you tell him?"

"Who doesn't like a good surprise?" Frankie said with a shrug.

Nolan looked over at her but didn't say anything.

"It's a Friday night. I don't think we'd be intruding by getting there in the early evening," Coda chimed in. They were back to business as usual. He never checked, but there wasn't an exact science on death and the protocol of talking about it. Would it have been better for Coda to dump his thoughts to Nolan and Frankie during the four-hour drive? Cathartic, maybe, but it's not usually how these things work. People like to return to normalcy and the status quo as quickly as possible after a traumatic event. Coda found himself sinking in the same boat.

"Do you think it's a residential address?" Nolan asked.

"Let me check," Frankie said.

"After Dallas, I'd rather not have to scour a wide area to find our person of interest," Nolan said, feeling a need to justify her inquiry.

Looking up from her phone, Frankie said, "The address is for the San Francisco Symphony Hall." The words came out in an unsure manner as if she didn't trust the information.

"Makes sense," Coda said.

"How so?"

"Ava was my next door neighbor during our senior year at TCSUM. She was *always* playing the violin. She said she started at the age of three and absolutely loved it."

"But why would Sam give us this address? Surely, Ava doesn't live at the symphony hall."

Coda shrugged, but Nolan and Frankie didn't see it from the front row of seats. "Does it really matter? It's Friday night and a good chance she will be there. Seems like it's another odd thread in a bundle of strangeness. Sometimes convenience comes free of charge."

The answer was acceptable enough that Nolan or Frankie didn't argue its merit. They continued traveling west at a steady pace.

Coda expected to enter the city on the Golden Gate Bridge but was disappointed when he caught the structure in the distance, glowing in the evening light. When he asked Frankie about it, she said that the Golden Gate Bridge took you north out of the city, which led to more confusion about their current geographical standing.

They pressed into the city and eventually found the symphony hall. It was a semi-circle of dirty white stone that took up the entire block. As Nolan navigated around to find a parking spot, Coda saw the box office lit up like an old school theater with pockets of people standing by. He couldn't tell whether they were waiting to go in or just coming out.

He wondered briefly if any of those stationary strangers had lost their mother a week ago and were on an extended road trip to escape the fear and shame of not being a better son. Yeah, probably not.

Shifting elsewhere, his friendship with Ava Babylon was as superficial as all the others. Their only conversations centered around what the tenants were doing in the building, how her violin lessons were going, and other pleasantries between neighbors that only saw each other in the hallway. The one time they delved into deeper territory was when Coda gave her *The White Meadow,* a poetry book by Sigmund Zula, who allegedly severed one finger and toe because he didn't like even numbers.[22] Makes you wonder if he had thoughts of piercing a lung or poking out an eyeball. At the time, Coda was combing through the book. His mother had given it to him years prior, but he never had an interest to digest the material after flipping to the last page and reading his rambling, metaphor-laced poem on the summer solstice.

Coda offered the book to her when she questioned him about it. She took it with gratitude and, as expected, life went on without either of

---

[22] By removing one finger and toe, Sigmund still had an even number of phalanges, so he didn't rectify his problem. Impossible to know what his end goal was though. People are strange.

them mentioning it again. Come the end of the school year, Ava moved out and ventured onto a new path without returning what was borrowed. Coda never considered that those people he lent books to assumed he was gifting it to them. There was no real etiquette when it came to that sort of stuff.

"Coda, I have a question," Frankie said, at some point while they were in Nevada the day prior, "Are these books you've been hunting down the only ones you gave away?"

"No. Not at all. They are the only ones I care about getting back."

In case anyone was curious to how generous Coda was with his empire of books.

Back in the present, Nolan found a parking spot five blocks away from the symphony hall. Frankie stressed that parking was an absolute chore in San Francisco and the words rang true after the fifteen minutes of parading around the streets.

As they retraced back to the hall, Coda said, "This is it. Hard to believe, right?"

"Yeah," Nolan said.

"Is everything alright?" he asked. Her short response likely had a long reasoning behind it.

"No, it isn't," she said, stopping in the middle of the block. They were surrounded by pawn shops and nail salons.

"What's wrong?"

"You . . . You . . ." she said, pointing at him. "You knew your mom wouldn't make it. That's fucked up, Coda. And then you lied about it for a week. Pretended that everything was okay like . . . like some sociopath. The amount of times you said she was still dying . . . It was your mother! How could you?"

"I'm sorry. It's complicated. Things got jumbled in my head."

"Algebra is complicated. Reading Mandarin is complicated. The relationship with your own mother is not. God, you were lucky to have parents that cared about you. You realize that, right?"

"Nolan. Coda. C'mon, this isn't how things are supposed to go," Frankie said, stepping between them.

"I'm not mad. Just confused," Nolan said. "And betrayed. But this isn't about me. You just lost your mom."

"I'm sorry. I don't know what else to say." He couldn't find the right justification for anything.

"I . . . I'll be fine. I know this trip wasn't about me, but I still feel drawn to this whole experience. Helping you find the books, meeting all the people from your past, hoping to bridge the gap in the relationship with your mom. And all the while, trying to discover what my next move should be, but—" she stopped herself. "Now's not the time for that. Let's just keep going. You never answered my three questions about this last person," Nolan said.

Coda explained about Ava and the circumstances around their spotty friendship. He wanted to say more to Nolan about how important it was that she accompanied him on the trip, but the timing of it would have felt cheap and forced.

He'd find a time to make things whole.

It was the one relationship he had left.

fifty

SEMIOTICS

How exactly Nolan, Frankie, and Coda skirted by security to make it backstage at the symphony hall was not as thrilling as you'd expect.

After purchasing three tickets for the show they watched in its entirety, Frankie found a door propped open that read EMPLOYEES ONLY, which was exactly where they needed to go. Symphony halls weren't doused in top-notch security, so they weren't questioned as they wandered around backstage asking for Ava Babylon.

Coda had confirmed during the show that Ava was in the third row, fourth seat. She looked as he remembered.

The third person they asked about Ava's whereabouts pointed them to the equipment room where he said Ava always went after a show. Inside, they found a woman going through the paces of returning the room to an orderly manner. Stacking chairs, arranging music stands, and shelving folders stuffed with papers seemed to be the majority of her menial tasks.

"Ava?" Coda questioned after taking several steps into the room.

The woman spun around with urgency and if there was any confusion as to who stood in front of her, it dissipated rapidly. "Coda Finn. Apartment 2B. What in the world are you doing here?" she said, almost out of breath.

"Long story or a condensed version?"

"Long story," Ava said.

Did anyone ever opt for the short version? No, it didn't seem like it.

Coda introduced Nolan and Frankie and then spoke his story for the umpteenth time.

"You're doing all this for your mom? That's incredible," Ava cut in at one point.

"We were too late," he said. "She died a week ago."

"And you haven't been back to New York yet?"

"Th-that's an even longer story. This is out last stop and I wanted to finish this. I know my mom would have understood." Coda heard Nolan shift behind him and lean against a desk that slid slightly across the floor. The noise was almost enough to cover her irritation at his response.

"I see," Ava said, clearly not under the same belief as Coda. "Remind me of the book again."

"*The White Meadow*."

"Right. Let me call my husband and see if he can find it. I only live a couple blocks from here, so he can bring it over."

"Thank you."

Ava stepped away and pulled out her cell phone.

"Coda, how are you feeling?" Frankie asked.

"I'm fine."

"I think that's bullshit," she said.

"I'm not here to argue my case," he said with a shrug. "Believe what you want."

"What's next after all of this? Are you two planning on driving back?"

"We have to. Nolan can't leave the car out here."

"Yup," Nolan said in a terse reply.

Frankie looked over but decided against pursuing any further conversation with her. She turned back to Coda. "How is it possible you managed to get back every book?"

"I couldn't tell you. Blind, dumb luck."

"No kidding. I've had a few people lend me books before and those got lost very quickly. It's actually incredible when you think about it."

"I try not to. This wouldn't be much of a story if we didn't get any of them back."

"A story for who?"

"I don't know. It was just hyperbole."

Frankie nodded and watched Ava walk back to the group.

"He found it and is on his way over now. Within an unpacked box. Thank goodness we labeled everything, or it would have taken several miracles to find it."

"Why did you keep it?" Coda asked, inspired by Frankie's disbelief in their luck.

"There's not some prophetic reason. It likely got placed on a bookshelf and shoveled into a box with everything else. To be perfectly honest, I don't actually recall what the book is about."

"It's a series of poems."

"Oh, that explains it then. Why'd you give it to me in the first place?"

Ava asked, squinting and looking up at Coda.

"I don't remember."

"It's annoying how much we forget with time."

"You just need to write everything down," Coda suggested.

"Is that what you do?"

"No. Maybe someday though. I'd have some stories to tell from this trip... But I'm curious. How did you end up here?" he asked, motioning to the space they were in.

"You know how much time I dedicated to playing the violin, so I needed to make it worthwhile. After college, I went to auditions. I found minimal success on the East Coast and my husband wanted to be closer to his family on the West Coast, so we moved out here and I stumbled into the symphony. I credit it to having a blind audition because if they saw I was a woman in my twenties, they would have rejected me immediately. It's insane how much of a man's world this is. I understand that it's gotten better, but still a lot more progress to make."

"Is this what you want to do as a career?"

"Absolutely. This is the first step. San Francisco is not the pinnacle, so I have higher aspirations."

"How come you haven't changed your last name after getting married?"

"Not everyone does that these days, Coda."

"Oh." He wondered whether Sam would have found Ava if she changed her name.

"Let's head to the front," Ava suggested. She led the way, talking to Nolan and Frankie as they navigated through the winding hallways.

Coda trailed behind and let them have uninterrupted conversation.

Once outside, they formed their own tiny pocket of people and waited for her husband. It took ten minutes for him to show up.

"Everyone, this is Derek. Derek, this is an old friend from college and two of his friends," Ava said, pointing to each person and reciting back the names.

The pleasantries went around as usual and, eventually, Derek presented the book and handed it to Ava.

"Is this what you were looking for?"

"If it has a symbol in the back, then yes."

Ava flipped *The White Meadow* open and let out a small laugh. "I remember this now. I always thought it was funny how on the nose that symbol is."

"What do you mean?" Coda said.

"You don't know what that symbol means?"

"No. I assumed it was something my mom made up."

"Definitely not. Was she into music at all?"

"Besides reading, it was her favorite thing."

"Did she sing or play an instrument?"

"I'm not sure. I never asked, and she never said anything."

"She must have been familiar with reading sheet music. There are a multitude of symbols that instruct the musician on what to do. Maybe it's to replay a section or what pitch the notes are in or . . . I can see I'm boring you. Let me speed this along. The symbol in the book means the musician is coming to the last section before the end. Any ideas what it's called?" Ava asked. She was enjoying this lesson.

Nolan shook her head.

Frankie shook her head.

Coda shook his head.

"It's you," she said, pointing to the face in the middle. "It's called a coda. I always thought your name was strange. People must ask you if Coda is short for Dakota because they can't rationalize a name like that. It seems like your parents knew what they were doing when they named you."

"He is the youngest of four. The only boy," Nolan noted.

"You're a coda in the literal sense," Ava said with another laugh.

"I'm sure they would have told me that if it was the case," Coda said.

"Look, I wouldn't get too hung up on this. The main point is your mom was using that symbol for a specific reason. I'm mystified as to how you never knew what its meaning was."

"I never bothered to ask."

"Now's the perfect time to!" Derek said with pure innocence.

Coda shifted his weight onto his left leg and then centered himself again. "Yeah, it is."

After a few more minutes, Ava politely said she was tired and ready to get home. She asked if they had a place to stay for the night and Nolan said they'd find a nearby hotel. Ava listed out several suggestions before saying her good-byes.

All the time, all the effort was reduced down to that final moment. The two weeks of travel and thousands of miles of driving to retrieve the seven (well, six) books was over.

Contrary to what was expected, there wasn't a big parade or a massive display of fireworks shot off into the sky. No, they parted ways from Ava without any fanfare.

Coda had what he came for, but the cost . . .

What now?

That question is actually answerable.

We keep moving forward to the coda.

fifty-one

SAUSALITO

They used the next day for exploring.

Things were still bitterly cold between Coda and Nolan as she rebuffed his attempts to talk at the hotel. It stung, but he understood.

Frankie agreed to tag along for part of the day but noted she needed to go see her boyfriend. Coda sensed the false urgency as if seeing him was a chore more than a relief.

They piled into the car and traveled north over the Golden Gate Bridge. From a distance the structure looked exciting, but while traveling on it, the experience was somewhat harrowing. One false jerk of the steering wheel and Nolan could have sent them careening over the edge. It would have taken considerable force, but Coda couldn't help but think of the disastrous scenario. Coda watched as Nolan gripped the steering wheel tighter as her brain determined how high above the water they were. Even though she didn't vocalize her discomfort, Coda knew she was working through a mild panic attack as it never materialized into anything more.

They crossed over without incident and Frankie advised Nolan to take the first exit after the bridge for a photo op. The 2008 Pinto Pinata climbed up a small hill and came to a stop in a tiny parking lot. From there, they followed a dirt trail that brought them out to an expansive grass field that overlooked the bridge. The light of day was muted by the dark heavy clouds, so the burnt orange shine to the structure was more of a gloomy red.

Ample pictures were taken. It felt like the first time Nolan and Coda had been tourists throughout the entire trip. Sure, they saw Chicago and Charlotte and the wonder of Easton and the stunning landscape of Yosemite, but none of those places inspired them to pose for pictures and burst out their largest fake smiles.

See:

Nolan's fake smile was the product of Coda's deception.

Coda's fake smile was a result of his mom being dead.

You know how these things go.

After the Golden Gate Bridge, they kept traveling northwest until they hit Muir Woods. Frankie gave the national park high praise and insisted they spend some time there. Nolan followed the caravan of cars until they were flagged down by an employee.

"Reservation time?" he asked with no joy.

"Since when do you need a reservation?" Frankie asked.

"Few years now. We get too many visitors in the park, so now they space out the timings. Do you not have one?"

"No."

"Tough break," he said with no sympathy. "I'll need you to turn around down there and head back the way you came. You can make a reservation online, but it's usually booked for days in advance."

Nolan rolled up the window and followed his instructions.

"Sorry about that," Frankie said. "You never expect things to change in your hometown."

"I thought you said you came here often," Nolan said, referring to their conversation on the drive over.

"Yeah . . . well . . . yeah . . . It's been a while since I came to Muir Woods."

"Hm, okay. When's the last time you were in San Francisco?"

"I don't know. Months, I guess. Over winter break."

Nolan nodded. "That's a long time to not see your boyfriend. Do you two talk every day?"

"Of course."

"On the phone or just over texts?"

"Both."

"Hm, okay. I just haven't seen you use your phone much."

"Is there a reason you're interrogating me?"

"No. Just trying to generate conversation. Where should be go now?" Nolan said, shifting the subject.

Frankie's expression softened as she thought. "There's a small *beach town* back south toward the city. It's called Sausalito. We could go there for lunch and walk around. Then you can drop me off after. I don't want to keep you from starting your drive back."

"I don't think we are in much of a rush, right Coda? I mean, if we had been, we probably wouldn't have wasted so much time at each location or maybe even done this fucking trip in the first place. I hear emails are a wonderful method of communication and the postage system in this country isn't too shabby either." It was impossible to ignore the venomous tone that Nolan spoke in, but Coda tried his best. He turned his head and watched as they emerged from the outskirts of the forest and back toward the highway.

An uncomfortable, elongated silence spread through the 2008 Pinto Pinata. Nolan occasionally glanced at Frankie's phone propped up on the dashboard; Frankie fiddled with the radio controls until the music reached the desired volume, which was practically nothing; Coda continued to watch the scenery flash by in a series of snapshots.

Sometime later, Frankie directed Nolan to a half empty parking lot near the main drag of Sausalito. The overcast skies and crisp breeze off the water kept many of the tourists away. Frankie rattled off several suggestions for lunch, but each one was met with indifference.

"Okay, I'll choose for us then," she said in disgust. "I didn't picture you two as petty people, but you're proving me wrong."

No response.

Frankie pushed out in front and led them across three blocks and down a side street before reaching the restaurant in mind.

The place was deserted, and the hostess seemed thrilled to move through the motions of showing them to a table. The waiter seemed equally excited to highlight the menu favorites and the day's specials.

As expected, lunch was a dismal affair of chewing bread, sipping drinks, and shifting food around on plates. Any effort to generate conversation was ignored as silence became the preferred choice.

Following lunch, Frankie led them along the path, listening to the water splash against the rocks. They came across a gathering of people chattering loudly while an old, distinguished gentleman picked up a megaphone.

"Thank you all. Thank you all. It has been an absolute pleasure to have worked with you and organized such a wonderful remembrance to life in 2024." His entire body trembled in sudden jolts. Nobody was concerned that he'd fall over and crack his skull. "We still have room left in the capsule, so please come talk to me if you haven't contributed yet." The man handed off the megaphone to a smiling face as he stepped down carefully from the bench.

"This was perfect timing," Frankie said. "Anyone interested in contributing?"

"No." The answer came quick from Nolan and Coda.

"Of all the ways you could have responded, you picked the worst one." Frankie left them and walked over to the man.

"Hello. New around here?" he asked.

"I grew up in San Francisco, but these two are just traveling through," Frankie said, pointing to the others who followed up behind her.

"Oh wonderful! We have some room left in the time capsule if you are interested in adding a memento."

Nolan and Coda both stammered out incoherent replies laced with lame excuses. The man listened and nodded politely, but it was quite obvious he wouldn't accept anything they said. "Look, we don't have much room left," he continued, "so even if one of you volunteer to include something, that would be helpful. No sense in going through the effort of creating a time capsule if it isn't filled completely, right?"

Nolan, Frankie, and Coda looked back and forth between each other.

"I think Coda should put something in," Nolan said, fully tossing him into the man's crosshairs.

"That's a great idea," Frankie said with a wide grin.

"What could I possibly add to a time capsule? I don't live around here or have anything worthwhile to give away." He was bobbing for an excuse that didn't exist.

The man stood with his arms folded and interjected with an idea. "Write me a letter. That won't take up much space. It can be about anything. Hell, it doesn't even have to be for me, but you should keep in mind that someone will read it when the time capsule is dug up. I'm no spring chicken, so who knows what will become of me," he said with a soft smile. Any concern about what laid beyond this plane of existence didn't bother the man.

"Why me?" Coda asked, looking around at everyone.

"Why not you?" the man countered. "It's a letter. Speak from your heart, kid."

Coda nodded concededly. "Do you have anything to write with?"

"Follow me. I live a block away." The man began to walk down the path without waiting for their response.

During their brief walk to his house tucked into the hills of Sausalito, they learned the man's name was Wallace, but preferred to go by Wally as it gave him a certain aloofness that fit his personality better. It may be hard to notice, he said, but he used to be an amateur daredevil, riding motorcycles through fire and catapulting off large ramps across a long row of beat up cars. While never gaining the notoriety of someone like Evel Knievel, Wally enjoyed the moderate level of success that afforded him a house in Sausalito. He explained that the time capsule had been an idea of his for years and took many conversations with the mayor as she didn't understand the purpose or reasoning. Once the green light was given, Wally found that while residents appreciated the idea, most didn't have enough gusto to contribute or help organize, hence the empty space within. He argued that adding something to a time capsule was as easy as putting on you pants in the morning, so the lack of participation was bizarre to him.

A lot of exposition in such a short time! That's Wally for you!

He led them into the house and searched through the junk draw in the kitchen until he found a notepad and pen. "Will this do?" he asked.

"Looks fine. Any requirements?" Coda asked as if it was a college assignment.

"However long or short you want it. Just write about whatever is on your mind. How's that?"

"Fair enough."

"Why don't you write in the dining room and we will stay in the kitchen and chat?"

Coda nodded and followed Wally's outstretched hand to see where the dining room was.

After Coda disappeared around the corner, Wally said, "Nervous fellow, isn't he?"

"It's been a long couple weeks for him. A lot of unresolved feelings," Nolan said.

"Tell me more, if you don't mind my prying. It's not often I hear fresh stories outside of the boring politics in this godforsaken town."

Nolan did. She gave him the long version. To Wally's credit, he never interrupted. He listened intently and urged Nolan to keep going with subtle cues.

It felt good to tell the story, as it helped her understand Coda's viewpoint better. She still didn't agree with his decisions, but she empathized. After all, wasn't the relationship with her parents as complicated as his had been?

Maybe.

Maybe.

Maybe.

When Nolan finished, she waited for Wally's onslaught of questions, but he only vocalized one. "Have you decided whether you want to stay in California?"

"I didn't think that would be your first question," Nolan said with a laugh.

"I appreciate you explaining to me what it's been like traveling across the country and the reasoning behind it, but it's clear what Coda's letter will be about, so I'll get to hear more from him in due time. If I'm lucky."

"Still undecided on what to do," Nolan said.

"I'm sensing a fear of leaving Coda behind."

"Why do you think that?"

"Well, why else would you go across the country for *him*? Your road trip has been largely about him, and you agreed to it because you undoubtedly care about Coda. Noble and true friendships like that are hard to come by, but there's also a point when you need to think about yourself. You staying in California seems to be much larger than finding your birth parents — it's rediscovering yourself. Still, it needs to be your decision, so don't let an old crow like me persuade you — just trying to give you another perspective."

"Thanks Wally."

"Here, take my number. In case you stay in California and need to escape to this paradise. I don't get many visitors these days, but maybe I could entice you by saying I have plenty of ridiculous stories to share — perks of being a daredevil." His tone was sincere. He was looking for people to pass the time with.

"Yes, I'd like that," Nolan said.

He turned to Frankie and began asking her questions about coming back to San Francisco. In typical fashion, her answers were vague enough to divert suspicion but lacked the sincerity of a true conversation Wally was seeking. At the end, he jotted down his number for her as well with the same reasoning.

They sat at the kitchen table for a full thirty minutes until Coda returned from the dining room. "Do you have an envelope?" he asked.

"Check the draw where I got the paper from."

Coda did as instructed and found a small chunk of envelopes buried toward the bottom, amongst the miscellaneous crap in there. It's amazing how many useless items can be crammed in one location. He plucked one out and folded the letter two times before placing it inside and sealing the envelope. Once completed, he handed over the final product to Wally.

"Hope it's worth it."

"It will be," Wally said. "You're too young to be jaded."

"Well, both my parents are dead, and I don't have a job to go back to, so things seem off-kilter now." That comment sucked all the air out of the room.

Wally gave a solemn nod. "I understand . . . Why don't we go back and place this inside?"

Back to the time capsule they went. It was a long cylinder with a handle on top to hoist it out of the concrete hole that was dug out in the grass. A small plaque commemorated the occasion with a projected date of when it would open.

Coda gazed into the future and wondered where he would be, what he would be doing, and whether he would be happy. What returned was total blankness. Starting each book by reading the last page always led Coda to think about the future. If he couldn't even read a book from front to back properly, how would he have the patience to live his own life that way? But aren't we all guilty of wanting to peek behind the curtain to see if a decision pans out or a relationship survives the trials or if success is ever in the cards?

Of course.

It's only natural, except life doesn't work like a book where all the pages are defined for you. Your story is constantly being written and edited without ever fully knowing what comes next.

Unless you believe in the script, which then means that everything is planned out in advance. You just need to find the master copy.

Wally handed off Coda's letter to a woman who opened up the time capsule and carefully placed it inside with all the other letters of various sizes.

Nolan, Frankie, and Coda stood around aimlessly, not sure of what comes next. Wally provided an answer.

"Well, it looks like I selfishly got what I needed. You're welcome to hang around here longer, but we won't officially get the capsule into the ground and sealed up until tomorrow."

That was enough motivation for them to say their farewells to Wally and return to the car. Nolan was the first one to speak as they all wondering what the next destination was.

"Frankie, is it time for us to part ways?" Nolan asked.

"I think so. I've intruded enough on your journey and you two need to have a nice, healthy chat."

Nolan peered back through the rear-view mirror toward Coda, but he was staring off, thinking about what he had written.

"Where should we drop you off?"

"It's a restaurant over in Cow Hollow."

"Cow Hollow?"

"Yes, it's a real area. Many young professionals congregate in the area. My boyfriend's choice," she said with indifference. "Let me pull up the address." Within seconds, Snoogle Maps was vocalizing the route for Nolan to take.

Nolan had more questions about the nature of Frankie's boyfriend and why she wanted to go to a restaurant when she ate a couple hours ago, but instead of the inane answers she would get, Nolan focused on crossing back over the Golden Gate Bridge and heading into the epicenter of San Francisco.

"Anywhere up here is fine," Frankie said as they inched closer down the congested blocks.

"You sure? I don't mind getting you closer."

"No, no. It's okay."

"This looks like a ritzy area. Your boyfriend has good taste," Nolan noted, thinking about how he supposedly didn't have enough money to fly to Denton.

"Thanks. I'll be sure to pass along the kind words when I see him."

Nolan pulled onto a side street, away from the main crux of traffic. She popped her hazards on, the melodic blinking sound filling the car as Frankie gathered her things.

Everyone got out of the 2008 Pinto Pinata and pulled Frankie's bags onto the street. They stood around aimlessly, stuck with uncertainty with what to do next.

"What do we do now?" Coda said, asking the important question on everyone's mind.

"Well, I'm going to give each of you a hug and make empty promises to stay in touch even though life will pull us in opposite directions as soon as I walk down the street. I'll thank you for being so kind and welcoming, and I'll tell you how I hope your friendship continues on after this trip since it's undeniable how much you care about each other.

How's that?"

Look:

Sometimes you need to be blunt with the truth to squash any awkwardness.

"Sounds perfect to me," Nolan said, stepping forward and giving Frankie a hug. "You have our contact information, so don't be a stranger."

"Yeah, of course."

Coda walked over and gave Frankie a hug. She whispered something to him that he decided wasn't worth sharing, so all we could do is speculate, but there's more important things to do than that.

Frankie clutched her bags, gave one last look, and turned to walk down the street.

They watched her drag the bags until she dipped around the corner.

"We need to talk," Nolan said, stepping back into the car. Coda followed and returned to the passenger seat, ready to tackle what was about to happen next.

fifty-two

OUT OF OPTIONS

There never was a boyfriend.

But you probably knew that already.

Frankie Lao took the first bus that brought her closer to the Bayview neighborhood of San Francisco. It took another transfer and five blocks of walking to reach her destination.

It was a far cry from the ritzy part of town she had Nolan and Coda drop her off in. She didn't lie out of malice, but shame.

See:

Everything she said was a lie. Subtle truths were hidden within, but complete strangers wouldn't know how to reveal them.

Frankie graduated from UNT the previous May — several semesters longer than what she claimed to Nolan and Coda. Student loans kicked in after six months and without any leads for a job in anthropology, Frankie began to drown. The motion of being evicted from her apartment was swift and effortless like an expert ballroom dancer. The money from the waitressing job wasn't enough to cover all her expenses and while Julio tried his best to get her additional shifts, at a certain level, Frankie had given up trying.

It was true her parents owned a business, but that didn't mean it was successful or still around. They grew up with a minimal income and Frankie assumed college was the answer. Maybe it's because she failed to ask, but no one told her getting a college degree wasn't an immediate ticket out of poverty. The loans made her time at UNT manageable, almost to the point she forgot what life was like back in San Francisco.

After being evicted, Frankie tapped on the few friends still in the area and they allowed her to crash on their couch. They were supportive, but there was only so long you could invade someone else's space.

She had less than a week left when Nolan and Coda showed up. Her friend asked her to find another place to stay and with no more options, Frankie settled on San Francisco. The last of her money would have been used for a flight or bus ride or something, anything to get her back.

The shame was insurmountable. Her parents mocked and ridiculed her on the latest phone call when she told them the situation.

Why couldn't you be more like your other siblings?

We told you that a degree in anthropology would get you nowhere.

What will you do back here? We expect you to help pay bills. You better find a job.

The list dragged on and on, but Frankie was desensitized to the verbal abuse and acidic vitriol that was always spewed at her.

The earliest memory of her father was in their kitchen, if you could call it that. The separation between each room was blurred. It was back when people still had landlines and cell phones weren't a common household item. Frankie's father was on the phone with someone and pacing around the kitchen. His temper was a short fuse with explosive results. She watched from the kitchen table as he placed a hand on his forehead and then thrust it out into the open air, pointing vigorously as if the person on the phone was standing in front of him. Frankie recalled her feet swinging in the chair as she tried to stretch her body enough to have the red shoes graze against the floor. It kept her occupied while her father began to lose control. Everyone in the house knew to seek shelter when he was about to unload in a verbal tirade or physical violence, but Frankie was young enough to see him as her father and not a monster. He hung up the phone in a fury. It fell off the receiver, dangling and swaying a foot off the ground. He picked it up and placed it on the receiver. Again, it fell. Again, he picked it up and placed the telephone on the receiver. Again, it fell. He picked it up one last time and slammed the phone against the wall.

Again.

And again.

And again.

A primal rage tore through the house as he continued to beat the phone into the wall until it was broken with sizable hole staring back at him.

"Daddy, please stop. You're being scary," Frankie said from the table. She cowered in her seat, stopping her legs from the leisurely swing.

He dropped the phone and moved toward her. The backhand against her face was quick like the changing of a stoplight from yellow to red. The rings on his hand tore open her skin as blood trickled down. "DON'T EVER TELL ME TO FUCKING STOP!" he screamed at her. His breath smelled like fish and cigarettes. She diverted her eyes to her feet that were so desperately trying to reach the floor. She watched as a droplet of blood fell from her cheek and onto the red shoes. It blended in perfectly.

Frankie cried. Deep, sorrowful wails as her dad stalked off to his room without any word of remorse. She'd seen him hit her mother and brothers but never her. Not his little girl.

Frankie's mom swept in from another room to console her child and whispered the senseless apologies that victims are beaten down into saying.

He didn't mean it.
You know how he can be.
He still loves you.
Things aren't easy right now.
The list dragged on and on.

As Frankie grew older, her mom abandoned the savior complex and joined in on the abuse when she realized Frankie wasn't determined to be a carbon copy of her parent's expectations. While her father relied on scare tactics, her mother was an expert at small jabs about her weight or intelligence or the way she ate her food or how she put the dishes away. It was endless ridicule and amongst it all, her mother had moments where she'd be stoic and tell Frankie how her children meant everything.

It took Frankie a long time to realize her mother only said that because her marriage was so miserable. If the only thing she had was her children, why was she so hellbent on alienating them at every turn?

A purely rhetorical question for there was not a coherent answer.

Whatever sympathy she had built up for her mother as a child, Frankie lost all of it. She viewed it as a trickle more so than a flood. Each day a few drips until all that remained was a dry husk.

Frankie stood across the street from the house. Every muscle willed her to keep moving, to find another place. Anywhere but there.

She had no choice though.

It wouldn't be long, she tried to tell herself. She'd find *something*. San Francisco was a booming city. If all else failed, she could move down to LA. Plenty of opportunities there.

In order to break the cycle of poverty, she needed to return to the last place she ever wanted to go.

Are you sure? Are you sure? There must be other options, her mind fluttered. Frankie grabbed her luggage and dragged them across the street. She opened the gate and lifted the bags up the three concrete steps. She'd thrown away the house key years ago, so she rang the doorbell. At first, the door opened a sliver and then wider and wider until she saw the full form of her mother. Worn down by age and a loveless marriage.

Frankie's mother stared at her for a long time before speaking. "Why are you here? I didn't think you were serious the last time we talked."

"I have no money and need a place to stay."

Her mother cackled with perverse pleasure. "And you think we have anything to give you?"

"I'm not asking for money. Just a place to stay for a couple weeks."

Her mother stepped aside and allowed Frankie to come in.

Frankie moved into the hallway with her luggage, back into the place of abuse and horrid memories all because she was out of money and options.

A sad reality for too many, isn't it?

fifty-three

BACK TO HOW IT WAS

Access to the hotel rooftop shouldn't have been as easy as it was, but it seemed San Francisco lacked real concern when it came to security.

Nolan swiped their keycard three times, but the door continued to show red. She then jiggled the handle in rapid succession until one of the attempts unlocked the door.

The rooftop dwarfed in comparison to the other buildings around it, but they didn't choose the hotel for the potential view.

They had some shit to sort out.

Coda sat down and crossed his legs with his back facing the giant skyscraper a block up the road. Nolan followed and sat across from him.

"So," he said.

"So," she said.

"I'm sorry. I truly am. I didn't mean to lead you on, but I knew you'd want to turn around and go back."

"No shit, Coda. Because that's the sensible thing to do. It's more than that though. You lied about how sick your mom was. Why bother with this trip if she was so close to death?"

"The books. It's always been about the books."

"But why?" she said, almost yelling at him. "They are just objects. Your mom . . . You can't go on another road trip and get that back."

"Nolan, the last however many years of our relationship being non-existent has been incredibly hard. Those books were my only way out."

"But it was your mother. She would have welcomed you back regardless. You didn't need to gather up the books to prove you were sorry."

"I know. I'm so stupid. I let the routine consume my life and I went so many days and months without thinking about her because of how unhappy I was with work and the commute and all the other boring parts of life," Coda said, knocking the side of his skull with an open hand two times.

He continued. "Above all else, it's shame. That is undeniable. As the months piled on, I began thinking about how I couldn't possibly go back and repair that relationship. I said I hated her and didn't think we could recover. The books were meant to be that gesture of apology. It wouldn't fix everything, but it was a start."

"Why did you say that to her in the first place?"

"Nolan, I'm fucked up. Do you think stabbing a classmate was an appropriate response to my dad dying?"

"I mean, he said something extremely racist and your emotions were running wild at the time."

"All true, but it doesn't excuse my behavior. On some level, I feel like I'm losing my mind. Or that I lost it a while back. The past week has been a blur and that blur is a continuation of all the floating I've done the past five years."

"You need to properly grieve."

"Back in New York I will."

Nolan exhaled sharply. "I'm still disappointed with you."

"I know. Nothing I could say would justify my actions and anything I do say will sound like a tired excuse."

"At least you are self-aware . . . I still care deeply about you obviously. You are my best friend and I hope our friendship carries on far into the future."

"Me too. Me too," he said, leaning in for a hug.

What more was there to say on the matter?

Plenty more for sure, but nothing that would change the tide. A longer explanation would have dug Coda into a deeper hole when the easiest, best choice was to own up to his misguided decisions and hope he could evolve from it.

He still had more to figure out — mainly the grief. That part was going to be a real chore.

"Nolan," Coda continued, "I can't thank you enough for driving me across the country. It's incredible to consider how many miles you're driven."

"You're welcome. It was worth it."

"Really? Why do you say that?"

"I'm not a fool. I understand I was a secondary character through all of this. We went places to meet people you knew and were trying to reconnect with. I'm not sure how successful you were or if it was even a goal of yours. In any case, my role was to provide support and I hope that was good enough."

"You have been much more than that. You had your own journey to go through. You've told me about your panic attacks and how you were adopted. The next step is to decide whether California is where you want to stay."

Nolan looked up into the sky. Nothing exciting was visible due to the light pollution. "I've thought for a while on what to do. My first instinct was to stay out here and start crafting a new life on the West Coast. But then I asked myself what the point was. I can't possibly rediscover my life by running away from the problems. California is the pipe dream, the last thoughts before falling asleep at night. And the vision is perfect. I'd find a beautiful place to stay in an affordable part of the state that doesn't exist. I'll stumble into a group of friends even though my social bone was tossed aside years ago; I'll hire a private detective to find my birth parents who will be eager to meet their discarded daughter. It's all crap, Coda. Total crap. My incentive to leave everything behind was blinded forgetting to solve your problems leads to more unhappiness than peace of mind. I need to go back to New York and have a conversation with my parents. I need answers and then I have to find that next step in my life. Maybe it will lead me elsewhere, but I can't run away before I even try. Do you recall what Murph told us as we left the bookstore in Denver?"

"Follow it."

"Exactly. Oddly enough, those words helped me realize I need to follow the questions before I seek the answers."

"Are you sure about all this?"

"Yes. I've made my decision."

"And this has nothing to do with me?" Coda asked.

"What do you mean?"

"I . . . I'm not quite sure. I have a lot of guilt for dragging you into this and lying and now I feel like my selfish needs are forcing you back to New York."

Nolan laughed. "I don't mean to be rude, but this is the one thing about the trip that has nothing to do with you. I am terribly sad you lost your mother, but I know you'd be okay to head back to New York if I had decided to stay here."

"I understand. Just trying to sort through all the things running through my head."

"It's okay."

"I'm happy you're going back — if only for a bit. Having you in the city will make the next few weeks easier."

"Of course."

Coda mimicked Nolan's move from earlier and gazed up into the hidden stars. "Do you think I have any chance of finding a job?"

"Without a doubt. It may take some time, but if you are persistent, something will surface. And this time, go with a job you will be satisfied with."

"You say that like I didn't think I'd be satisfied with JEC."

"Well . . . true, I guess. But you now know a major corporation isn't the path you want. You could always work at a bookstore or freelance programming or find a startup or write a book if you come up with a unique idea. The options are out there, but you need to seek them out."

Coda nodded. "Lots to consider. As always. Is there ever a time in someone's life where they feel completely content and not second-guessing every decision they make."

"Oh sure, those people exist . . . in fiction. Coda, you have to understand nothing will ever be easy and the reason you quit your job was because you wanted better for yourself. It was a bold step, one that some people never have the confidence to take. Make sure it was worth doing."

He stared back at Nolan, watching her expression soften and waiting for him to propel the conversation forward. "Are we okay?"

"We will be. Just another obstacle for our friendship to overcome."

"How are we going to get back to New York?" Coda asked.

"I've thought about that too. Considering my parents haven't called once over the past two weeks, I'm thinking they don't care much about the car. With everything that's going on, we can't waste any more time. I suggest we fly."

"What will you do with the car?"

Nolan shrugged. "Who gives a fuck about the car?"

"We have to take the car somewhere. Maybe we can sell it."

"Or, maybe we can give it to Wally. For safe keeping. I'd consider asking Frankie, but I'm unsure what her deal is."

"Sounds like a long term plan if Wally takes it."

"Could be, but I don't give a shit about that car. It's an object. Just another status symbol for my parents. They have other toys to capture their attention."

"I'll trust your judgement."

"Good," Nolan said, wiping her hands on her pants. She began to stand, ready to rid herself from the rooftop. She paused, taking in the sights around here. "It's different out here. Almost makes me miss New York."

"We will be back there soon enough." Coda stood up and wrapped his arm around Nolan as they walked toward the door.

"This was the adventure of a lifetime, wouldn't you say?"

"We have plenty more to go."

They disappeared back into the building, leaving behind the cloudless sky and millions of stars hidden beyond the lights of San Francisco.

Their cross-country trip was complete. It was time to go home.

IV

LET IT ALL OUT

fifty-four

A MATTER OF PERSPECTIVE

Buying a ticket for a cross-country flight the night before you leave is a costly and annoying affair. Many were sold out, and the ones that remained had astronomical prices on the shitty airlines no one wanted to fly.

Coda Finn and Nolan Treiber were crammed in middle seats on opposite ends of the American Airlines flight from SFO to LGA. They were charged for their extra bags and the six inches of additional leg room their seats were so lovingly blessed with. The flight attendants threw stale snacks and half opened beverages at them like they were mimicking a t-shirt cannon. The plane was full of crying babies, sneezing toddlers, and bladder-challenged adults who used the bathroom every hour.

Coda kept to himself the entire flight. He watched a bit of news, feeling the need to catch up on world events, but quickly turned it off after realizing everything was still — supposedly — in the same state of calamity with no salvation. At one point, he scrolled through his phone and looked at all the new numbers he had saved. He wondered if he would contact any of them. They had been so welcoming and incredibly helpful that Coda felt obligated to continue a friendship — or whatever it should be classified as. The main problem was in Coda believing he had nothing to offer. Their time together was centered around a clear, concise objective. Once completed, he carried on with life to the next stop of his tour. Their conversations thrived because of the time spent apart, and aren't some of the best friendships that way? Two opposites coming together because the months or years apart allowed for enough events to occur that made conversation flow.

Until Coda had a job and significant hobbies and exciting tales from the city, he had nothing to give anybody.

So he thought.

That eternal doubt crept in and latched on without fear of being shaken off. The trip was the beginning. Coda's evolution would happen in phases and he only finished the prologue.

He locked his phone and tilted his head back. Coda closed his eyes and pretended to fall asleep.

Toward the front of the plane, Nolan was alert and enthralled by the movie. She used it as a distraction from thinking about the joys that awaited her in New York. Like Coda, her story was in its early stages and the narrative rested entirely on her shoulders. She alone determined where it went next.

After descending from the rooftop the night prior, Nolan called Wally and explained the situation about flying home and asked if he would take the 2008 Pinto Pinata. Sadness laced his voice as he agreed to, but she understood he didn't necessarily think New York offered her much value anymore. They dropped the car off with no fanfare. The logistics of maintenance and other oddities weren't discussed as if Nolan was dropping off the car for only a few days. It was hard to believe she had driven the car for thousands of miles across the United States. She'd never sit back and think about the countless miles of boring swatches of land with no sights to see. She'd never consider how much her lower back ached after particularly long stretches of driving or how it took her three days to figure out the cruise control. We have an inherent ability to tune out the mundane moments and create a sizzle reel of the highlights. It's been said at nauseum that the trip belonged to Coda Finn, which is highly debatable. What would she think back on? Time would tell because not every picture is clear at first glance.

Following their excursion to Wally's house, they grabbed a rideshare to the airport. Somewhere amongst the skyscrapers and heading south, Nolan turned to Coda.

"The viewing was on Friday. What about the funeral?" The question came to her suddenly. Maybe Coda's urgency to get back was to make it for the funeral.

"It was yesterday," he said flatly.

"Oh." So much for that hope.

"I can see your judgement."

"I'm not trying hard to hide it."

"And what would you have done if the roles were reversed?"

"I wouldn't have left New York. I'd have repaired the relationship as fast as I could, but you have been shy on the details regarding you and your mom's falling out, so I imagine it's more complicated than what I'm thinking."

"It's funny to me how everyone always pictures themselves doing the heroic thing and never making a mistake. If you ever find yourself in my situation, I hope you make the right choice. But like you said, it was more complicated than I could describe."

Nolan wasn't trying to pick another fight, so she didn't pursue the conversation further. Coda was right though. It was incredibly easy for a passive audience to judge and criticize a choice when they showed up late to the party. Nolan imagined his sisters had an opinion on the situation just like his mom and amongst all the stories and emotions hid the truth. How much did the truth matter now? The decisions had been made and the outcome was final.

Instead of fixating on Coda's life, she turned inward and considered her own. That occupied the first couple hours of the flight until her head became so swelled with information that she turned on the first shitty rom-com movie she found and turned her full attention to it. The worst part of such a long flight was when she finished the movie, they still had another two hours left until they landed.

The remaining time slid by in a haze. It was the first time Nolan had been on a plane since she was adopted. She inched forward and looked out the window. Far out in the distance was a storm cloud, dark and heavy and full of malice. She watched as the lightening shot out in a flash and waited for the thunderclap that never came. From her vantage point, the scene was beautiful. For those below it, there may have been concern.

It was merely a matter of perspective.

During their descent, the New York City skyline came into view. Even from that height it was hard to ignore the complexity and cramped nature of how everything intertwined. A fresh blanket of show was visible across the boroughs as winter seemed to impart one last storm before spring sprang in. The boats on the Hudson and the cars on the expressways and all the other moving parts seemed to glide with no urgency, but of course, that was never the case. The leisurely drive they spent weeks doing would be replaced by the scrambling denizens and constant urgency to be somewhere.

It went mostly unspoken, but Nolan and Coda missed the city.

It was home after all.

For now.

After landing and parking at the gate, Nolan disembarked and waited for Coda in the crowded terminal. All around her, people blitzed in every direction to make a flight or escape the confines of the airport. She tried to focus in on one person, but they would quickly get lost in the maze.

Coda tapped her on the shoulder, bringing her back. "Ready?"

She nodded and led the way through the terminal, following signs for the subway.

"Are you going to the cemetery?" Nolan asked as they waited for the train.

"I plan to."

"I'm here if you need some support."

"Thanks. I'd appreciate that. I'll give you a call when I go."

"Also, considering our current job prospects are zero, we could make it to The Wobbling Stool for all of happy hour and get properly drunk," Nolan said.

"I drank more these past two weeks than I ever did in college, so I'll pass on the getting drunk part, but I'm all in for spending some evenings at The Wobbling Stool. As long as we both promise to search for jobs during the day."

"Agreed."

The train arrived on time as Nolan and Coda pushed their way into the subway car and found two seats in the corner. They created a perimeter with all their luggage, much to the annoyance of the passenger sitting across from them.

They remained in silence for most of the ride, opting to listen to the squealing of metal and the soothing voice that notified them of each stop.

Anyways, what was there to talk about?

They had driven thousands of miles together over the course of two weeks. They had more car chats than captured. They met a wild blend of people whose stories ranged from traumatic to outrageous. They retrieved seven books from seven strangers all in the hopes of using them to reunite Coda with his estranged mother.

Look where hope got them.

During all that, we didn't glimpse the countless times they laughed at each other's jokes or bickered over where to stay for the night or who would pay for the meal. For all that we read about, there was so much more they'd never share because we wouldn't understand. The best relationships tend to work that way, huh?

Nolan glanced up at the electronic board and gathered her things. Seeing as they were adept subway riders, they stood up without the need to brace themselves for the heavy-handed braking the conductor was fond of.

"Got everything? Sure you don't need any help?" Coda asked.

"I'm fine," Nolan said with a laugh. "Don't worry about me. I only need to drag this shit a couple blocks."

"Okay," he said, pulling her in for a hug. There was a finality to it like they wouldn't see each other again, but that couldn't be the case. Their relationship was the only one Coda had figured out how to get right. "Thank you for everything," he whispered.

Nolan said something back that was blurred by the squealing. Her comment made Coda laugh and reduced the stress of the moment.

As Nolan moved to the opening door, Coda said, "Let's do this again sometime . . . Under different circumstances."

"Who doesn't like a sequel?" she said, stepping out onto the platform and blending into the shifting wave of people.

fifty-five

FOR CODA

Slightly messy and dotted with books.
 His apartment was as he left it.
 When Coda made it back from the airport, he collapsed into his bed, not bothering to unpack any luggage. It could wait. Maybe he could leave it all packed for the next trip . . . when or if that ever happened.
 It wasn't until the next morning that Coda made some semblance of human movement and rolled himself out of bed and to the bathroom. He shaved off the patchy stubble that resembled a bad season of crops at the homestead and returned to the babyface that forced him to present his ID at any bar. He twisted and jerked his jaw and watched as the mirror repeated the gestures back to him. Sometimes he needed to check if his body had been invaded by foreign entities because why else would a sane person do what he'd done over the past three weeks? Scratch that. How about five years?
 He smiled for the mirror with nothing in return except a loud creak from the radiator as it kicked on. The noise snapped him back to the present. He stepped out of the bathroom and dug through the closet until he found the appropriate jacket to brave the cold weather.
 Coda walked to the subway station underneath the Barclay's Center and watched as the other platform was stuffed with people trying to make their way into Manhattan. That was him not so long ago. It would probably be him again, but he was thankful for the reprieve.
 Instead, he took the subway deeper into Brooklyn toward familiar territory. Things changed as they always did, but he could easily spot the corner stores and coffeeshops that would survive any disaster. It was more peaceful in this part of the city. The noise was slightly less as the traffic was a moderate drip compared to the constant flow by him. The side streets offered solace and shortcuts. And the sidewalks had enough room for people to walk without smashing into one another. Even in a city such as New York, you could drift from the chaos.
 His feet carried him to his destination without conscious thought. He climbed the steps and pulled the key from his pocket. It had always been

on his coffee table, begging for use. The invitation went unheeded.

He stepped into the foyer and was greeted by questions of concern.

"Hello?"

"Clem, is that you?"

The voices stepped around the corner. "Ah. You finally showed up," his sister Cecilia said, taking one look at him before retreating back to where she came.

Cassandra glanced back at Cecilia before deciding not to follow her lead. She moved toward Coda with her arms spread wide. "Coda."

They hugged and he felt some of the tension escape his body. Still more to get rid of though.

"You're back. I'm glad you're safe. We have been worried about you," she said, craning her neck to get a good look.

"You know everything that's been going on?" He hadn't spoken much to Cassandra during his trip westward.

"Cecilia filled me in."

"She's mad, isn't she?"

"Devastated may be the right word. But probably mad too. She feels like you abandoned the family and let petty differences stop you from having a relationship with mom."

"And what do you think?"

They continued to stand in the foyer with no urgency to move elsewhere. Coda felt the cold air whisk into the room from underneath the front door. He tried to block out the high wispy sound and focus on Cassandra's incoming answer.

She gave a long sigh and folded her arms. "I . . . I . . . It's complicated," she said. "You were always different from us. The only boy, the only one who showed interest in learning and not on a surface level to get through school. When dad died, we were at a different place physically and emotionally than you were. We had the large groups of friends to fallback to or sports or those other distractions to make the pain subside. You didn't. And because of that, you didn't process the event which led to the long, subtle decline in your relationship with mom. When I think of it that way, I understand why you left. I understand why you felt the books would mend the gap and be the ultimate peace offering, but what bothers me is that you think our mother would have expected something like that. She was as selfless as people get. She spoke about and praised you constantly to the point of annoyance. It lessened when you two stopped talking, but that was only because she didn't have any news about you. We can't go back and change the outcome of your relationship with her, so I hope you find solace and are able to move forward."

Hope.

That silly word always pops up at the most inconvenient time.

Coda absorbed the information. He could feel the disappointment wafting off his sister, but the direct words would go unsaid. "Did mom say anything at . . . at the end?"

Cassandra shook her head. "She drifted off. For all the suffering she had, it felt like a quiet, peaceful end."

"I should have been there," he said.

"You made your choice." It wasn't a comforting answer, but an honest one.

"How was the funeral?"

Each question made his stomach twist into tighter knots. Coda felt like someone was mining out his chest to find one nugget of gold.

"I wouldn't repeat it again."

"Did anyone ask about me?"

"Of course. Some people aren't going to understand and will look at you differently. Needless to say, there aren't many people who skip out on one parent's funeral, let alone both."

"I didn't want my last memory of mom to be of her on a hospital bed or in a casket."

"Let me ask you then," Cassandra said. "What is your last memory of her? Because it's not like you made any new ones in years."

The jab caught him off guard. No memory came to mind. Everything was clouded and scattered.

"I don't know," he managed to say.

"So yeah, while my last memory of mom is her in a casket, at least I have a thousand others to think about."

Coda's face contorted to some blend of shame and regret. He dipped his head and then craned it toward the ceiling. Feeble attempts to stop the tears. Cassandra took notice and tried to backpedal, slightly.

"I'm not trying to call you out, but we can't ignore what happened. All we can do now is move forward. You need to come back into this family, Coda. We miss you. We miss your smile and your ability to relate life back to a book you read and the compassionate nature you got from dad. Mom is gone but we aren't."

She was right. In the midst of the feud with his mom, Coda lost sight of the periphery. He knew practically nothing about his sisters because he'd never taken the time to ask questions. He never shared anything about his life because he didn't think they would care. And for what? Coda had no reason to treat his sisters any differently than the multitude of people he met during the trip. He sought answers and divulged his story to anyone who asked. Cecilia, Cassandra, and Clementine only wanted the best for their little brother, and it was long, long, long overdue for Coda Finn to recognize that.

Would he ever be able to forgive himself for the lost time and the choices he made?

Add it to the burn pile. The answer isn't worth knowing. Sometimes, too many questions become inhibitive of the ultimate goal — whatever that may be.

He looked at Cassandra and felt the tears running down his face. "I'm sorry," he said, giving her another hug. "I'm sorry. I'm sorry," he kept repeating. They were the only words that made sense.

Cassandra wiped her face and said, "Let's get dinner this week. I want to hear about your trip, and it looks like you may need some help finding a new job. You're a brave kid, Cod. I wouldn't have had the courage to quit like that."

"It was a reckless decision — one of many I suppose," he said with a smile. "And yes, I'd like that. You won't believe all my stories though," he cautioned.

"Oh yeah?"

"When you drive as much as we did, you're bound to meet some . . . strange individuals. Some moments felt like a fever dream."

Cassandra laughed. "I can only imagine." She turned to walk down the hallway. Coda was unsure whether it was an invitation for him to join or not.

"Cass?"

"Yeah?" She stopped and faced him once more.

"Any advice on how to handle Cecilia and Clem?"

"Cecilia gets in her own head too much. Once she realizes your intentions weren't laced in malice, she will come around. I don't think she will ever understand why, but she isn't going to cast you out. As for Clem, she has been quiet about your absence. You need to figure out that one on your own."

Coda decided to follow her down the hallway as she turned away from him once again. "What are you going to do with the house?"

"Sell it," she said, the answer traveling over the sounds of their footfalls.

"Really? This was our childhood house."

"And?"

"I . . ."

"It's got a mortgage none of us can afford, so unless you'd like to take on that responsibility . . ."

"I understand."

Coda followed Cassandra into the kitchen. Cecilia was in the living room doing a fantastic job of ignoring her brother as she scrolled through her phone.

"How did mom pay for this house anyways?" Coda asked.

"One of life's great mysteries. There were rumors about an inheritance from a distant relative or those couple of years where she was a card shark down in AC before we were born."

"You're joking."

"No shit, Cod," Cassandra said with a laugh. "Maybe you forget but mom worked and the death benefits from dad probably helped for a while. What does it matter now?"

"It doesn't," Coda said. He leaned against the counter and remembered a time when his head couldn't even see over it. A lifetime ago.

Cassandra looked over at Cecilia and as it became clear her sister had no intention of joining the conversation, Cassandra motioned to Coda. "There's something upstairs for you." Leading the way, Cassandra continued on. "We have been cleaning throu—"

"I can help with anything you need," Coda cut in. He needed her to know he wouldn't be absent any further.

"Thanks," she said with indifference. "So . . . Yeah, we have been cleaning the house and came across a box with your name on it. Well, actually, it's addressed to you. 'For Coda' is written on the side in mom's handwriting. You know how unmistakable it was."

"Yeah."

"It was sealed up. I didn't check to see what was inside."

Cassandra pushed open the door into his old bedroom. The same pinstripes lined the wall with the posters for inconsequential movies he'd only watched once.

The box sat atop the twin sized bed he'd outgrown back in middle school. They didn't have enough space for anything bigger. It was a minor miracle he had his own room — perks of being the only son.

Coda moved toward the box and grabbed at the tape. There could only be one thing inside. Briefly, he imagined a snake was hiding in there or a magic bullet meant to make him suffer one last time for being an ignorant jackass. Cassandra stood in the corner and looked on with vague interest. The past week had worn her out. She was in the main chunk of grief where acceptance feels like it's three marathons away.

Inside, books were stacked on top of one another in uneven columns. His mom had stuffed some into the side and tried to fill up as much space as possible. It was a combination of paperback and hardcover books of various sizes and age. Coda spotted yellow, crinkled paper that gave off an indistinct smell. He reached in and pulled out the first book his hand landed on. A Swill Grenning novel. He'd never heard of the author. He twisted the book in his hand and flipped it open to the inside cover. No note. He moved to the last page. No symbol.

Of course.

Not every book his mom gave him was adorned with a message and symbol. If anything, they were the vast minority. Only twelve over his lifetime. He'd have to comb through the entire box to find if there were any additions to his valued collection.

The pain hit him all at once.

That was it. No more.

He'd never get another book from his mom. The passion they shared was snuffed out unless he carried on with it. He waited for the tears to come again, but they never breached the surface. They would with time. You can't outrun grief forever. You know all about that, don't you?

Coda placed the book back amongst the piles and resealed the box as best he could.

"That was to be expected," he said, turning back to Cassandra. "I should have known she was collecting more books for me over the years."

"I'm surprised it was only one box," Cassandra noted. In all fairness, the box was crowded and Coda would have a hell of a time carrying it.

"I almost expected a letter to be in there. Something that would provide some finality."

"Finality to what?"

"Why she chose the books she did. Mom gave me dozens, but only a select few had a message in them and the symbol in the back. I tried to find a connection but there wasn't one."

"You're expecting to find an answer to something that doesn't need one."

"I guess so," Coda said, conceding the books were a gesture of love and nothing deeper. Did it need to be anything more?

"Did mom play any instruments?" he continued. The urge to ask surfaced suddenly.

"The violin. When she was a kid." Cassandra's face twisted in confusion. "Did you not know that?"

Coda shook his head and considered what else he never found out. He began to ask if she knew the meaning of his name. Coda stopped himself because on the off chance Cassandra didn't know, he wanted it to remain a secret.

"Just thought of how you'd find her either reading or listening to music. I was curious if there was an origin to either," he said, defending his initial ask.

He grabbed the box, balanced the weight in his arms, and followed Cassandra out of the room.

"Really, don't be a stranger. I expect to hear from you this week and you're buying me lunch as repayment for my patience and unending support," she said as they went downstairs.

"Yes, yes. I heard you the first time," Coda said, focusing on not dropping the box.

"Cod?"

"Yeah?" he said, peeking his head over the box.

"I love you. She loved you. We will always be here for you, wherever you go."

He put down the box and gave his sister one last hug. "Thank you, Cass. I love you too. I'm going to be better. I promise," he said, taking the first step to repair one of the things that had been lost.

fifty-six

LEND

The box of books challenged every unworked muscle in his arms, but Coda still deviated from the direct path back to the train.

He wanted to walk by one place. Just to see.

Four blocks away from the house, Coda saw the sign flash in the early afternoon light.

Uncle Sal's Pizza Palooza & Planetarium, the original location of the moderately successful New York chain restaurant and where his working career began.

Coda contemplated going inside and seeing if Cousin Sal was still working there, but fear of dreadful news kept him from doing so. Cousin Sal was an obese, soda-sucking man that was surely suffering from diabetes or some other ailment. Coda couldn't stomach the idea of hearing about another death.

Instead, he peered in through the window and saw the layout was the same. The red chairs that made an awful grating sound across the floor; the tables that wobbled anytime an ounce of weight was applied to them; the checkered floor that was perpetually sticky; the ludicrously high counter that the workers stood behind so they could peer down menacingly at the patrons.

What pizza place didn't share the same characteristics?

He remembered the countless afternoons he spent holed up at a table in the corner reading a book because his homework wasn't as interesting. He remembered how Cousin Sal praised him for his double douse method of cleaning methods and scolded the other employees for not following Coda's example. He remembered that besides his brief stint at the fire station, the pizza shop was the only other job he enjoyed. No offense to Eve and the college bookstore.

With the reminiscing behind him and his arms shaking heavily, Coda picked up his pace and reached the subway. His wait was short and soon he was heading back north.

The man across the subway car took three stops before he mustered up the courage to ask Coda his question.

"What's in the box?"

"A severed head," Coda said.

The man recoiled at the thought. "That's not something you joke about."

"You're right. My apologies. They are books." Coda reopened the box and showed the man to prove his truth.

"Well shit. I didn't think anyone read still."

"A mighty few of us left."

"You know the last book I read?" the man asked.

What an insensible question. For all the questions Coda pondered over the course of his journey, that one right there may be the dumbest one he heard.[23]

"I'm stumped," Coda said, throwing up his hands in surrender.

"Me too. I can't remember what it was called."

"What a shame. Must not have been a good book."

"Actually, the book was great. Eight hundred pages of pointless family drama written by some Russian guy that everyone drooled about back in the Stone Age or some shit. Huh, I guess I know more than I thought. No clue about the title though . . . Definitely not being sarcastic or anything," he said with a knee slap to show his sarcasm. "What are you going to do with all of them?" the man asked, switching topics.

"Read them, most likely."

"Ah, a sensible man. How long will that take you?"

"Hard to say. It depends on how motivated I am. But I intend to read them from front to back."

---

[23] A quick Snoogle search tells us the first *published* book was the Gutenberg Bible (no surprise there) in 1455. That isn't considering how people had the cognitive ability to read for thousands of years and told stories by the fire for longer than that. It is the year 2024 so that gives us 569 years of literature being published for the masses to read. Now, it is impossible to accurately state how many books (fiction, non-fiction, and any other delineation your heart desires) have been published each year, but let's go with an easy number of 50,000. That will make up for the countless years in the beginning that didn't have a number that large and for the recent years where that tiny number is wildly inaccurate. Beep, bop, boop. Math is fun. By multiplying our two numbers together, we get 28,450,000 books, which—this cannot be stated enough—is an outrageously conservative number. But this tells us that while Coda's options aren't exactly limitless, the odds aren't in his favor of guessing the correct book. Actually, Coda is more likely to become a saint (1 in 20 million) and he isn't even religious! If that doesn't prove the wackiness of the man's question, go read the Bible or something because you need to save your wretched soul.

"Uh huh," the man said in confusion. "As opposed to the other way people read books."

Without thinking, Coda divulged more information than necessary. "I've always read the last page of a book first. The idea of not knowing what would happen from the very start would wear away on me. I didn't have much patience as a kid, but I don't have a good excuse for why I continue to do it now."

"What's the point of reading a book if you already know the ending?"

"The emotion."

"The emotion of what?" the man asked.

"The story, of course. Even if you know the ending, that is only a small part of the experience. And I've learned that reading the last page first rarely spoils the ending. But really, does anyone remember the details of a novel? I doubt it. Instead, they are more likely to recall how they felt."

The man nodded his head. It was hard to determine if the nod was in agreement or just acknowledgment. "Well, you have plenty of opportunities to read a book the *correct* way," he said, motioning to the box.

"You want to borrow one?" Coda asked. "As you said, I have plenty here."

Before the man could answer, Coda dug into the box and pulled one out. It was a crisp paperback by another author he hadn't heard of. He held it up for the man to see. "What do you think?" Coda asked.

"Toss it over. I'll give it a shot. I'm not much of a snob even though the cover is somewhat unappealing. Is that clock trying to show noon or midnight?" the man wondered.

Coda opened the front cover and then flipped quickly to the back. It wasn't one of the elites.

He underhanded it to the man who caught it like a Venus flytrap slapping down on an unsuspecting insect.

"And by borrow, you can keep it or pass it on to someone else. I doubt we will cross paths again," Coda said.

"You never know. Stranger things have happened. That's a deal though."

A surge of dopamine tore through Coda. Lending out books was the lamest drug for him. He imagined finding a dealer with the following exchange blitzing through his mind.

"Hey man, you got any lend?"

"Be discreet. Be discreet. Yeah, I got it. What do you want? I have a Kilgore Trout paperback or the new Stevie Queen hardcover, but it isn't cheap. I've sold ten copies just this morning."

"Give me the Trout. That high always hits the best."

"Five days. If you don't bring it back, I'll scratch your corneas!"

Coda shook off the odd thought. The man opened up the book and skimmed through the first page.

They continued on together for several more stops before Coda scooped up the box and shuffled off the train. The man yelled out one more thank you that was muffled by the closing doors.

Back at his apartment, Coda placed the box down next to his luggage, not ready to deal with any of it yet.

He returned to the bathroom mirror, watching himself as the façade slipped away, and the tears fell like rain.

fifty-seven

WHY?

On the other side of the East River, Nolan Treiber was pacing back and forth inside her apartment.

After a night similar to Coda's, Nolan woke up refreshed and ready to engage with the one string keeping her in New York. Her parents were creatures of habit, so Nolan knew they'd be getting massages at the penthouse. Why leave when the peasants come to you?

The nerves coursed through her faster than a midnight joyride. The deep rooted panic settled into her bones like the familiar face you passed by on the street. Nolan tried a series of affirmations, but they failed to deviate her thinking.

Down.

Down.

Down she went.

She sat on the couch and focused on her breathing, trying to bring it back to a normalized state. Her vision blurred as everything swam around in undistinguished loops.

You are nothing.

You are lucky to have been adopted and now you want to question that?

Go ahead, try to leave New York. You wouldn't last two months on your own.

Your non-existent group of friends will certainly miss you.

On and on.

On and on.

On and on.

Nolan squeezed her eyes shut and counted back from a hundred. She could dig through her bag for the pills, but the effort seemed implausible. Nolan was paralyzed.

Eighty-nine.

Eighty-eight.

Eighty-seven.

But what about the Ferris Wheel and the waves? She thought that moment had been a breakthrough and the panic attacks would never surface as drastically again.

How foolish.

It was a mantra for her, at least that's what she told herself. She was foolish for quitting her job. She was foolish for having such a vendetta against two people who gave her a home and a stable upbringing. She was foolish for considering a move across the country was the answer to her problems. She was foolish for thinking her birth parents would have any interest in seeing her. She was foolish for not having any friends. She was foolish for being scared of heights. She was foolish for suffering from panic attacks.

But this is how they worked. They tore into every facet of her life and made her believe she was worthless. What a terrible routine. What an awful perfect circle of self-hatred.

It had to end.

Sixty.

Fifty-nine.

Fifty-eight.

Nolan casted aside all her doubts and continued her countdown. Ten numbers later, the same disgusting thoughts wormed their way back in.

Things weren't always so easy and convenient to fix.

Nolan unstuck herself from the couch and considered whether any of this was part of the script.

What script? she echoed back to herself.

She didn't even know anymore.

Nolan combed through her toiletries until she found the orange bottle. She twisted off the cap and tipped it until one pill slipped out.

Much like how everyone had a story, everyone was fucked up in some way. For Nolan Treiber, her struggle was internal. The short wirings in her brain were destructive, but it could be managed in one way.

Time.

The pills were an escape; the affirmations were a partial solution; the small wins like the Ferris Wheel were great, but she'd need many more to overcome the struggle.

With time, it would be possible.

Twenty-seven.

Twenty-six.

Twenty-five.

She could only control so much, and the most obvious example was eight subway stops away sitting in a penthouse suite getting pampered.

After she reached zero and started over again from fifty, Nolan grabbed her jacket and left the apartment.

To say she felt better would have been a lie, but she knew the medication would kick in and the madness of the city would be enough to distract her until she made it to her parent's place.

Unlike Coda, Nolan's experiences with the subway weren't likely to have encounters with random passengers. She kept to herself and avoided conversations. Between wearing headphones and her eyes locked on her phone, it was easier than expected for people to not interrupt her.

The penthouse was near Central Park, in one of those nondescript buildings a tourist may have assumed was home to some company they'd never heard of. Nolan walked into the main lobby and went to the counter.

"Miss Treiber! It's been a long time. How are you?" the man asked.

"Hi Freddie. I'm doing well. I'm surprised you remember me."

"It's part of my job! I can still picture you running in through that door for the first time. The look on your face . . . like a kid getting free run of a toy store."

"Hard to believe that was almost twenty years ago."

"We've been lucky to have you for that long," Freddie said.

Nolan was never fond of praising herself, so she cut straight to the point. "Do you know if my parents are in?"

"Well, the . . . the massage people came an hour ago. Right on time. So they should be up there. Still have a key?"

"It hasn't been that long," Nolan said with a laugh.

"Of course. Of course. You know the way then. Good seeing you, Nolan. Come back more often."

"I will," she said, moving toward the elevator.

Inside, Nolan pushed the button and the elevator zipped up to its destination. One perk of being a millionaire was whenever you pressed the button for the penthouse, the elevator wouldn't stop at any other floor. Those poor souls could wait.

The elevator opened to a stubby, dull hallway with a singular door at the end. Sometimes there was a bodyguard standing outside as if the Treiber family had rabid fans who clamored to see Pierre and Diane Treiber for an autograph.

Nolan pulled out the keycard from her pocket and used it to swipe into the penthouse.

The allure of the place was undeniable. Extravagant art was tossed up on every wall, the meaning of each piece a complete mystery. If Nolan had an eye for interior design, she could better explain how each room had its own theme while blending together for one cohesive unit. It reminded her of a museum, but one she wasn't very fond of.

Of course, her parents had no hand in decorating the space. That's what they had money for.

Nolan heard the sound of soft music filtering in from the living room. Two tables were being folded up and stuffed back into bags for easy transport. The masseuses had a look of gratitude that they were done and on their way out.

"Au revoir!" her father called out with a small wave. He was always in his best mood following a massage. Something about the nasty toxins getting hammered out of his body.

The masseuses said nothing in return and headed for the exit, ignoring Nolan as they passed by, likely mistaking her for a maid.

Nolan rounded the corner and came into full view. Her parents stared at her with confusion before deciding to speak.

"Nolan. What are you doing here?" her mother asked. A dull start to their conversation.

Nolan looked past them, out the floor to ceiling windows that covered the entire back wall. The sky beyond was in a state of confusion as to whether it wanted to be cloudy or let the light shine through. The choice made no difference to Nolan.

"I had a few questions to ask you both." Was there a need to run through the pleasantries or could she just jump right into it? She'd let them decide that.

"You picked a good time," her father said. "We are refreshed from our weekly massage. Isn't that right, Diane?"

"Yes."

"How long has it been?" he asked. "Two, three weeks?"

"Almost three months. I haven't been home since Christmas."

"That long? My goodness. Sometimes I forget the world still turns whether you are paying attention or not."

"What have you two been up to?" Nolan asked. She was falling into the trap of wading through the pleasantries before getting to the goal. Oh well, she'd suffer through it.

"The usual stuff. Charities, parties, real estate deals, and other oddities. All dull affairs, right Diane?"

"Yes."

"Some things never change I suppose," Nolan said.

"What about you, darling? Tell us about everything." This is what they did. They showed enough interest in Nolan's life that she would give them information and then the conversation would end in frustration as they couldn't relate to anything she said.

They sat down on the ornate couch (if such a thing was possible) in their expensive robes and gave her their undivided attention.

"I quit my job and drove across the country in the Pinto."

"Our Pinto?" her mother said in confusion, focusing on the least important part of Nolan's statement.

"Yes."

"Oh my. We didn't even notice it was gone."

"I figured. I left it out in California with someone who said they would look after it."

"Oh my," her father echoed. "That poor car."

Nolan was enjoying this. She felt her parent's discomfort over losing a car they didn't even know was gone. A car! Imagine that!

"It's in good hands. I've been thinking about moving out to California," Nolan said.

"Why is that?"

"I have nothing here."

"Now that's not fair," her father said with disdain. "You have us and all the friends you met at the parties throughout the years."

"I made no friends at those parties. You used me to . . . to . . . I don't know . . . show other people that you actually had a human side or something."

"It's more complicated than that," he said. Not the best defense to Nolan's claim.

"What does that even mean? You two dragged me to all those parties and pushed me out to meet strangers for your own benefit. I cried all the time and told you I didn't want to go, but you never took my side. All you were concerned about was the image of a perfect family that was artificial from the beginning."

"Nolan, that's not fair," her mother said. "As your father said, it's more complicated than that."

"I want an honest answer."

"We have always been honest with you," her father said.

Nolan saw through the lie. "Why me? I've never understood or had the courage to ask. Maybe I was afraid of the answer, but not anymore. How was it possible that a couple in New York would fly out to California and stumble upon the foster home I was living in? The odds of that happening are . . . unfathomable."

Pierre rested a hand on Diane's leg. It wasn't a movement of affection, but one of worry and an urging for Diane to speak.

"You're right. It wasn't by chance," she said, trembling with the words. "Oh Nolan. You are never going to forgive us."

Nolan felt the rush and dread seeping back into her body. It was happening all over again. The wave was going to crash and drag her under. "Forgive you for what?"

"Never telling you the truth about your parents."

Oh God. Was she in the middle of some soap opera or something?

"It's okay, honey," her father urged.

"Your mom was my sister," Diane said with sadness.

Nolan's vision flashed as she tried to keep herself afloat. *What the fuck is going on?*

"We hadn't been close in years," Diane continued. "She resented my marriage to your father and felt I abandoned her out in California. I tried my best to get your mother to come to New York so we could get her the proper care, but she was fiercely independent and fought any help."

"Care for what?" Nolan managed to say.

"Your mom was schizophrenic. She would be fine for periods of time then suddenly lapse into an episode where she would disappear for months. One of those times she resurfaced and was pregnant with you. She never told us, but I believe she was involved in prostitution to support herself.

"It became clear after you were born that she wasn't able to properly care for you. We looked for you for years, but she lied about your name and whereabouts, and with a name like Nolan, it's almost like she purposely picked that to confuse us further."

"Why? Why would she do that?" Nolan's voice cracked as the words came out in a jumble.

"I wish we knew. Nolan, your mother wasn't well. Her actions were . . . misguided. She put you up for adoption and like we've told you, that first place didn't work out and then you were put into foster care. I'm so sorry. I'm so sorry," Diane said.

"Nolan," her *father* said, "we have argued for years on whether to tell you. The truth is painful for us, so we couldn't imagine the toll it would have on you. I guess you saw the parties and lifestyle as a pathetic attempt to get you involved, but we saw it as a way to distract you from asking questions, from wondering what your life was before this. For a while, your mom and I wanted children, a family of our own, but life isn't always so kind. Years went by and we made peace with it. The money helped distract us from our own sadness of not having kids, so we extended that thinking to you. But then, we finally found you and flew out to California. I was so nervous. So incredibly nervous. I will never forget meeting you for the first time and the smile you had. You invited us to play with your toys and explained all about how your doll never got along with the pink elephant. The feud ran deep apparently. I watched you and kept wondering to myself that you should have been broken. Absolutely shattered from all the horrible things that happened to you during your short life, but that wasn't the case. Nolan, you were perfect. You *are* perfect. Everything we ever needed. And I think we wanted to preserve that innocence and give you a meaningful life. We made mistakes — God knows we did — so I hope you can forgive us. The best intentions are sometimes covered by lies."

Nolan looked at her parents and the grief they didn't bother to hide. It was similar to how Coda looked on that RV in Yosemite. He always talked about the routine, the perfect circle. Was her life any different?

She asked, "You don't know who my father is?"

Diane shook her head. "I'm sorry. We don't, but we can help you find him if that's something you are interested in."

"What about my mother?"

Pierre squeezed Diane's hand, urging her to speak again. Diane looked at everything in the penthouse except for Nolan until her eyes eventually rested on her daughter. "Your mother committed suicide a few years ago. She wasn't meant for this world, Nolan. The help she needed was never enough."

The wave crashed. Her overriding reason to run to California dissipated into smoke and then nothing. "Why didn't you tell me?" Nolan tried to feel the sadness she should have at the news, but it never came.

"Ignorance is bliss, as terrible as that sounds," Diane said. "You kept speaking about how much you loved your job and enjoyed the work and how you finally settled into a routine. We didn't want to disrupt that. Again, we did what we thought was best."

"But it was my mother and you made that decision for me," Nolan said, the tone somewhere between anger and disbelief.

"I know," Diane said, the pain abundantly clear in her voice.

"Would you have ever told me?"

"Yes," Pierre said. "You deserved the truth."

"But only when I asked for it."

"That's not fair, Nolan. You never asked us questions about how we *found* you."

"So this is my fault?" Nolan said.

"No. No, please don't say that," Pierre said. "I don't want this to distance you from us. We love you and only wanted to give you the best life possible."

"Right. By drowning me in money to forget that pain exists in this world. Do you know the reason why I never made friends in college except for Coda? Because everyone saw my last name and figured they could either get a handout or that I was a vapid, stuck up bitch. I didn't ask for any of this and that's exactly why I wanted to leave it all behind for California. I don't want this name or the money. None of it."

"I understand, but I hope you'd still have room for us in your life. We care about you so deeply," Pierre said.

"Look, I have a lot to process. This did not go as I expected, but I could never ignore that you are the only family I have. I watched Coda throw away the relationship with his mom for no discernable reason and I could never make that same mistake. For our entire trip, he always talked about living in a perfect circle and I never understood what he meant. You fail to realize you're in the midst of one until you step back and reevaluate your life and that's what I did on the trip. I know now my perfect circle is this city. I spent my childhood combing through the streets and examining the buildings and exploring the same coffeeshops on every corner. And I loved it, but there is so much more out there. I need to follow it. I don't know if I'll succeed or fail, but what's the point of never trying? I've saved money and made good connections at my old job, so I'm confident an opportunity will turn up. I finally have what I need to leave this place. I just need your support."

"You have it," Pierre said. "Forever."

"Without a doubt," Diane said.

The guilt would never go away for Nolan. The guilt of having more money than any human needed. The guilt of never asking about her birth parents and hearing the truth long before she did. The guilt of blaming her adoptive parents for not being enough when they were doing the best they could . . .

The list dragged on.

Her panic attack subsided. The wave receded into the blackness, likely to return again at the most inconvenient time. A worry for another day.

For all the guilt Nolan harbored, she felt none over her decision to leave New York.

The world was too vast and populated with people of superior knowledge to her own. If there's one thing she picked up from Coda Finn, it was that asking questions granted you a more fulfilling life. Every single person had a story worth sharing, but Nolan had to go seek them out.

Most importantly though, she had to create her own.

<u>fifty-eight</u>

FRONT TO BACK

Two weeks passed before Coda unpacked the box or his luggage from the trip. He pushed the pile around the apartment until it was impossible to ignore.

Prior to all that, he at least followed through on several of his promises.

He got lunch with Cassandra and they spoke about the trip, more about what happened between him and his mom, and what was next for him. It was cathartic, which settled in as a clear theme for Coda during that time. Coda felt confident their relationship would thrive and he could work through any differences with Cecilia and Clementine.

Outside of family, Coda met up with Nolan at The Wobbling Stool three times that first week where she gave him the full story about what happened at her parent's house. He empathized with her pain and could see that she was processing all of it. On the third day of their happy hour adventures, she confessed her intentions to move to California. Coda listened as she rattled off the reasons for her choice — which were more expansive than what they had been during the trip — and he knew there was no longer any hesitation. He believed their friendship would survive, but distance was one of two dastardly reasons why a relationship fails.

After that first week, Coda worked up the courage to visit the cemetery with Nolan tagging along for moral support. They braved the cold for a long time as they searched to find the grave, which was a difficult task considering the headstone hadn't been placed yet.

At the grave, he spoke to his mom, saying all the things he should have when he had the chance. He wiped the last remnants of snow off of his dad's grave and spoke to him about how things are going.

It was the quietest and worst family reunion ever.

Nolan stood nearby road and watched her friend, unable to hear what he was saying. Whatever happened at those graves was only for Coda, but she knew the good-bye was long overdue. Would she have that moment of crying about the loss of her biological mom? Was it possible to be sad for someone you'd never met? For Nolan, her best course was to keep asking questions as she thought of them and try to learn what she could.

On the train ride back, they spoke of happier topics like how Coda wondered which water station was winning the eternal battle at JEC, how the job hunt was going, and how they had no other choice but to remain friends for eternity because the script wouldn't demand anything less.

As they parted ways, Nolan suggested their next hang out should be a throwback — one of their legendary subway trips.

"Of course," he said as Nolan moved to the exit. "We haven't done that in years."

"Nothing like a little adventure, huh?"

Following his trip to the cemetery, Coda merely existed until he worked up the courage to clean the apartment. He knew the finality that rested in the box and his luggage. Slowly, he ripped off the tape and lifted up the flaps. He pulled the box in closer and began taking out each book as if they were a Fabergé egg. Coda developed a system where he'd scour the first and last pages of each book to see if his mom left behind a note or the symbol. If so, they went in pile A. If neither etching was found, they went in pile B.

This method continued on for almost an hour. He wasn't in a rush to skim through the last set of books his mom would ever gift him.

At the end of his sorting, there weren't any books in pile A. It was a perfect representation of how rare the elite books were. A bit of a letdown though.

He moved onto his luggage and pulled out a combination of clothes and books. The clothes went in the hamper while he created a new pile for the books that were picked up from the trip. It was a boring affair. One that could be summed up as such:

He had a shit ton of laundry to do and needed to find a new home for lots of books.

The laundry would be a nuisance, but one he was familiar with. As for the books, that took some creative maneuvering. For the ordinary ones, Coda placed the newest additions on top of the fridge and in a cabinet that had some space.

All that remained on the floor were the special books. He flipped open each one, thinking about how they were in somebody else's possession for so long. Halfway through the pile, he opened up *The White Meadow* and his highlighted list fell to the floor. He placed the paper on the table and returned to the question at hand: What should he do with the books?

He could burn them. It would be a symbolic gesture that nothing lasts forever. Coda could gather up the ashes and display them on his shelf or ship them off to a museum that would pay him handsomely for such a donation. The thought fluttered by and was replaced by another.

He could donate the books to a local bookstore or library. A safe but unfulfilling outcome.

The last option he considered was slowly lending out the books over time and then repeating the same adventure again in another ten years or so. Like Nolan said, who doesn't like a sequel?

All those shitty options led him back to the most obvious one: He needed to keep the books for himself. If he didn't, what was the point of anything he and Nolan went through? Fine. He could manage that.

If he were to follow his previous trend, the books would be stowed away in the cubby hole within the closet to be chewed on by rats. That seemed disingenuous now. Again, why would he have gone through the effort to retrieve them if he was just going to hide them away like they were cleaning supplies?

Coda cleared off the top shelf of his bookcase and began placing each of the books in order of when he received them. He crosschecked between his lending ledger and the highlighted list on the table to ensure he was correct. As for the books that were previously there, they found another home in the apartment.

When Coda was done, he stepped back. The shelf was almost full, but something felt off. He cross-referenced his lists again and synced up the counts. The highlighted entries in both sources totaled twelve. He only had ten on the bookshelf.

He went to the list and quickly saw one of the culprits was *Harrison Spotter and the Pebble of Grave Importance* — the first elite book his mom gave him.

His brain clicked and he remembered it was the one book he had in his possession before the trip. It had only been a month ago when Coda looked at it, but you could have convinced him it'd been years. He opened the closet and bent down to the cubby hole. Coda popped it open and stared down at the dusty copy. The cover was of a quirky kid with a tree shaped scar on his forehead. Inside the front cover was a long note from his mom. He had no recollection of the contents, so he read it slowly, trying to analyze each word.

> *Coda,*
> *I've watched your passion for reading expand over the past year. Every moment you are tucked in a corner and burning through the pages of another book. I miss the days when I was able to do the same. Life carries you away from your passions sometimes, but if you fight hard enough, you can always circle back to them. There is so much to learn from books — different perspectives, inspiring stories, new knowledge — that I want to help guide you to the best ones. You'll get countless books from me in the years to come, but some will be more special than others. Like this one. Anytime you see your name in the back, it's a reminder that there's a lesson in the book I think you can learn from. Some may be obvious, but others will be harder to understand. That's okay. Sometimes we only realize the lessons long after we've closed the book.*
>
> *G.F.*

If there was ever any doubt as to why his mom went through the effort of marking certain books, the answer was always in front of him, buried away. She wanted him to learn. No overarching mystery or clues leading to a globetrotting adventure, just a simple desire from a parent to their child.

Maybe you were expecting something more, but would anything else have made sense?

A wonderful thing about books is how subjective they are. Coda didn't believe every book his mom gave him was great, but it'd been so long since he read any from the highlighted list that maybe he'd break his rule and jump into them again. To rediscover why.

Coda closed the book and placed it on the far left of the shelf. Only one more to go. He looked at his highlighted list one last time and skimmed through the entries, hoping he hadn't missed a location they needed to stop at. His answer came quickly and stopped any worry as it was under his nose.

He left the apartment, walked downstairs, and knocked on his neighbor's door.

"Coda! Hello, how are you?" Ms. Harris asked.

"I'm doing well. Wanted to see if you were finished with the book I gave you."

"Oh yes, it took me quite a while, but like I said, I never give up on a book," she beamed with pride. "Come in! I need to find where I put the damn thing." She hobbled away from the entrance and deeper into the apartment. Hers was much larger and comfortable than Coda's. He stood awkwardly next to the couch, waiting for further instructions.

"I haven't seen you in a while," she continued. "Is everything okay? We usually run into each other at least once a week."

"It's been a long month," Coda confessed.

She rummaged within a stack of books until she found what she was looking for. "Ah, got it! In perfect condition too." She took her time walking back to Coda and handed over the book. *Empty Stands* by Stevie Queen. Her magnum opus — so she says.

Out of instinct, Coda turned to the last page and saw the infamous symbol perched in the corner. The final movement in this journey was done.

For real this time.

Ms. Harris noticed what he was searching for and said, "You know what that means, right?"

"I recently learned."

"Pretty clever if you ask me."

"You're familiar with the symbol?"

"Oh yes. Of course. Believe it or not, I used to do a lot more than sweep the front porch here. I lived a rather exciting life, but there's a point where . . . things change."

"For as long as I've lived here, I don't know anything about you, which is unlike me. I like to understand people better than that."

"Don't dwell on it, honey. I'm here all the time. You come by whenever and I'm happy to answer any questions. But something tells me you have a story to share, so I'm here to listen today," she urged him.

Coda took the bait because he could either let the pain fester inside or expel it out into the world.

"My mom had been sick for a long time and she . . ." he began. Coda spared no detail to Ms. Harris. She looked on with extreme interest and sat quietly as he spun a tale that twisted and curved.

When the vocalized the bulk of it, he asked, "Do you think I'm a bad person for abandoning my mom? I need the truth."

"You're not a bad person. That is clear by your other actions. You care for others and will continue to grow with time . . . Life is hard, Coda. No other way to put it than that. We all make choices and not all of them will result in the outcome you want."

"I feel so much regret and pain. Will it ever go away?"

"It will. Nothing lasts forever, at least in my experience," Ms. Harris said. "All you can do now is move forward. I know it sounds cliché, but there's a reason people always advise to do that."

Coda looked down at the book and back over at Ms. Harris. He felt himself breaking. He could deny the emotion as he became adept at doing or let it bubble over the surface. He chose the latter.

"I miss her so much," he said, placing the book down and sobbing into his outstretched hands.

"It's okay. It's okay," Ms. Harris said. "Let it all out. You don't have to carry onto any burden." She stood up and grabbed the box of tissues to bring over.

Coda found it odd that he was able to cry in front of his neighbor but not in front of Nolan or at the cemetery. Grief is an entity of little definition and understanding.

He took a tissue and wiped his face. The sobs turned into hiccups until they eventually subsided to silence.

"All I wanted to do was break the cycle. That perfect circle was ruining my life. I needed to get out of New York . . . I knew that she didn't have much longer, but I . . ."

"It's okay. It's okay," she repeated.

"Ms. Harris, have you ever felt that life is just one massive routine?"

"Of course. I didn't mind it though. It brought stability for me."

"Am I an idiot for hating the routine?"

"Absolutely not," she said in a strict voice.

"The books were the excuse, and that's a hard thing to admit to myself. It wasn't until we picked up the first one that I realized how much I *needed* them back, but my intention was never solely about the books."

"You have them now."

"And look at what it cost . . . Seeing my mom one last time . . . My job . . . Any chance at a good future. If I don't find som—" Coda stopped himself. He didn't want to play out the scenario if he couldn't find another job.

"Based on what you've told me, I think you got a lot out of the trip. Isn't that right?"

"Yeah," he said, wiping his nose as the snot kept flowing down.

"What did you learn then?"

"I wrote it in the letter for the time capsule. I'm not sure I could recap it any better than I did there."

"Okay, so why don't you hold onto that memory then? To remind yourself what the purpose was."

"I'll try." He felt like he was being nurtured by a grandparent, which was a welcomed change to going through everything alone or keeping people like Nolan at a distance.

"What's next for you? I'm sure you've been thinking about that nonstop."

Coda nodded. Besides the guilt surrounding his mom, some variation of that question had been floating around his mind since they landed back in New York. He could have rattled off a thousand answers, none of which would have had an iota of truth. His desire to understand the ending before reading all the pages was a worthless endeavor he needed to break. Coda had no other choice but to create his story from front to back, just like anyone else.

He looked over at Ms. Harris and smiled for the first time in what felt like months. Newfound peace poured into him like air after emerging from a crashing wave.

Coda Finn gave an honest answer.

"For once, I don't know."

<u>epilogue</u>

ALL THERE IS

His day always started the same.

A sudden jolt of awareness but overshadowed by a creeping sense of disorientation until he reminded himself that any of the nightmares were already forgotten.

The pattern had been unchanged for years, long before he moved into the house by the water.

He lifted off the three layers of blankets — he was always cold — and reached for the cane that was propped up against the nightstand. He didn't need an alarm clock because his responsibilities had no timetable. Anyways, he woke up well before the working class. He pulled himself up to a seated position and felt his spine realign. He sat in the darkness with no earnest desire to remove himself from it.

This was the routine.

You know how these things go because these things don't change.

Time passed, likely more than he realized, before he used the cane to hoist himself up. He slowly moved toward the bathroom, which was always the first true test of each day.

Afterward, he walked down the hallway, turning on lights out of habit, but they didn't help much. His sight had been diminishing for years to the point where he was declared legally blind. All the lights did was blur his vision further and create halos around every object. No matter though. He knew the layout of the house well enough that if his eyes actually crapped out, he'd still be able to take care of himself.

If you bothered to get anyone else's opinion on the matter, they would have scoffed at him for still living alone. His options were limited. He'd managed to outlive the rest of his family, so moving in with relatives wasn't feasible unless he settled into a grave next to them. He became irrationally annoyed at the mention of moving into an assisted living facility, which people witnessed enough times that they stopped broaching the subject. What was left then? Just continuing down his current path until something swept him away.

Some days he wished it would finally happen, but today wasn't one of them.

He reached the stairs, gripping the railing with one hand and using the cane to feel the step below. He repeated this process twelve times at a snail's pace until he reached the bottom.

He walked into the kitchen and began prepping his breakfast which consisted of apple cinnamon flavored oatmeal. With the exception of going out, he never deviated from his breakfast of champions. His twist to the traditional meal was adding chocolate milk to fatten up the oatmeal. The sugar always got his heart pumping and if he didn't have a bum leg, bum lung, bum heart, bum spine, bum eyes, and so on, he may have even done some calisthenics afterward.

He made his breakfast and ate it without issue. He cleaned his bowl and spoon, returning both to their proper place. No sense in leaving a mess when he was having company over.

He was a popular man inside the small *beach town* of Sausalito, but he still didn't find himself getting too many visitors. Maybe it was the location of the house or that every other resident was dealing with as many physical ailments as he was, but he thought himself to be a pleasant man who made good company on the occasions when others sought it out.

Normally, he'd sit on the couch and listen to the morning news for an hour. That would give him plenty of insight into the disasters, riots, genocides, and other atrocities he would be leaving behind.

Did anybody have good news to report anymore?

After sitting through it, he'd feel a combination of rage, sadness, and yearning to have done more with his life. It was the high quality cocktail anyone would sip on.

Like already mentioned, today was different though. A day he'd been anticipating for ten years. Crazy, right? Wallace Winger — his preference being Wally — was already old enough to be commemorated on a coin or stamp the first time we saw him, so how the hell did he live another ten years?

His secret was deceptively simple. When you follow a routine, you tend to avoid mistakes. He didn't always adhere to that logic — especially during his days of being a daredevil — but he settled into it around the time he became a permanent resident of Sausalito, after his wife died of cancer and his two children took their love elsewhere.

Anyways, we could listen to the rambles of a wizened wizard all day, but that is not the point!

Instead of watching the news, Wally turned on his Bluetooth speakers and played his favorite band, The Killers.

It's true that Wally Winger wasn't familiar with the band during the height of their popularity, but that didn't stop him from gaining a huge hankering for them after Nolan introduced him. She was a peach, always checking in on Wally to make sure he had everything he needed.

Often times she referred to him as her second adoptive parent, as if her folks back in New York weren't enough. It warmed his heart to be looked at in such high regard. When you get old, you find that the greatest pleasure in life is knowing somebody still gives a damn about you. It's far too simple to be tossed away into a nursing home and left to rot on a bed until a priest walks in and forgives you for all the things that you've done.

Wally started up the *Hot Fuss* album from the top and tapped along to the beat. He tried to mimic the lyrics but found is brain couldn't keep up with the flow, so the words came out in a mumble of syllables reminiscent to a baby finding their voice. When the words failed, he resorted to humming, which was a cheap man's massage of the nervous system — at least that's what someone said at some point somewhere.

He made it through two albums before the doorbell rang. Before he had a chance to move toward it, Wally heard footsteps down the hallway and a familiar voice.

"Good morning Wally!"

"Nolan, you made it," he said as if it was a surprise that she showed up.

"Of course I did. I wouldn't miss this. Ten years in the making and you've been reminding me every opportunity you get."

"Well, I was foolish to not ask you to include something. We had enough space."

"I forgive you," she said with a smile.

To say that Nolan Treiber looked the same as when we last saw her in 2024 would imply that we even knew what she looked like to begin with.

They killed some time by speaking through the pleasantries that two friends did, but the details aren't important. Jumping ahead into the future wasn't an excuse to peek back into the lives of Nolan, Frankie, and Coda.

It was to . . . well, let's rediscover why.

Wally checked his watch and announced it was time for them to walk down. He hooked his arm into Nolan's as she led the way.

The March weather was brisk with a heavy fog laying over the water. The cloudy sky made Wally's vision slightly more bearable.

A small crowd gathered around the concrete hole with the locked compartment. As Wally anticipated, many of the locals didn't show up. Some had a good excuse because they died somewhere along the way, but for the others that were still around, they'd just lost interest. What was the point of a time capsule anyways? With the internet, people had the ability to search Google for what was popular ten, fifty, or even a thousand years ago.

Wally wasn't a fool. He understood the inherent silliness of the time capsule, but he wasn't interested in the objects.

It was the letters.

As the pioneer of the event, Wally sifted through the crowd until he made it to the front. There wasn't any applause or recognition of who he was, but everyone still quieted down, sensing he was the one with the key. He leaned against his cane and gave a short speech about the history of the time capsule and what it was meant to symbolize. While the majority seemed unenthused, Wally found Nolan and her constant nodding that urged him to keep going. It was important to him, so all the others be damned!

After his speech, Wally presented the key and Nolan walked over to assist.

He leaned in and whispered, "I thought Frankie was going to make it."

"You know she can be," Nolan said. "Always preoccupied with something new."

"Yeah . . . Yeah," Wally repeated to himself.

Nolan removed the padlock, tossed it aside, and flipped open the time capsule cover. With one hard yank, she pulled out the cylinder and placed it upright on the nearby bench. It stood nearly two feet high and, from above, looked like a perfect circle. Wally stepped over to the capsule and placed it on its side. Some of the crowd dispersed, expecting more glitz and glam.

Fuck 'em, Wally thought. *I did this for me. I just didn't expect to be the one opening it ten years later.*

Together, they removed the contents and placed them on the bench. It quickly turned into an assortment of sentimental objects and piles of papers — letters, notes, apologies, confessions, and other oddities. Wally set aside the three papers that were addressed to him, and once they were finished sorting, he began showcasing what was in there. The crowd went mild.

Eventually, Wally removed himself as the centerpiece and allowed others to peruse the objects from 2024. He hobbled over to a bench with Nolan and looked down at the letters.

"Three? I didn't think you were that popular," she said.

"Coercion is a useful tactic to implement sometimes," he said with a smile.

"Which are you going to read first?"

"Here's the thing . . . You know my eyes aren't good. Would you be able to read them to me?"

"Of course. Unless you think there will be personal information in them I shouldn't see."

Wally shrugged. He didn't care if there was. "Start with this one," he said, pulling out the middle letter. It was addressed to Wallace in small, blocky font.

Nolan tore into it and read the contents. The letter turned into a confession of missed opportunity for an admirer of Wally's that lived in Sausalito. She spoke of his pearly white hair and his chivalry and how he engaged her in each conversation they were a part of. The letter flowed and flowed with no proper point to be made. It ended abruptly with Wally showing indifference to what Sharon had written him. When Nolan pressed him further, Wally said the letter was nice, but Sharon had died four years back and there was nothing to fret about now. She was in a more peaceful place, if that's what you believed in.

The second letter was one he'd written to himself, mostly as a joke. At the time of writing, Wally was eighty-four years old and could hardly envision himself living into his nineties. But the world wasn't ready to let him go. Nolan read the letter aloud and paused several times as if she was trying to make sense of what he'd written. For Wally, it didn't make much sense to him either. He stared out ahead and watched the electric cars zip by without a sound, only half listening to what Nolan was saying. He wasn't concerned about his own words. They wouldn't have amounted to much, since he knew they weren't even honest. The pain he'd felt in losing his wife and having a shitty relationship with his kids was never a lock anyone was able to open.

Regrets. It's impossible not to have some when you live for nearly a century.

Sensing his disinterest, Nolan folded his letter, returned it to the envelope, and picked up the last one.

It was addressed to Wally with the initials C.F. on the back.

"How is he?" Wally asked suddenly.

"Wally, we've talked about this before," Nolan said like a mother soothing her child.

"Yes. Sorry. I forget sometimes."

Without saying anything else, Nolan opened the envelope and pulled out the letter. She read it aloud with little urgency as if she didn't want it to end.

> Wally,
>
> You asked me to write a letter without any guidelines. I guess I'm too engrained between work and school that when I get an assignment, I expect the criteria to be clear. That's okay though. I'll give this my best shot, and like you said, I'll speak from the heart.
>
> My life has always been a perfect circle, a predictable routine that anyone could pick up on in a matter of days. Of course, there hasn't been just one circle or routine, but dozens.
>
> Growing up, the first routine I encountered was going to school, doing my homework, and being whisked off to bed while my brain was still actively churning. I'd lay in bed and wonder about a time when I wouldn't be walking from classroom to classroom and sitting through boring topics of history and molecules and whatever the hell they tried to teach me in calculus. It felt never-ending, but I guess to a kid, time moves slower until you look back and realize how fast everything whipped by. I tried my best to alter the routine by getting a job, but all it did was expand the circle and absorb new activities into the routine.
>
> That circle collapsed when my dad died. I found him on the bathroom floor with a broken neck. His eyes were red and staring straight ahead at the wall as if something important lay hidden behind it. The image will always be here. How could it ever go away? As that first circle went away, it was replaced by another. The grief I felt was indescribable. I lived in a household where it was my dad and I versus four women. We were always at a disadvantage in terms of getting to

watch what we wanted on TV or where to eat on the rare occasions we went out, so we banded together to create a united front. I lost my first friend that day and spiraled into a perfect circle of hate and anger and frustration at everyone around me.

That circle broke after an incident at school only for — you guessed it — another one to form.

Again and again and again new routines took shape. They would eventually break with a more boring, bleak one to fill in the void.

This continued on through college. It got to the point where I enjoyed nothing. When I started work at JEC, that turned into the sourest routine with employees who worked endlessly to impress management and create bigger, bolder profits. And for what? To kill more innocent civilians or build more planes where the safety features were hidden behind a paywall? It ate away at me until there was nothing left.

And then this trip happened. I don't need to recap every moment of it, but it's worth saying how selfish I have been. Knocking on stranger's doors, begging for books back when I haven't spoken to them in years, and all under the guise of rushing back home to see my mother one final time before she died. It was all lies for a majority of the trip. I lied to every single person, including the one friend who dropped everything to come along with me. I know Nolan has her own reasons were tagging along on this journey, but you don't offer to drive thousands of miles with a friend if you don't care immensely about that person.

You know what's funny? Even the trip turned into a perfect circle. Each stop yielded the same results with the same conversations and the same wacky individuals or heartfelt stories.

The whole time I continued to ask myself one question . . . Is this all there is? Just one routine after another until we die.

No, that couldn't be the case, but for a majority of the trip, I had no answer. I resigned to the notion that I may never find out, and I had to be okay with it.

But then we made it to Yosemite.

And Frankie, Nolan, and I were on top of that RV and the answer began to form. It wasn't the scenic display laid out in front of me; it was something much simpler than that.

What do you think matters most in this world?

Money? Maybe. I'd consider that answer since we can't survive without it.

A job? It would make sense if more people actually enjoyed what they did.

Family? That's close, but it's even more basic than that.

It's people and the relationships we build, Wally! God, the answer is so trite and silly that I knew it had to be the right one.

As we sat there on the RV, I knew it was impossible for me to be where I was if it hadn't been for every single person along the way. Nolan for agreeing to come on the trip . . . Frankie for bringing us to Yosemite . . . Muscle for being in juvie the same time I was . . . Eve for talking to me when we worked at the bookstore . . . and on it goes. Every person and relationship that formed — regardless of its brevity — led me to that moment.

Where would we be in this world without building relationships?

I know the answer is silly. Believe me, I let myself live in a bubble for far too long, but there isn't any reason to.

This trip was always about more than the books, more than the opportunity to break my newest routine.

This was about rediscovering all there is, all that matters. And I fucked up, Wally. I fucked up with my mom and I cannot go back to alter my choices, but I can better myself moving forward.

I've always found that the best stories are the ones where the protagonist finally realizes they want to change, not the journey of how they accomplish it.

I hope I go back to New York and build upon the relationships I have and begin forging new ones. I hope I never stop meeting new people and learning their stories. I hope I give up my crusade about living a dull routine and just focus on what matters.

I know that the world is more complicated than just hoping for change or to not be concerned about things like money or a job, but I need to start somewhere.

It will take time — years even — but I'm not in a rush.

After all, what's the point in getting to the end if you didn't enjoy the journey?

Until next time,
Coda Finn

Wally stared up into the sky. The clouds broke apart and his glassy eyes saw more halos than they normally did. He took a deep breath, held it in, and controlled the exhale.

He swiveled his head toward Nolan, who was lost in a state of longing and sadness. She cleared her throat like she was ready to read the letter aloud for a second time, but instead, she continued to sit on the bench, clutching it tightly.

Wally smiled and said the first words that came to mind, ones he read long ago in a book.

"If that isn't nice, what is?"

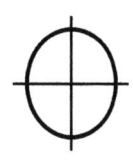

Made in the USA
Middletown, DE
09 August 2021